What Reviewers Have Said About *Ferren And The Angel*, Book 1 in The Ferren Trilogy.

"Richard Harland's approach to entwining the perceptions, lives, and clashes between very different peoples is thoroughly engrossing... [*Ferren and the Angel's*] powerful, unpredictable brand of fantasy is highly recommended for young adult to adult readers and for libraries seeking something refreshingly new in the fantasy genre."
  –*Midwest Book Review* (Diane Donovan, Senior Reviewer)

"The worldbuilding here is addictive ... This story has a great plot, some incredible conflict, and secrets just waiting to be revealed. Dystopian fans are in for a treat."
  –*Independent Book Review* (Alexandria Ducksworth)

"A richly developed fantasy that will rise quickly into a beloved classic ..."
  –*Reader Views* (teenage reviewer)

IFWG's Masters of Fantasy
line of titles

Ferren and the Invaders of Heaven

The Ferren Trilogy
Book 3

By
Richard Harland

IFWG Publishing International
Gold Coast

www.ifwgpublishing.com

ACKNOWLEDGEMENTS

My deepest thanks to Australian fans of the original *Heaven and Earth* books, who refused to let those stories die. Your enthusiasm and dogged determination have been my greatest inspiration for this trilogy!

Equal thanks to Gerry Huntman of IFWG Publishing, who saw the potential and backed it all the way. Always encouraging, always supportive—much appreciated, Gerry!

More thanks to the team that brought the book to its final shape: to editors Noel Osualdini and Stephen McCracken, and to Elena Betti for another mind-blowing cover. I can't think of the Ferren books without Elena's visual imagination! Additional thanks to Jeanette Taylor for checking the Latin phrases of angelic speech.

Outside of the book, my retrospective gratitude to Liana Burrage for the great video clips she created for the first two volumes of the trilogy. And the same to my partner, Aileen, for her indefinable but absolutely invaluable contribution—as ever!

The Story So Far...

Miriael

is an angel who was shot down and fell to Earth in the thousand-year war between the armies of Heaven and the armies of Earth. She should have winked out like a light, but Ferren fed her mortal food, which kept her alive while altering the purely spiritual nature of her being.

Ferren

is a young Residual tribesman, one of the surviving remnants of the original human race. Like all Residuals, he believed that his tribe was allied to the artificial Humen fighting on the side of the Earth. Then he found out what the Humen really do to the Residuals they select for 'military service'.

Doctor Saniette

was a giant computer-minded Doctor, composed of many individual Doctors, who came in as leader of the Humen. He captured Miriael as a sample angel to dissect and analyse, but Ferren and a rescue team destroyed him in the process of saving Miriael.

The young Nesters

led by Kiet, they include her family (Tadge, Rhinn) and her friends (Flens, Bross, Gibby, Ethany). They joined Ferren in the rescue team that broke into the Bankstown Camp.

The Bankstown Camp

is a military-industrial complex that will be the launching point for the greatest ever offensive against Heaven. Inside the Camp live the unnaturally preserved or created Humen types: Doctors, Hypers, Queen-Hypers and Plasmatics.

Shanna

is Ferren's sister, who was taken for 'military service', escaped in the Humen Camp and operated for two and a half years as a solitary saboteur. The rescue team discovered her by accident when searching for Miriael.

The Residual Alliance

is an alliance to resist the Humen and their Selectors. Before Miriael was distracted by Asmodai, she and Ferren were going round and joining up all the Residual tribes. Each tribe agreed to send a representative to a great assembly, which will be held at the People's Home Ground.

Asmodai

is a fallen angel, forgiven by Heaven, who visited Miriael and promised to raise her back up into Heaven. Instead, he traded her off to the Humen. A being of pure spirit, he's incapable of the human kind of love, but rather enjoyed watching Miriael fall in love with *him*.

Peeper

is the Morph who was left behind when Asmodai trapped the rest of his colony to serve as a new form of energy to power his flying wing. Only angels like Miriael can see Morphs, but Kiet cares for and communicates with Peeper.

Zonda

became the leader of Ferren's old tribe after her father died and after the People survived through a terrible terra-celestial battle. She once betrayed Ferren and once saved him; he's never been able to work out her feelings towards him.

Uriel

is one of the four greatest archangels. Like all angels, he follows strict ethical principles, and couldn't justifiably execute Miriael even though he disapproved of her 'corrupted' spiritual state.

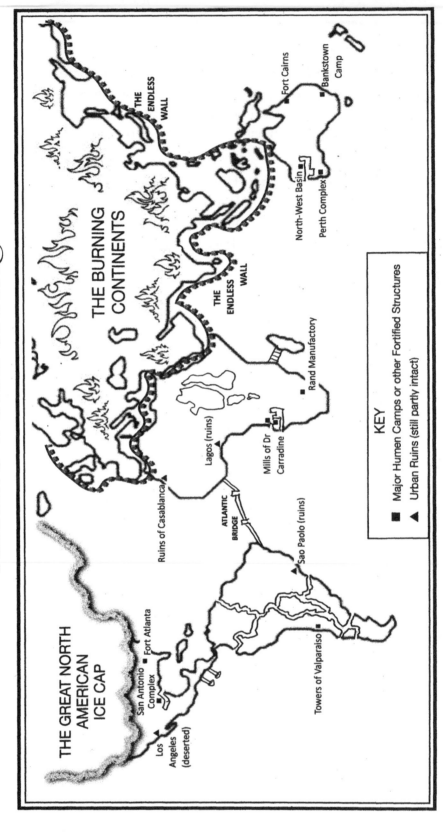

PART ONE

THE FLYING WING

1

The night sky lit up just as the rescue team reached the edge of the trees. Ferren and Kiet were in the lead, followed by Shanna, Flens, Bross, Rhinn, Tadge, Gibby and Ethany, along with Miriael, who'd been rescued. They turned and looked back at the sudden radiance now appearing above the Bankstown Camp.

A banner had been unfurled across the sky, a vast, glittering banner with gold lettering. It hung in folds like a curtain, held up by a score of angels. Other angels with long heraldic trumpets flew down alongside. While the auras of the angels lit the darkness, the rays of some greater brightness shone out from behind the banner.

None of the rescue team could read the language of the gold lettering. "What does it say?" asked Ferren.

Only Miriael understood. "*Concedite nunc aut accipite dira fata vestra,*" she read out. "It means, *Surrender now or suffer your fate. Your terrible fate.*"

Tadge clapped his hands in excitement. "They're going to fight! Heaven against the Humen."

"I expect—" Miriael's voice was drowned out by a fanfare of golden trumpets.

TARAAAAAAAAAAAAHH!!

Very slowly, the angels holding up the banner lifted it higher into the sky. Behind was a great rift of light, a glowing, cavernous opening framed by pillars and an arch. In the next moment, a horde of angels poured from its depths.

"They've opened up the Fourth Portal!" breathed Miriael in wonder. "Just look at those warrior angels!"

The angels wore silver casques and breastplates, and carried bright spears and shields. There were many thousands of them, and they streamed forth, spread across the sky and formed up in row upon row facing the Humen Camp. Their commanders took up position before them, and flag-bearers next to the commanders.

"Will they attack the Camp?" Kiet asked Miriael.

"Eventually. They're giving the Humen a chance to surrender first."

"Some hope!" sniffed Shanna.

"It's the usual procedure." Miriael shrugged. "Twelve hours' warning. Ah—watch this!"

Out from the Fourth Portal drove a chariot with wheels of fire. The driver was a tall archangel with sixfold wings who held the reins in one hand and a mighty sword in the other.

"It's Uriel!" cried Kiet.

"Yes, the Regent of the South and one of the four greatest archangels." Miriael nodded. "All the forces for this continent are under his command."

As she spoke, Uriel's chariot swung and swept along before the front line of the angelic army. Leaning out at the side, he extended the tip of his sword and drew a line parallel to his troops. The line lit up and widened and became a line of flames.

"What's this now?" Ferren demanded.

"It's a line of demarcation between Heaven and the Humen," Miriael explained. "No angel will cross that line until the period for surrender expires."

"Pointless." Shanna sniffed again.

"Yes, but it's Heaven's way," Miriael agreed mildly. "Unfortunately, it gives the Humen time to activate their defences."

She dropped her eyes to the ground, and the Residuals did the same. Everyone could feel it. There was always a faint throbbing underfoot this close to the Camp, but the throbbing had now intensified to a stronger, pounding vibration. The rotating wire canopies that protected the Humen weren't visible from here, but they were surely cycling round faster and faster.

Then beams of light shot up and raked the sky in all directions. Everyone raised their eyes again.

"Both sides are preparing to fight," said Miriael. "But nothing will happen for many hours yet."

They stayed watching for a while, until Miriael said, "We need to make some decisions. Let's go in under the trees."

"Yes, new plans," Ferren agreed. "This changes everything."

Miriael shook her head. "Not everything. Some things, though."

2

Thirty paces into the forest, they found a small clearing where the ground formed a hollow. Moss covered the trunks of the trees at their backs and the boughs over their heads—everything was padded and rounded and soft. They unslung their backpacks and sat down in a circle.

The young Nesters of the rescue team had changed a great deal since they'd first volunteered for a doomsday mission. When they'd set off to break into the Bankstown Camp and save Miriael from Doctor Saniette, it had seemed like a tremendous adventure. Perhaps it still seemed that way to twelve-year-old Tadge, since he and his sister Rhinn had stayed guarding the team's base in the construction site outside the Camp. But for the others who'd broken in, they'd faced and cheated death too often to hold any illusions. Their mission had become a matter of survival rather than excitement.

At the same time, they had *proved* themselves. Not only had they completed their mission of saving Miriael, but they'd had two more extraordinary successes as well. Before the rescue, they'd discovered Ferren's sister Shanna, who'd been hiding and sabotaging equipment inside the Camp. Then, at the end of the rescue, they'd brought down Doctor Saniette, the giant figure who'd turned out to be made up of hundreds of ordinary Doctors wired together to create a computational super-mind. For months, Ferren had been telling all the tribes that Residuals could and should stand up for themselves—and now they had. Even the armies of Heaven could never have inflicted so great a defeat as the destruction of Doctor Saniette.

Their faces were pale blurs under the shadowy trees as they sat round ready to discuss the next step. Instinctively, they turned to Miriael. Although she was the one who'd needed saving, she was also the one with the widest knowledge of terra-celestial warfare.

She raised a hand for attention and began. "I think Heaven must've seen the fallen body of Doctor Saniette. Since he ended up collapsing out beyond the canopies, he'd be visible to any observer angel. I think they aim to seize this opportunity to wipe out the Bankstown Camp."

"*We* did it for them!" cried Tadge. "Do they know that?"

Rhinn hushed him, and Miriael smiled.

"No, they couldn't know, and they'd hardly believe it if they were told," said the angel. "All they know is that the Humen will be relatively disorganised without a leader, so the Camp may be more vulnerable. They've tried twice in the past to attack and failed both times. This could be their best chance."

Everyone listened intently. They'd seen the Camp's defences for themselves, and understood how hard it would be to overcome them.

"They have to try, because this is where the next great offensive against Heaven will be coming from," Miriael went on. "The Humen have been building up forces on this continent, planning some great new operation. Doctor Saniette would've been part of the build-up, along with the Queen-Hypers and secret weapons he brought in. Heaven hopes to strike first."

"They should've struck without announcing it," said Shanna. "They've lost the advantage of surprise."

Miriael sighed and shook her head. "Ethical principles. Heaven's always very rigid about following ethical principles."

Shanna grunted. "Winning's what matters, not ethical principles."

"But they'll still win, won't they?" Gibby asked Miriael.

"Maybe, maybe not. Either way, the Residual Alliance is what matters for Residuals. That hasn't changed. You need to look after your own interests." Miriael turned to Ferren. "The representatives from the tribes will be gathering at the Home Ground very soon now. Some may have already arrived. You need to be there for the assembly."

"Me?" Ferren almost jumped. "What about you?"

Miriael's expression was unreadable in the dim light. "That's what's changed. Someone needs to stay here to watch what happens. If Heaven's attack succeeds, it'll be great news to report to the assembly. I'll come and report it, probably after the assembly's well under way."

"I thought you'd be coming to help with the representatives."

"No, you'll do better by yourself. You can speak as a Residual to other Residuals. I'm only a distraction as a Celestial. Well, a hybrid sort of Celestial." Miriael swallowed and cleared her throat. "In any case, I'm the best to stay and watch because I know about terra-celestial fighting. I'll be able to understand what happens."

"That makes sense." Shanna addressed the circle of faces without looking at Ferren. "And I'd like to stay, too."

Ferren frowned. "Don't you want to meet up with our tribe again? Meggen and Oola and Zonda and Urlish and everyone? They'll all be there in the Home Ground."

"Yes, but I'd be a different sort of distraction, wouldn't I?" Shanna stuck out her jaw. "I haven't been involved with the Residual Alliance, I wouldn't be much help. I've been two and a half years away from the People, I can wait a bit longer."

"I'd be glad of the company," said Miriael, then turned to the young Nesters. "How about you? Do you want to go back home or go the assembly or what?"

"The assembly," Kiet answered at once. "I'll go with Ferren. I want to see our Residual Alliance set up and working."

"I want to watch the fighting here," said Tadge.

"No." Rhinn shook her head at him. "Kiet's our sister. We're family, and we stay together. And I need to keep an eye on *you* especially."

Tadge was ready to protest, but Miriael spoke first. "It won't be fighting like an open battle, you know. It'll be a siege. A slow sort of fighting, not an instant attack. What about everyone else?"

The other young Nesters looked at one another.

"Not home," said Gibby. "Definitely not home."

"I vote to go with Kiet," said Flens.

Bross nodded. "Keep the team together."

"*We'll* help with the Residual Alliance," said Ethany. "We know all about it."

A tiny voice piped up from the musical instrument on Kiet's backpack. "Me too-o-o!" It was Peeper, the invisible Morph attached to the pegs of the zither. "Me with you-oo! Plea-e-e-e-ease!"

Everyone laughed. Kiet bent over the zither and spoke in the special crooning tone she used for talking to Peeper.

"Of course you shall come," she told him. "I wouldn't leave you behind, little one."

Ferren jumped to his feet, and the others stood up too. "So, all decided!" He pointed deeper into the forest. "To the assembly and the Home Ground!"

Apart from Miriael and Shanna, everyone turned to walk on.

3

Ferren was hugely relieved that the young Nesters had chosen to accompany him. Bonded by dangers shared, they'd become closer than friends over recent weeks. Daredevil Flens with his bugle of a nose...muscular Bross the wrestler...cheery, round-faced Ethany... Gibby with her fierce determination so ill-matched to her dainty features. Then there was Kiet's family: Rhinn of the long face and endless worrying, spiky-haired Tadge with his boyish enthusiasms. And Kiet herself, of course... Ferren felt more comfortable talking to Kiet than to almost anyone else in the world.

He no longer felt as comfortable when talking to Miriael, or even Shanna. There had been a distance between Miriael and himself ever since her secret meetings with the angel Asmodai. As for his sister, she had once been the most dearly loved person in his life—companion, mentor, mother, everything. But her years as a solitary avenger and saboteur had changed her, and her new, grim, hardened personality seemed unfamiliar to him. He could laugh more easily when chatting with Kiet...

It was midday when they finally came out onto a plain of tall grass. They'd had no clear view overhead while walking in the forest; now they looked back over the trees and saw that Heaven's battalions still remained in their ranks, drawn up behind Uriel's line of fire. The angels' spears, shields and breastplates were as bright as ever, though they stood out less sharply against the daylight sky.

"Still waiting to attack," commented Ferren.

"I hope they smash the whole place flat," said Kiet. "And every Humen with it."

Ferren was surprised by her sudden intensity. Her eyes were flashing, her hair flying, her teeth gritted. Deep brown eyes, dark red hair, brilliant white teeth...

She lost both her parents to the Selectors, he remembered. *Like I lost mine.*

He looked away and surveyed the landscape before them. The tall grass and scattered ruins of brick and stone put him in mind of the Plain around the Home Ground. The Plain as it used to be before the great battle...

They had slowed in their walking, and the other young Nesters had almost caught up. Ferren pressed forward once more, and Kiet came with him.

"This is the Tunnellers' territory," he told her.

She seemed to have left behind her moment of anger. "A tribe called the Tunnellers? You visited here before?"

"Yes. They joined up to the Residual Alliance. They'll be sending a representative to the assembly."

Her eyes swept in all directions. "Where are they?"

"They stay mostly hidden by day. Because of being so close to the Humen Camp, I suppose. They have their fields and crops, but they tend them by night. The rest of the time, they live in their burrows under a mound of bricks and stones. A huge mound like a mountain, collected up from all the ruins around." He made the shape of a pyramid with his forearms.

"Like over there?" Kiet pointed.

Ferren followed the line of her finger to a faraway hump on the horizon. "That's it, yes."

"Can we call on them? They sound interesting."

"Better not. It's three days' walk to the Home Ground, and I don't want to be one of the last ones there. You'll meet their representative at the assembly."

"Not the same." She pulled a face. "All right. You mustn't be late."

As it turned out, they met the Tunnellers' representative that very afternoon. They saw him at first as a tiny silhouette cutting through the grass on a route parallel to their own. They veered and came closer, then Ferren called out. The Tunneller stopped and waited until they came up.

"Ferren of the People!" Ferren announced himself at thirty yards' distance. "Remember me? I came and talked about the Residual Alliance two months ago."

"I remember," the Tunneller called back. "I'm on my way to the People's Home Ground now. Pinnet of the Tunnellers."

Ferren gathered the group around him before covering the last thirty yards. "He'll stink of smoke," he whispered. "His tribe does all its cooking underground. But don't say anything, right?"

Pinnet not only stank of smoke but seemed to have been cured in it. His skin was darkened and creased, and his face looked like old leather. When he addressed them, his accent was strange and his voice was hoarse and rough.

"What's happening back there?" He jerked a thumb towards the angelic battalions lined up in the sky. "Do *you* know?"

"Yes, Heaven's going to attack the Humen Camp," Ferren told him. "In a couple of hours."

"Brr! Heaven…the Humen…" Pinnet shivered. "I don't like it."

"It's no threat to us," said Ferren. "And if the Humen are defeated…"

"Whooo!" Tadge brandished a fist. "All thanks to us! We started it with Doctor Saniette!"

"We'll tell you the whole story as we go," said Kiet.

4

Positioned under the eaves of the forest, Miriael and Shanna waited for the attack to begin. They were shielded by foliage from above, while looking across a wide, weed-covered wasteland towards the Humen Camp. But they couldn't see the Camp itself, nor even the wire canopies rotating on masts above the complex. Instead, they faced the construction site outside the Camp, where they'd hidden and rested through the previous day. High stacks of girders and pipes and building materials blocked their view.

Eventually, Shanna grew bored—and hungry. "Nothing's going to happen for a while yet, is it?" she said. "I'll go find us some food."

She went off into the forest and was gone for a couple of hours. Miriael was starting to worry, when she suddenly reappeared, grinning from ear to ear. She held out the bundle she carried in her arms.

"I've done well. Look!"

The bundle was Shanna's own jerkin wrapped around a great stock of provisions from the forest. Miriael saw nuts, mushrooms, berries and fruit.

"That's enough for days and days," she laughed.

"Yes, why not? Let's eat some now."

For the next half hour, they sampled every kind of nut, berry, mushroom and fruit. By the end of the meal, their stock of provisions seemed hardly smaller than when they'd begun.

Afterwards, Shanna had a question to ask. "I knew *you* ate food, but… Is that normal for angels?"

"Not mortal food, no." Miriael smiled a little sadly. "Proper angels only consume the manna of Heaven. I'm not a proper angel."

Shanna didn't ask any more, but Miriael chose to continue. "I was shot down and lost my aura, you see. I should never have survived in your terrestrial atmosphere. But your brother found me and fed me *his* kind of food, which somehow kept me alive. It's not meant to work like that. I'm a baffling case."

"Are you grateful?"

"To your brother? Yes, on the whole, I am. Why do you ask?"

"I don't know. You seem a bit awkward with him."

Miriael considered a moment before answering. "I was very close to him. But I spoiled it." She drew a deep breath. "I suppose I might as well tell you the whole story. Only please don't judge me. I do enough of that for myself."

"I wouldn't. I couldn't."

"It was an angel called Asmodai who led me into a trap." There was a bitter taste in Miriael's mouth even as she uttered the name. "Every other angel despised me for letting my body change into something less pure and spiritual. But he visited me on Earth and seemed to take my side. I thought he was so kind and compassionate. And very, very beautiful. We met in secret for weeks. I suppose I fell in love with him."

Shanna let out a little gasp. Miriael looked at her, then quickly away again.

"Yes, I thought he could love me back," she went on. "Because of the things he said… But it was all deception. He only wanted information from me, to help gather Morphs to power his flying wing. And when I'd helped, he traded me off to the Humen, so that *they'd* help him with constructing the wing. I was utterly stupid. I should have known he could never love me."

"Why not?"

"Angels never feel that personal kind of love, only angels like me. For all proper angels, love is a communal experience. And not even that for Asmodai. I think his love is all for himself. And loving to have someone fall in love with him. He told me how much he enjoyed watching me helpless with love for him."

"When?" asked Shanna. "I mean, when did he tell you?"

"After he'd traded me off, when I was waiting in Doctor Saniette's surgeries."

"He kept visiting you even then?"

"Yes." On reflection, it seemed odd to Miriael too. "I suppose he still wanted to bask in my adoration."

"Phah!" Shanna spat at the ground. Her prematurely lined face with the scar down one cheek looked quite fearsome when she wasn't smiling. There was a long moment of silence.

"So now you understand the problem between your brother and me," said Miriael at last. "I betrayed him."

"He was jealous?" Shanna frowned. "But how could he love you?"

"Oh, a strange kind of love, I think. Service and devotion and loyalty. But I didn't return the loyalty."

"He still led the rescue team to save you."

"Which makes me feel even more unworthy."

Shanna raised her eyes and looked Miriael full in the face. "I'm glad you told me, anyway."

"I'm glad I told you. I think I needed to tell someone."

They fell silent once more, but it was now an easier kind of silence.

The sun sank lower as the afternoon wore on. The battalions of angels shone out more brightly in the dimming sky; the line of fire that Uriel had drawn across the sky faded to a dull, smouldering red.

Must be very soon now, thought Miriael.

Although she expected it, the start of the attack took her by surprise. A mighty, resonant note rang out as though a great gong had been struck. The vibrations still pounded in her eardrums even when she put her hands over her ears.

"That's the Great Patriarchs!" she shouted to Shanna, who also had her hands over her ears. "The Proclamation of Battle!"

Then Heaven's battalions burst suddenly into action. They swept across the red line and swooped down upon the Bankstown Camp. So swift was their flight that the eye caught only the coruscating trails of light they left behind. Thousands and thousands of trails of light…

In the next moment, the angels had all vanished behind the stacks of the construction site. The sky was empty.

Shanna took her hands from her ears. "We can't see from here," she lamented.

Miriael also groaned, but for a different reason. "Listen!" she said.

A distinctive kind of hum had started up. Louder and louder it rose, a sound somewhere between a drone and a shriek. Miriael shuddered.

"That's a force-field," she told Shanna. "A psycho-affective force-field."

"A what?"

Miriael didn't try to explain. "They'll never get through now. Too late to disable the canopies. That's what comes of giving the Humen advance warning."

Glows of light showed out above the stacks of building materials, but not the sources of the light.

"They're still fighting, though," said Shanna.

"Yes, they'll be probing for weaknesses."

"I wish we could watch. I wish we could go close for a better look."

"Back to the construction site, you mean?"

"We could hide where we rested up yesterday. The same place under the girders."

"Hmm." Miriael knit her brows and thought about it. "I suppose we won't have much to report if we don't go closer than this."

"Yes, then?" Shanna's face lit up with a grin.

"Yes, all right. But wait until nightfall, then we make a move."

5

Kiet spent a restless night. So much had happened during the day, and she kept running over and over it in her mind.

First there'd been Pinnet of the Tunnellers, then they'd met up with Dwinna of the Clanfeathers. Dwinna, who wore a headdress woven out of twigs like a bird's nest, was another representative on her way to the assembly. Unlike Pinnet, who kept a constant check on his tongue and his actions, Dwinna was open and talkative, gesturing constantly and pulling faces. She seemed to communicate as much with her arms and hands as her words. At moments, she broke into an odd, trilling laugh that had nothing to do with humour so far as Kiet could understand.

Naturally, the representatives had been amazed to hear the story of the doomsday mission in the Humen Camp. Kiet had taken the lead in telling it, and it grew more dramatic with every telling. Their journey through watery tunnels underground...their near-fatal encounter with Ferren's sister...the Hyper they'd disabled by pulling the plug from his forehead...their trampoline escape under the great dome...their flight through flamethrowers in the bucket-train...then finally setting fire to the giant Doctor Saniette himself. Kiet made it sound incredibly heroic, though for the sake of inspiring by example rather than boasting. The representatives needed to believe that Residuals like themselves could achieve great deeds against the Humen.

For hours, she slept and woke and slept and woke. Towards dawn, she made the mistake of rolling over on her side and looking in the direction of the Humen Camp. Even from this distance, she saw strange glows at the bottom of the sky and heard faint sounds of battle in the silence of the night. After watching for a while, she knew she would never fall back asleep.

She rose from her place on the ground and surveyed the other sleepers. Then she decided to take a walk.

The landscape here was a maze of ponds and marshplants. On one side were the glows above the Humen Camp; on the other, the first glimmer of a new day peeped out above the horizon. A quarter-moon hung low in the sky, while a million stars sprinkled the darkness overhead.

She wandered past ponds and smelled a new, intoxicating perfume in the air. Miraculously, the marshplants had opened their blossoms under the moon and stars—huge white blossoms, a handsbreadth wide. Pale yellow stamens seemed to bend and bow at the centre of each blossom.

She stopped after a while and stood inhaling the perfume. Her mind quietened until soon she was thinking of nothing at all. There was only the sense of something impending, something that was meant to be.

"Hullo? Couldn't you sleep either?"

Ferren's voice made her jump. She made a vague sound in her throat, but didn't turn when he came up beside her. *No need to talk,* she wanted to say.

"Did you leave Peeper behind?"

It seemed such an irrelevant question! She had to force herself to think out a response.

"Yes, he's happy where he is."

"Good." There was a long pause…yet still he wanted to talk. "Best not to draw attention to him. Your family and friends are used to him, but you remember your aunt. She couldn't bear to be near a being she couldn't see. He was still like some sort of ghost to her."

"Mmm."

"I'm thinking of the representatives from other tribes. They might react the same."

"Mmm."

"We don't want to unsettle them."

She continued to gaze straight ahead. The surface of the ponds gleamed black and lustrous under the moon and stars. A memory floated into her mind…of what she'd been told about Ferren's behaviour after the rescue mission. When he and the others had escaped from the Camp, then discovered that she was missing, he'd wanted to go straight back and search for her. If Bross hadn't knocked him out, he'd have walked right in among all the Hypers and Queen-Hypers. *Frantic to save you,* according to Rhinn.

She turned to face him. Perhaps this was what was meant to be…

At that moment, a dark shadow cut across the moon and glided across the sky. Ferren let out a gasp, and Kiet felt the hairs rise up on the back of her neck.

It was vast, it was sinister. The shadow passed on beyond the moon and covered the stars overhead. It was invisible in itself, black against the black night sky, yet Kiet saw where the stars should have been. It was like a moving hole in the shape of an enormous delta.

She flinched and shivered. Her dreamlike mood of a moment ago had been shattered. In absolute silence, the shadow swept across on a wide, curving path. Below it and behind it, the air seemed suddenly chill.

Then it passed over, and the stars reappeared.

They stayed watching long after it had gone. Kiet realised she'd forgotten to breathe, and gulped in air.

"What was *that?*"

But Ferren had no answer.

6

"It's called a psycho-affective force-field because it mimics all the most violent kinds of emotion," Miriael explained. "Hatred, spite, malevolence, utter insanity. The Humen have machines to weave the exact frequencies."

She and Shanna observed the Bankstown Camp from an aisle between towering stacks of pipes and girders in the construction site. They were close to the rescue team's old base, a safe refuge to which they could retreat at any time. Their view took in the moat and embankment encircling the Camp and the rotating wire canopies that protected the

Camp from above. At present, the embankment and canopies appeared blurred, as if seen through a haze.

"What you see are waves of vibration in the air," Miriael went on. "A barrier of artificial emotional energies. No angel can survive flying through that intensity. They'll have to wait."

"Wait for what?" Shanna asked.

"Wait until the force-field exhausts its power sources."

They watched as Heaven sent down squadron after squadron, always one at a time. Groups of angels swooped down close to the canopies, touched spears together and fired great flashes of light towards the Camp. Miriael and Shanna couldn't see exactly where the blur of psycho-affective energies ended, but the angels could—and stayed just out of contact.

"So what's Heaven trying to do?" Shanna asked at last.

"Encourage the Humen to maintain their force-field at full strength. Those are all feint attacks. If the force-field keeps going like that, it'll run down sooner."

"How long?"

Miriael shrugged. "No idea."

They had deposited their stock of food in the old base, which was a trench with a huge stack of girders piled across it. Miriael now wore Shanna's jerkin over her head; as Shanna had explained, "Your hair's so bright, it'll give us away if anything does." So far, though, there had been no Hypers or Humen vehicles in their part of the construction site. All the activity and sounds came from the fighting over and around the Camp.

The feint attacks continued through the day. At one time, the chanting of choirs drifted down from the Fourth Portal high in the sky. Another time, there was a long percussion like the roll of a drum from the battalions lower down. In the afternoon, plumes of steam rose spiralling through the canopies of the Camp.

Later in the afternoon, the Humen began firing projectiles that flew up like fiery bolts. The hovering angels mostly broke ranks to let them pass through, but a few were hit. Miriael winced in sympathy as she remembered the sickening blow when she'd been shot down herself. But the angels shot down now plummeted into the force-field and met a very different fate. Instantly incinerated, each went out in a single flare of flame.

Still the feint attacks continued. The afternoon was almost at an end before the force-field began to fail. It didn't fail all at once; the high-pitched, droning hum of the machines cut out for a moment, then restarted. The first time it happened, there was no reduction in the blur of emotional vibrations. But when it happened again and again, the unnatural haze lost intensity, the features of the Camp became more and more distinct. Miriael and Shanna exchanged looks of elation.

Finally the machines fell silent for good, and the force-field petered out altogether. From the battalions of angels came a mighty battle cry.

"Hosanna! Hosanna! Hosanna in the highest!"

Then the battalions of angels made way for a stream of Cherubim descending from the Fourth Portal. No ordinary warriors, the high-ranking Cherubim had fourfold wings and wore robes of the deepest blue. As they approached, Miriael saw that they cupped sparks of what looked like red fire in their hands.

"This is it!" she cried. "They're going to break in!"

"The real attack?"

"The real attack. Those sparks of fire are to disable Plasmatics. They'll be aiming to disable Plasmatics inside the masts that rotate the canopies."

Shanna snapped her fingers. "We need a better view. We ought to go up higher."

"Higher?"

"We could climb one of these stacks. We'll see everything from on top."

Miriael laughed and surveyed the stacks. "Which one?"

7

Shanna chose a stack of huge metal pipes that went up higher than any other stack. Although the pipes were smooth and rounded, they had holes for bolts that made them easy to climb. But no climbing was easy for Miriael, and it took many minutes before they both reached the top.

From this height, they could look out far and wide. Stacks of construction materials rose like mountains all around them. An overbridge passed close to one side of the site, and on the same side was a fenced-off zone where machinery worked on automatically, regardless of the state of the battle. Miriael and Shanna took up a position screened from the zone, just in case any Hypers were there with the machinery.

Meanwhile, the battle had progressed. The Cherubim had already finished applying their sparks of fire—with some success. Although the majority of canopies continued to rotate, three had been immobilised, and one was tilted completely out of alignment. While the Cherubim hovered at a distance, ordinary warrior angels took over the attack.

The tilting canopy was their particular target. A score of angels descended upon it, and began lifting and pulling to bend it further sideways. Other canopies sped up and rotated in a frenzy, all except the canopies that had been immobilised. As a hundred more angels circled round to give cover, the attack party directed their flashes to weaken and warp the metal. The gap between the tilting canopy and its neighbour grew steadily wider.

Then a new means of defence came into play on the Humen side— Queen-Hypers. No doubt they had swarmed up the supporting masts. Miriael and Shanna had seen these elite troops before, with their special augmentations and athleticism. Now four of them launched themselves up onto the canopies to confront the attack party.

They carried no flamethrowers or other visible weapons. Leaping in great bounds from wire to wire, they advanced upon the angels and swung their arms. Piercing screams rang out—not from the angels but the Queen-Hypers. Yet it was the angels that fell.

"How did they do that?" cried Shanna, as four angels seemed to come apart before their eyes. "Did they throw something?"

Miriael was horrified. It was as though the victims had been sliced by knives, yet nothing had been thrown that she could see.

The surviving angels seemed stunned. The Queen-Hypers leaped forward and drew back their arms to strike again.

"*Desist!*" thundered a mighty voice overhead. "*Desist from your presumption! Desist from your profanity!*"

Miriael recognised the voice of one of the Great Patriarchs. But the Queen-Hypers paused only for a second. Then they screamed their aggression and struck a second time. More angels fell.

"Stop them!" Miriael groaned. "Do something!"

Heaven's answer took the form of a sudden snowstorm of white wings. A great flock of them appeared out of nowhere and flew at the four Queen-Hypers, flapping and fluttering in their faces.

Shanna cheered at the sight. "What're they doing to them?"

"Nothing." Miriael wasn't cheering. "They can't. Those are Blessed Souls. They're only a distraction."

Still, the distraction worked. For a few moments, the Queen-Hypers were blinded by the white flurry of wings. They couldn't swing their arms or get a clear view of the surviving angels. They were still trying to brush away the wings when their opponents regrouped and fought back.

The angels were charged with light, but they also had spears. They jabbed at the Queen-Hypers and flashed with light—and the spears directed the flashes along their shafts and forward from their points. Lances of dazzling light struck the Queen-Hypers' rubber-clad limbs from all directions.

The cat-like beings staggered and lost their footing. One rolled and slipped right off the side of the canopy, dropping to the depths of the Camp below. The others remained caught in the wires.

The angels jabbed again to finish them off. This time they struck at heads and chests, and the explosions of light broke the Queen-Hypers apart.

Whumpf! Whumpf! Whumpf!

Three shattered bodies discharged colours and psychic images into the air. The angels stood back and watched, then returned to their task of widening the breach between canopies.

Shanna whooped and turned to Miriael with shining eyes. "They're winning! They're winning!"

Miriael saw the battalions of angels above preparing to enter through the breach. She couldn't help herself. She rose to her feet and spread her wings in triumph.

"Hallelujah! Hallelujah!" she cried.

She was still celebrating when a vast and black shadow shot across over their heads. At tremendous speed, it made straight for the Bankstown Camp. It was shaped like a great delta and cast an instant chill where it passed.

Miriael stared in shock. *A flying wing...*

"It's blocking them off!" Shanna gasped. "It's closing the gap!"

The great delta had decelerated to a stop above the Camp, and was now lowering itself over the breach that the angels had opened up between canopies.

But Miriael was still wrapped up in her own dire thoughts. "He was building a flying wing with the Morphs," she said.

Shanna turned to her. "What? Who?"

"Asmodai. It must be."

Shanna pondered the name. "The angel you fell in love with?"

"Yes. He's back in his flying wing."

8

Miriael felt sick to the stomach with guilt. *She* was the one who'd made this possible by helping Asmodai in the past. Not only had she directed him to the Morphs in the City of the Dead, she'd also shown him how to win their trust by singing to them. He hadn't even been able to communicate properly until she'd taught him the trick of it. So very, very stupid!

The angels who'd been working on the breach had flown up out of the way of the wing. They wheeled in the air like baffled gnats, while many more squadrons swooped down to join them. Heaven was clearly amassing forces for another attack. Miriael and Shanna held their breath.

But the attack was a failure from the start. The angels were ineffectual against the great delta. Every time they tried to dive down onto it, they were repelled by some invisible force. Their flashes were equally ineffectual, even when they touched spears for a combined burst of light. After a dozen attempts, they gave up and withdrew.

For a minute, the delta remained motionless. Then it lifted away from the canopies and shot forwards and upwards. Its leading edge must have been sword-sharp because it cut through the hovering angels like a scythe through wheat. Wings severed, auras bisected, limbs sheared through...

"It's the ultimate destroying machine," moaned Shanna.

The delta swept round in a circle, now heading in their direction again. Miriael was still frozen in mid-celebration, still standing with out-spread wings. Shanna tugged at her hand.

"Down! Get down!"

Miriael dropped down just in time. Asmodai's flying wing skimmed over the construction site as he continued to harry the defeated angels. Miriael glimpsed a globe of light underneath the point of the delta. Like a huge, glassy eye! And inside it—

In the next moment, the wing had shot off into the distance again. But she couldn't have been mistaken. Inside the globe was a black-robed figure, the dark centre of the eye. Asmodai! He had changed his colours from white to black.

She turned to Shanna. "Did you see him?"

"Yes. But he didn't see us."

"He's fighting for the Humen."

"Fighting and winning." Shanna's mouth was a grim, tight line. "And we need to hide before he comes round again."

Miriael could hardly think about the danger, but Shanna surveyed the huge metal pipes of the stack they'd climbed on top of.

"We could hide up here if we could fit in *there*." Shanna gestured towards the circular mouths of two pipes near the top. "I'm sure I could. What about you?"

She scrambled across and slid into her pipe with ease. It was more difficult for Miriael, who had to furl her wings very tight against her body. But soon they were both hidden in side-by-side pipes. The curved metal felt cold to the touch, and echoes amplified every sound.

"He's coming again!" Shanna called out.

Miriael drew back deeper into the pipe. A moment later came a dimming of the light and a chilling of the air.

He's passing above us, she thought. And what was that noise? She strained her ears…

It might have been almost anything, but it put her in mind of the wail of a Morph—many hundreds of Morphs. Wails of pain like souls in torment! Was she hearing the cries of all the victims that Asmodai had trapped in his flying wing?

She was still wondering when Shanna's voice called out again. "All clear! He's gone!"

Miriael slid forward and stuck her head and shoulders out from the pipe. Shanna was already partway out from the pipe alongside.

The scene had changed. High overhead, the Fourth Portal had now closed, sealing the rift in the sky. Lower down, not a single angel remained—all had fled if not annihilated. On the wire canopies of the Camp, a whole troop of Queen-Hypers strutted and swaggered like conquerors. And Asmodai…

"Where is he?" she asked.

Shanna pointed, and Miriael followed the line of her finger. From the height of their stack, they had a view not only of the overbridge that ran by the construction site but also of a further overbridge beyond it. Between the two overbridges, close to the Camp, was an expanse of bare, flat ground—where Miriael now saw a vast delta shadow coming in to land. She watched as it sank lower and lower, then finally touched down.

"What's he going to do?" muttered Shanna.

9

For a long time, Asmodai did nothing. The flying wing remained motionless, and Asmodai remained invisible. No doubt he was still in his bubble of glass under the point of the delta.

Shanna turned to Miriael. "Tell me about him," she said.

"Who? Asmodai?"

"Yes. I know he deceived *you*, but there's more to him than that, isn't there?"

"A lot more. He has a very long history."

"I'm listening."

Miriael sighed. "Well, he was a Fallen Angel and a follower of the Satan. The Supreme Trinity cast him down into Hell along with all the others. That was back when the Supreme Trinity still ruled, before the Millenary War between Heaven and Earth. Then he was one of the Fallen Angels allowed to return, some time after the start of the War. They were allowed to return if they were truly repentant. Of course, Asmodai must've always been good at pretending to be what he wasn't." Miriael paused. "You don't really understand this, do you?"

"Enough. I get the general idea. Keep going."

"So, when he was back in Heaven, he was lower in rank than before, but very, very clever. When the Humen in North America threatened us with electrical storms high in the sky, he invented techniques to control the weather and turn it against them. Rain, snow, wind, the Hundred Years' Blizzard. You've never heard of the Weather Wars, have you?"

"No."

"He believed his techniques made all the difference, but he was never given due recognition. According to him. Then he started doing his own research in secret."

Miriael broke off. Something was happening on the far side of the flat ground where the wing had landed. A great procession of Hypers streamed out from the Camp along the distant overbridge. They looked like black ants on the march, thousands upon thousands of them.

"They're coming to see *him*," Shanna commented.

The procession advanced to a ramp at the side of the overbridge, then descended to the ground below. Now Miriael could see how they were waving their arms, cheering and singing, glorying in the victory that Asmodai had won for them. Still there was no sign of movement from the wing itself.

The Hypers came forward and formed a circle around the delta. Now they were no longer cheering and singing, but hushed and expectant. There were a few Queen-Hypers also among the throng.

"And that's the product of his secret research," Miriael went on, nodding towards the flying wing. "Nobody ever realised that the souls of the Residual dead could be a source of spiritual power. They'd been shut out of Heaven since the start of the war, and nobody gave them a thought. But *he* did—and he found out how to harness their power for his own evil purposes."

She broke off again as one of the Queen-Hypers began to clap. More and more joined in, while ordinary Hypers began stamping their feet on the ground. The applause reached a crescendo and turned into a roar of acclamation.

"They're trying to bring him out," said Shanna.

Finally Asmodai condescended to appear. He emerged stooping from underneath the delta, then rose to his full height. Though his robes were black, his wings were still brilliantly white, and light streamed from his head and limbs like a many-pointed star. He was more radiant and beautiful than ever.

Miriael heard Shanna's muffled exclamation beside her. She sucked in breath and felt a churning in the pit of her stomach—one of the new physical sensations that had come with her part-physicalised body. She hated Asmodai with an absolute, violent hatred, yet there was a kind of helpless weakness in the feeling as well.

"Are you all right?" Shanna turned to her with a look of concern.

Miriael managed a nod and forced a smile.

The circle of Hypers and Queen-Hypers gazed at Asmodai in awed amazement. Then the applause redoubled and became a thunder of clapping, stamping and cheering. Miriael couldn't bear to watch him celebrated and surrounded by his new admirers.

A few minutes later, the procession reversed direction and headed back up the ramp and along the overbridge.

"He's going into their Camp with them," commented Shanna.

"He's chosen the Humen now," Miriael agreed. "A far more dangerous enemy than Doctor Saniette ever was. He knows all about Heaven. And with his cleverness…"

Still she couldn't bear to watch, but kept her eyes on the sunset on the other side of the sky. Shades of pink coloured a few solitary wisps of cloud, then deepened gradually to a dull red.

10

The Plain around the Home Ground was covered in grass, but there were differences to the way Ferren remembered it. The grass that had sprung up since the great battle was still only knee-high, and the ground rose and fell in folds that had never existed before.

"We must be close now," he told Kiet, as they marched as usual ahead of the others.

"Didn't you say something about ruins?" she asked.

"That's how it used to be, yes, but the ruins got buried under silt. I don't know what Zonda's done to the Home Ground since."

Then Flens called out from behind. "Hey! Isn't that a field over there?" He was pointing to a dip in the ground and a square of freshly turned soil.

"And there!" Ethany pointed in another direction. The field she'd spotted had green plants growing in tidy rows.

Soon they were seeing more and more fields in all directions. Ferren clapped his hands.

"The People's new territory!" he cried. "We've expanded out over the Plain."

"Soil looks fertile enough," commented Dwinna of the Clanfeathers.

"But where does your tribe sleep?" Gibby demanded. "They must have some shelter."

Ferren laughed and shrugged. He was sure the People no longer huddled under a blanket overnight, but he had no idea what sort of shelters Zonda had constructed. The representatives would need shelters too...

Suddenly, a question rang out from a different voice: "Who's that?" Then the tone changed. "Are you more representatives for the assembly?" Then the tone changed again. "*Ferren!*"

Two heads had bobbed up above the next ridge. Ferren recognised them at once: his aunt Meggen and her friend Oola. As they came over the ridge to meet him, he ran towards them.

Meggen squeezed him in a hug until he could hardly breathe. He hugged back, delighted and surprised. His aunt had done her best to bring him up after the Selectors had taken his family, but she'd never been obviously affectionate. Now she was like a new person, more animated altogether.

By the time he escaped her hug, Dwinna, Pinnet and the young Nesters had gathered around Kiet, and more of his own tribe had come over the ridge. Mell, Shuff, Unce, Dugg, Burge and Tunks—everyone wanted to hug him or clap him on the back. Their faces were as familiar to Ferren as his own hands, yet they smiled and laughed and seemed light-hearted in a way he didn't remember. They were all trying to speak to him at the same time.

"We knew you'd be back soon!"

"Soon as the representatives began turning up!"

"So many tribes in the Residual Alliance!"

"You've really made it happen!"

"Where's the angel who was helping you?"

The last question came from Dugg, and Ferren was about to give a long response telling them all the news they didn't know. But his response was cut short when a new figure sprang forward and clasped him in the fiercest hug of all.

Zonda?

His past relationship to the tribe's current leader had always been a mystery to him. Why she'd picked on him yet snuggled up close to him…why she'd helped him escape after getting him tied up in the first place… Now suddenly she was hugging him like a long-lost friend! He could hardly believe it.

Finally she disengaged and held him by the wrists at arm's length. She'd hardly changed in the time he'd been away, still plump and pert and voluptuous.

"How do you like what I've done with Home Ground?" she asked. "I've done wonders, haven't I?"

"Er, more fields and crops."

"Of course."

"What about shelters?"

"We live in caves now. So easy to dig in this new earth! And so snug!" She turned and looked back the way she'd come. "You can't see from here. We dug them in the slope by the side of the Creek."

"Where's the Creek?"

"Come and see." She swept a hand to include the newcomers along with the People. "Everyone! Follow me!"

She led the way up the next ridge with Ferren, while Kiet and the rest trailed behind.

"Who have you brought with you?" she questioned him in a loud whisper. "They're not like the other representatives here. Much younger."

"They're Nesters, not representatives. They've been helping me. Except for the older two, Pinnet and Dwinna—they represent the Tunnellers and the Clanfeathers."

"Oh, right." Zonda wasn't interested in the details. She stopped when they came to the crest of the next ridge. "There! How about that!"

Ferren looked down over an altered landscape. The Creek still ran across the Plain, but now followed a different course. On this side, where the land slipped sharply down, there were paths, lawn, a cooking area and patches of flowers. On the other side, which was flatter, there were crop fields bigger than any he'd seen so far. He gaped at the bright, golden array of sunflowers next to the Creek and the rows of corn beyond the sunflowers.

"Mature plants already!" he enthused.

"It was a good summer," said Zonda complacently.

"And ten times as many as we used to have!"

"I had channels dug to carry water to the plants. No one ever thought of that before."

Ferren whistled in admiration. Zonda preened and talked on.

"All new except for the old Swimming Pool. Remember? Where we made the shelter to protect us through the great battle. I kept it the same as it was, to remind us of the first thing we ever built. Our totems are in there, too."

"Right, our totems from the Good Times." Ferren nodded. "Seems like you're bringing the Good Times back."

Zonda grinned and preened some more. "I've only just started."

27

For Ferren, the new Home Ground was like a vision of the future, when all Residuals would create a better world for themselves. He felt almost as proud of the achievement as Zonda herself.

"Come!" She grabbed him by the hand. "Now you have to see our caves. I'll give you a tour of *everywhere!*"

Pulled by the hand, Ferren laughed and ran down the far side of the ridge with her. This time she didn't invite the others to follow, but they tagged along anyway.

11

Miriael and Shanna hadn't discussed their next step, and Miriael was glad to postpone the subject. They stayed overnight on top of the stack and slept curled up in their side-by-side pipes. In the morning, when Shanna pushed for a decision, Miriael had her arguments ready.

"Yes, the plan was to go and report the results of the attack to the assembly," she agreed. "But we haven't seen all the results yet."

Shanna frowned. "What else is there?"

"I don't know. What happens with Asmodai and the Humen."

"You said it last night. He makes the Humen more dangerous than ever. The assembly ought to hear about it."

"Maybe not straightaway, though. The representatives will have hardly held their first meeting if we go and report now. The news will dishearten them before they've even started. I think we ought to give them time to get the Residual Alliance fully established before we turn up with the bad news."

"There is that, I suppose."

"And we may have more news in a few days anyway."

"A few days…" Shanna considered. "All right. Then we go."

Miriael couldn't have said why she wanted to stay longer. Her arguments were convincing enough, and she didn't scrutinise her own personal reasons.

Asmodai's wing remained where it had landed on the open ground beyond the nearby overbridge. On the canopies of the Camp, gangs of Hypers worked under the supervision of Queen-Hypers, repairing the wire shield that had been twisted out of alignment.

Later in the morning, Shanna went down to collect their stock of food from the trench under the girders. By the time she returned, new developments were under way. Miriael pointed.

"Look! Humen coming towards us," she said.

It wasn't as large a group as yesterday's procession, and it was advancing along the nearby overbridge rather than the one on the other side of the flying wing.

"They're not coming *here*, are they?" muttered Shanna.

The two of them crept into their metal pipes, where they could observe without being seen. From the height of the stack, they looked down onto the deck of the overbridge. At its closest, the deck passed just a hundred yards from their observation post.

The first thing they observed was the radiance of an angelic aura— Asmodai again, in the middle of the group. Then they recognised Queen-Hypers at the front, loping along with their distinctive springy gait. Lastly, as the group came almost level, they saw that some of the ordinary Hypers at the back were pushing wheelchairs. In the wheelchairs sat half a dozen small, wizened Doctors, their grey, crumpled-looking faces showing out above white medical coats.

Those must be survivors from the fall of Doctor Saniette, thought Miriael. She'd seen Queen-Hypers cutting individual Doctors free from the giant body. *How many more survived?* she wondered.

It looked as though the group would march on past, but then they veered to the other side of the deck. For the first time, Miriael noticed a ramp going down. She stuck her head out further to watch, and Shanna did the same. The group descended the ramp, cut through under the overbridge and entered the construction site.

"It's that special zone," said Shanna. "That's where they're heading."

She was right. The Queen-Hypers opened gates in the high wire fence, and the rest of the group followed them through. The machinery in the zone that had never stopped operating, even during the battle, continued to chug-chug away now.

"What's so important about that place?" Shanna mused aloud.

Miriael hardly heard. Her attention had swung to Asmodai—she couldn't help it. As he came through the fence, she saw him for the first time clearly: his solemn, beautiful face, his curling, floating hair… What she couldn't actually see she imagined. Her pulse rate quickened, and a painful constriction rose in her throat.

She watched as he accompanied the Queen-Hypers to a low structure of massive tubes and girders at the centre of the zone. It looked like some kind of frame, about eighty feet long by thirty feet wide, rising fifteen or twenty feet above the ground. It was clearly unfinished at the top, with ends of tubes and girders projecting upwards.

Whatever it was, Asmodai was obviously very interested in it. When the Doctors arrived, they pointed and appeared to be explaining particular features of the structure to him.

A few minutes later, he began an inspection, circling the tubes and girders. The Doctors in their wheelchairs went round after him.

"Know what I think?" said Shanna—then repeated the phrase more loudly to catch Miriael's attention. "Know what I think?"

"What?"

"I think your evil angel has taken over. He hasn't just joined the Humen, he's their lord and master."

"Oh? How do you know?"

"Because they're all so subservient towards him. Watch the Doctors. Watch their body language."

When Miriael thought about it, she had to agree. The Doctors behaved like underlings, Asmodai behaved like a commander. She was still studying the interactions when Asmodai suddenly flicked a glance towards the stacks—towards the top of the very stack that was their observation post.

Miriael drew back at once to hide in her metal pipe. It was as though he'd looked straight at her! Had he known? How could he have known?

"What's the matter?" She heard Shanna's puzzled voice outside. "Nobody saw us."

Shanna hadn't retreated into *her* pipe. Miriael thanked her stars that she'd been wearing the jerkin over the bright gold of her hair. Perhaps he hadn't been looking straight at her after all… But a disturbing memory had jumped into her mind.

"Now there's a connection to me in you, and to you in me."

Asmodai had said that to her after what he'd called an imprinting. The imprinting was supposed to establish a line of communication between the two of them, so that she could summon him merely by reciting, *Veni Asmodai, veni ad me.* She'd welcomed it at the time, and he *had* come when summoned. But now...

She remembered the feel of two hands pressing gently against her head, she remembered the darkness opening up before her and drawing her out...then the tiny, bright figure in the darkness...then a burning light that shot forth and pierced her, penetrated her...

She shuddered at the recollection. What if the line of communication was still there? Although she'd rejected him utterly, had that connection remained inside her?

She refused to come out from her pipe when Shanna announced, "Looks like they've finished." She stayed hidden even when Shanna told her, "They're returning to the ramp now." Only when she heard Shanna say, "They're on the way back along the overbridge," did she feel it was safe to come out.

12

By his second day in the Home Ground, Ferren was familiar with all its new features. The hub of the tribe's life was a community area between the Creek and the steeply sloping bluff into which they had dug their caves. Each cave typically held two, three or four occupants, whether families of the People or representatives of the Residual Alliance. Only Zonda, as leader, had a cave to herself.

Ferren found himself sharing a cave with the young male Nesters, Bross, Flens and Tadge, while Kiet, Rhinn, Gibby and Ethany were put into a separate cave. Their caves had been used for storage, but the stores were soon moved out and the interiors refurnished. Their beds were hollows in the ground, with a layer of woven cloth over a layer of feathers over a layer of soft, green rushes.

By his second day, Ferren had also visited all the representatives' caves and talked with all the representatives. He had met them before when joining tribes up to the Residual Alliance, but some he knew better than others. In one cave were Shillow of the Sandlings, Clerty of the Greycaps and Heskie of the Homekin. Another held Chervis of the Truebloods and Pedge of the Skinfellows. Then there was Rance of the Baggers with Scobbs of the Upbreed and Hove of the Claydwellers. Pinnet, who'd arrived with Ferren, moved in with Nye of the Treetoppers. The other latest arrival, Dwinna, joined the other female representative, Briall of the Waymakers.

Ferren was disappointed, though not surprised, that the representatives were mostly older members of their tribes. Young Residuals were typically more receptive to new ideas than their seniors. So far, the assembly's single young representative was Zonda, who had nominated herself to speak for the People.

It was Zonda who took Ferren round from cave to cave and introduced each representative to him as though he'd never set eyes on them before. She also backed him up when he raised their morale by describing the rescue team's triumph over Doctor Saniette.

"We left the whole Camp helpless and leaderless," he told them. "So now Heaven's attacking to finish them off."

"They're done for!" cried Zonda, clapping her hands. "No more Humen, no more Selectors!"

"That's the sort of thing Residuals like us can achieve," said Ferren.

"We're the best!" Zonda clapped her hands again. "Our assembly will change the world!"

She spoke glowingly of the assembly in general, but she was less complimentary about individual representatives when talking about them afterwards. She found them comical, as though she had nothing in common with any of them.

"They're so weird, aren't they?" she confided to Ferren. "That Heskie of the Homekin with a live snake wrapped round his waist! He must be out of his mind!"

"All the Homekin do it," Ferren told her.

"All out of their minds, then. Phuh!"

She was even more scornful of Scobbs of the Upbreed. "Do you know why he speaks so funny? It's because he has a peach stone in his mouth. All the time, eating or talking or whatever. Don't tell me his whole tribe's the same."

"Yes," said Ferren.

Similarly with Rance of the Baggers. "Guess why he carries that little bag round his neck. He keeps all his nail clippings and hair clippings in there. A whole lifetime's worth of them!"

And similarly with Pedge of the Skinfellows. "Did you ever see anything so crazy? With those weights on his ears, pulling them nearly down to his shoulders. Why would anyone do that?"

Ferren passed over her scoffing comments until she made one within earshot of Nye of the Treetoppers. "What does he think he is, a possum? Does he really believe that hanging a tail between his legs—"

"You seem just as weird to him," Ferren hissed at her out of the side of his mouth.

"Me? I'm normal. Me and you and the People—we're the only normal ones."

Ferren shook his head. "Every tribe thinks it's normal. They could make fun of us for the things *we* do."

Zonda looked at him for a moment, pouted—then laughed. "All right, if you say so. I won't make fun of them again."

"For the sake of the Residual Alliance."

"For the sake of the Residual Alliance," she repeated. "I promise."

From then on, she held back the scoffing comments and put all her energy into spreading enthusiasm. "This is our time!" she told everyone. "All of us together!"

13

There had been no angels in the sky since the attack on the Camp had been thwarted. Miriael knew that Heaven usually kept a few angels hovering on high as observers, but no longer. It wasn't hard to guess why. For the first time in all the years of terra-celestial warfare,

Heaven had lost control of the sky.

The threat of the great delta wing was enough; Asmodai didn't need to fly around in it. While he exercised his new powers inside the Camp, the wing remained on the ground outside. Surveying it from the height of their stack, Miriael noted that its upper surface was a different colour to its surface below: a dull charcoal grey underneath, but a glittering white on top. Sometimes she imagined she could see Morphs attached to its upper surface, their snowflake-like patterns shimmering in the sunlight. But, in truth, she couldn't tell how or where the Morphs were attached. She couldn't see anything clearly at this distance.

She wondered if Heaven knew that Asmodai was now the leader of the Bankstown Camp. They probably knew he was responsible for the flying wing and probably suspected that he'd chosen the Humen side for good. But whatever they suspected, they surely didn't realise the tremendous danger he posed. He wouldn't be content with just a successful defence!

Should she try to warn them? She could go up to Heaven in a visionary dream, even though it was hard to make herself visible up there. But would they listen to her? They'd despised her before, and if she had to explain why she knew so much about Asmodai… She had so much more to be ashamed of now! On the whole, she was glad that Heaven had forbidden her to communicate through visionary dreams.

It was the day after Asmodai's visit to the fenced-off zone, and Miriael was lying curled up in her pipe when Shanna called out, "Come and see! You have to see this!"

Miriael emerged and looked where Shanna was looking. It was another kind of procession approaching along the overbridge that ran by the construction site. There was no sign of Asmodai this time, and if there were Doctors and Queen-Hypers, they were lost among the vast mass of marching Hypers. But even the Hypers were dwarfed by the monstrous transport machines accompanying them.

"I don't think it's an army for fighting," said Shanna.

Miriael understood what she meant. The Hypers carried what appeared to be tools rather than weapons, and none of the vehicles had a military look about them.

The rumble of engines and pounding of boots swelled to a thunderous volume. The head of the procession was just two hundred yards away, yet more Hypers and machines continued to pour out from the Camp. Miriael and Shanna retreated into the safety of their pipes.

"They're all workers! A labour force!" Shanna shouted across.

"I can guess where they're going," Miriael shouted back.

Her guess proved right. As the head of the procession reached the nearby ramp, shouts and orders rang out, and the note of the engines changed. Then Hypers with their transport machines descended to the ground, passed under the overbridge and entered the construction site.

They spread out far and wide across the site, but there was no doubt about their focus: the special, fenced-off zone that Asmodai had visited—and within the zone, the structure of tubes and girders he'd particularly inspected. Miriael watched as they congregated around it and began setting up equipment.

"What *is* that thing?" Shanna shouted across to her.

Miriael shook her head, equally baffled. "We'll have to wait till they build more of it," she shouted back.

14

Day by day, more representatives arrived at the Home Ground for the assembly. Kiet found them all fascinating, with their curious accents, customs and styles of dress. She would never have thought people could be so different!

She met Moireen of the Sea-folk, who smelled strongly of fish, wore a necklace of pierced seashells and tied her sun-bleached hair up in a topknot. Then there was Jerrock of the Longheads, covered from head to foot in tattoos of what looked like moths or butterflies. With his guttural accent and brusque, blunt manner, he was the very opposite of polite, soft-spoken Floy of the Fusselfolk. Floy's lips were stained purple, and he wore bracelets and anklets of black, velvety fur.

Most surprising of all was Anniga of the Nod-bodies. Anniga's face and shoulders were daubed with mud, and she seemed to live in a state of perpetual motion. Even as she stood and talked, she tapped her fingers against her hips or the satchel she carried, as if marking the beat of some inaudible rhythm.

The only representative Kiet didn't like was Zonda of the People. At first, she accompanied Ferren when Zonda took him round from cave to cave, but she soon gave up. She went off to a quiet spot with the zither to tell Peeper all about it.

"She takes over all the time," she complained. "Everything's always about her. You'd think she broke into the Humen Camp with the rescue team herself. *And* saved Miriael. *And* destroyed Doctor Saniette."

Peeper uttered soothing, cheeping sounds, but nothing in words. From Kiet's point of view, he made the perfect listener.

"So pushy, so full of herself. She ignores me like I wasn't even there. Just her and Ferren. It's as though they've been best friends since forever." She scowled and thought about it. "Perhaps they have. I thought he was more of a loner, but they grew up together in the same tribe. There must've been some sort of closeness between them... They seem to share so many experiences. What do you think, little one?"

Peeper's only response was another consoling cheep. Kiet sighed. She had Peeper to talk to, along with her sister and brother and young Nester friends. Yet she still felt excluded and somehow unhappy.

With family and friends, one thing discussed was the representation of their own tribe at the assembly. The Nesters were supposed to have two representatives because of their large numbers, but so far nobody had appeared.

"Maybe *we* could be representatives," Flens suggested. "Two of us."

"Me!" said Tadge at once.

"No, you're too young," Rhinn shut him down. "Kiet would be one, of course."

There was no argument about that, but a great deal of argument about who the other should be. Flens or Bross or Ethany or Gibby or even Rhinn herself? They debated it and grew quite heated about it, without ever knowing if stand-in representatives would even be allowed.

As it turned out, there was no need. Kiet was alone with Peeper in their cave when Flens stuck his head in at the doorway.

"Our Nester representatives have arrived," he announced. "You'll never guess who!"

"Who?"

"Skail and Stogget."

Kiet groaned. Skail was the Guardian of her own stock, Bloodstock; although not as old in years as most representatives, he was old in cunning. He'd been negative about the whole idea of a Residual Alliance until he'd suddenly decided to switch sides. Stogget was the Nesters' established champion wrestler, whom Bross had been planning to challenge.

"I can understand how Skail got himself chosen," said Flens. "He could arrange it if he wanted it. But Stogget? He doesn't have a brain in his head."

Kiet considered. "Maybe Skail arranged that as well."

"Why? Why him?"

"Because he'll do whatever he's told. Skail will be the brains, and Stogget will be the brawn."

"Hmm. Not good, then, is it?"

"It's the worst. Were you talking to them?"

"Yes, with Ferren and Ethany and Bross. We told Skail about rescuing Miriael and destroying Doctor Saniette. But…" Flens spread his hands in a resigned sort of gesture. "Not impressed."

Kiet rose to her feet. "I suppose I'd better go and show myself, too."

She found Skail and Stogget beside a storage cave that was being emptied out to serve as their residence. Skail was questioning some of the People who were doing the emptying, Stogget stood watching with arms akimbo. When Kiet came up, Skail swung towards her, his lips pinched tight, his pale, wide forehead creased in a frown.

"Ah, you," he said. "I thought it wouldn't be long."

"What?" Kiet bristled at the note of accusation in his tone.

"The ringleader shows up. Kiet of Bloodstock. You encouraged your friends to sneak off without telling their families. You didn't even tell your Guardian. Don't you have *any* sense of duty and behaviour?"

"You'd have stopped us."

"Perhaps. Perhaps not. I'm responsible for you, remember."

Kiet understood the accusation, and also felt the injustice of it. "We all survived, didn't we? What about what we achieved? Doesn't that count—"

"What counts is foolish, thoughtless behaviour. And even now you haven't returned home. I suppose it was you who encouraged the others to come here? Sneaking your way into an assembly that's none of your business."

Kiet could hardly speak for the temper building inside her. He was turning everything upside down, refusing to open his mind…

"I'm glad Bross is here, at least," he added.

For a moment, surprise outweighed her anger. "What's that supposed to mean?"

"It means you need to complete your bond to him. You've done First Intimacies with him. The sooner you do Second and Third, the better."

"Oh, I see. Then I'll be more obedient, is that the idea?"

"You'll settle down in Nester territory and start a family. It's my job as your Guardian to make sure you do. I know Bross will protect you."

"*Protect* me? Don't lie. You want him to keep me in line."

Stogget, who'd been silent until now, unfolded his arms and spoke. "As it should be."

Skail narrowed his eyes and confronted Kiet face to face. "We all remember that tendency in you," he said. "We've been working to control it since you were fourteen. You'll endanger us all if it comes out again."

Kiet bit her lip and walked off before she could explode. She knew what he was referring to: the time when the Selectors had taken her parents for military service, and she'd run to attack them with a length of wood. She might have done something similar right now—but then she'd have proved Skail's point, of course.

"He can't force me to do anything," she told Peeper afterwards. "Ferren and the others won't let him. We're here for the assembly, and we're staying put."

Later that same day, the representatives from the two last tribes turned up: Corm of the Basketmen and Bertel of the Handmates. With all twenty-one representatives now present, the first meeting of the Residual Alliance assembly was set for the following morning.

15

Ferren rose to his feet to launch the meeting. At last the moment had arrived! He scanned every face and clapped his hands for attention.

Even the weather was favourable: sunny, with a light breeze and not a cloud in the sky. The representatives sat in a semi-circle in the community area between the bluff and the Creek. The young Nesters were there too, sitting further back, along with all the members of the People not busy working.

Ferren began by echoing Zonda's phrase. "This is our time! The time of tribespeople like us! The end of the Humen! You heard what *we* did to their giant Doctor Saniette, and the angels have probably done the rest by now. But we don't depend on Heaven any more than we depend on the Humen. We look after our own interests. That's what the Residual Alliance is all about."

There was a general nodding of heads and a murmur of approval.

"Yes, we take the place of the Humen because it's our place by right." Ferren went on. "We're descended from the original inhabitants of this world. We call them by different names—Ancestors, Old Ones, Lords of the Earth or whatever—but we've all kept the memory. Long, long ago, they built cities of tall, white buildings, they lived in peace and prosperity and happiness. We've all seen their ruins and preserved their relics."

He was repeating what he'd said when joining tribes up to the Residual Alliance, but it was good for them to hear it again.

"These are hands"—he displayed his outspread hands—"like the hands that did the building! This"—he tapped a finger to his forehead—"this is a brain like the brains that invented moto-cars and electrics and shop-shops! We've done it before, we can do it again! All of us! It was our past—and it *will be* our future! We begin to create it with the decisions of this assembly!"

Applause broke out, and the young Nesters waved their fists in the air.

Then Skail rose to his feet. He had been applauding and continued to applaud. He gave Ferren a look that said as plainly as words, *If you've finished…?*

Ferren remained standing a moment, then realised he *had* finished. He sat down and yielded the floor to Skail. Skail kept on clapping until everyone else had stopped.

"Well said, well said." He turned first to Ferren, then addressed the representatives. "Many decisions to be made. And the very first is, how do we decide decisions?"

Puzzled frowns appeared on the representatives' faces. Stogget cried, "Hear, hear!" though it wasn't clear that he understood either.

"It's what everyone agrees," said Zonda.

Skail turned back to Ferren. "How do we know what everyone agrees?"

Ferren shrugged. "When they say yes."

"What if some say no? How do we decide between them?"

Ferren compressed his lips. He felt he was being played with. "Then we all take a vote. People raise their hands to be counted."

"Yes, a counting of hands, and the majority wins." Skail nodded and smiled. "When you said, 'We all take a vote,' it sounded as though you were including yourself."

"How do you mean?"

"Well, your tribe of the People has one representative, doesn't it?" Skail pointed to Zonda. "I thought she was the one."

"She is."

"Wouldn't it be unfair if your tribe had twice the vote of any other tribe?"

Ferren thought of mentioning the Nesters' own double represent-ation, but since he'd made that arrangement himself…

Moireen of the Sea-folk spoke up. "But he started the Residual Alliance. He *is* the Residual Alliance."

"You want to allow an exception?" Skail pursed his thin lips, as though considering.

"Yes!" cried several voices. "Why not?"

"We *could*," said Skail. "By a majority vote. But does he get to vote in that vote?"

Now there were voices for and voices against, all speaking at the same time.

"And would there be any more exceptions?" Skail went on, raising his own voice. "Look at all the other members of his tribe sitting here too. *And* other members of my tribe, too." He swung an arm to encompass the young Nesters and People sitting further back behind the representatives. "I could ask for an exception and have many more Nester votes. But would that be fair? I'd rather stay with what our tribes agreed to when we joined up."

Ferren scanned the semi-circle of representatives. The meeting was in danger of falling into chaos and confusion.

"It's all right," he called out. "I don't have to have a vote. Let's stay with what the tribes agreed to."

"I think that's fair," said Skail, and Stogget backed him up with another, "Hear, hear!"

The hubbub subsided. The representatives looked from Ferren to Skail, then back again.

"We have to remain unified," Ferren told them. "That's the most important thing."

"Exactly," said Skail. "So let's say that only representatives can speak and vote in the assembly."

Ferren didn't pick up on the word, but another voice burst out immediately. "What do you mean, *speak?*"

It was Kiet, sitting with the other young Nesters. Skail frowned at the interruption. He didn't address his answer to Kiet but to the representatives.

"We don't want endless speeches by onlookers who can't vote." Again he swung an arm to encompass the young Nesters and People. "There's as many of them as us. Everything would take twice as long."

"He's already spoken, hasn't he?" objected Dwinna of the Clanfeathers, indicating Ferren.

"Of course. And very right and proper," Skail agreed at once. "I'm not saying onlookers can't speak, only that they speak by invitation of the assembly."

"After a majority vote, of course," Ferren put in ironically.

"If necessary." Skail smiled, though the smile never reached his eyes. "Of course, you'd have been invited, no problem about that. But it has to be the same rule for everyone, don't you agree?"

"That's nonsense!" cried Flens, springing to his feet. "You always want to impose rules and regulations! We know all about you!"

The other young Nesters backed him up. "Always the same!" "Wants control!" "*He* doesn't care about the Residual Alliance!"

Skail dropped the smile and turned to the representatives. "You see? This is what happens if we allow onlookers to speak whenever they like. Exactly what I was talking about. Shouting and disruption and—"

He broke off as the clamour rose to a crescendo. The representatives joined in, and everyone jumped up and began yelling over everyone else. Some of the loudest yells were pleas for "Quiet!" "Enough!" "Stop it!" Ferren was one of those shouting for calm.

Finally, calm returned. Skail seized the opportunity to go on with his speech.

"As I was saying. If you let people speak who don't have a vote, they can bully those who do. Bringing pressure. Improper influence. We wouldn't want that."

"You expect us to sit in silence?" Kiet demanded. Like most of the young Nesters, she was still on her feet.

"Yes." Skail's voice was a venomous hiss. "You're too young to speak anyway. The assembly doesn't want to listen to *you.*"

Kiet scanned the representatives and clearly didn't find the signs of support she was seeking. "Then I don't want to listen to *them!*" she snapped—and swung on her heel and strode off.

In another moment, the other young Nesters followed her.

Ferren watched in dismay. The situation had played out in the worst possible way. *We have to remain unified,* he thought. *That's all that matters.* Then he realised Skail was addressing him.

"What about you?" Skail's mild tone didn't match the glint of victory in his eye. "You don't agree with them, do you?"

Ferren *did* agree with the young Nesters, but he didn't want to create more disunity. He couldn't say yes, and he wouldn't say no. Skail had him trapped, and they both knew it.

"There's no need for you to go," said Skail, suggestively.

Ferren rose to his feet with a shake of his head. "No need, but I think I will. I've made my speech, and I'll speak again when invited. The important thing is for you all to make decisions and advance the cause. I leave you to it."

He walked out of the semi-circle and away from the community area. *For the sake of the Residual Alliance,* he told himself. *That's all that matters.*

16

The young Nesters had gathered in the cave where Kiet, Rhinn, Gibby and Ethany slept. Ferren's feet took him there almost of their own volition. Everyone inside was jabbering away about Skail and the assembly.

"You walked out too!" cried Kiet, seeing him enter the cave.

"I sort of walked out," he said. "Not like you."

"You did the right thing!" she proclaimed.

"I wish it hadn't happened," he muttered, more to himself than her. The noise in the cave drowned his words out anyway.

He was already having doubts about his choice. Should he have stayed on as a silent onlooker? Could he have influenced the representatives merely by his presence? Would it have been wrong if he did influence them?

He listened with one ear to the furious chatter in the cave, but he also looked out from time to time towards the assembly. So far as he could tell, Skail was doing most of the talking while the representatives listened. He hoped they were making some good decisions, though for a long while he didn't see any hands raised.

When he did see hands raised, it wasn't good at all. Zonda had been arguing with Skail, but she must have lost the vote. The members of the People who'd been sitting near the semi-circle of representatives rose slowly to their feet and walked away.

"He's got rid of them too," said Kiet, who happened to look out at the same time. "No observers. No one to watch what he does. *That's* what he was aiming for."

It was an hour later before hands were raised for another vote. Then the first meeting of the assembly broke up. The representatives mostly wandered off to their own caves, but Zonda came looking for Ferren.

"Huh!" she snorted, entering the cave. "Huh!"

Everyone bombarded her with questions, but it was Ferren's question she answered. "Was it as bad as it looked? It was stupid and boring, that's what! Nothing about building a better future. Only little things."

"We saw the People having to leave."

"Yes." Zonda scowled. "Stupid and boring *and* annoying. Skail claimed they were influencing decisions. We didn't make any real decisions!"

She reported the discussions and speeches, so far as she could be bothered to remember them. Ferren quizzed her patiently for details. It was obvious he wouldn't be invited to speak again in a hurry.

"You're our eyes and ears at the assembly now," he told Zonda. "We rely on you to tell us what goes on."

"Mmm, you depend on me, don't you?" The thought seemed to please her. "All right. I'll come here again after the next meeting. Wait for me here."

The next meeting was the following morning. Once again, Ferren and the male Nesters joined the female Nesters in their cave; once again, Zonda came in both bored and frustrated. There had been many trivial decisions about the operation of the assembly—along with one significant one.

"Now he says we have to have someone responsible for calling the votes and counting hands raised for or against. An 'overseer', he calls it."

"And he wants to be it," said Rhinn. "Of course."

"I argued against it, but they outvoted me. We haven't voted on *who* yet." Zonda pouted. "I'm going to stand against him."

"When?" asked Ferren.

"Tomorrow morning." Zonda flounced her hair and swivelled her hips. "I'll show him who's popular! The little squirt! I'll walk all over him!"

"He doesn't have to be popular," said Kiet. "He's cunning."

"He hasn't got what I've got," Zonda asserted with supreme

confidence. "I'll go round all the representatives this afternoon and win them over.

"I think it's a good idea," Ferren agreed. "You're our only chance."

Zonda looked at Kiet. "*She* doesn't think so."

Ferren also looked at Kiet, who drew a deep breath. "We really appreciate anything you can do. All of us here. You'll do it if anyone can. I'm just saying it won't be easy."

Zonda was mollified. "It'll be easy for *me*." She turned to Ferren. "You can watch from my cave if you like. Don't let the representatives see you, though. Be there when the assembly starts."

"I will." He accepted at once. "Thanks."

17

Whereas the cave that Ferren shared with the young male Nesters was further along the Creek, Zonda's cave looked directly down onto the community area. When Ferren set off for it in the morning, Kiet appeared as if by magic out of *her* cave and walked along with him.

"You don't mind if I come too?" she suggested.

Ferren looked at her. A blustery wind had sprung up overnight, and her dark red hair billowed out spectacularly round her head.

"Er, yes, should be all right," he agreed.

Zonda's cave was less bare than most, with pots and baskets, cast-aside clothes and a woven rug. The walls were covered with scratch-marks for counting the days, while an inscribed diagram of the Home Ground took up one third of the floor. Ferren and Kiet stood on either side of the doorway, where they could spy out without being seen...

Even before the meeting began, they discovered a problem. Although they could see the representatives gathering, they couldn't hear when they spoke to one another. The wind was too strong and blew the words away.

"Just our luck!" Kiet snorted in disgust.

They watched the whole meeting as a kind of dumb-show. Representatives stood up to speak, then sat when they'd finished. Skail stayed on his feet throughout and spoke more than anyone. Everyone seemed to be shouting against the wind, but their words still didn't carry to Ferren and Kiet. Meanwhile, Stogget prowled around with a menacing expression, or positioned himself very close to certain representatives until they had second thoughts about standing to speak.

One representative he couldn't quell was Zonda. She bounced up and down, strode to the centre of the semi-circle, flung out her arms and grew increasingly passionate. But it wasn't clear whether her passion had more effect than Skail's quiet insistence.

The assembly took several votes. Ferren and Kiet saw hands go up, but had no way of knowing what was approved or rejected. They could guess the purpose of the final vote, however—Zonda's furious reaction was enough of a giveaway, and Skail's bow of acknowledgement confirmed it. The final vote had decided who was to be the new overseer, and Zonda had lost out to Skail. The meeting closed soon afterwards.

Ferren and Kiet were still talking it over when Zonda came storming back to her cave.

"He fixed it beforehand!" she raged. "He went round the representatives and turned them against me!"

"How?" asked Ferren, and immediately drew her rage onto himself. "How should I know?"

"He'd find ways," said Kiet. "He's sneaky like that."

Zonda swivelled. "What's *she* doing here?"

"I invited her," said Ferren. "That's all right, isn't it?"

Zonda glowered and changed the subject. "I'm sick of the whole thing! Assembly, representatives—phah! I'm through with it!"

"But you're our eyes and ears—" Ferren began.

"You *can't* drop out!" Kiet was outraged. "You can't be sick of the Residual Alliance! You *have* to keep going to the assembly!"

Zonda focused on her again. "You don't tell me what to do!"

Ferren saw Kiet grit her teeth, then suddenly felt her eyes upon him. In another moment, she swung right around and walked out of the cave.

"Wait!" he cried, but she'd already disappeared. What did that look of hers mean?

"Back in a minute," he told Zonda, and hurried out after her.

She had gone twenty paces, but slowed to a stop when she heard him following. Face to face, she confronted him, still with that strange look in her eyes. Anger was definitely a part of it...

"Go back to her!" she hissed.

"What?"

"I left so you could be alone with her."

"I don't understand."

"Someone has to make her keep going to the assembly. And it won't be me. Only you can persuade her. She doesn't like me."

"She doesn't like me much right now, either."

"Yes, she does. She will. Be nice to her. Talk about old memories. Talk about all the things you share. You can win her over if you try."

"All right. But why are you—" He was going to ask why she had to be so angry about it, until she silenced him with a glare.

"Just do it!"

In the next moment, she had walked on again. Ferren shrugged and went back to Zonda in her cave.

18

In the construction site next to the Bankstown Camp, the work continued at a feverish pitch twenty-four hours a day. Arc-lights shone, Hypers milled around like ants, tools sprayed bright cascades of sparks. All through the nights, Miriael and Shanna heard the sounds of machinery whirring and hammering, clanging and clanking. The focus of activity was the special fenced-off zone, but transport vehicles moved among the stacks carrying construction materials to the zone from all parts of the site.

Miriael still couldn't work out what they were building. The central frame-like structure had risen no higher than before, the ends of tubes and girders still projecting at the top. At most, it appeared perhaps a little less skeletal, a little more filled-in. So far as Miriael could see, the construction materials going into the zone were simply swallowed up.

Shanna hadn't revived the subject of going to report to the assembly, and Miriael was happy to let it lie. As the days passed, their original stock of food ran out, but Shanna had the answer. She climbed down from their observation post at night, went scouting around the site and came back with two bottles filled with a strange, syrupy liquid.

"Try it," she urged Miriael. "It's as nourishing as a meal. It's what the Plasmatics live on."

Miriael thought about it. "And since the Plasmatics are made from Residual organs and tissue…"

"What works for them works for us." Shanna nodded. "And probably you too. It's what kept me going all the time I lived by myself in the Humen Camp."

Miriael took a cautious sip. The syrup tasted pleasant enough, very sweet and thick on the tongue.

She was curious about Shanna's life as a saboteur, and, over several conversations, she heard the whole story. There had been countless adventures and misadventures, risky exploits and hairbreadth escapes, trials and emergencies and self-imposed missions. Shanna told it all, from her original escape out of the baths in the pit to her first small nuisance acts of revenge to ever more ambitious feats of sabotage—up to her ultimate achievement of blacking out power over half the Humen Camp. Miriael listened in amazement.

Shanna was equally curious about Miriael's past as a warrior angel in Heaven. Miriael did her best to describe it, but she didn't get very far. It was almost impossible to convey the communal togetherness of angels, the touching of spirit to spirit—and soon her eyes were wet with the memory of times to which she could never return.

"It's all right," said Shanna. "Enough. Stop now."

Miriael shook her head. "I'm not what I was as a warrior angel. I need to leave memories of Heaven behind."

Shanna didn't question her again, but she must have continued thinking about it. Another time, she brought up the past in a different way.

"We're similar, you know," she said. "We're both outcasts."

Miriael didn't understand. "*I* am. I'm exiled from Heaven. But you're with your own people again."

"Not really. I've been too long away. Two and a half years, living a completely unnatural, solitary life. I had to make myself hard and cold and ruthless to survive. I don't think I can ever get back to what I was."

"You will. Give it time."

"Maybe. But I don't seem to be fully human right now."

"Ah, we're similar from opposite sides, then." Miriael nodded. "You're not fully human, and I'm not fully angel."

"A pair of freaks is what we are!" cried Shanna, and burst out laughing.

Although the frame-like structure in the special zone never appeared to change, they observed two new developments outside the construction site. Shanna was first to notice that Asmodai's flying wing wasn't in quite the same position on the bare, flat ground between the overbridges.

"You see?" She pointed. "Yesterday it was more facing *that* way, and today it's more facing *this.*"

Miriael saw what she meant. "I wonder… Do you think Asmodai flew off somewhere in the night?"

"We'll have to stay awake and keep watch."

They observed the second new development later the same day, when a far-off thunder of engines and marching boots drew their attention. The sound came not from the overbridges on either side of the flying wing, but from another overbridge further around. They shielded their eyes and stared into the distance.

"It's an army marching out from the Camp!" said Shanna.

Miriael, with her sharper angelic sight, was already counting the armoured machines, transport vehicles and companies of Hypers. "A big army. Asmodai must be up to something."

"Maybe it's connected to him flying off," Shanna suggested. "If that's what he's doing."

When they stayed awake that night to watch, there was no doubt about it. They tracked the glowing oval of Asmodai's aura all the way to the wing, then saw the great delta shoot off into the sky. Once again, it came back before dawn.

19

Ferren watched from Zonda's cave as the representatives gathered for their next meeting. Zonda herself was among them, after he'd successfully persuaded her to continue attending. In fact, he'd done better than persuade her, he'd filled her with new determination. Today, she intended to push for discussion and decisions on issues that really mattered for the Residual Alliance.

Yesterday's wind had died down, and he could hear every word uttered when the meeting began. It wasn't long before Zonda rose to her feet and launched her campaign for action.

"We have to talk about the purpose of the Residual Alliance. We've settled the details of how this assembly runs." A hint of a grimace appeared, then disappeared, on her face. "Now it's time to deal with the big issues."

There were many nods and murmurs of agreement. Ferren saw a silent exchange of looks between Stogget and Skail: a quizzical look from Stogget, a faint shake of the head from Skail. The overseer had judged the mood of the meeting and had opted to go along with it.

"Indeed, well said." He took up his favourite position in the middle of the semi-circle. "I'd like to offer some ideas…"

But Ferren was distracted from Skail's ideas by an unexpected arrival. Kiet slipped in suddenly through the doorway of Zonda's cave.

"Thought I'd come and watch again today," she said, with a false sort of brightness.

Ferren was troubled. Zonda hadn't been pleased to find Kiet in her cave yesterday, and keeping Zonda pleased had become a priority. Even Kiet had said so. But now she saw the look on his face and scowled.

"Why not? Why should you be the only one to know what's happening?"

"Yes, but…" He could see she was spoiling for a fight, and let the sentence drop.

"Don't worry," she jeered. "I'll be gone before *she* gets back."

He shrugged and went back to watching the assembly. Kiet in this state of mind was a total mystery to him.

Down below in the community area, Skail was now wagging his finger as he addressed the representatives.

"The purpose of the Residual Alliance is to look after our own interests, isn't that right? We're not with the Humen and we're not with Heaven. Whatever works to benefit the tribes…"

Ferren nodded to himself. He agreed with the basic principle. But he stopped nodding when Skail went on to give his view of the tribes' position.

"There are two great forces fighting this war. We're small and insignificant in comparison. But if we keep our heads down and don't antagonise them, we'll be able to play them off against each other."

Keep low, keep small, keep out of sight, Ferren thought ironically to himself. Skail's language reminded him of old Neath's phrase, the motto by which his own tribe had lived in the past.

Zonda was back on her feet again. "Maybe there won't be two forces anymore," she said. "Haven't you heard? The angels are attacking the Humen Camp. If they wipe it out, we won't have the Humen round here anymore. No Humen, no Selectors, no military service."

Many representatives cheered at the prospect. But Skail held to his point of view.

"*If* they wipe it out," he said. "That's a big *if.* And would it benefit us if they did? If Heaven becomes all-powerful, we lose our leverage. How can we negotiate if they don't need to keep us onside?"

"I want to see the Humen finished for good," said Moireen of the Sea-folk.

"Me too," agreed Pedge of the Skinfellows. "They took my daughter for military service."

"And we know what *that* means!" Zonda shook her fist. "Siphoned off! Dismembered!"

"You *can't* negotiate with the Humen!" cried Rance of the Baggers

"What would you negotiate?" Anniga of the Nod-bodies demanded. "An end to military service?"

Skail flapped his arms for silence. "Enough! Only one at a time! You have to stand before you speak!"

Half a dozen representatives jumped to their feet. Stogget moved round towards them, but they remained standing. Again, Skail signalled with a small shake of his head.

"We can negotiate with anyone if we have to," he insisted.

"Negotiate an end to military service?" Anniga repeated her question.

"Possibly. But we shouldn't be too greedy at first. Small steps, not asking too much."

Ferren heard Kiet's snort of contempt. He shared the feeling completely

The debate among the representatives went endlessly back and forth. Skail produced further arguments, and many in the assembly were inclined to listen to him. Others followed Zonda's lead and opposed everything he said.

Finally, Zonda strode to the middle of the semi-circle, jostled Skail aside and demanded in a loud voice, "Who's ready to take a vote?"

Skail jostled back and tried to out-shout her. "I'm the overseer here! I decide when to take a vote! You don't even have a proposal to vote on!"

"Yes, I do!"

"What?"

"I propose…I propose…I propose…"

At first, Ferren thought Zonda was struggling to formulate a proposal. Then he realised she'd lost her train of thought. She was staring towards the top of the bluff, at something above the cave where he and Kiet were hidden.

The representatives had all been facing the other way, but they swivelled to stare in the same direction. Jaws dropped and eyes widened. Some gasped, some flinched, some pointed.

"What *is* it?" Kiet muttered.

Ferren stuck his head right out of the doorway and twisted to look up—yet still couldn't get a view of whatever was there above them.

"Don't let them see you!" Kiet hissed at him. "We're not supposed…"

He ducked back inside. He suspected that the representatives *had* seen him, but they weren't thinking about forbidden observers. They continued to gape in horror, frozen as if paralysed.

The horror transferred to Ferren, though he still didn't know the cause. The hairs stood up on the back of his neck.

Then the cause came into view. In great springy leaps, a tall, black, rubber-clad figure descended the bluff. It was one of the special, new Hypers with augmented powers. A Queen-Hyper!

Her shadow passed by just to the left of their doorway. Now Ferren could see the plastic blister on her back, the copper circuitry on her shoulders, the curls of blonde hair painted on her head. She carried a bag slung over her shoulder like a handbag, and a weapon with a cone-shaped nozzle. He knew that kind of weapon: a flamethrower.

He shrank deeper into the cave, and Kiet shrank back, too. They'd both had past experience of Queen-Hypers with flamethrowers when rescuing Miriael.

Peering out again a few moments later, they saw that the Queen-Hyper had displaced Skail and Zonda in the middle of the semi-circle. She addressed the representatives in a silky, sibilant voice.

"Greetings to you all from the Humen of the Bankstown Camp. And from our great and glorious leader."

20

Ferren's heart sank. So Heaven hadn't conquered the Humen Camp after all! The Queen-Hyper proved it by her very presence here. He looked at Kiet in dismay.

"They've got themselves a new leader too." She sounded no less numb and shocked than he felt himself. "Destroying Doctor Saniette didn't stop anything."

Down below in the community area, the representatives were starting to recover their voices. Zonda was the first to speak up.

"We thought you were under attack in your Camp. We were told you were going to be…you know…"

She faltered over the word, and the Queen-Hyper said it for her. "Defeated? Us defeated? By Heaven? I don't think so! They thought they could take advantage and tried to attack. Phah!" A blob of iridescent spittle gleamed in her mouthslit. "We have a new leader now, and we're stronger than ever."

"Oh, right." Zonda's shoulders slumped.

The Queen-Hyper swung her flamethrower casually in Zonda's direction. "Are you in charge here?"

"No," said Zonda, and pointed to Skail. "He's our overseer."

Skail had backed away to the side, apparently trying to become invisible. The Queen-Hyper took two long, lithe strides towards him.

"You're the overseer? Stand up straight, no need to be afraid. What's your name?"

"Skail. Skail of the Nesters. *I* never thought you'd been defeated."

"Very wise of you, Skail of the Nesters. Because we never will be." The Queen-Hyper turned from him to the representatives in general. "And here you all are, gathered together. Perfect! Representing many different tribes all in the one place. It'll save so much trouble."

"How did you know?" Zonda asked. "Who told you about a representatives' meeting?"

The Queen-Hyper smiled—or at least her mouthslit curved upwards. The garish lipstick around the slit made it more like a mockery.

"Our leader knew because he knows everything. Why? It's not a *secret* meeting, is it?"

"No, no," Skail put in quickly. "We weren't doing anything against you."

"Very wise again, Skail of the Nesters. Our leader knows everything— and he approves of your meeting. Representing many different tribes, you can make a decision for all at once." The Queen-Hyper paused and scanned the semi-circle. "You can decide on a new alliance between Humen and Residuals."

The representatives exchanged looks of amazement. "New alliance?"

"Yes, that's why I'm here, to offer you a new alliance. Our new leader has been reviewing the partnership between Humen and Residuals. He thinks it's time for a fresh start."

Everyone in the community area held their breath and waited to hear more. Up in Zonda's cave, Ferren and Kiet also waited to hear more.

"The fact is, we Humen haven't been the best of allies. We've taken too much and given too little. It's time for an alliance equally beneficial to both parties." The Queen-Hyper produced another garish smile. "We wouldn't want you to switch allegiance to the other side, would we?"

For a long moment, the representatives were too surprised to speak. Up in the cave, Ferren could hardly adjust to this complete change of heart.

"Exactly what Skail wanted," Kiet murmured in disbelief.

Down in the community area, Skail had recovered his confidence. He addressed the Queen-Hyper in a firmer voice.

"You're saying we should negotiate a better kind of alliance?"

"Yes, negotiate."

"What would be the terms? What would you offer us?"

"An end to military service."

If the representatives had been surprised before, they were thunderstruck now. "An end…?" "Does she mean…?"

"I mean no more Selectors. No more contributions for military service."

"What do you want from us in return?" asked Skail.

"Only your support. So that everyone on Earth presents a united front."

"Because you don't want to lose us to the other side…" Skail struggled to hide the smirk on his face. "Of course, we'll have to discuss it and take a vote."

"Of course." The Queen-Hyper purred. "An alliance is a solemn commitment—no one expects you to rush into it. Take your time, discuss it thoroughly among yourselves. Our leader imposes no deadline. I can wait."

The representatives were in a daze, but a happy sort of daze. The Queen-Hyper showed no impatience as she surveyed them.

"Why don't I go off somewhere nearby and leave you to your discussion?" she suggested. "You don't want me listening in to your speeches."

"Somewhere nearby?" An uneasy look replaced the smirk on Skail's face. "I don't know…"

"You're worried about leaving me to wander about on my own?" The Queen-Hyper smiled at him and nodded. "Perfectly understandable. We haven't done much to deserve your trust in the past. You're welcome to set a guard to keep an eye on me, if you like."

"You don't mind?"

"Not at all."

"What about your weapon?" Zonda called out.

"This flamethrower?" The Queen-Hyper hefted it in her hands.

"A guard can't really be guarding you when you're armed."

"Very well. I shall surrender my weapon. Skail of the Nesters…" She turned to him. "Please take care of this flamethrower for me."

She held it out. At first Skail was reluctant and held back, but in the end he had to accept it.

"Think of it as a peace offering between us." The Queen-Hyper spoke as if making a proclamation. "From our new Humen leader to the leader of this assembly. From Asmodai to Skail. In expectation of an improved partnership in the future."

Then she swung away and swept off in springy strides towards the Creek and the sunflower field.

21

"Did you hear?" Kiet demanded.

Ferren had registered her gasp of indrawn breath, but not the reason for it. "What?"

"She just named their new leader. 'From Asmodai to Skail.'"

"Yes, I heard that."

"*Asmodai!* Have you forgotten who Asmodai is?"

The name was somehow familiar, but he couldn't place it.

"He's the angel I saw with Miriael," Kiet went on. "The angel who handed her over to the Humen. You remember, when we met Uriel with the other angels, and they worked out who'd betrayed her. They called him Asmodai."

Ferren thought back, and the name slotted into place. "Mmm, I remember."

"So now the Humen have an angel leader in place of Doctor Saniette. An *evil* angel."

They were still talking about it when a crowd of young Nesters burst into the cave.

"Was that a Queen-Hyper?" Ethany's round features were red with excitement, her eyes wide with shock and horror.

"She said she saw a Queen-Hyper!" cried Flens.

"I *did!* Like the ones in the Camp!"

"Is it true?"

Flens, Gibby, Rhinn, Bross and Tadge were all clamouring for answers. Ferren and Kiet took turns telling the story. When they came to the name of the new Humen leader, Rhinn knit her brow.

"Asmodai? Didn't he have something to do with the fire in the City of the Dead?"

"Yes, he wanted to drive out the Morphs and trap them in his flying wing," Kiet answered. "Peeper told me. Asmodai cheated the Morphs like he cheated Miriael."

"And this new alliance must be a cheat too," said Gibby.

"But why?" asked Bross. "I mean, what's the purpose of it?"

The young Nesters turned questioningly to Ferren and Kiet, who could only shrug.

"No purpose I can see," said Ferren.

Everyone tried to think of possible purposes, but none of their guesses made much sense. Then Tadge, who stood closest to the doorway, called out, "Zonda's coming!"

In one corner of his mind, Ferren wondered if Zonda would be annoyed about so many uninvited guests. But it hardly seemed important now.

She turned up a minute later. She had to elbow young Nesters aside to enter her own cave.

"What do you think?" Ferren asked her at once. "An end to military service—it's too good to be true. It *has* to be!"

"Most of the representatives believe it," Zonda replied, scowling.

"We know who their new leader is," put in Kiet. "An evil angel."

"A lying, deceiving angel," added Ferren, and explained about Asmodai's deceptions in the past. "So you *can't* trust his offer," he concluded. "The assembly has to reject it."

Zonda pulled a face. "They're already going to accept it. Nobody's opposed. Except me, of course," she added.

"Get me and Kiet invited to talk to them," Ferren urged. "We'll change their minds."

"You and Kiet!" Zonda responded with a puff of derision. "Do you know what they're saying about you right now?" She jerked a thumb towards the community area and assembly.

"What?"

"They're saying *you* deceived them. You made them think the Humen were bound to lose. You told them Heaven had as good as conquered the Camp. Nobody believes in you anymore."

"We were a bit over-optimistic, but…" Ferren began.

Zonda shook her head. "No, worse. Your credit is zero."

It's probably true, Ferren realised.

"You need to keep away from the assembly," Zonda went on. "If you tell me all the things you'd have said to the representatives, I'll try and say them for you. But don't get your hopes up."

22

By next morning, the representatives were ready to make their decision. Perhaps Zonda's objections had caused debate and slowed them down, but nothing more. Ferren studied their faces when they met in the community area, and groaned.

"They're still going to say yes to the offer."

Kiet was there with him in Zonda's cave. They waited to watch the assembly take a final vote and seal the alliance with the Queen-Hyper. But their watching was cut short when Stogget appeared suddenly before them.

"Onlookers forbidden," he growled. "You know that. You showed yourselves once too often."

Ferren was prepared to argue, but Kiet pulled on his elbow. Stogget folded his brawny arms and looked menacing.

"Out now!" he warned them. "Skail doesn't want you here."

"All right, all right," said Kiet, and pulled again on Ferren's elbow. "Come on." She dropped her voice. "Idea."

Stogget watched them walk away in the direction of the visitors' caves. Ferren bent to listen to Kiet as they went.

"What idea?" he asked.

"We can cross the Creek and observe from the other side instead. They won't see us in the sunflowers."

"Long way," Ferren whispered back. But he nodded agreement.

They had reached the visitors' caves when Stogget finally gave up watching and headed back to the assembly. Still they couldn't cross the Creek until they were well out of sight from the community area. Then, after splashing across, they were forced to make a wide detour through the grass of the Plain before they could risk approaching the cornfield behind the sunflowers.

"Hurry," muttered Ferren. "It'll be over before we get there."

At last, they circled back towards the Creek. The corn was tall enough to hide them from view, but the sunflowers had grown only chest-high and offered less cover. The huge golden heads had shed most of their petals and were starting to run to seed. Ferren and Kiet scurried forward bent almost double, stumbling in and out of irrigation channels between the plants.

"Shush now," hissed Kiet, as they glimpsed a gleam of water ahead.

They crawled the last twenty yards flat on their bellies, came up to the Creek and peered out through a screen of sunflower stems and leaves. The banks of the Creek were low here, and the community area on the other side was right in front of them.

"Too late," muttered Ferren. "We've missed the vote."

The Queen-Hyper had already arrived and stood facing the representatives, who sat in the usual semi-circle. Skail was on his feet, and had evidently just finished making a speech.

"Excellent." The Queen-Hyper responded to Skail's speech. "On behalf of Asmodai and the Humen, I accept your acceptance. A new start for a new alliance."

The representatives cheered and called out. "No more Selectors!"

"No more military service!"

"Indeed," purred the Queen-Hyper. "Now all that remains is to make the final arrangements. An exchange of monitors."

The celebrations faded. "Monitors?" "What are monitors?" "What does she mean?"

Ferren and Kiet looked at one another, equally puzzled.

After holding the representatives in suspense for a moment, the Queen-Hyper took notice of their questions and explained. "Monitors are an obvious requirement for any alliance, especially when there's been mistrust in the past. *You* need to be sure that *we're* keeping our side of the bargain, and vice versa. So we send someone to attend and report on your assembly here, while you send someone to attend and report on any decision-making meetings in our Camp. Monitors don't participate, they're simply observers and witnesses."

The representatives considered the idea. "One of us goes into their Camp?" "One of *them* sits in on our meetings?"

The more they digested it, the less they liked it. They muttered and shook their heads.

"We didn't know about this." Skail spoke up at last.

"No?" The Queen-Hyper appeared surprised. "What else did you expect?"

"We never had monitors in the old alliance."

The Queen-Hyper snapped her fingers. "Exactly. And that's what went wrong with it. If both sides had known what the other was doing, there could have been objections raised and issues resolved. We have to do better this time."

Ferren boggled at her language. Objections raised and issues resolved? When the Humen were dismembering Residuals for their psychic deposits and body parts?

"Perhaps you should take time to consider the arrangement," the Queen-Hyper went on smoothly. "I suggest you discuss it until you feel comfortable with it. Then decide who you want to send as your monitor."

She turned to leave. "Take as long as you like and call me when you're ready. You know where I'll be."

23

Ferren was sure the representatives wouldn't agree to an exchange of monitors, and Kiet thought the same. Any Residual sent into the Humen Camp would become a kind of hostage, while the presence of a Humen monitor at the assembly would paralyse all discussion. They were still talking about it when they became aware of a rustle in the sunflowers.

"It's *her*," whispered Kiet.

The Queen-Hyper made her way to the middle of the sunflower field and sat down. Ferren wriggled a little closer until he could see her black shadow, then wriggled back.

"No one guarding her," he reported. "Maybe no one wanted the job today."

"This must be where she stays and waits." Kiet pursed her lips. "What about us here?"

"We'll be all right as long as we keep our voices down."

They remained close to the Creek, and the morning passed slowly, very slowly. In the community area, the representatives huddled in small groups and muttered among themselves. Although Ferren and Kiet couldn't hear what they were saying, their voices sounded dull, their faces looked dismal and defeated. The way they hung their heads expressed the same old hopelessness that had been the normal condition of Residual life before the Residual Alliance.

Ferren wriggled over several times to check on the Queen-Hyper. She had stretched herself out full length on the ground and lay as if comatose. Then, in the middle of the day, came a change. He tensed at a strange, scratchy, burring sound from the middle of the sunflowers. Was she talking to someone?

He wriggled over to inspect, and this time Kiet came with him. The Queen-Hyper had propped herself up on one elbow and was speaking into a thing like a black box with a spike at one end. The scratchy, burring sound was the voice she was speaking to.

Ferren and Kiet nudged one another. They remembered seeing a similar black box with a spike in the Humen Camp, when they'd been rescuing Miriael. The Hyper chasing after them had called up reinforcements with the same sort of communication device.

The conversation on the Queen-Hyper's side told them nothing. "Understood," she said, and "I'll do that," and "On to the next stage. Right."

Then she pressed a switch on the device and ended the conversation with a click. Ferren and Kiet crept back to their spot at the edge of the sunflower field.

"Who was she speaking to?" wondered Kiet.

Ferren couldn't begin to guess. "It's not good, whoever it was."

The afternoon wore on. Ferren thought he heard rumbles of thunder, very faint and far away. The sun still shone, but the weather was changing on one side of the sky. Through the sunflowers, it looked like a band of very black cloud rising up behind them.

Eventually, the small huddles of representatives came together in a single larger group and appeared to reach a decision. Ferren and Kiet watched as they all went back to their positions in the semi-circle.

Soon there was a rustle in the sunflowers, and a shadow passed by them on the way to the Queen-Hyper. The voice that addressed her belonged to Stogget.

"We're ready now," he announced.

"You're sure?" came the Queen-Hyper's response.

"Ready," he repeated, and hurried off back to the assembly.

The Queen-Hyper herself was in no hurry. Leisurely, she rose to her feet; leisurely, she retraced her route through the sunflower field. Ferren and Kiet lay low and held their breath until she'd gone. Only when they heard her splash across the Creek did they swing back to look out over the community area.

Skail was the sole representative on his feet, holding the flamethrower by his side. The Queen-Hyper raised an eyebrow as she surveyed the semi-circle, then turned her attention onto him.

"So. You have your answer for me?"

Skail seemed unwilling to meet her gaze. "Yes. We accept your monitor attending our assembly. But we trust you. We don't need to have our monitor at your meetings. If that's all right with you."

The Queen-Hyper laughed. "You trust us already?"

"Yes," Skail replied miserably.

The Queen-Hyper laughed again and shook her head. "I'm afraid not. It has to be the same on both sides. Don't you want a partnership of equals?"

"Yes…no…um," Skail mumbled. He looked round for support, but none of the representatives reacted.

"Well, let me see. What could we do?" The Queen-Hyper made a great show of thinking it through. "You'll have to send a monitor, but it doesn't *have* to be a Residual." She rubbed a black-clad finger against her black-clad chin. "It could be an angel, for example. If you have a suitable angel to send."

Hidden among the sunflowers, Ferren stifled a gasp.

24

The growl of thunder came again, louder, deeper and much closer than before. Out in the community area, the representatives shivered and looked over their shoulders.

"Yes, an angel as your monitor," The Queen-Hyper went on with a nod. "That would solve your problems."

Skail appeared nonplussed. "We don't have an angel."

"Oh, I think you do. Asmodai thinks you do. What about an angel who visited your tribes and helped arrange this meeting? An angel who isn't quite a proper angel?"

Ferren was ready to rush across to the community area and halt the questioning. But Kiet's arm came down on the small of his back and restrained him.

Skail spread his arms helplessly. "We can't, we don't know where—"

"An angel called Miriael!" The Queen-Hyper thrust out a finger and jabbed Skail in the chest. "Where are you hiding her?"

Ferren couldn't hold back any longer. He knocked Kiet's arm away and rose to his feet.

"You'll make things worse!" she hissed at him.

But he was already out above the sunflowers, head and shoulders exposed to view. He ran forward, plunged into the Creek and splashed across to the other side.

"You don't know anything!" he yelled at the representatives. "You can't say! Don't talk about her! They don't want her as a monitor in their Camp! They want to cut her in slices and dissect her for analysis!"

He rushed up into the community area, dripping water. The Queen-Hyper swivelled towards him with an uncanny glare in her eyeslits. He drew breath and yelled again.

"It's all a lie! They only want—"

The Queen-Hyper opened her mouthslit and screeched. On and on, the sound poured out of her, a terrifying, eardrum-shattering screech. Ferren couldn't shout over the top of it, couldn't even think for the ringing in his head. The representatives clamped their hands over their ears.

Finally satisfied, the Queen-Hyper stopped as suddenly as she'd started.

"That's better, you can uncover your ears now," she told the representatives in her normal voice.

Then she swung towards Ferren. "So, the angel Miriael. *You* know the one I'm talking about, at least. Is she somewhere nearby? Where are you keeping her?"

Ferren shook his head. He resolved not to respond to any questions, not even to say that Miriael wasn't nearby at all. He became aware that Kiet had come up behind him—and she too was shaking her head.

The Queen-Hyper stared at the two of them. Then her gaze shot out further to take in many more Residuals who'd just emerged from their caves. No doubt aroused by the screech, young Nesters and members of the People had come forth to see what was happening.

"Hah! How many more do you have skulking away?" The Queen-Hyper beckoned to them imperiously. "Come here. All of you. Come forward where I can see you."

Step by reluctant step, the young Nesters and People obeyed. The Queen-Hyper hissed softly as though her suspicions had been confirmed. She waited for them in silence, then directed them to line up behind the semi-circle of representatives.

Ferren, meanwhile, was looking out at the sky beyond the sunflowers and cornfield. He had a clear view of the cloud now, like a black wall rising to swallow the afternoon sun. The rest of the sky was bright and blue, but the cloud itself was impossibly dark. And not only impossibly dark but impossibly fast-moving...

"That's not natural cloud!" he exclaimed to no one in particular.

The Queen-Hyper heard him and laughed. "Of course not. It's been created by a master of clouds. It'll be here in a minute, and so will he."

"What do you mean, *master of clouds?*"

The spittle gleamed in the Queen-Hyper's mouthslit, and her laugh had a horrible, wet quality. "I mean, he has the power to control the weather."

Ferren continued to study the cloud, which rolled and churned inwardly upon itself. It was like a black, liquid sea, with eddies and whirlpools, billows and currents...

"There's something in it," muttered Kiet, who was studying it too. An edge of fear came into her voice. "Something in it!"

In the next moment, a triangular shape slid forth from the blackness. A mere arrowhead at first, it grew larger and larger, wider and wider.

It's the same! thought Ferren. *The same great delta that passed over once in the night!*

As it emerged fully from the cloud, the delta darkened even the bright, blue part of the sky. Closer and closer it came, until its point was directly above the community area. Then it stopped, hovering, no more than thirty or forty feet from the ground.

Just behind the point was what looked like a bulging bubble of glass. Ferren saw a figure inside the bubble—and heard Kiet's horrified gasp in his ear.

"It's *him!* It's Asmodai!"

The figure was a winged angel wearing black robes and a black circlet round his forehead. Filled by his radiance, the bubble resembled a glowing, luminous eye with a jet-black pupil. Ferren had the impression that the eye was looking down at the Queen-Hyper—and it was the Queen-Hyper whom the angel addressed when he spoke.

"Well, have you found my little Miriael yet?"

The Queen-Hyper was looking straight up with her head tilted back. "Not yet, my leader. But some of these Residuals know all about her. They were saying we planned to slice and dissect her for analysis."

"Ah, Doctor Saniette's plan." Asmodai's voice was like sweet, solemn music. "You didn't tell them I have quite different plans?"

"No, my leader. I doubt it'll make any difference, though. They seem very protective and possessive about her."

"How touching. Is she here with them?"

"I think so, but they haven't admitted it yet. We may need to interrogate them."

"Mmm, I'm sure we'll find ways to encourage confessions."

"Shall I give the word for the envelopment?"

"Yes. Whoever we flush out, bring them all in. Start the envelopment."

The eye seemed to rotate and redirect, the surface of the delta seemed to ripple. Then the great wing shot forward and swept off low across the sky.

25

For a moment, the sun was uncovered and shone down once more on the community area. The Queen-Hyper produced her black box with the spike and began speaking into it. The representatives were stunned, the young Nesters and People were stunned, Ferren and Kiet were stunned.

Then the day went dark again. The black wall of cloud moved up in front of the sun, the rumbling thunder swelled to a roar like a ravening beast. In no time at all, the fast-moving cloud had blotted out every ray of sunlight.

Skail turned in desperation to the Queen-Hyper. "Please! We can still negotiate that new alliance. If we find that angel you want, we'll tell you where. We can promise…"

Holding the black box to her ear, the Queen-Hyper ignored him and listened to the scratchy, burring voice on the other end.

Ferren turned to the young Nesters, the People and the representatives—and he was desperate too. "We have to escape! No more negotiations! No more lies! We know who our enemies are now! We escape them first and fight them afterwards!"

The Queen-Hyper finished speaking into her communication device and switched it off with a click. Skail was still struggling to attract her attention.

"We'll be the best of allies," he pleaded. "Anything we can help you with, we'll do it."

The Queen-Hyper eyed him with amused contempt. "You think we care about Residuals as allies? I was only playing for time."

She turned to address everyone in the community area. "Stay where you are, the lot of you. You've left it too late to save yourselves now."

"No!" shouted Ferren. "Run for it!"

"Let's go!" cried Kiet

Zonda clapped her hands. "We're with you!"

The young Nesters had already made their choice. The People weren't so sure, but Zonda made the decision for them. The representatives rose to their feet, then looked around uncertainly. The Queen-Hyper merely folded her arms and smiled.

"Come on!" yelled Ferren, and swung away from the approaching wall of cloud. "This way! Follow me!"

"Get moving!" yelled Zonda, motioning to the representatives with furious gestures.

Ferren raced for the bluff. When he glanced back over his shoulder, the young Nesters were at his heels, the People weren't far behind and the representatives were finally starting to follow.

He went up the slope at full speed, passing Zonda's cave on his right. He was half running and half scrambling. Then he reached the top, and saw what lay beyond. His spirits plummeted.

Kiet and the young Nesters pulled to a halt beside him.

"Trapped!" gasped Rhinn, and Ethany groaned.

A vast Humen army advanced in a glittering arc all across this side of the Plain. Ferren saw black-clad Hypers with their bizarre metallic decorations, monstrous machines on wheels and caterpillar tracks. They were less than three hundred yards away, converging steadily towards the Home Ground.

Ferren took one look, and understood there had been another kind of thunder behind the thunder of the storm: a pounding of boots, a growl of engines, a rumble of wheels and tracks. He also understood that there was no chance of evading the arc. He swivelled to face the other way.

The black cloud was at a similar distance, stretching like a curtain all across the bottom of the sky. Roiling and boiling, it was terrifying in its unnatural energy. Already, its leading edge almost touched the People's cornfield.

Kiet was looking out over the same scene. "Better to die in a storm," she said.

"Right," he agreed. If the storm killed them, at least it would be a clean, quick death. Better than being tortured for information by the Humen.

"Other way!" he shouted. "Into the storm!"

He raced back down the slope of the bluff, yelling to the represent-atives and People who were still climbing up.

The Queen-Hyper stood as before with folded arms. "Don't do it," she sneered. "Give up now. You don't have a hope in a storm like that. It's designed for total destruction."

Ferren ignored her. He ran across the community area, then paused on the bank of the Creek while the others caught up. The black wall of cloud had swept across the cornfield and was approaching the sunflowers. As he watched, it tore up whole plants and flung them about in a lashing , thrashing frenzy.

He was momentarily mesmerized by the violence. As if from a distance, he heard Kiet say something like, "I'll just be a minute." On his other side, the Queen-Hyper said something like, "I'll have that back that now." Ferren didn't try to work out what was going on.

He raised an arm aloft. "*We can do it!*" he yelled, and rushed straight into the Creek.

He had the impression that the black wall was rushing to meet him. He splashed across, came out on the other side and kept going through the sunflowers.

Twenty paces in, a sudden wind plucked at his hair and whipped his face with grit and leaves. The roar of the storm was incredible. Total destruction? He braced himself and plunged on into it.

PART TWO

HUNTED

1

"**H**ang on tight, little one! We're leaving, you and me!"

Kiet snatched up the zither and ran back out of the cave. Peeper let out a little peep of surprise, alarm—and perhaps thankfulness, at not being forgotten.

Her detour had taken only a few moments, but already the black wall of cloud had reached the far bank of the Creek, while the community area was almost empty. Only three figures remained: the Queen-Hyper, Stogget and Skail. As she sprinted back past all the other caves, Kiet saw that some kind of tussle was going on between them. The Queen-Hyper had one hand over Skail's head, clutching his hair; with the other hand, she pulled at the flamethrower he still held onto.

Trying to reclaim her weapon, Kiet thought. She couldn't tell whether Skail was deliberately holding on to it or whether he had his fingers caught in the trigger guard. His mouth was wide, and he appeared to be howling in fear and panic, although no sound was audible above the roaring storm.

Help Skail or follow the others? It wasn't really a choice—she couldn't abandon her own kind to the Humen. But before she could run up, Stogget flung himself at the Queen-Hyper from behind and tackled her round the legs.

The tall, black figure crashed to the ground, bringing Skail and the flamethrower down with her. At once she began flexing her body like a snake, thrashing furiously back and forth. The bag over her shoulder flew through the air and landed ten feet away. Skail's face was a blur as his head was thrown from side to side. Yet his fingers remained in the trigger guard, and Stogget clung on to the Queen-Hyper's legs.

Kiet skidded to a halt a few yards away. She wanted to intervene, but the three bodies flailed about in such a welter, she couldn't see where to dive in or take hold.

Then it happened. Skail's fingers must have caught on the trigger, because a great jet of yellow flame shot from the nozzle of the flamethrower. It could have gone anywhere, but it happened just when the nozzle was pointing up towards the Queen-Hyper. She let out a terrible screech as the flame caught her full in the face.

She fell back, releasing Skail's head and the flamethrower, rubbing at her eyes. She wasn't dead or destroyed, but seemed to have been blinded. The flame from the nozzle had already died as Skail wriggled away, dragging the weapon behind him. Stogget also wriggled away.

Kiet was aware of an overwhelming smell of burning rubber. She stared at the scene, then turned as a sudden gusting wind blew her hair across her face. The wall of cloud was coming across the community area, roaring as it came. She looked up and saw it towering high over her head.

No time to set off after the others; the unnatural storm had reached her first. She narrowed her eyes, planted her feet wide apart, held the zither tight against her chest and waited for the blackness to engulf her.

2

Ferren fought for breath. The rain was a waterfall pouring on top of him, slamming down on his head and shoulders. He ploughed on with outstretched arms, expecting to be knocked off his feet at any moment.

He had started running through sunflowers, but already the plants were gone, beaten flat by the deluge. He felt their fallen stalks under his feet, but couldn't see them, or anything much, through the water that streamed down over his eyes.

Many times, the wind made him stumble. Like a raging animal, it attacked him from left, then right, then left again. Although he tried to run in a straight line, he might have been running in circles for all he knew.

The corn was sturdier than the sunflowers, and the stems brushed against him on his way through. But it was only the bare stems still standing, after every leaf had been stripped away.

"This way! Keep going!" He swung his arm and yelled to those following, hoping they saw his signal. If they could all live through this storm and come out on the other side... At least it wasn't the certain death that the Queen-Hyper had promised them.

The People's irrigation channels had long since burst their bounds, and water flowed everywhere. Ferren often found himself calf-deep in pools or wading through surging torrents. When the ground wasn't running with water, it was thick, clagging mud.

Coming out at last beyond the cornfield, he stopped and looked back at those following. They came forward like shambling hulks: Zonda right behind him, then Rance of the Baggers, then Jerrock of the Longheads. Further back were half a dozen more: mere grey, unrecognisable outlines through the curtaining rain. He could only hope there were others trailing after the small number he could see.

He continued on across the Plain. The grass would have given them no cover when it was knee-high, and even less now it was beaten down— but the rain and cloud were all the cover they needed. The storm that was their enemy was also their friend.

They were trudging along at a walking pace when the nature of the storm changed. Ferren felt the change as a succession of blows to the top of his head and his shoulders. Savage, ice-cold blows! It was hailing!

He wrapped his arms over his head for protection. Looking back over his shoulder, he saw Zonda doing the same—and no doubt everyone else all the way down the line. But he could no longer see beyond Zonda as the hailstones multiplied and grew larger. Soon they came down so heavily that even Zonda vanished from view.

He thought he heard cries of pain behind him, though it was hard to hear anything through the drumming of the hail. He cried out himself at times, when particularly sharp stones cut into the flesh of his forearms. Even where he wasn't cut, he was battered and bruised.

But he was still upright and moving forward, until the hail came down twice as hard. Suddenly he found himself down on his hands and knees. He would have kept crawling on all fours, except that a hand clamped round his ankle.

It was Zonda, who was also down on all fours. She came forward to yell in his ear.

"Stop here! Let it pass! Hailstorms never last long!"

Ferren wasn't so sure about *this* unnatural hailstorm. But if everyone else was stopping behind Zonda... He nodded, and prepared to wait it out.

For three, four, five minutes, the hail was unrelenting. He felt he was being pounded into the ground. He glimpsed hailstones as big as fists bouncing and rebounding all around. Then came lightning, accompanied by violent cracks of thunder. Ribbons of light slashed at his eyeballs and lingered in after-images long after the strike had passed.

But Zonda was right: the hail soon dwindled away. The lightning continued, and the rain and wind returned in full force. Sore and aching, he struggled to his feet. Zonda rose too, and others behind her.

"Everyone okay?" he yelled. "Let's move on, then!"

In spite of the rain, he could see a little better in the on-off flashes of lightning. Their advance was different now, with white mounds of ice to detour around and even more water everywhere. Hailstones floated on top of the water and lay over the ground, which had become more treacherous than ever. So easy to skid and fall, so easy to roll an ankle!

Struck by a sudden idea, Ferren paused and swung round. "Everyone support everyone! Hang on to the hand of the person in front of you!"

Even shouting at the top of his voice, he knew his words wouldn't carry far through the wind and rain. But hopefully people would see what those ahead were doing, and the idea would travel to the end of the line. He stretched out a hand for Zonda to take hold, and she trailed a hand for Rance behind her.

This way we won't lose anyone either, thought Ferren, as he trudged forward again.

On and on they went, zigzagging around piles of hailstones and pools of water. The ground was more up-and-down than before, but they still seemed to be crossing the Plain. Ferren had lost all sense of direction; he could only pray they weren't looping back round towards the Humen army.

After a while, they came to a wider expanse of water that lay right across their route. More like a river than a pool, its surface seethed with a million ripples under the rain. Ferren shielded his eyes and looked out, but couldn't see where the water ended.

When he led the way forward, it flowed like a river too. Still, the flow was gentle, and the water only a few inches deep. If they were lucky, it would stay shallow all the way across. He kept on going, and the others followed.

For thirty paces, their luck held. Then the water grew rapidly deeper—up to their calves, up to their knees, as high as their thighs. Ferren considered turning back. But looking ahead, he thought he saw dry land rising again on the other side. Not so far, so long as they could keep wading…

But as he pressed forward, hidden currents sprang up suddenly in the water.

"Hang on!" he shouted, and felt Zonda's grip tighten on his hand. He braced himself against the underwater surges pushing against him. The drowned grass was slippery underfoot, and the water was up to his waist. It was impossible!

He was about to shout "Go back!" when a cry of panic came from further down the line. He couldn't see who or where, but someone must have lost their footing.

Would the human chain hold?

Another cry, then a wail, then many despairing wails. They were all getting swept away. Ferren felt a sharp tug on his hand as Zonda lost her balance, pulled over by Rance. He tried to haul her upright, but his own feet went from under him. In the next moment, he was carried away with the rest.

3

When the hail struck, Kiet was in the sunflower field. She had lost contact with Skail and Stogget, and hadn't wasted time searching for them. After the first onslaught of driving wind and rain, she had set out to follow Ferren and the others. But she couldn't go on in the hail.

She dropped to the ground and bent forward over the zither. Tucking herself in as small as possible, she protected Peeper with her body while wrapping an arm over her head. Hailstones pummelled her limbs, back and shoulders in a million hammer-blows. She had no doubt she was cut and bleeding...

At the first flash of lightning, she jumped and gasped. At the second flash, she looked out from under her arm and saw something approaching from behind. Looming through the screen of hail was a dark and monstrous shape. Surely a Humen machine, surely one of the military machines they'd seen from the top of the bluff!

She stayed motionless where she was. No Hypers rode on the outside of the machine, but doubtless they were peering out from inside. She prayed she was as shadowy to them as the monster was to her. It was going to pass by a little way to her left.

She saw the ugly lumps and protrusions of its silhouetted outline, felt the vibrations of its tracks crunching over the ground, heard loud, metallic pings as hailstones hit and rebounded from its armoured surface. She held her breath until it had gone past. Nobody had spotted her.

"It's all right, safe again," she said to Peeper, with her mouth very close to the strings of his zither. The Morph cheep-cheeped in response.

But she knew in herself that the danger was ongoing. Now it wasn't just the hail and lightning, it was the Humen army in pursuit. They must have come over the top of the bluff and crossed the Creek, charging straight on into the storm.

In fact, the hail had already passed its peak and was losing intensity. Soon it died away, and the rain came back. Kiet staggered to her feet and continued on through the sunflowers into the cornfield.

The strikes of lightning remained as frequent as ever. The world around her leaped in and out of existence, though only to a distance of twenty or thirty yards. Successive strikes came down on either side of her, hitting leafless stumps which were all that was left of the corn.

No, it can't be targeting me, it's just random, she told herself sternly. *Even this storm can't be that unnatural.*

The stumps that had been hit flared up like torches before the rain dowsed them a moment later.

She pushed on, wondering how far ahead Ferren and the others would be by now. Though she urged herself to go faster, her legs refused to obey. She narrowed her eyes and peered forward into the obscurity.

Then, in one flash of lightning, a scene to her right caught the corner of her eye. She swivelled—and the scene was instantly swallowed by darkness. But she couldn't have been mistaken! Three figures, and one of them was a Hyper! The other two looked very much like Skail and Stogget.

She crouched low and waited for the next flash of lightning. When it came, she took in all the details. The other two *were* Skail and Stogget, and they stood with their arms pinned to their sides, bound around by some sort of glistening thread or cord. Skail still held the flamethrower that the Queen-Hyper had tried to reclaim, while Stogget carried the bag she'd dropped in the struggle. Clearly, Skail was unable to use the flamethrower with his arms immobilised.

As for the Hyper, he had his back turned to Kiet as he faced his captives. He was jeering at them, but she couldn't hear his words even in intervals between the cracks of thunder. He wore a spiked metal helmet and carried a long weapon with a perforated barrel.

Kiet crept up closer until she could catch some of what he was saying.

"Done up nicely, hey?... Ready for delivery... Yeah, extra psycho-litres for you two..."

He laughed an ugly, rasping laugh, then hefted his weapon and slung it over his back. Kiet froze, but he didn't look round.

She studied the weapon on its strap across his shoulder. How long would it take him to unsling it and aim it? He would need to lift the strap over the top of his head...

Perhaps this was her chance? Skail and Stogget stood only a dozen paces beyond the Hyper, who couldn't see her so long as she stayed directly behind his back. She focused on Skail's flamethrower, remembering what it did to the Queen-Hyper. Skail couldn't use it, but with luck *she* could.

She placed Peeper's zither on the ground, then crept quietly forward.

She didn't look out again. Skail and Stogget hadn't yet noticed her, and it was better they didn't. She rose on the balls of her feet and waited for the darkness following the next flash of lightning.

SPAAKK! The lightning struck very close, the thunder came a split second later. Her eyes were still blinded by the dazzle when she took off. She swept forward past the Hyper and raced up to Skail. Her sight was just clearing as she halted before him.

The flamethrower was trapped vertically next to his arm, encircled by the same cord that bound him. She grabbed the barrel and yanked sharply upwards. Behind her, the Hyper let out a bellow of surprise and rage.

"Let me have it!" she yelled at Skail. "Let go!"

But it wasn't Skail who was holding on—the cord had a strange sort of stickiness. She gave a more savage jerk, and the flamethrower came partway out, then snagged again. Kiet could almost feel the Hyper's weapon trained on her back. She made a supreme effort—Skail howled as though she was hurting him too—and finally the full length of the flamethrower came free.

With a sob of relief, she whirled and raised the stock to her shoulder. The Hyper had just finished lifting the strap of his weapon over his head. She found the trigger, aimed at his chest and fired.

Nothing happened.

There was a faint wet click, and she felt a mechanism move inside the weapon. But no flame burst forth. Skail's frantic voice called out behind her.

"Won't work! I tried! Waterlogged!"

All she could do was use the flamethrower as a club. The Hyper now cradled his weapon in his arms, and the perforated barrel was swinging towards her. She reversed the flamethrower in her hands, hoisted it high and prepared to charge.

SPAKKKK! Out of nowhere, lightning jagged down and hit the spike on the Hyper's helmet. A ribbon of light ran through from the top of his head to the boots on his feet.

The explosive force of it knocked Kiet backwards and sent her sprawling—but not before she saw the black-clad body split and fly apart in a dozen separate pieces.

4

For a minute, Kiet lay winded. She heard a burst of hysterical laughter close by—Skail relieving his pent-up terror.

"It got him on his spike!" he gasped. "Lightning loves metal!"

He and Stogget had also been flung to the ground. Kiet looked at them, then rolled over to look at the Hyper. All that remained of him were scattered chunks of charred, honeycomb-like material. His spiked helmet lay among the chunks, melted to an amorphous, metallic blob.

She rose to her feet. Skail stopped cackling, and he and Stogget struggled to rise too, but the cord pinning their arms prevented them. Kiet pointed to the strands of glistening, sticky stuff.

"How do I cut it?"

"Knife," said Stogget. "In my belt at the back."

He rolled over to present the back of his belt to her. Kiet drew out the knife and set to work on cutting him free. The cord was flexible but very tough, and her arm was aching by the time she broke through a single strand. But with a single strand parted, it was easy to unwind the rest of the coil.

"We had to surrender when my flamethrower wouldn't work," Skail told her—and Kiet noted how he now claimed ownership of the weapon. "He had a gadget to bind us up in this stuff. So quick, we never knew what was happening."

Stogget took over the knife and sawed at Skail's bonds. Kiet circled back round the remains of the Hyper and gathered up Peeper, unharmed on his zither. Then she kept watch for any more Humen while Stogget finished the job. As the cord fell from him, Skail rubbed at his arms— and immediately looked for the flamethrower. It lay in the ground where Kiet had dropped it.

"Ah, I'll take that again now."

Kiet was puzzled. "Even though it doesn't work?"

He picked up the flamethrower and nodded at the zither in Kiet's hand. "More use than that," he said.

She let it pass. Perhaps he'd forgotten about the Morph attached to the pegs, or perhaps he didn't care anyway.

"We should move," said Stogget. "Get clear of the Humen army."

"*And* catch up with the others," added Kiet.

Skail and Kiet had slightly different ideas of the direction to go. But, since Stogget agreed with Skail, their preference won out. Kiet wasn't eager to walk on alone.

They came out from the cornfield and continued on across the Plain. The lightning still flashed, the rain was as heavy as ever. Kiet's doubts about their direction increased when they crossed a succession of small ridges and valleys.

We're heading off to the side, she thought. *We'll never catch up with the others now.*

But Skail and Stogget walked on fast, and seemed mainly worried about escaping the Humen. The ridges grew higher and the valleys deeper. Icy masses of hail had accumulated in the bottoms of the valleys.

Then Stogget suddenly stiffened, halted and raised an arm to halt Kiet and Skail too.

"Who? What? Hypers?"

Narrowing her eyes against the rain, Kiet saw half a dozen figures ranged along the top of the ridge ahead. Mere grey shadows, they could have been anyone. But not quite anyone…

"Not tall enough for Hypers!" she whooped, and ran forward.

The figures had been facing the other way, but turned as she ran up. She recognised Flens, Bross, Tadge, Gibby, Rhinn and Ethany—all her friends and family!

"Found you!" she cried.

"And *you!*" cried Tadge.

She hugged her brother Tadge, then her sister Rhinn. Skail and Stogget came up behind her.

"Where are all the representatives?" asked Skail.

Kiet stopped hugging and looked around. "Where's Ferren? Where's his tribe?"

Rhinn shook her head. "We got separated. We stopped when we realised *you* weren't with us. The others kept going, but we hung back a while waiting for you."

"Then we went on again, hoping you'd turn up," added Flens.

Kiet grinned. "And now I have!"

"Now you have." Flens grinned back. Then the grin faded, and he pointed ahead. "But we're stuck here."

Following his pointing finger, Kiet looked down the descending slope on the other side of the ridge. This was a much deeper valley than any they'd seen so far, with water flowing along at the bottom. As she squinted through the curtains of rain, she saw how wide the water was.

"It's a river," she said.

"And look at the strength of the current," said Bross.

They had raised their voices above the ongoing storm, but suddenly fell silent. They had all heard the sounds from upstream. Many cries, many people calling out!

It was sharp-eyed Gibby who spotted them first. A dozen and more heads bobbed in the water, splashing and spluttering and calling for help. The fast-flowing river swept them along at tremendous speed. In no time at all, they had come level with the young Nesters on the ridge.

"It's them!" yelled Tadge. "Is it? Is it?"

None of the people in the water looked up—and in the next moment, their bobbing heads had been swept right past.

"I saw Dwinna!"

"I saw Zonda!"

"What do we do?"

"Join them!" cried Flens, and set off running down the slope.

"Join them!" echoed Kiet, and set off after him.

The others weren't far behind. They plunged into the water and gave themselves up to the current.

5

Rotating in the current, round and round, Ferren doggy-paddled to stay afloat. Everyone else was doing the same, kicking their legs and beating their arms. They were over their initial panic.

On and on, the river carried them. He had been the last one in, and still floated after the other doggy-paddlers. The water was icy cold, no doubt chilled by the hail. All kinds of flotsam accompanied them downstream—plants and leaves, bits of bark and wood.

Then one huge mass of vegetation bore down upon them. It looked like a floating thicket, and must have been very light because it was travelling faster than they were. Ferren's first thought was to get out of the way of it; his second thought was to catch a ride on it.

He sucked in breath and shouted to the others ahead. "Grab hold! Grab hold!"

Then he swung round in the water and grabbed hold himself. The floating thicket was made up of hollow canes, twigs and foliage. He hauled himself higher and leaned his elbows across a length of cane almost as thick as his arm.

"Grab hold!" he shouted again, as the floating thicket began to overtake the others. "Grab hold! Grab hold !

One by one, they got the idea and clung on to canes and bunches of twigs. Soon they were all travelling rapidly downstream, recovering their breath and resting tired muscles.

What a slice of luck! Ferren thought. *This way we escape from the storm faster than we could ever have gone ourselves.* He suspected they wouldn't have been able to keep doggy-paddling for much longer anyway.

The river narrowed and flowed faster as it crossed the Plain. The Plain itself was hidden behind the rain, but Ferren saw stormwater pouring into the river over the banks on either side.

Then the unnatural storm ended almost as abruptly as it had begun. In one moment, they were enclosed in an opaque world of cloud and wind and rain; in the next moment, they were out in the open, and the sky was clear, the air was still. But the light remained dim. With surprise, Ferren realised that the sky had darkened and the day was almost over. A glowing strip of orange above the horizon showed where the sun had just dipped down out of sight.

"At last!" said someone, and someone else gave a quiet cheer. Ferren sensed the relief all around.

A few of the survivors had raised themselves higher in the floating thicket, right out of the water. Moireen of the Sea-folk looked down on

Ferren from a kind of seat she'd created among the canes and twigs. At the sight of her looking so comfortable, Ferren laughed the first laugh he'd laughed in a long while.

"Come up into the dry!" she called.

He started to hoist himself up towards her—then froze. From the hollow end of one of the canes that made up Moireen's chair came the head of a snake. Yellow-green eyes, flickering tongue... Moireen saw it too, and screamed.

The snake hissed and swivelled its head towards her. It slid out further, revealing black scales and red underbelly. It was about to strike.

Ferren was half in and half out of the water. He snatched up a handful of leaves and twigs and flung them as hard as he could. They fell harmlessly, barely touching the snake, but they worked as a distraction. The yellow-green eyes swivelled from Moireen to Ferren.

He scrabbled frantically, blindly, for a better weapon. He couldn't tear his eyes away from the snake's eyes. The creature slithered forth like liquid pouring out of the cane: one foot, two feet, three feet of glistening black and red. As it reared up over him, his hand closed over a length of cane.

He pulled it loose and swung it up in the same moment that the snake struck down. He had a momentary vision of fangs and gaping mouth plunging towards him—but the mouth closed over the cane's end, the fangs bit into the wood. He had skewered the snake just inches above him.

He pushed upwards and drove the cane further into the creature's gullet. It writhed and thrashed, but couldn't jerk free.

"Get away!" Ferren shouted to Moireen, to everyone. "Snake! Back in the water! Snake!"

Moireen launched forward from her sitting position and leaped right over Ferren into the river. The whole glistening length of the snake emerged, five feet from head to tail. Nothing could now stop it from jerking free. He threw the cane with the snake still attached into the depths of the floating thicket. Another pair of yellow-green eyes lurked in the thicket, too.

He kicked off and thrust himself backwards into the river. By now, everyone was shouting the alarm and diving for safety. Splash followed splash as bodies hit the water, more splashing as they doggy-paddled away.

Their ride was over. The lightweight thicket floated on in the current and left them behind. Ferren scanned the bobbing heads around him. How much longer could they keep going? How much longer did they *need* to keep going? Already they must be several miles away from the Home Ground…

The current was as strong as ever, though less turbulent. As they drifted downstream, Ferren struck out and came closer to the front of the group. The leading swimmer looked a lot like Zonda.

Meanwhile, the Plain was coming to an end. Scattered single trees appeared to their left and right; then the dense, dark mass of a forest loomed ahead. Ferren heard Zonda's voice call out from the front of the group, but couldn't tell what she was shouting.

The last of the twilight had nearly gone when the forest closed it off altogether. The river passed into darkness, with massive trees overhanging its banks. Zonda shouted again, and this time her words came clearly.

"Out now! Out here!"

The river swept round in a great loop, and Ferren felt the current carrying him to the far side of the curve. Those ahead of him began paddling their way towards that side, where one particularly massive tree drooped its branches low over the water.

"Take my hand!" Zonda shouted.

She had already pulled herself out of the river and sat astride one of the low-hanging branches. As Ferren watched, she caught hold of someone's hand and helped them to dry land, then reached towards someone else.

He trod water and waited for his turn to be fished out.

6

After being fished out himself, Ferren sat on the branch with Zonda and helped her bring others to dry land. The survivors included Dwinna of the Clanfeathers, Floy of the Fusselfolk, Pinnet of the Tunnellers, Rance of the Baggers and Dugg, Mell and Burge of the People. But not Kiet or any of the young Nesters.

Ferren scanned as far as he could see in the dark, but there were no more bobbing heads. A sudden fear gripped him: had they ever been part of the group at all? He'd assumed they'd been following back in the line on the way through the storm, but he couldn't remember seeing any of them in the river afterwards. Had he lost them right from the start? Had he lost Kiet?

The horrible void in his stomach was like the feeling when he thought the rescue team had lost Kiet in the Humen Camp.

"More coming!" Zonda announced.

Again Ferren scanned upstream—and now a second group of bobbing heads had appeared. His heart leaped. As they approached, he saw that they were holding onto floating logs and other flotsam so that they didn't need to paddle so much. The young Nesters, of course they were! They'd cheated death so often already, of course they'd come out alive!

He and Zonda helped them out of the water: Rhinn, Tadge, Ethany, Gibby, Bross, Flens and Kiet. Surprisingly, Skail and Stogget were with them as well.

Kiet called out to him over her shoulder as Zonda drew her towards the river bank. "We saw you and jumped in after you!"

Ferren had a dozen questions to ask, but was too busy helping with the rest of the young Nesters. He followed her with his eyes as she went to sit with the other survivors under the trees.

"That's all," said Zonda, when they'd fished out the last of the second group. Her voice sounded very flat, and Ferren understood why.

"What about our tribe?" he asked. "Only Dugg, Mell and Burge?"

"And Oola, before you got here." Zonda shook her head. "Maybe the others are waiting it out somewhere. It's our territory, they know places to shelter and hide."

Ferren hoped she was right. His relief over Kiet and the young Nesters had soon dropped away.

"Go and check on them all." Zonda waved an arm towards the survivors. "I'll stay and see if anyone else turns up."

Ferren nodded and went to check on the survivors, who sat slumped and huddled on the muddy riverbank. Only the young Nesters didn't appear miserable. They sat in a circle with Kiet at the centre and windmilled their arms vigorously. They were clearly trying to warm themselves up.

He walked around and counted the numbers. He had to peer closely to recognise water-streaked faces and bedraggled hair in the dark. As well as those he'd seen and Oola whom he knew about, there were just four more representatives: Pedge of the Skinfellows, Moireen of the Sea-folk, Jerrock of the Longheads and Anniga of the Nod-bodies. Anniga sat rocking from side to side, her face in her hands, pouring out a low rhythmical note of lament. No doubt it was a form of mourning for the dead.

He didn't interrupt Anniga, but tried to speak words of encouragement to everyone else. Since the young Nesters were least in need of encouragement, he left them till last. By the time he came round to them, they'd finished windmilling their arms and were listening to Kiet.

She broke off mid-sentence and turned to Ferren. "Did you know the Humen army came right on after us into the storm?"

"She saw a Hyper and a huge machine!" put in Tadge.

Ferren chewed at his lip. "Do you think they'll be still coming after us now?"

"Yes. They weren't expecting us to run into the storm. But they still have orders to capture us."

A worried frown appeared on Rhinn's long face. "We should go and look out from the edge of the forest."

"Surely they couldn't have come so far already," said Bross. "Could they?"

Gibby jumped up. "I'll go!"

Tadge jumped up too. "And me!"

"No." Rhinn rose more slowly to her feet. "You stay. *I'll* come with you," she told Gibby.

Ferren was wondering whether to go with them when Zonda appeared, pulling a gloomy face over the heads of the young Nesters. She seemed to want to talk, so he went with her instead.

"Nobody else, then?" he said. "No more People, no more represent-atives?"

"No. If there are People, they'll never find us now. And the rest of the representatives are definitely gone for good."

Wandering away from the circle around Kiet, they stopped by the massive trunk of a tree. Ferren shook his head at himself.

"I should never have tried to wade across the river," he said. "Or I should have turned back when it got deep and I felt the current."

"Who knows? Maybe the rest weren't even following then."

"No, I blame myself."

"Don't."

"Yes, *do*," said another voice. "Blame yourself for the whole thing. You could've stopped it."

The voice belonged to Skail. He and Stogget had been sitting by themselves on the other side of the tree, but now rose and came round to confront Ferren. Ferren noted that Skail still carried the Queen-Hyper's flamethrower, while Stogget had acquired the bag she'd worn.

Zonda spoke up on Ferren's behalf. "What's that supposed to mean?"

Skail continued to address Ferren. "That angel they wanted. That Miriael. You went and rescued her, you know where she is."

Ferren shrugged. "Not exactly."

"Why?" asked Zonda.

Skail turned his bitterness on Zonda. "He could've told them what he knew. We couldn't say anything because we didn't know. But he could've told them enough to satisfy them. He could've saved us."

Ferren was too amazed for anger. "You think I should've given Miriael away?"

"They only wanted her as a monitor."

"Whose side are you on?" demanded Zonda.

"*Our* side."

"That's mad," said Ferren.

"Everybody thinks the same." Skail spat dismissively. "But it's too late now, of course."

He turned away, but Stogget still stood protecting him. He flexed his arms and looked ready for a fight.

At that moment, Gibby and Rhinn came dashing back from the edge of the forest.

"Run!" cried Gibby.

"Humen army!" cried Rhinn.

"Lights and engines!"

"Coming straight towards us!"

Everyone was on their feet in an instant. Despair and apathy vanished as the instinct for self-preservation took over.

"Run!" Ferren echoed Gibby's cry, and so did Skail and Zonda.

Gibby raced on ahead, and they all followed her deeper into the forest.

7

Miriael and Shanna were still in their observation post on top of the stack of pipes. Shanna often went off scouting and scavenging at ground level, while Miriael stayed watching developments in the construction site and around the Camp.

One interesting development was that, after the one big army marching out, all of the troop movements were now coming *in*. They were mostly in small groups and companies, but a massive number in total. Day after day and night after night, they converged along the overbridges and streamed into the Bankstown Camp.

Miriael also watched the comings and goings of Asmodai's flying wing. His flights were mostly at night, but sometimes he took off and returned during the day. She saw him as a distant oval of light as he made his way to and from the glass bubble under the wing, and the mere sight of him was unsettling. Old memories agitated her with a tremulous, queasy feeling.

"I can't work out what he's up to," she told Shanna. "Where could he be going?"

"Who cares?" Shanna dismissed the subject with a sniff.

Shanna herself was more interested in the fenced-off zone in the construction site. The frenzied activity there went on without a break, and endless quantities of materials were transferred into the zone from stacks around the site. Yet still there was no visible result to show for it all. The low structure in the middle of the zone remained exactly the same height and width as before.

Shanna shook her head in frustration. "It's hopeless. We'll never learn anything from this distance. How long have we been here now?"

"Two, three weeks?" Miriael answered vaguely.

Shanna was growing more and more restless over the delay, and finally she could wait no longer.

"It's time to tell the assembly that Heaven's attack failed and the Humen have a new leader. We can't keep putting it off. They'll have the Residual Alliance well established by now."

Miriael pointed to the fenced-off zone. "We still don't know what they're building down there."

"No. So I'm going to break in and take a proper look."

"What? How can you?"

"I've been spying it out. There are main gates at the front, but also smaller gates round the back. I've chosen one in a quieter spot."

"You're really going to do this?"

"Yes. Tonight. Then we can go."

Miriael could see that Shanna's mind was made up, and stopped arguing. "I'll come with you," she said.

"*You?*" Shanna shook her head. "I have two and a half year's practice at slipping around unseen. You'd be a liability."

"Some of my senses are sharper than yours. And you can tell me what to do."

Again Shanna shook her head, but less vigorously.

Miriael pressed home her advantage. "Two's always better than one. One to act and one to keep lookout. We'll work as a team."

"A team." Shanna's expression was part-grimace, part-grin, part-resignation. "All right. But follow my lead, promise?"

8

The fence was a barrier of crisscross wire, ten feet high. The gate was a rectangular frame in the wire.

"Do you think it'll be unlocked?" asked Miriael dubiously.

"No, locked. If it wasn't locked, it'd be guarded."

"So…?"

"A lock's the same as any Humen machinery, operated by a Plasmatic. Live nerves and muscle tissue inside the mechanism. I can give instructions to Plasmatics."

Miriael was amazed. "What, in mathematical formulae?"

"No, that's the way Hypers do it. I do it by tapping and touch." Shanna reached in the pocket of her jerkin and brought out a small screwdriver. "I'll unscrew the plate of the lock and communicate with the Plasmatic inside. Don't you remember the bucket-train, when we rescued you?"

Miriael thought back. "You were up at the front, behind the engine."

"Yes, controlling the Plasmatics. I wasn't steering with a steering wheel, you know."

"I never thought about it."

"I learned how to do it when I was sabotaging equipment in the Camp. It usually works. Not always." Shanna clicked her tongue. "Stay here and wait for my signal."

Five minutes later they were inside the fenced-off zone, hiding behind a pile of sheet metal rolls. Shanna had closed the gate behind them without relocking it. They peered out towards the strange, low structure at the centre of the zone.

The floodlights were concentrated there, as were the gangs of working Hypers. Trains of flat-topped trolleys came in through the main gates laden with construction materials, circled around the zone in procession, then made their way to the central structure where the gangs unloaded them. All Miriael could see of the structure itself was the top of its frame and the tops of several huge cylindrical tubes.

"So how do we get closer?" Shanna mused aloud.

Miriael heard orders shouted in mathematical formulae to the engines pulling the trains, and an idea leaped into her head. Plasmatics in the engines…trains travelling to the structure they sought to investigate…

"If we could hide in under those trolleys, we'd get taken right there," she said.

Shanna scanned the trains of trolleys and nodded. "Yes, we could hide in the undercarriage out of sight. But we'd need a train to stop before we could slip between the wheels."

"You," said Miriael.

Shanna looked at her with dawning realisation. "You mean, I could control the Plasmatics in the engine?" She returned her gaze to the slowly circling trains. "Yes, I could take one train right out of the line and stop it close to you here. Hmm. It might work..." Her face split into a broad grin. "You'll turn into a real saboteur yet!"

They planned the details. Shanna would need to climb up behind an engine soon after it had entered the main gates...but she couldn't remain there or she'd be seen by Hypers unloading the trolleys...so she'd jump down and join Miriael in the undercarriage while the train was stopped...

"That's it, then," said Shanna. "We'll *make it* work."

She sped off round the edge of the zone and vanished almost immediately into the shadows. Miriael composed herself to patience.

She imagined Shanna sneaking up onto the footplate behind her chosen engine, then opening the engine cover, touching and tapping the Plasmatics inside. Miriael wouldn't even know which train she'd chosen until it veered out of line towards the pile of sheet metal rolls.

Train after train circled round in slow procession. Each was three, four or five trolleys long, laden with coiled hoses, cables, steel brackets, flanges, rods, or items of equipment whose purpose Miriael couldn't begin to guess. The wait seemed endless.

Then one train left the procession, approached and drew to a halt just yards away from the sheet metal rolls. Miriael's pulse raced. She didn't need a signal from Shanna—she sprang from her hiding-place and ran to the nearest trolley. It was the middle one of five, and its wheels were solid metal with rubber rims.

She crouched low and squeezed through, holding her wings tight to her body. Once under the trolley, she could see all the way along between the wheels of the train—like a long, dark tunnel with light coming in at regular intervals. The axles between the wheels were two feet above the ground; then springs above the axles; then the undercarriage of heavy struts and crossbars over her head.

She stayed bent down and listening. There was a clatter of boots as

Hypers ran towards the wayward train, shouting questions. They were all on the side turned in towards the centre of the zone, she noted.

Where was Shanna? Miriael moved back to the wheels on the outer, darker side of the train and peered out, craning her neck to look forward to the engine. She saw a shadow spring down from the footplate just as the Hypers ran up on the other side. They had stopped shouting questions and were now barking out mathematical orders to the Plasmatics in the engine.

Miriael waited no longer. She swung herself up over the nearest axle and clambered in among the struts and crossbars. There was no way to lie comfortably, but she could lie safely with no risk of being dislodged. She looked back down, but Shanna still hadn't appeared in the tunnel between the wheels. The Hypers were barking out a single mathematical formula, repeated over and over again.

Miriael twisted over, searched for a peephole and looked out through the metalwork on the darker side of the train. There was Shanna, still approaching, still out in the open. What was she doing?

Then Miriael realised. Shanna was pausing every few paces, peering in under the trolleys, looking for *her!* Miriael threaded an arm between struts and crossbars, found a space to stick out her fingers and flapped desperately.

In that same moment, the trolley gave a lurch, the wheels and axles turned and the train rolled forward.

Miriael saw the startled look on Shanna's face, saw her stare at the wheels going round in front of her. Too late for her now to dart between them!

Hide, thought Miriael. *Hide before the rest of the train goes past. Hide before you're left in full view of the Hypers.*

Shanna must have recognised the danger because she leaped suddenly away and disappeared behind the pile of sheet metal rolls. For a moment, Miriael was relieved—until she considered her own predicament. All by herself now…

Still, she had to go through with their plan, so far as they'd planned it. She surveyed the scene through her peephole and saw that the train was curving around to rejoin the procession. She glimpsed a stack of empty pallets…a gang of Hypers rolling copper-coloured cylinders over the ground…a column that held up overhead floodlights…

And now the train was now heading back towards the centre of the zone. The noise around grew deafeningly loud: banging and clanging, booming and hammering. She heard a new kind of voice too, giving mathematical orders—not the rasp of a Hyper, but a crackling, amplified, artificial voice.

She couldn't yet see the tubular legs of the central structure. The train's smooth, continuous motion changed, and its advance became a series of jerky stops and starts. Then came another change: a hollow, resonating sound from under the wheels. Suddenly they were passing over a surface of metal grilles.

Miriael shifted position for a better look down through the slots in the grilles. But the slots were passing too fast to give a clear view of what was below. She formed only an impression of some underground emptiness.

Then the amplified voice rang out again. *"4ab + 2.35 x 30%."*

With a grinding and creaking of wheels, the train came to a halt. Miriael gasped at the sight suddenly revealed through the grille. The underground space was *vast!* Far below, there were lights, machinery, gleaming cables, tubes sliding telescopically one over another. She couldn't even see to the bottom!

She hardly paid attention to the thumps and bumps from the flat top of the trolley over her head. No doubt the train's cargo was being unloaded. She focused on the subterranean world under the grille—and now she saw figures moving about in the depths.

Most were in black, the usual Hypers, but one wore a white medical coat. She remembered those coats—as worn by the ten original Bankstown Doctors. Also by the many individual Doctors strapped into the giant body of Doctor Saniette. Like the ten original Doctors, this one sat hunched in a wheelchair.

As her eyes roamed further afield, she spotted a second white medical coat, then a third, then a fourth. So many, and all so busy down there!

What unimaginably huge construction were they building for Asmodai? And were they building it *up* or *down?* She was still wondering when another amplified order rang out.

"3xy – 4.42 x 30%."

Her train, now unloaded, started forward again. As it picked up speed, her view through the grille was once more obscured. She wasn't sure whether or not she'd passed through the low structure at the centre of the zone.

By the time she shifted position to look out through her peephole at the side, she was on her way to the main gates. The train was leaving the fenced-off zone, and she had no idea where it was going. How would she get down from it now?

Her spirits sank as the problem of her own predicament came back to her.

9

The train rolled out through the main gates and on through alleys between stacks in the construction site. A single Hyper strode along by the engine and called out mathematical orders. Under his orders, the train made a ninety degree turn to the left, then a similar turn to the right.

What would Shanna have done? Miriael thought back to what they'd planned. They'd expected to be carried out through the main gates, but their escape after that depended on Shanna's expertise. Miriael could only hope that the train would stop in some quiet spot where she could slip out between the wheels.

The construction site outside the fenced-off zone was generally less well lit, with fewer Humen machines and Hypers moving around. Through her peephole, Miriael watched stack after stack go past. The Hyper giving orders was directing the engine to some specific destination…and finally they arrived.

Their destination wasn't a quiet spot at all. Half a dozen lights played over a stack of concrete slabs, and twenty or thirty Hypers approached the train on both sides. As soon as the train stopped, they began loading it up with slabs. Miriael heard every sound of concrete sliding over the flat trolley top inches above her head. She gritted her teeth and prayed for a single moment when there would be nobody nearby.

But the moment never came. The loading process seemed to last for ages—far longer than the unloading process before. Then, as soon as the workers stepped back, the Hyper in charge shouted a new mathematical order, and the train rolled forward again. It swung in a U-turn and headed back along the route it had just come.

Back to the fenced-off zone, thought Miriael in despair. Would she be trapped in this undercarriage going round and round forever?

She watched the same stacks going past, heard the Hyper striding alongside bark out an order for a ninety-degree turn. Then the engine rounded the corner—and suddenly he burst out in a volley of curses. He broke off cursing just long enough to bring the engine to an emergency stop with another order.

Miriael hung on to the struts and crossbars as the train's trolleys jolted and banged into one another. She wondered and waited.

"What fool idiot did that?" the Hyper snarled. "Smack in the way!"

The train had halted in a particularly dark part of the site, and Miriael couldn't see what was ahead from her peephole. She swung herself down to the ground and looked out from between the wheels.

Now she saw it: a bucket-train similar to the one in which she'd once made her escape from the Humen Camp. Someone had parked it across the route, completely blocking their passage between the stacks.

She heard the stamp of the Hyper's boots as he marched forward to investigate. More cursing followed, and mathematical orders directed at the engine of the bucket-train. Then came a succession of dull clanging sounds as the Hyper kicked at the engine's wheels in his frustration.

Now or never! Miriael darted out from under her trolley and raced for the rear of the train. At any moment, she expected a shout to ring out. But she was in luck. She'd taken barely a dozen paces when a gap opened up between two stacks of construction materials at the side. She dived into it—and brushed past someone who'd been standing in the gap looking out. She pulled to a halt and swung round.

"That went well," said a quiet, familiar voice.

Miriael could have wept with relief as Shanna materialised out of the darkness.

10

Miriael was bursting with questions, but Shanna wouldn't answer until they were safely away from the Hyper. They passed on down the gap between the stacks, turned left into a wider alley and finally stopped at a secluded spot beside a great mound of box girders.

Only then did Shanna explain how she'd sprinted to the back gate in the wire fence and run all the way round outside the zone to the main gates. Then she'd watched as Miriael's train emerged, followed it to the stack of concrete slabs and set up a barrier to block its return journey.

"You'd have got down somewhere sooner or later anyway," she said, dismissing Miriael's thanks. "What about you? Did you find out what they're building?"

Miriael told her story, describing the vast underground space with the machinery and Doctors. "But I still don't know what it's for," she concluded.

Shanna shrugged. "Oh, well, we did the best we could."

Miriael bit her lip. "It doesn't bother you, what Asmodai might be doing?"

Another shrug. "He's finishing off what Doctor Saniette started. Whatever that is."

"It'll be far more terrible with *him* doing it."

Shanna shot her a penetrating look. "Will it? Maybe you have too much respect for your evil angel."

Miriael frowned and changed the subject. "Is it far from here to our observation post?"

"No, but why? We don't need to go back there now. We can start off to the Home Ground straightaway."

"Not tonight."

"What's wrong with tonight?"

"I've had enough for one night. And I want to see what's happened with the flying wing. It flew off not long before we left, remember."

Shanna stuck out her jaw. "No, I don't remember. It comes and goes all the time. Why does it matter?"

"Because he's up to *something*." Miriael turned away, not meeting her gaze. "So, can you lead the way back to our stack now?"

"More delays, more excuses," Shanna muttered under her breath.

"What was that?"

Now Shanna was the one avoiding Miriael's gaze. "It's always about him, isn't it?" she said.

"Who?" Miriael paused, but Shanna said nothing. "You're talking about Asmodai?"

"You know I am."

Miriael felt she was on the defensive, though there was no reason she should be. "It's not Asmodai, it's the threat he represents."

"No, I think it's him. I think you're still half in love with him."

Miriael scoffed. "Still half in love? After what he did to me?"

She spoke dismissively, but the memories churned inside her. Asmodai's beauty...her need and desperation...the depth of his deceit...the depth of her own stupidity... She hated him in a way she'd never hated anyone before.

"Hatred can be the other side of love," said Shanna, as though she'd read Miriael's mind. "You're obsessed with him."

"No."

"Prove it. Come with me to the Home Ground, and we'll report to the assembly."

"I will. Of course I will. But not tonight."

Shanna curled her lip. "And you'll probably say the same tomorrow night."

The churned-up feelings in Miriael's breast were turning into anger. "You go off by yourself, if you want to go tonight."

"And you'll go back to our stack?"

"Yes."

"You don't even know where it is."

"I'll wander round till I find it."

"You can't. You *can't*." Shanna was staring hard at the ground. "All right, we'll go back for one more night. But only one."

Miriael said nothing, and they set off in silence. With Shanna leading, they kept well away from lighted areas, Hypers and passing transport vehicles. Miriael's journey in the undercarriage of the train really had brought her quite close to their observation post.

"Nearly there." Shanna spoke for the first time in many minutes. "That's strange."

She was looking up at the sky ahead. Miriael saw nothing strange, unless perhaps there was more light in the sky than before…

They were passing a mountainous pile of drums when Shanna stopped so suddenly that Miriael bumped into her. Above the drums, the great arm of a crane had come suddenly into view. It swivelled slowly round as they watched, tilting upwards, then downwards.

Step by cautious step, they advanced to the next corner. Miriael heard Shanna's hiss of indrawn breath, peered out over her head and saw the stack of pipes where their observation post had been. The stack was in the process of being dismantled.

A battery of lights…dozens of Hypers high on the stack and down on the ground…a train of flat-topped trolleys similar to the one she'd just escaped…

Of course, Miriael told herself. *Our stack was never permanent, just construction materials waiting to be used. It was bound to happen.*

Already the top part of the stack had disappeared, including the part that had served as their observation post. As they watched, Hypers attached cables to pipes, which the crane lifted, carried across and lowered to the ground.

"That settles it, then," said Shanna in a whisper. "We leave tonight."

Miriael could only agree. They backed away into the shadows, and Shanna led them off in a new direction, heading out from the site.

11

All day, Ferren and the surviving Residuals had been crawling through endless weeds. They had emerged from the forest before dawn and started across a series of weed-covered ridges. But when the sun rose, they had been forced to get down on their hands and knees. They would have been too easy to spot walking upright in the light.

They were aching in every muscle by the time they came to the end of the weeds. Their salvation appeared late in the afternoon: at first as a band of light, bright green, neither tall grass nor bushes. Studying it from the tops of the ridges, they couldn't work out what it was.

Only when they came close did they realise that the plants were light green ferns. They came in under them, and the fronds made a roof over their heads. They could even stand upright, since the ferns grew six feet tall.

They looked back, saw no signs of pursuit and moved deeper in. Soon they discovered a rivulet of fresh running water, with shoals of tiny gudgeon swimming about in it. They stopped, ate and drank; then Zonda patted her belly.

"You all do what you like, but I'm going to sleep," she announced.

No one disagreed. Exhausted from all their crawling, they flopped down and fell fast asleep.

Ferren slept through the night and into the next morning. He was woken by the sound of nearby voices.

"Aren't they darlings?"

"So tiny! So perfect!"

He opened his eyes, and a soft, green light fell over him, filtered through the tracery of the fronds. The voices belonged to two of the young Nesters, Gibby and Ethany. They were on the other side of a nearby clump of ferns.

What are they talking about? he wondered. He stretched, rose and went round to the other side of the ferns. Gibby and Ethany had been peering in among the fronds that fanned out at the top of the clump, but drew back as he approached. Their faces were radiant.

"What is it?" he asked.

They pointed without a word, and he stepped up to look where they'd been looking. There, nestled at the base of the fronds, was a small transparent sphere.

"Like an egg," he commented. "A glass egg."

"Look closer," said Gibby in a whisper.

He took another look. Inside the transparent egg was a miniature fern, hardly more than an inch high. Infinitely fine, infinitely delicate… and at the same time, an exact copy of the plant on which it grew.

"Other ferns are the same." Ethany was also whispering. "They all have an egg with a baby fern inside it."

"Beautiful," murmured Ferren.

"I like this place," said Gibby. "We ought to stay here."

"Yes." Ethany addressed Ferren, no longer whispering. "You ought to persuade everyone. We've done enough running away."

Ferren completely agreed that they'd done enough running away. But a memory from the night before last cast a shadow in his mind. *Blame yourself for the whole thing*, Skail had said. *Everybody thinks the same.* Would people listen if he tried to persuade them?

He turned to Gibby and Ethany. "Do you think I could've saved us?" he asked. "Should I have told that Queen-Hyper about Miriael?"

"Told her what?" asked Ethany.

"Where we left Miriael spying on the Humen Camp."

"We could've told her too," Ethany pointed out. "Why would we?"

"Then the whole thing might not have happened. The storm and the Humen army."

The two young Nesters looked puzzled. "But then they might've gone and captured Miriael," said Gibby.

"All over again," added Ethany.

It was obvious they didn't understand why he was even asking them. The idea of betraying Miriael was unthinkable to them…as it *ought* to be unthinkable to anyone. Reflecting back, Ferren wondered whether Skail himself had seriously meant it. Frustrated in his aims and momentarily despairing, Skail had been looking for someone to blame, so he'd picked on Ferren. But if he'd considered the consequences of giving away Miriael's whereabouts—surely not!

"So everyone thinks I did the right thing?" he asked.

"We all do," said Gibby. But of course she was speaking for the young Nesters…

"What about the representatives?"

"Probably," said Gibby.

"Except Skail and Stogget." Ethany was less positive. "And maybe not Pinnet or Pedge."

"Most of them probably haven't thought about it," said Gibby.

Ferren pursed his lips. If the survivors from his own tribe followed Zonda's lead, and Zonda was on his side, then it wouldn't matter if a small number of representatives opposed him. Apart from the young Nesters, he didn't think anyone would be ready to fight back against the Humen yet, but he should be able to halt the running away. He decided to call a meeting...

Someone cleared their throat behind him. He swung round and saw that Floy had come up and was waiting politely for attention. The representative of the Fusselfolk wore his fur anklets and fur bracelets, and a long, pointed stone on a cord round his neck.

He cleared his throat again. "I came to tell you... Skail has called a meeting."

Ferren frowned. "When for?"

"It's already started."

Ferren's frown deepened.

"Coming," said Gibby. "Lead the way."

12

It seemed that everyone else was already there at the meeting. They sat squeezed in between clumps of ferns, all facing towards Skail, who carried the flamethrower and also the Queen-Hyper's bag that Stogget had previously carried. When Ferren, Gibby, Ethany and Floy arrived, some sort of argument was going on about seating arrangements

"We have as much right—" Rhinn was saying, then broke off when she saw Ferren. "*He'll* tell you."

But Ferren didn't want to get into an argument about seating arrangements. He shook his head and came forward to where everyone could see him.

"I have something to propose," he began at once. "We've left the Humen behind by now, and they'll never find us hidden in the ferns. I propose we stop running away and stay here."

"*You* don't decide," said Skail.

Ferren held back a surge of irritation. "I didn't say I did. Only if everyone's in favour. Let's take a vote."

Skail continued to scowl. "I'm the overseer. I decide when to take a vote."

Kiet was sitting on the ground right at the front and challenged Skail before Ferren could speak. "You *were* the overseer, when there was still an assembly. Now we're all just survivors together."

There was a flurry of raised voices. The argument that had begun over seating arrangements was boiling over into something bigger.

Skail shouted above the raised voices. "The assembly still exists! Representatives are still representatives!"

"All together!" Kiet shouted back. "All equal!"

Skail had been standing while Kiet was sitting. He stepped closer to loom over her.

"You're a member of my stock, girl, and a member of the Nesters. I represent the Nesters—with Stogget here—so you don't need to speak. You don't have a vote."

Uproar followed. Young Nesters sprang to their feet, as did Zonda and some of the People—but none of the representatives.

"Only representatives get to vote!" shouted Skail, and Stogget echoed him. "*Only representatives get to vote!*"

"Who says?" demanded Zonda.

"I do!" Skail retorted. "The Residual Alliance does!"

Zonda pointed to Ferren. "He founded the Residual Alliance! What does he say?"

Red spots burned on Skail's pale cheeks. "No! That's in the past now!"

"So is the assembly and only representatives voting!" cried Kiet.

Ferren tried to push forward, but there were too many bodies in the way. "Can't we agree on anything?" he appealed. "Who thinks only representatives get to vote?"

"Only representatives decide on that!" Skail's voice was almost a screech.

"This is stupid!" exclaimed Zonda. "Can't you see how stupid it is?"

She was much closer to the front than Ferren. She waved her arms, and the uproar subsided to a degree.

"I heard a good proposal before," she said. "We ought to stop running and stay here. Let's get back to that."

"Only representatives can make proposals," Skail insisted.

"All right. I'm a representative, and I'm making it." Zonda put her hands on her hips and glared at him. "Don't you like the idea?"

"That's not the point."

"No? Does that mean you want to keep running away? How long for? Another day? Another week? Forever? What sort of coward are you?"

The burning spots on Skail's cheeks had gone from red to white. "The point is, I'm the overseer here."

"Oh? And is the overseer a coward?"

Skail didn't answer. Instead, it was Stogget who stepped forward and thrust his face in Zonda's face. He was built like a bull, his brawny arms as thick as thighs.

"Take that back!" he growled.

Zonda didn't move a muscle. "Or what? What if I don't?"

Stogget raised a fist. "Take it back!"

"Are you going to hit a girl? Is that what you do?" Zonda advanced her face an inch closer to his fist, defying him.

Stogget's aggression dissolved into uncertainty. When his threat failed, he didn't actually want to hit a girl. He looked round to Skail for guidance.

Meanwhile, Skail must have made a rapid calculation. When he spoke again, the anger had gone and he sounded like the voice of quiet reason.

"No call for violence. Let's all calm down." He addressed himself to Stogget first, then to Zonda. "You asked me what I wanted to do, stay or keep running. If you'd just asked the simple question, none of this would've happened. And my answer is, I think we've come to a good, safe place, with food and water, and we should stay here to rest and recover. As overseer of the assembly, my advice for representatives would be to vote in favor of the proposal."

The friction had evaporated as quickly as it had sprung up. In the end, there was hardly a serious vote at all. When Skail asked those in favour to raise a hand, every hand shot up. He made a show of counting only the representatives' hands, but it was a half-hearted show.

Ferren was left with the feeling that nothing had been satisfactorily settled. He had won on his immediate proposal, but it was no more than a temporary victory. The task of building support for revenge against the Humen seemed more difficult than ever.

13

Maybe she's not so bad, Kiet reflected, thinking back over the way Zonda had put Skail and Stogget in their place. When she came upon Zonda sunning herself in a patch of sunlight under the ferns, she squatted beside her.

"You did so well there," she began. "Standing up for Ferren against Skail."

Zonda huffed contemptuously. "Skail's a worm."

"Yes, but he's my Bloodstock Guardian. I wish I could speak to him like you do."

Zonda patted the ground beside her. Accepting the invitation, Kiet stretched out alongside.

"The People here will always support Ferren, won't they?" she asked after a while. "Since he's the same tribe."

"They'd better," said Zonda.

"You grew up with him, right? Same age?"

"Yes."

Kiet closed in on a subject she'd been wanting to broach for a long time. "Tell me about him. What was he like, growing up?"

Zonda considered. "I never had much to do with him until later on. I was the daughter of the leader of the tribe, and he was a nobody without parents. My father thought he was odd and not to be trusted. He wasn't very popular back then. But there was something about him… I discovered he was doing things no one else would've dared to even think about."

"*He* would."

"Mmm. I stood up for him with my father. And then I set him free when he was tied up and going to be handed over to the Selectors."

"Who wanted to do that?" Kiet was horrified.

Zonda didn't answer directly. "You see, he'd been going out exploring where he wasn't supposed to go. And after he found the angel—"

"Miriael."

"Yes, Miriael. He'd been seeing her in secret. A boy from our tribe with a different kind of being like her. It was too weird."

Kiet moved up closer and lowered her voice. "He told me once he was in love with her."

"Phah!" Zonda snorted with derision. "Him and her! I bet he never even kissed her. How could he?"

"I don't think it was about kissing. I think it was about devotion and service. He said he was going to spend his whole life like that."

"Stupid!"

"It was all in his head."

"Typical boy."

"All on his side."

"No sense of themselves."

"No sense of reality."

"No sense!"

They chimed in on the last phrase together and laughed. Kiet loved to hear Zonda confirming what she thought herself. They lay side by side in comfortable silence.

"Maybe he's learned his lesson now," Zonda mused aloud.

Kiet was thinking about the story of Ferren's life. She was eager to ask more questions—about his parents, his sister, his early years. They'd hardly started on the full story yet...

"Maybe I should give him another chance," said Zonda thoughtfully.

Kiet hardly took it in at first. When she did, a cold draught blew in on her comfortable feelings. She held herself very quiet and waited to understand.

"Yes, him and me," Zonda mused on. "It's possible now. Nobody thinks of him as odd anymore."

"You make it sound like you and him..."

"Oh, he wanted to. He was always hot for me, you know, always sniffing around. He used to like to snuggle up close at night."

"*Before* he thought he was in love with an angel, of course."

Kiet's tone was sharp, but Zonda didn't seem to register the sharpness. "That was different. He'd still have jumped at the chance with me. Any boy would. But he's the only one who might deserve it."

"You're very confident about yourself, aren't you?"

Again, the intended barb bounced right off. Zonda merely nodded. "We're so much alike, him and me."

Kiet had lost all urge to hear about Ferren growing up. She rose to her feet, muttered an excuse of a farewell and went off. Did Zonda so much as notice she'd gone? Kiet had never met anyone so completely wrapped up in themselves.

Even the memory of Zonda's language left a bad taste. 'Hot for me' and 'sniffing around'—like talking about a dog! And then, unbelievably, 'Any boy would'! The girl believed she was irresistible! Kiet grimaced. Her first impression of Zonda had been the accurate one.

14

Kiet couldn't stop stewing over her conversation with Zonda. Next day, when she saw Bross doing press-ups under the ferns, she decided to ask for an independent opinion.

"Hi!" She sat down beside him.

He let out his breath and lowered himself to the ground. "Hi."

"You're still in training, then?"

"A wrestler never stops training. I aim to be the best."

"You aim to beat Stogget, you mean?"

"Yes. I'll challenge him when the time's right."

Might be a long time, thought Kiet, and moved on to her real question.

"What do you think of Zonda?"

"Zonda?"

"As a girl. Is she attractive?"

"She's all right."

"Only all right?"

"She's a real looker, of course she is."

"And you'd be attracted if she gave you the chance?"

Bross shook his head, but his eyes said something different. He kept his mouth shut even after he gave up shaking his head.

"No need to answer," she said, and thought, *You just gave your answer anyway.*

She made a move to leave, but Bross rolled over and sat up.

"Wait a minute," he said. "Has Skail said anything to you?"

"No. What about?"

"He was on at me before. After the meeting yesterday. And when we were back at the Home Ground. He said you and me ought to complete our Intimacies and become bonded."

Kiet sniffed. "He still wants to settle me down."

"And you don't want to be settled down. I know. But if he pushes for Second Intimacies..."

"Then we fake it. Same as we did for First Intimacies. You want to be a champion wrestler, and I've got other things to do."

Bross was grinning at the memory of their fake First Intimacies, when he'd rubbed his body with oil, and they'd pretended Kiet had done it. Kiet grinned too.

But her humour didn't last, and Bross's answer about Zonda stayed longer in her mind. She was still mulling it over when she almost walked into Ferren coming the opposite way.

"I've just been with Oola and Burge," he told her. "Zonda's been encouraging them, and they're all in favour of fighting."

Kiet hardly took in a word he said except the name "Zonda'.

"Fighting against the Humen, I mean," he explained in response to her silence.

"What do you think of Zonda?" she blurted out before she could stop herself.

"Zonda? She's doing a wonderful job. All the People are onside. Now it's the representatives we have to persuade."

Was he deliberately answering the wrong question? Kiet frowned.

"*We?* You and Zonda, that is?"

"Er, yes." He seemed puzzled. "What's the matter?"

"You used to rely on me for help."

"And I do, with your friends and family. But I'm sure they want to fight the Humen already. Don't they?"

"Why Zonda?"

His eyebrows shot up in surprise. "You know why. She's a representative, so she can talk to the other representatives. Better than you, better than me. It's the same as when we couldn't attend the assembly in the Home Ground. You *wanted* me to work through Zonda then."

"Working through her?" Kiet tried to look on the bright side. "That's what you're still doing, then?"

Ferren shook his head. "You say it as if it was some sort of calculation. I really like Zonda."

The bright side went dark again. "You don't mind when she throws her weight around?"

"Not when she does it against Skail. Of course not. I wish I had her confidence."

"I think you admire her."

"I do. She knows what she wants, and she goes for it."

And what she wants is you, thought Kiet. Somehow she couldn't quite manage to ask the real question she was desperate to ask. *Do you want her?*

She was afraid she might not like the answer. She went away in a worse mood than ever.

15

There was one being to whom Kiet could always reveal her inmost feelings: Peeper, the Morph on his zither.

"They're always going off together, little one. I know they have to talk to the representatives, but often it's just the two of them."

Another time, she reported a conversation with Ferren. "They're making plans to win against Skail, according to him. He makes it all sound so innocent, but I bet it's not innocent for *her.*"

And another time again, "I wish he'd stop saying 'we'! It's all 'we think' and 'we suspect' and 'we decided'. I'm sick of hearing that word!"

Peeper was a great consolation, although he never said much for himself. Even his peeps and chirrups were supportive. In the past, Kiet had had to soothe him when he was sad and lonely; now, in his own way, he did the same for her.

One day, she was frantic with worry, when Ferren and Zonda went missing completely. "She must've got what she wanted, little one. She must've been right about him being hot for her. Maybe she *is* irresistible."

Later, though, she saw the two of them sitting talking by the side of the rivulet, further downstream. She hurried back to Peeper, where she'd left his zither propped against a clump of ferns.

But, for once, the Morph was too distracted to be supportive. When she began to tell him how relieved she felt, he let out a long wail of distress.

Kiet forgot her own problems. "What's the matter, little one?"

"Oh...oh...oh ...oooh!"

At first, she couldn't coax an explanation out of him, only wordless sounds. He had gone back to the state he'd been in when she'd first found and rescued him in the City of the Dead. So she too went back—communicating with him in song, as she'd communicated then.

A few minutes later, she rushed out to Ferren and Zonda with the zither under her arm. They still sat by the rivulet, now dangling their toes in the water.

"You have to hear this!" she cried, and held out the zither. "Tell them, Peeper!"

Zonda scowled at the zither. "What's that? What's Peeper?"

"Peeper's a Morph we rescued," Ferren told her. "Attached to the pegs of that instrument. Morphs are the souls of humans who've been shut out of Heaven since the start of the war. All they want is to be allowed up into their true Heavenly home."

Kiet shushed him, then softened her voice to the Morph. "Tell them what you told me, little one."

"I know about Morphs," said Zonda. "My father's Morph floated off to join with a colony of them somewhere."

Ferren nodded. "Because they can't get up to their true—"

"*Shush!*" Kiet turned on them both. "Shut up and listen!"

But when Peeper made a sound, it was only a wordless wail. Kiet snapped her fingers in frustration.

"Peeper got left behind when Asmodai tempted the City of the Dead colony up onto his flying wing," she explained. "Now they're all trapped there—"

Peeper's wail, which had been dying down, rose suddenly to a squeal of absolute terror. Kiet stared up through the ferns, and Ferren and Zonda automatically followed her gaze. But the sky beyond the fronds remained blue and empty.

"He can *sense* them!" Kiet hissed. "That's what he told me! Their pain and crying! He senses them very close!"

A great shadow swept across overhead, cutting off the sunlight. It was travelling low and very fast—here one moment and gone the next.

Peeper let out a low whimper. Ferren and Zonda looked at one another, then at Kiet.

"Asmodai!"

"He's found us!"

"We have to run!"

They leaped up and raced to where the other survivors had been resting under the ferns. But nobody was resting now. They were all sitting up and muttering in alarm.

"It was him!"

"That delta shape!"

"Did he see us?"

Ferren spoke up firmly. "No, he didn't see us. But we need to go now."

They had just started to move when the shadow flew back in the opposite direction. Everyone froze, instinctively ducking their heads. With the speed of the wing and the green fronds in the way, Kiet couldn't see the actual bubble of glass, but she pictured the black-robed angel scanning the ferns below.

He's searching for us, she thought.

The shadow passed and the sunlight returned.

"Let's go!" cried Ferren. "Go, go, go!"

16

Miriael and Shanna had left behind their quarrel about Asmodai. Miriael had lost out over leaving their observation post to report to the assembly, but it was Shanna who was more contrite.

As they came towards the Plain and the Home Ground, Shanna talked about the old Home Ground she remembered, and Miriael talked about what to expect now. After the great terra-celestial battle, falling silt had covered over the tall grass and the ruins; still, even Miriael couldn't guess what Zonda and the People had created in the many months since.

"There'll be great changes," she told Shanna. "Be prepared."

The great changes didn't live up to her hopeful anticipation, however. The first ominous signs appeared when they were still several miles away. All at once, the ground on which they were walking was littered with bits of twig, broken branches and small piles of stranded vegetation.

"It's like there's been a flood through here," said Shanna.

"And dried up again since," Miriael agreed. "Strange, when there's not even a natural watercourse."

As it turned out, there *was* a natural watercourse, but when they came to it, it was no more than a shallow stream. Shanna shook her head in amazement.

"It must've burst its banks by miles and miles. What sort of deluge did they have here?"

Miriael considered the flow of the stream. "Whatever it was, the worst of it happened ahead."

"Which is where we're going," Shanna groaned. "Please not the Home Ground!"

A couple of miles further on, they saw the direct effects of the storm. Bushes were smashed to the ground, trees uprooted, branches left bare of foliage, grass flattened and weeds shredded. Many blackened, blasted stumps bore witness to lightning strikes.

Miriael said nothing to Shanna, but she had a bad feeling in the pit of her stomach. This had been no ordinary weather—a storm of such violence could hardly have been natural. She knew of only one being with the power to shape unnatural weather...

"Let's turn off to some higher ground before we get to the Home Ground," she suggested. "I'd like to survey the whole area first."

Shanna didn't ask for reasons why. By the look in her eyes, she already dreaded the worst.

In fact, the reality proved worse than the worst. When they climbed a small hill to look out over the Plain, what they saw was total devastation. The land was bare and featureless, the grass flattened as if pasted to the ground. Instead of one single Creek, numerous small flows of water meandered here and there among pools and ponds.

But the greatest shock wasn't the landscape. In the middle of the Plain, where the Home Ground had been, there now stood a dozen black tents and a larger black marquee. A dozen masts rose up around the marquee, some flying flags but most bearing metal dishes like upright saucers.

"It's the Humen," Shanna muttered in shock. "They've taken over."

"And Asmodai generated the storm and flood to make it possible." Miriael nodded. "He had his special techniques from the North American Weather Wars."

"But where are the People?"

"Yes, and the representatives of the assembly."

"What about my brother?"

"Or his Nester friends who rescued me."

For a long time, they remained staring in silence, revolving similar thoughts in their heads.

"We don't *know* yet," said Miriael at last. "Maybe they escaped before the Humen came."

"Maybe," Shanna agreed grimly. "I'm not giving up hope. We'll have to find out."

There was another long silence. Several Hypers moved about between the marquee and the tents, like black, glittering ants in the distance.

Then Shanna said, "I'll go down among the tents after dark. I'll spy around for clues, see what I can learn."

Miriael didn't ask to accompany her. She would definitely be a liability on this mission.

17

That night, Miriael waited what seemed like an eternity. She'd expected Shanna to be gone for an hour, but hour after hour went by, and still there was no sign of her. The sliver of a moon climbed up on one side of the sky and down on the other.

Her only solace was the quietness of the night. Surely she would have heard cries and shouts if Shanna had been captured?

She'll be fine, she's an expert at this, she told herself over and over.

Then finally a figure materialised out of the darkness. Miriael breathed a sigh of relief as Shanna huddled down beside her. Then another sigh of relief at her first words.

"It's good news. Some of them got away. I don't know how many."

"You heard that?"

"I eavesdropped on dozens of conversations. Going round from tent to tent—the fabric's thin, I could hear every word through the walls. But most of the talk was about other things. It took ages to gather any real information."

"I was worried about you."

"Sorry." A smile had appeared on Shanna's face in the darkness. "I'll give you the information without the other things, shall I? Just let me sort it out in my mind."

So Miriael heard how a Humen army had come against the assembly and encircled the Home Ground with the aid of an artificial storm. But many Residuals had managed to escape and hadn't been recaptured yet.

"They went through the storm," Shanna explained. "The Humen weren't expecting that."

"You said not recaptured *yet,*" Miriael interrupted. "Does that mean they're still hunting for them?"

"Yes. It's not *all* good news. You see that marquee with those dishes on the masts?"

"Of course."

"Well, that's their command centre for coordinating the hunt. I eavesdropped on the marquee most of all. There were always dozens of voices talking—not only to each other, often it was like they were talking to someone far away. But when they were talking to each other, they didn't sound happy at all."

"Because the hunt's not going well?" Miriael suggested hopefully.

"More than that. They didn't see the point of keeping on with it. A 'sideshow' they called it. And a 'needless diversion of resources.' They just wanted it to be over."

"They didn't care about escapees from the assembly?"

"Not really. I think they saw it as some little distraction from a few troublesome Residuals. Hardly worth bothering about. But they were under orders from 'him at the top'."

"That would be Asmodai."

"I suppose so. He wanted something from the escapees and wouldn't give up on it."

"What?"

"They never said. Maybe they didn't know. They didn't understand, anyway. They were annoyed because they were expecting to be back at the Humen Camp by now. I think about half the army's gone back already."

"Mmm. While the other half stays out here hunting."

"Yes, but not for much longer. They were very sure about that. 'We'll all be needed soon,' they said."

"That's good. If our friends can stay out of reach until the hunt's called off... What?"

Shanna was shaking her head. "Not so good. The Humen have discovered the location of the escapees. It came in just now while I was listening. New orders are going out to the Humen army."

Miriael sat up at once. "Why didn't you say? We have to warn them!" She bit her lip. "If we can find them."

Shanna nodded. "The Humen were talking about a 'forest of ferns'. And it was due south of here.

"That's a start." Miriael rose to her feet. "Come on, then."

She started back down the slope of the hill, and Shanna hurried after her.

"If Hypers are following them, it's easy to track where Hypers have gone," Shanna remarked. "They trample everything with their boots."

"Yes, as long as we're not still tracking behind when *they* find them," said Miriael.

18

Ferren and the survivors hadn't sighted the flying wing again, yet they kept on running. By the end of the first day, they were still in the ferns, but the clumps were rapidly thinning out. They arrived at a new kind of landscape just as the sun set: a bare rock platform divided by strange walls.

They paused only until the light went out of the sky. Luckily, the moon that night was the thinnest of new moons. They advanced in the shelter of the walls, which turned out to be composed of rubble, bricks and broken concrete. Ferren guessed that the area had once been a city of the Ancestors, and the fallen materials had been reshaped into these long, high barriers. Breaks in the barriers allowed them to pass through, and no wall blocked their way for long.

The walls came to an end a little before dawn. Now there was only the rock platform—but not completely bare of vegetation. A line of trees ran forward across the rock in the direction they wanted to go. They sprinted towards it and took shelter before the new day could catch them out in the open.

The trees grew on either side of a gully like a deep crack in the rock. There was no water flowing through at present, and the trees dangled their roots in the empty air. Flens spotted ripe, red berries in bunches overhead, and everyone ate their fill.

Then they started forward again. They were too tired to run, and the floor of the gully was lumpy with loose stones. Still they stumbled forward. The young Nesters, Skail and Stogget led the advance from the front, while Ferren brought up the rear, checking on stragglers.

As the sun climbed higher, the rock platform showed its true colours. It was blotched all over with lichen: green, yellow, brown, rust-red, salmon-pink and a blueish sort of grey. The survivors saw it between tree-trunks, looking out over the sides of the gully.

Later they saw something even more remarkable: metal plates, staples and wire stitches fastened over fissures in the ground. It was as though the rock had been provided with surgical dressings over its wounds. Ferren remembered something similar from his very first journey, when he'd been walking towards the Humen Camp by the side of an overbridge.

For a long time, no one paid attention to the huge circular holes they saw in the rock, nor to faint, dull booming sound in the distance. Then someone realised that the sound wasn't so distant, and the holes were the source of it. They were passing one particular hole, and the booming was much louder, though still somehow remote.

In the next moment, young Tadge jumped out to investigate. Ferren, thirty yards further back, saw him scuttle across the rock, bent almost double.

"Get back here!" cried his sister Rhinn, and jumped out after him. Then his other sister, Kiet, jumped out to help. But Tadge was too far ahead for them to catch.

Ferren groaned and joined in too. He ran straight for the hole, hoping to cut Tadge off. But Tadge got there first, then Rhinn, then Kiet, then Ferren.

The hole was ten feet in diameter, lined on the inside with some kind of white ceramic. By the time Ferren came up, Tadge was staring down into it, while Rhinn gripped his arm and Kiet had hold of his shoulder. The hole seemed bottomless, with no visible end.

"Look!" Tadge leaned forward, almost as if he meant to throw himself into it. "It goes down forever!"

Rhinn and Kiet pulled him back, and Ferren helped them manhandle him further away. Rhinn started to give him a lecture on staying under cover, when an almighty voice boomed forth from the hole.

"FOREVER-EVER-EVER-EVER!
FOREVER-EVER-EVER-EVER-EVER!"

They sprang away in a panic. The volume was deafening, and Ferren, Kiet and Rhinn clapped their hands over their ears. Tadge tumbled over on his backside, then bounced up and flew back to the gully as if all the hounds of hell were after him. Ferren, Kiet and Rhinn returned more slowly.

"It's an echo," said Kiet, as if trying to convince herself. "That's what it is."

"An underground echo," Ferren agreed. But they were all white-faced and shaken.

The voice continued to boom out of the hole as the survivors continued forward along the gully. It diminished only when they had left it far behind. But when they approached another hole half a mile later, there it was booming out again.

"FOREVER-EVER-EVER-EVER!
FOREVER-EVER-EVER-EVER-EVER!"

It sounded as loud and terrifying as ever. Anniga of the Nod-bodies, who was walking ahead of Ferren, turned round to him in disbelief.

"That's not possible. How is that possible?"

He had no answer for her. Something was going on deep down under the ground, but something caused by the Humen? It didn't seem likely. And probably not caused by the Ancestors either.

They trudged on along the bottom of the gully, and the same voice was booming out of every hole they passed. Always the same word, always at the same volume. Ferren had to shake off the impression that it was directed personally at them.

The mystery remained mysterious, but repetition gradually dulled its impact. By late afternoon, they were all dog-tired, and many of the older representatives were falling asleep on their feet. They had been awake for two days and a night, and running or walking almost the whole time. The decision happened spontaneously in one of the quieter intervals between the booming holes. The survivors sat down to rest, closed their eyes, slumped lower and dropped off asleep.

They were hidden by the sides of the gully and still under cover of the trees. *As good a place as any,* said Ferren to himself, and sank down too. The thought that had been worrying him for two days and a night passed once more through his mind.

How did Asmodai know to search for us in the ferns? What gave us away?

But he couldn't hold on to any thought for long. In the next minute, sleep overwhelmed him.

19

When Ferren woke to a new day, his muscles were still sore from so much running and walking. He looked along the bottom of the gully and saw representatives, People and Nesters still curled up with their heads on their arms. But someone was growling at them and shaking them awake.

"Come on, rouse yourself, we're moving on."

It was Stogget, and he was rocking Pedge of the Skinfellows back and forth with the sole of his foot. Pedge wasn't young; if the walking had left Ferren sore, it must have been twice as hard on Pedge. But Stogget, who seemed to be enjoying the role of enforcer, rejected all protests. He went round from sleeper to sleeper until he'd woken everyone up.

They ate a breakfast of berries, then continued on along the gully. The scenery was the same as yesterday, with the lichen-coloured rock platform, the staples, plates and stitches, and, every now and then, the circular holes that still boomed with the same voice: "FOREVER-EVER-EVER-EVER!" As on the previous day, Skail, Stogget and the young Nesters led from the front, while Ferren brought up the rear.

The sun was high in the sky when finally, thankfully, they left the rock platform and its mysteries behind. Emerging from the gully, they entered a forest of tall trees. Now they were better hidden than ever—though not by any ordinary foliage. The canopy that sheltered them here was a canopy of flowers, not leaves. Every tree in the forest bloomed with bright masses of pink or orange blossom. Even the light filtering down was a soft glow of pink and orange, and pink and orange petals lay sprinkled over the grass.

They pressed on into the afternoon. The trees that had been tall from the start were towering giants by now, their tops completely invisible from the ground. Petals drifted down through the air like pink and orange snow.

But Ferren could see that the representatives at the back of the advance were tiring fast. They walked with lowered heads, and their steps grew increasingly laboured. Still they continued to do their best— until Moireen of the Sea-folk lost her footing and went sprawling.

"I can't," she told Ferren when he offered to help her up. "I've had it."

Anniga of the Nod-bodies plumped down beside her. "Me too," she said. "I need a rest."

Ferren called out to those marching on ahead. "Wait up! We need a break here!"

Representatives and People dropped back and gathered round. Skail, Stogget and the young Nesters turned up a moment later.

"What's wrong with them?" Skail gestured towards the women on the ground with the nozzle of his flamethrower. Ferren noted that he now also carried the Queen-Hyper's bag, which Stogget had previously carried.

"They can't keep going at this pace," he said. "I'm calling a halt."

"Why not make it a permanent halt?" put in Kiet.

Skail, as usual, ignored Kiet and responded to Ferren. "Only the overseer can call a halt." He looked round and took in the general mood of sympathy for Moireen and Anniga. "Right, I *will* call a halt. A temporary break to rest and recover."

"And eat, too!" cried Tadge. "I bet we can find nuts and fruits in this forest."

Ferren liked Kiet's idea of a permanent halt. He couldn't push for it yet, but it gave him an idea of his own.

"There'll be a good view from the top of these trees," he said. "I'll climb up and see if the Humen army's still following us. Then we'll know how safe we are here."

He chose the tree with the broadest trunk, hoping it would be the tallest as well. There were plenty of closely spaced branches to swing himself up by.

In a minute, he was twenty feet high and approaching the masses of pink and orange blossom. Below and behind him, some survivors disappeared into the forest, while most had flopped down on the ground. He plunged into the blossom and lost sight of them.

Ten minutes later, he was still climbing. The tree seemed to go on forever, and so did its flowering canopy. He was starting to wonder if he would ever emerge to a clear view.

Another five minutes' climbing brought him above the tops of the neighbouring trees. He wasn't yet at the top of *this* tree, but there were plenty of spaces for looking out through its branches and blossom.

The view was breathtaking. He was looking out exactly where he wanted to look out, back over the route they'd come. There was the rock platform with its cracks and circular holes; further in the distance were the long, straight lines of rubble walls. And nowhere was there a single Humen soldier or machine in sight!

He grinned to himself. Now he could argue for a permanent halt!

But he still hadn't finished climbing. The tree he was on was surely the tallest of all. He kept on going and finally stuck his head up above the topmost mass of flowers.

If the view had been breathtaking before, now it stretched out further than ever—and panoramic as well! Now he could see right to the end of the flat, rocky area with the walls, and beyond to a light green expanse that was surely the ferns.

But he could also see the vanguard of the Humen army.

He shielded his eyes and squinted at black spots and specks moving through the light green of the ferns. At such a distance, he couldn't identify soldiers or machines, but he saw how they moved in military columns and formations. Two formations had even advanced beyond the light green expanse to the edge of the grey stony area with the walls.

Except...unless...could it be? He stayed watching with his heart in his mouth. At first, it was no more than an intuition...which grew little by little to a real possibility...then turned at last into a certainty. The two formations weren't *advancing* beyond the ferns to the area with the walls, they were *withdrawing* from the area with the walls to the ferns!

Observing as the formations passed across the boundary between grey and green landscapes, he felt more and more convinced that all the other black spots and specks were moving further away too.

This changed everything! No one could oppose a permanent halt when the Humen army had given up chasing them. Now he'd be able to take the next step and argue for ways to fight and avenge themselves against the Humen.

He had been many minutes staring at the withdrawing army when something made him want to turn and look in a new direction. Like a shiver or the hairs standing up on the back of his neck... He readjusted his position on the branches and gazed out over a different part of the panorama.

Now he saw overbridges converging towards a dark smudge on the horizon—no doubt the Humen Camp. Enough to cause a shiver in itself. But it wasn't the Camp, it was something rising above it that held his attention. Something that looked tiny from here, but was clearly huge in size close up. It rose some way into the air, then stopped and swung off in a sweeping curve. Unmistakably, the delta shape of Asmodai's flying wing!

It came out of its sweeping curve and arrowed straight towards him.

20

Ferren ducked down low and hid in the blossom. He had a sense of the delta growing larger and larger, closer and closer.

When it passed over, it seemed to skim the top of his head. He clung more tightly to the branches and refused to look up. The eye-like bubble of glass was surely scanning all the nearby trees—but not just the tree he was on, not exclusively.

Then, with a swoosh, the wing was gone. The petals around him stirred in the wind of its wake.

What gave us away this *time?* he wondered. Did Asmodai have some kind of supernatural power for tracking them down?

A few moments later, the wing swept over his head again. Asmodai was still searching, circling the area. It was as though he'd tracked them down, but only approximately. He knew the area but not the exact location—the same as when he'd tracked them down in the ferns...

The wing came round several more times, but in gradually widening circles. Asmodai was extending the radius of his search, so he hadn't found anyone yet. Ferren hoped the other survivors below were hiding and staying hidden.

After a dozen circles, the wing seemed to abandon the search. Ferren remained motionless and counted to a hundred, then counted to a hundred again. When he looked out above the blossom, there was no sign of the great delta anywhere.

He climbed back down in a fraction of the time he'd spent climbing up. Often he saw a branch below, and half-slid, half-dropped down onto it. He was taking calculated risks in his hurry.

His elation over the withdrawing Humen army had vanished. The threat of the army might have gone, but the threat of Asmodai was greater than ever. He had no good news for the others after all.

But where were they? When he came down low enough to see through the canopy, there was no one visible at the bottom of the tree. Were they still hiding?

He jumped the last part, landed on soft grass and sprang to his feet again.

"Danger's over!" he called. "You can come out now!"

Only two figures appeared. Zonda appeared from behind one tree-trunk, and Kiet from behind another.

"The others have gone on ahead," Zonda told him. "I said I'd wait for you."

"So did I," said Kiet.

Zonda pointed. "They went that way. They'll be far ahead by now."

"Let's go," said Kiet.

They set off at once, walking fast. Kiet explained that her family and friends had promised to leave signs to guide them; they just had to keep walking straight until they came to the next sign.

The first sign was a line of four twigs planted upright in the ground, with another twig placed flat at the end of the line.

"See, here's the pointer to show the direction." Kiet indicated the twig lying flat. "This is how we leave signs in the Nesters."

They found more similar signs over the next half-hour. By now, the sun was sinking, and the light through the canopy grew dusky and dim. They had to keep their eyes wide not to miss the signs: always five twigs, four planted upright and one placed flat.

Then the forest came to an end. All at once, the trees were behind them, and they stood facing a thick, white mist. It seemed to billow as they watched, rising ten feet up in the air.

"What *is* that?" Zonda demanded.

Ferren had no idea. "The others must've gone right into it."

"If they could, so can we," said Kiet.

She marched straight into the mysterious vapour, and called out a moment later. "It's not mist, it's *plants!*"

She had gone no more than a few paces in, but already she was no more than a vague silhouette in the whiteness. Ferren stepped forward to investigate and saw bulb-like plants poking up through the ground. The top of each bulb opened up in a million tiny filaments, so very fine and light that they floated upwards in the air.

"Keep close!" Kiet's voice sounded muffled and blanketed. "I'll lead the way!"

Ferren pushed through the whiteness after her, and Zonda followed behind. The filaments swirled at the slightest draft of movement. He felt their touch as a feathery tickle on his skin, and their smell was a dry sort of mustiness. His eyes began to water, his nose began to itch, and his head began to throb with a faint, dull ache.

How can we ever find the rest of the group now? he wondered.

Thirty paces in, Kiet sneezed. A violent explosion of a sneeze! In the next moment, Ferren sneezed too, and Zonda a moment later. One after another, the dry tickle of the filaments set them off.

Ferren's head was still ringing from his sneezes when he heard voices calling out.

"Here we are!"

"Wait there!"

"We'll come and get you!"

It was the young Nesters. A minute later, dark silhouettes showed through in the whiteness ahead. They beckoned, and Ferren, Kiet and Zonda followed. By now, everyone was holding their hands over noses and mouths.

Another fifteen paces, and the whiteness parted like a veil. Ferren,

Kiet and Zonda found themselves at one side of a shallow bowl with a pool in the middle. The young Nesters clustered around them.

"We knew we'd hear you start sneezing!" cried Gibby.

"We stayed awake to listen for you," said Ethany.

"Being close to water stops the tickle," added Rhinn. "Floy told us. He knows all about plants like this."

Ferren understood why Ethany spoke of 'staying awake.' Around the pool, representatives and People lay stretched out full length on the stone. They were either sleeping or settling down for sleep. Several voices murmured, "Hush" or "Quiet" or "No more talking."

The young Nesters shrugged and settled down too. They made a place for Kiet to sleep beside them, while Zonda went across to join the People. Ferren found a place for himself not far from the pool. The urge to sneeze had passed, along with his watering eyes and the throb in his head.

His own bit of news wasn't urgent or important anymore.

21

"Wake up!"

Ferren opened his eyes and discovered Kiet kneeling beside him, shaking his shoulder.

"What is it?"

"They've started a meeting."

He sat up. In the early morning light, Skail and the representatives had gathered on the far side of the pool. They kept their voices down, and Skail, as usual, seemed to be doing most of the talking.

"Trying to leave us out," said Kiet.

"Like he did before," Ferren agreed.

"But we won't let him."

"Right."

As Ferren rose to his feet, he saw that the young Nesters were also on their feet. All in a group, they came round the side of the pool to break in on the meeting. Skail saw them coming.

"You don't need to speak," he told Ferren. "No one wants to hear anything from you. You've been wrong too often."

Ferren kept his calm. "What about?"

"About places to stop where you say we'll be safe. But we never are. They're still always hunting us."

Ferren wasn't optimistic, but he had to say it. "Not the Humen army. I saw them from the top of the tree. They've turned back."

"So you tell us." Skail sneered and appealed to the representatives. "So he tells us, but do we believe him? It's all a distraction. That angel Asmodai is still hunting us, and we can't get away from him." He swung back to Ferren. "We can't, can we?"

Ferren couldn't deny it. "He seems to know where we are. But if we could discover how—"

"Distraction!" Skail jabbed an accusing finger at Ferren, then turned to the representatives again. "So, as I was saying... We need to negotiate an end to being hunted. It's all a misunderstanding. This angel Asmodai—you heard him over the Home Ground. Asking the Queen-Hyper about 'my little Miriael' and had she been found yet. That's why he's hunting us, because he thinks we have the other angel with us. He doesn't care about us, only about his 'little Miriael'."

Ferren frowned. Perhaps it was true, it probably was, but how could Skail be so definite about it?

Moireen of the Sea-folk raised a hand. "He still wants to get information out of us, though."

"Yes, information about Miriael. Exactly." Skail nodded approval. "That's why we need to negotiate, to clear up the misunderstanding."

"Like last time?" Everyone turned as an aggressive new voice cut in. Zonda had come to join the meeting, along with Dugg, Mell, Burge and Oola.

Skail scowled at her. "What last time?"

"Last time when you thought you were negotiating an end to military service. That didn't go so well, did it?"

Ferren joined in the attack. "You *can't* negotiate with the Humen. Or Asmodai. They only pretend to negotiate, when really they're taking everything they want."

"You'd have to be stupid to trust them," added Zonda.

"Remember what the Queen-Hyper said afterwards?" Ferren went on. "'I was only playing for time.' She never cared about making an alliance with Residuals. She said so."

Skail's shook his head. "I don't remember that."

"I do," said Dwinna of the Clanfeathers.

There were murmurs of agreement, not only from the young Nesters and the People, but from several representatives as well.

"That Queen-Hyper was only an underling anyway." Skail's face wore an angry, defensive expression "She didn't know what was going on."

"And you did? You do?"

"More than you," muttered Skail. He raised his voice to the representatives. "They *will* negotiate now."

Ferren raised his voice too. Everything he'd been wanting to say for a week poured suddenly out of him. "The time for negotiation is over. Asmodai and the Humen are our enemies. They've proved it once and for all. After their last cheat… It's madness to talk of negotiation. We have to fight them! We have to make them pay for what they've done!"

"Ah, heroic revenge," mocked Skail.

Ferren overrode him. "We can fight! We're not so weak and helpless! They couldn't crush us before, and they can't crush us now!" He brandished his fist. "They'll *never* crush us!"

He looked around. The young Nesters supported him completely, the People had been won over, but the representatives? He sensed that, with a little more persuasion, they might be won over too.

At that moment, a two-note whistle came to their ears. It came from somewhere nearby, somewhere in the mist of filaments. Everyone heard it, swung in the direction and froze.

22

"Is it the Humen?" breathed Rance of the Baggers.

"They've followed us again," muttered Rhinn.

"Quiet!" growled Stogget, a finger to his lips.

They stared into the whiteness, searching for shadows that might leap forth upon them. The whistle came again—closer than before.

There was instant panic. Everyone jumped to their feet, fled from the pool and scattered into the mist. Anywhere to escape!

Ferren cursed and ran too. He didn't understand how any Humen troops could have arrived here after he'd seen their army marching away. Unless there were small bands or advance scouts he hadn't spotted…

His vision reduced to a few feet in front of his face. Shadows passed before him, rushing right to left and left to right. One bumped into him, and a face flashed before his eyes. He recognised Anniga of the Nod-bodies, but she was in too much of a panic to recognize him. She let out a whimper of fear, jumped back, flung out her arms and shot off the other way.

Again he heard the two-note whistle. Was it coming from a different direction now? Were they signalling to each other as they surrounded their quarry? He swept filaments aside with his arms as if swimming through cobwebs. The dry, musty smell was in his throat, his nose itched and his eyes watered. Many times, he trod on the bulbs of plants and almost lost balance.

Then he went over completely, falling flat on his face. It wasn't a bulb that had tripped him this time, but an outstretched body. Someone had gone sprawling on the ground before him. He twisted round and found himself looking into the familiar eyes of Mell of the People.

He couldn't see the rest of her face because she had her hand clamped tight over her nose and mouth. She was desperately struggling not to sneeze. He felt an urge to sneeze rise in himself and tried to clamp down on his own nose and mouth.

Then Mell lost her struggle. Her features contorted, and a muffled sneeze exploded out of her. She wasn't the only one; other muffled sneezes came from here and there in the mist. When she made a move to jump up and flee, he put an arm across her shoulder and shook his head at her. Better to lay low for now.

Besides, he was wondering about those two-note whistles…

Even as he wondered, another whistle split the air. It was louder than ever, but cut off short on the second note. The whistler was sneezing too!

Ferren peered around in the mist. Could Hypers sneeze? They weren't like real human beings, they didn't have internal organs, so where would a sneeze come from?

Then a voice called out. "Show yourselves! Where are you?"

Mell gasped and pushed Ferren's arm aside. "Lemme go!" she hissed.

"It's all right," he said, and laughed.

She goggled at him laughing. "You're mad!"

She gathered her legs under her and took off running. He was still laughing as she disappeared into the white mist of filaments.

He scrambled to his feet and looked in the direction where the voice had come from. Somewhere near the pool...

"It's all right, everyone!" he shouted. "Come back! Back to the pool!"

The urge to sneeze fought with the urge to laugh as he headed back himself. In no time at all, he stepped out into the open space around the pool. There was no one there—until he shouted again.

"I'm here! This way! *Here!*"

One moment later, the filaments parted on the other side of the pool, and his sister Shanna appeared. A huge grin broke out on her face, and she ran forward with Miriael right behind her.

23

"We thought...Humen...didn't realise..." Ferren emerged breathless from a hug with his sister. He could hardly speak, and nor could she. Miriael, who hung back smiling in the background, explained.

"We've been trying to catch up for days. We went to the Home Ground and saw the destruction, but we knew you'd escaped. Shanna found out which way you were going."

Shanna held Ferren by the elbows and gazed into his face. "You thought we were Humen? Didn't you recognise the special whistle?"

Ferren thought back. "You taught it to me."

"Yes, when the Selectors were coming for me, and I hid in the Rushfield. It was our signal."

He *did* remember, but it seemed a very long time ago. "I never used it, though. I never heard you use it either, not really loud."

Shanna tilted her head back and whistled the two notes at full volume. Ferren pretended to cover his ears, and they both laughed.

They were still laughing when the white curtain of filaments parted in several places. Kiet stepped forward, along with all the other young Nesters: Flens, Bross, Gibby, Ethany, Tadge and Rhinn. They stared in amazement at Miriael and Shanna.

"It was *you!*" Kiet cried.

Miriael nodded. "We weren't sure about you, either. We found twigs planted in the ground like some sort of sign. We just hoped they might be something to do with you."

"We've been lucky," Shanna came in. "We started by tracking after the Humen army. Then our best clue was Asmodai's flying wing. Twice we saw it circling like it was searching in a particular spot. We guessed that was you."

Ferren grimaced. "Yes, he keeps finding us, we don't know how. Or almost finding us, but never the exact right place."

While they'd been talking, more Residuals had emerged from the mist of filaments: Zonda, Dugg, Burge, Mell and Oola. They clustered immediately around the long-lost member of their tribe.

"Shanna!"

"We heard!"

"So good to have you back!"

Zonda said nothing, just stepped up to Shanna and clasped her in a fierce embrace. Shanna's eyes were shining.

Miriael turned to Ferren. "Is this all of you? Any more?"

"There's two dozen of us. The representatives are still hiding." He scanned the white mist around the pool and saw shadows in it. "Come on out, it's Miriael and my sister!" he called to them.

There were whispers in the mist, but the shadows remained shadowy.

"It's safe!" Ferren encouraged them. "Everything's fine!"

More whispers. Then Stogget came forward, followed by Jerrock, Rance, Pinnet, Dwinna and Floy, followed by Anniga, Pedge, Moireen and Skail. Ferren gestured towards Miriael and Shanna. "You see?"

But Stogget planted his feet and shook his head. "It's not fine," he said. "You're fools if you think it's fine."

"What?" Ferren didn't understand why he was glaring at Miriael.

"We don't want *her* joining us. You all heard it in the meeting—that angel in the wing is after *this* angel. How can we tell him we don't know where she is?"

Skail stepped forward. "On the other hand..." he began, and silenced his henchman with a shake of the head. "On the other hand, this creates a whole new situation. Maybe it'll end up working in our favour."

He swung to address the Residuals in general. "Our meeting this morning was cut short. Let's have a proper meeting now. Everyone included."

Expressions that had darkened following Stogget's negativity cheered up once again. Skail himself appeared very pleased indeed. But Ferren was not relieved. He suspected that Skail's idea of what worked in their favour would be very different to his own.

24

They gathered on the same side of the pool as before. Skail shepherded the representatives into their usual semi-circle, but didn't try to exclude the People or young Nesters. Ferren positioned himself next to Miriael, while Shanna stood on her other side. Miriael was observing Skail with a puzzled frown.

"Where did he get that flamethrower?" she asked Ferren under her breath.

"From a Queen-Hyper who came to the Home Ground. He turned up with it afterwards. That bag belonged to her too."

Miriael pursed her lips. "It's not good to take over Humen things. They're designed to serve Humen purposes."

She broke off as Skail rapped the butt of the flamethrower on the ground for attention. The meeting was beginning, and Skail intended to speak first.

"What we have here is a whole new situation." He repeated his phrase from before. "And a much more favourable situation. I said earlier that we should try to negotiate with Asmodai and the Humen. Now I say we *can* negotiate. No question that they'll be willing. We can negotiate an end to being hunted—and I believe we can negotiate an end to military service as well."

There were wondering gasps all around. Skail visibly repressed a smirk.

"Yes," he went on. "The very thing we've always dreamed of. It didn't seem possible before, but now it is. We have what they want, and they'll have to offer what we want in return."

Ferren understood, and his heart froze. The other Residuals and Miriael herself still waited for Skail to explain his miracle.

"Do you want it to come true?" he demanded dramatically. "Do you want a peaceful life and freedom from oppression? It's in our grasp! So simple! All we have to do is trade them this angel!"

He swung an arm and pointed at Miriael.

Two dozen mouths fell open in shock. There was a long moment of absolute silence.

Then Shanna found her voice. *"No! Never!"*

'She'll only be going as a monitor." Skail addressed the representatives rather than Shanna. "You heard what that angel Asmodai said to the Queen-Hyper. He said he wasn't going to cut her up like some Doctor Something. He had different plans for her. He won't hurt her."

Young Nesters, People and representatives all began shouting at once. "You don't know that!" "They could do anything to her!" "You can't trust him!"

Then Miriael took a step forward, and the hubbub stilled. "Why would he want me?" she asked Skail.

"Don't know, don't care." Skail faced her, though he didn't look her in the eye. "He's been hunting us because he thought we could tell him where you were."

Miriael turned to Ferren. "Is this true? I'm the reason he's been hunting you?"

Ferren confirmed the fact reluctantly. "Yes. I think so."

Skail addressed the representatives again. "And now we *can* tell him. But we do it on our own terms. Let's take a vote."

Stogget moved to stand shoulder to shoulder with Skail. "Yes, a vote," he growled. "Now."

Moireen of the Sea-folk raised a hand. "Who votes? It's never been decided."

"Only representatives of the Residual Alliance ," suggested Pinnet of the Tunnellers.

"No, everyone!" cried Kiet at once. "Otherwise it doesn't count."

Skail focused a death's head sort of smile upon her. "It seems there are still strong feelings on the matter. Very well, not only the representatives. Everyone gets to vote."

Stogget gaped. "But they outnumber us!"

"Of course, it still has to be fair," Skail went on smoothly. "Remembering that each representative was chosen by the votes of all their tribe. So each representative's vote counts for as many people as they have in their tribe. In the case of the Nesters, that's two hundred and five people."

The representatives looked thoughtful, and several nodded. But the young Nesters were all on their feet.

"You call that *fair?*"

Moireen of the Sea-folk directed another question to Skail. "So if I have thirty-three in my tribe, that means I have thirty-three votes?"

"Exactly."

"Good. That'll be thirty-three votes against handing the angel over, then."

Skail's face fell. "Did you say 'against'?"

"Yes."

"Why?"

"Because she helped defeat the seagulls for us." Moireen looked at Miriael. "And a Selector too. My tribe is in her debt. They wouldn't want me to vote for trading her off."

Once more, the representatives looked thoughtful, and several nodded again. But the nods had a different meaning now.

"Same for the People," cried Zonda. "We owe her our lives from long ago. We'd have been wiped out if she hadn't shown us how to build a bunker and protect ourselves. So that's another twenty-eight against.

Skail shook his head. "You can only count those still alive. Here's you and four survivors." He pointed to Dugg, Mell, Burge and Oola.

"The rest are probably dead."

"No-o-o!" Zonda's cry of protest was like an animal howl.

A dozen disapproving voices spoke up against Skail. "That's heartless!" "You can't say that!" "They could've survived!"

Skail scanned the meeting and seemed to decide he was losing support. Even the representatives might not be on his side.

"All right, all right." He made soothing gestures with both hands. He was all calm sense and reason now. "Maybe we should postpone the vote until I negotiate the terms of a deal. Then you can know exactly what you'll get in exchange. If it's an end to military service, then you can decide if you want to turn that down."

Shanna advanced on him. "You try to exchange her, you do it over my dead body."

Stogget raised his fists, Skail raised the flamethrower.

"If that's how you want it," said Skail, and pointed the nozzle of his weapon at Shanna's chest.

Shanna halted, but she was still on the balls of her feet, still ready to lunge.

"He's bluffing!" Kiet called out. "His flamethrower's waterlogged! Doesn't work!"

"Is that so?" Skail responded with a sneer, his eyes still fixed upon Shanna. "Who wants to try? You don't know as much as you think you do."

Miriael spoke to Shanna, defusing the situation. "It's all right. Nothing's happened yet." She turned to Skail. "I'm curious. How do you expect to negotiate? If you meet with the Humen, they'll just collect me and everyone else. Once they know where we are, what's to stop them?"

"They won't know, and I won't meet them." Skail lowered the flamethrower with a superior look on his face. "I negotiate at a distance."

"That's very clever if you can find a way to do it."

Skail responded to her irony with a mocking laugh. "You don't know as much as you think, either."

He reached inside the Queen-Hyper's bag that he wore over his shoulder. "I negotiate with *this*," he said, and drew out a black box with a silvery spike at one end.

25

Ferren remembered how he and Kiet had seen the Queen-Hyper speak into that very same box. It was a communication device for communicating at a distance. Others were also nodding their heads in recognition—perhaps they'd seen such devices used by Selectors in the past.

Mirlael seemed to know about them too. "So you talk to the Humen with that?" she asked Skail.

"Yes."

"You've already tried it, haven't you?"

Skail continued to look superior. "Yes."

Zonda rounded on him. "You've been communicating with the Humen *in secret?*"

Others were equally outraged. "You never told us!" "We should've had a meeting!" "We should've taken a vote!"

Skail's voice went up a notch. "You voted me to be your overseer! I was acting as overseer. I'd have reported as soon as I had anything definite to report."

Everyone was on their feet now, clamouring. "No!" "We never agreed to that!"

Skail retreated a step, and Stogget came forward as his human shield. Skail raised the black box in one hand while gripping the flamethrower with the other.

"I was acting in your interests!" he shouted. "Don't you understand? I was trying to help us all! And now I can! You'll see!"

There was a click as he pressed a button on the black box.

"Stand back," warned Stogget. "Let him talk."

Skail turned away and raised the black box to his ear. When someone answered at the other end, he spoke with his mouth very close to one end of the box so that nobody round the pool could hear.

Stogget spread his arms out wide to stop them coming closer. For the moment, they just watched in disbelief.

Then Miriael addressed a question to Stogget. "Were *you* there other times when he talked to the Humen?"

"Always. We went off by ourselves, and I stood guard. It didn't work at first."

"What, the communication device?"

"It must've been waterlogged from the storm and the river. Then it dried out. It connected to someone as soon as he pressed the button."

"Who?" asked Miriael.

Stogget's only response was a shrug.

"The last person the Queen-Hyper was talking to," Ferren suggested.

"Some Humen officers," said Stogget. "I don't know who."

Skail had finished speaking into the box. He covered one end with his hand, then turned.

"They're putting me through," he announced. "I'm going up higher this time. I'll be negotiating with the top Humen commanders. Maybe even that angel Asmodai."

"It was only officers before," Stogget explained to the onlookers. "They used to ask where he was, but he was too smart, he never gave anything away."

"Shush!" hissed Skail, as a scratchy sound came from the box. "I've been connected."

"Shush!" Stogget repeated the order in a menacing growl.

Skail uncovered the box and turned away again. But his voice soon grew louder and sharper, and this time everyone could hear.

"No, not you, your superiors! This is important. That angel you keep asking about—we have her now. That's right. Your commanders will want to talk terms with me, don't you think? Please do. And quickly."

Once more he covered the box with his hands. "That'll hurry them up. They know what it's about now. They're always asking me to wait and keep the channel open while they consult with their superiors. It's always *hold on, hold on, just a little longer.* This'll make them change their tune."

Miriael's brows creased in a frown. "How long do you keep the channel open?"

Skail must have thought he heard something, because he turned away and raised the device once more to his ear. Stogget answered on his behalf.

"A few minutes. Three or four."

Skail lowered the box again. "No, nothing," he muttered.

"Still taking their time," said Stogget.

Miriael looked from Stogget to Skail and back again.

"Of course!" she cried suddenly. "I should've seen it!" She pointed to the black box. *"Get that thing from him!"*

Shanna moved first. She dodged past Stogget, caught hold of Skail's hand and prised the box from his grip. Skail was still blinking in surprise.

"Now turn it off!" cried Miriael. "Find the button and *turn it off!*"

'Give that back!" Skail demanded, and stepped forward to reclaim the box.

Shanna held it out of reach of his clutching hands. She was still searching for the button.

"Fool!" Again he grabbed, again Shanna kept it away from him. "If you lose the connection, I'll have to start all over again. Give it—"

There was a decisive click as Shanna pressed the button.

Skail snarled in frustration. "Fool! Siding with Celestials instead of your own people. Angel-lover!" He raged on, but no one was paying much attention.

Ferren watched Miriael, who was scanning the sky.

"I think it's time for us to hide," she said.

Her tone was calm, but her manner was urgent. Ferren took up the call in a louder voice.

"Hide! Hide! Everyone hide!"

The only place to hide was in the white mist of floating filaments. There was a frantic scurry as they all dived for cover. One minute later, the clearing round the pool was deserted, while the mist was filled with shadows. Everyone had guessed what they were hiding from.

It wasn't long before Asmodai's flying wing passed across overhead. But it wasn't especially low or close, nor directly above them either.

He's really missed his target this time, thought Ferren, peering up from the edge of the mist.

"He didn't have long enough to locate us," said Miriael, nearby. She spoke to herself, but it was as though she'd read his thoughts.

Unlike the Residuals, Miriael hadn't clamped her hand over her nose and mouth. Apparently, the dry mustiness given off by the filaments didn't affect her. Everyone else soon started spluttering and sneezing.

Asmodai, though, was far too high in the sky to hear such sounds on the ground. He flew over once more to the left of them and once more to the right. It was only a matter of time before he gave up altogether.

26

When they were sure it was safe, the Residuals re-emerged and stood by the side of the pool again. Skail launched immediately into blame and accusations.

"You see?" He pointed a finger at Miriael. "This is what happens because of her. We'll always be hunted while we're connected to her."

Miriael sighed. "You still don't understand, do you?"

Skail banged the butt of his flamethrower on the ground. "She's a danger to us all!"

"No, you're the danger," she replied. "You and that Humen communication device."

Shanna, who still carried the black box, held it up for inspection. "This?"

"It's mine!" cried Skail.

"No, it belongs to the Humen." Miriael turned to Ferren. "You told me Asmodai kept finding out where you were. When?"

Ferren hardly had to think back. "Yesterday was the last time. I was up a tree and he flew right over."

"And where were these two?" Miriael indicated Skail and Stogget.

Ferren spread his hands and looked round for assistance.

"They went off into the trees while you were climbing," said Kiet.

"So. Communicating with Humen officers?"

Stogget nodded; Skail shook his head.

"'Course you did!" Zonda snorted. "And came back moments before that wing thing flew over!"

Skail stopped shaking his head. "I never told them where we were! I swear it!"

"No, it wasn't from anything you said." Miriael addressed Ferren again. "And there were other times?"

Zonda jumped in. "The time in the ferns! We were completely hidden, but he knew where to search for us."

Stogget was sucking his lips, looking thoughtful. "I remember." He turned to Skail. "It *was* the same, you know. You were talking to them two minutes before."

"Shut up," Skail snapped back.

"And then you gave up and switched off."

"Shut *up!*"

"It sounds as though you broke contact just in time," said Miriael. "You were incredibly lucky, more than once. When you pressed the button on that box, it sent a signal—and continued sending a signal until you pressed again to switch it off. You didn't need to give anything away, the signal gave you away. The Humen could trace where it was coming from."

There were gasps all around.

"I should've guessed as soon as I saw that device," Miriael went on. "It only takes them a little time to home in on the exact location."

Stogget nodded his head slowly. "That's why they wanted the channel kept open."

"That's right." Miriael swung from Stogget to Skail. "He understands now. Do you?"

Skail's mouth twisted in an ugly expression. "He's a fool."

"*You're* the fool!" Kiet called out in a loud voice. "Because you thought you were so smart!"

Skail's eyes darted in all directions, seeking support and finding none. He wouldn't admit to being in the wrong, Ferren could see.

"It's foolish to play around with Humen devices." Miriael gestured towards the black box in Shanna's hands. "Smash it!"

There was only a single gasp this time—from Skail. But it made no difference. Shanna threw the device to the ground and stamped on it. There was a crunch of metal and glass. Again and again she stamped, until the box was a flattened mass of fragments.

Skail half-raised the flamethrower, though he didn't try to use it. But the weapon drew Miriael's attention.

"That too," she said.

Shanna stepped towards Skail, reaching for the flamethrower.

"It doesn't work—" Kiet began.

With a tremendous, hizzling roar, a great jet of flame shot from the nozzle. Shanna flung herself to the side, but the nozzle hadn't been aimed at her or anyone in particular. Tongues of yellow fire licked along the ground, then went out.

"It was waterlogged too," Stogget explained in the silence that followed. "It worked when it dried out."

Everyone had retreated several feet away, but Miriael now took a step towards Skail. "All the more reason, if it works," she said. "You shouldn't have that."

Skail raised the flamethrower, this time with purpose. "You think you've won, but you haven't." He pointed the nozzle straight at the angel. "You're not going to smash *this*. I'll burn you first."

Several voices cried out in horror. "No!" "Stop!" "You can't!" Even Stogget protested.

"You know you don't really want to do that," Miriael told him, and advanced another step. "Come on. Give me the weapon."

Skail merely snarled—a noise without words.

Ferren had started to creep forward on one side of Skail, Shanna on the other. Stogget, who'd been standing next to Skail, was closest of all. Skail's eyes remained locked upon Miriael's.

"No one blames you for your mistake over the communication device." Miriael continued to speak calmly and reasonably. She made another small advance. "You couldn't know about them tracing the signal."

She advanced again, now barely three arms' lengths from the flamethrower. Skail's hands shook, the nozzle wavered this way and that. Ferren prepared for a desperate rush.

But Skail acted first—and so did Stogget.

Skail's finger tightened on the trigger in the same moment that Stogget stepped round and gripped him from behind. A jet of fire burst from the flamethrower and caught the edge of Miriael's wing. Tiny flickers of flame lit up on her white feathers.

Skail struggled to free himself from Stogget's embrace, but he had no chance against the wrestler's powerful arms. Still he kept a hold on the flamethrower and wriggled furiously.

"Stop it," Stogget grunted. "Enough. Let go." He was trying to persuade Skail to release the weapon.

Skail only wriggled all the more, pulling the bigger man off balance, dragging him from side to side. He shifted the flamethrower in his arms and aimed it back over his shoulder in the general direction of Stogget's face. He couldn't see, but he fired anyway.

Another jet of flame spurted from the nozzle. Stogget screamed as the flame burned the side of his head and his hair. Ferren flung himself forward at the pair of them and knocked the weapon away. He crashed to the ground—and so did the flamethrower.

When he picked himself up and looked round, Stogget was lifting Skail bodily up in the air. With one hand under Skail's crotch and the other holding his leg, he hoisted him high, swung him over and drove him down with tremendous force. Skail's head hit the ground with a sickening crack.

Shanna rushed forward and knelt to inspect. Stogget straightened, breathing heavily, and clamped a hand to the burnt side of his scalp and his ear. Ferren joined Shanna over Skail's motionless body.

"I think his neck's broken," said Shanna.

Blood seeped from split skin on the crown of Skail's skull, but it wasn't the blood that told the story—it was the impossible angle of his head in relation to his shoulders. When Ferren and Shanna rolled him over on his back, his head flopped loosely and his eyes were fixed in death.

27

For Miriael, the pain when the flame caught the edge of her wing had been a horrible new kind of physical sensation. She examined her charred, singed feathers—luckily, only half a dozen of them. She asked Shanna to pluck them out, and experienced a second new physical sensation, though not so painful. Shanna had tears in her eyes as she performed the task.

Stogget's burns were worse. The outer parts of his ear were a red and black mess, and the skin on that side of his head was puffed up and shiny. But he didn't moan or groan for himself, only over the fatal act he'd committed.

The young Nesters consoled him, and grieved in their own way too. Miriael was curious to note how they put aside previous feelings towards Skail and now lamented his death as the loss of a fellow-member of their tribe.

Their funeral rites lasted all morning and into the afternoon. Non-Nesters weren't excluded, but weren't invited to participate either. Watching from a respectful distance, Miriael observed a great deal of chanting and singing of dirges.

Later in the afternoon, the young Nesters dug a deep grave among the white filament plants, coughing and sneezing but carrying on regardless. Next, they undressed the dead man and smeared mud and dirt all over his nakedness until not a patch of bare skin remained.

Perhaps because he's going into the earth, Miriael speculated. *So they coat him with earth in preparation.*

The body had been buried but the dirges were still going on when Floy of the Fusselfolk came up to Miriael, Ferren and some of the others.

"I know where we are," he told them. "I suspected it before, so I went for a walk, and now I'm sure."

Dwinna of the Clanfeathers was one of the others sitting around. "Ah! You knew all about the sneezy, white plants, didn't you?"

"Yes, they grow near the territory of my tribe," Floy agreed. "It's a day away from here." He turned to Miriael. "We can't be followed now, can we?"

"Not since we smashed the Humen communication device, no."

Floy made a small bow. "Then I'd like to offer everyone the hospitality of the Fusselfolk. You're all welcome to stay with us."

"Thank you." Miriael surveyed the others and sensed positive reactions all round. "We're very grateful," she told Floy. "It'll be a pleasure to be among friends."

"We can have a meeting when we get there," added Ferren. "For planning our next step."

Miriael nodded agreement. "We'll start out first thing tomorrow."

She thought back over the scene when she lay down to sleep at the end of the day. She'd taken the lead and made the decision—and everyone seemed to expect it of her. Of course, they were impressed by the way she'd uncovered the truth about the black box. But even before that...

She remembered how they'd all stood up for her when Skail proposed to trade her off to Asmodai. It wasn't only the young Nesters who'd disliked the idea, but the representatives and People too. Skail had assumed they wouldn't care about her because she wasn't a Residual, but they *had* cared about her. The memory gave her a feeling that warmed her all over.

I never realised, she thought. She'd always had the impression that Residuals viewed her as a being utterly unlike themselves and wanted to keep her at a distance. But after today, after they'd refused to trade her off for their own benefit, she felt a sympathetic connection as never before.

She went to sleep in a happy frame of mind and woke the next day in the same state. Everyone else was in high spirits too. When they set off to walk to the home of the Fusselfolk, Zonda shouted a grand proclamation at the top of her voice.

"The Residual Alliance is back on track! We're going to do great things! We'll make that Asmodai wish he never messed with us!"

PART THREE

THE TOWER

1

Kiet hadn't changed her opinion of Zonda. It was good that the leader of the People had opposed Skail and supported the Residual Alliance, but in herself she was as objectionable as ever. And as for her claims on Ferren...

For most of the day, they were walking in single file through the white-filament plants. Although Floy led the survivors along creeks and watercourse as far as possible, Kiet had her hand over her nose and mouth most of the way. She could hear Zonda's belligerent-sounding sneezes close behind her, with every loud sneeze followed by an even louder curse.

"Typical, she has to let the whole world know," Kiet murmured to Peeper on his zither. "Can't even keep her sneezes to herself."

It was late afternoon when they finally left the white mist behind. They came out onto a wide riverbank, where the creek they'd been following joined in with a much larger river. Now they could bunch up and talk freely again.

Looking ahead, Kiet saw that Ferren, Miriael and Shanna had formed a group immediately behind Floy at the front. Then Zonda barged past, bumping elbow to elbow as she pushed her way forward to join them.

"Excuse *me*," Kiet said sharply. But Zonda's didn't hear her or didn't pay attention.

Of course, she has to force herself into the same group as Ferren, Kiet thought, and clenched her fists as they all followed Floy downstream along the riverbank.

Half an hour later, Floy pointed ahead to an island in the middle of the river. "The home of the Fusselfolk," he declared. "Nearly there now."

Five minutes more, and they stood facing directly across to the island. It was a low hump, a hundred yards long, velvety black in colour and bare of all vegetation. A row of tall poles stuck up from the ridge of the hump, and about three dozen tents. When Floy called out, the Fusselfolk themselves appeared and stood in a line to observe their visitors. They wore fur anklets and fur bracelets like Floy, had similar purple-stained lips and carried similar pointed stones on cords round their necks.

The water wasn't deep between riverbank and island, and the survivors splashed in and waded across. A surprise awaited them on the other side. Kiet was still on her way across when she heard whistles and shouts of amazement ahead.

"It's *furry!*"

"What *are* they?"

She soon discovered for herself. As she came up out of the river, she felt a strange softness underfoot. She stared down and saw that the island was entirely composed of what looked like small, furry balls.

She bent and scooped up half a dozen. They gave off a sour, fishy smell—and moved in the palm of her hand.

"They're alive!" she exclaimed.

The survivors had collected together by the water's edge, all examining the small, furry balls. Ferren had a broad grin on his face.

"They're fur-snails," he explained. "Or *fussels* for short. They go down many feet deep, millions and millions of them."

Kiet turned a puzzled expression upon him. "How do you know?"

Zonda weighed in before Ferren could answer. "He's been here before, of course. Him and Miriael, they went round all the tribes joining them up to the Residual Alliance. Didn't you know that?"

Kiet *did* know, and wished she'd thought it out for herself before speaking. She couldn't decide whether Zonda was being deliberately hostile or just being her usual self.

"Yes," Ferren confirmed. "We were here for three nights a couple of months ago."

A gasp and a cry drew everyone's attention. It had been a sound of shock, not pain, and it had come from Dugg of the People. He lay flat on his back on the black, furry ground.

"It pushed me over!" he protested.

Ferren laughed outright. "You have to learn to keep your balance on the fur-snails. They won't make it easy for you."

Kiet understood what he meant. The fur-snails were rolling over one another in a continuous, almost imperceptible motion. What had seemed solid and fixed under her feet wasn't the same as it had been a minute ago. She was rotating slowly to her left, and her feet were spreading further apart.

Floy cleared his throat. "Here's our Fusselfather," he announced. "Now we'll make arrangements for you to stay with us."

Half a dozen Fusselfolk were coming down from the ridge of the island. The Fusselfather was distinguished by the lines of age on his face and his long, purple-stained beard. He stopped twenty paces away, and Ferren and Miriael went with Floy to make arrangements.

Kiet didn't try to listen to the conversation, but it sounded very formal and dignified. After several minutes, Floy left the others talking and returned to the survivors by the water's edge.

"Yes, you're all very welcome for as long as you like," he told them.

"'Course we are," said Zonda. "Now how about something to eat?"

2

The meal was served in bowls: a purple-coloured, fishy-flavoured soup. The taste was sour, yet Kiet found it oddly pleasant. Ferren, Miriael and the Fusselfather sat a little apart and went on with their conversation. After the meal was over, Floy came forward with another announcement.

"Your tents are ready, if you'd care to rest now."

The Fusselfolk had erected a new row of tents for their visitors while they ate. Each tent held only one person, so there were twenty-four in all. They were made of fusselfur stretched tight over frames of curved ribs.

"They're all the same," Floy told them. "Please call me if you need anything else."

He went off and left everyone to select a tent for themselves. Since Ferren and Miriael were still with the Fusselfather, Shanna selected a tent for the angel. She probably intended to select for her brother as well, but Zonda jumped in first.

"This one's for me, and this one's for Ferren," she said, pointing.

Side by side, Kiet noted with a grimace. Perversely, she selected the tent on the other side of Ferren's for herself.

It was very snug inside. There was a rolled-up blanket of black fur, but nothing for lying on. Still, no mattress could have been more comfortable than the natural, velvety ground of fur-snails. She placed Peeper's zither on the blanket, then turned round on her hands and knees, and stuck her head back out through the flap at the front.

The sun had sunk below the horizon, but its pink and orange glow continued to light the sky. Ferren still hadn't turned up, so no doubt his conversation with the Fusselfather and Miriael hadn't yet finished…

"What are *you* doing here?" The angry question came from Zonda, whose head and shoulders had just appeared through the flap of her own tent.

Kiet restrained the impulse to bite back. "Why not?"

"You could've chosen some other tent."

"*Somebody* had to choose this tent."

Zonda harrumphed and changed her angle of attack. "Why are you looking out now?"

"What, I'm not supposed to look out?"

"You're waiting for Ferren."

Kiet saw no reason to deny it. "Yes, I want to talk to him about the meeting tomorrow."

"Oh? Well, I'm talking to him first. And I don't think he'll be wanting to talk about meetings after that."

"So important, huh?"

"Important to me and him. Something special between us. Nothing to do with you."

"You think there's special between you and him?" Kiet sniffed. "Sure you're not imagining it?"

"It's going to happen now we have time for it. You just keep out of the way, all right?"

Kiet shook her head. "I'll talk to Ferren whenever I like. We're friends."

"*Friends!*" Zonda put a world of scorn into the word. "I think he's getting a bit beyond wanting your sort of friendship."

"Why don't you let him make up his own mind what he wants?"

Zonda snorted as if struck by a sudden new thought. On all fours, she came right out of her tent and moved round to confront Kiet eyeball to eyeball.

"You're not getting ideas yourself, are you?" she demanded. "You're not hoping that you and him...? What a joke."

You're a joke, thought Kiet, and held back her mounting anger.

"Is that why you're always hanging around?" Zonda went on. "It is, isn't it?"

She thrust out her jaw and came closer. She was very well developed, and her breasts were full and prominent under her breast-band.

And don't you love to make a show of them, thought Kiet savagely.

Zonda laughed derisively. "Don't kid yourself. He'd never look at you twice *that* way. You don't have what he wants."

"Nothing to do with me," Kiet brought out between gritted teeth.

"No, nothing to do with you." Zonda's breasts seemed somehow more on display than ever. "Go back into your tent, why don't you?"

Kiet was on the edge of her greatest rage since she'd run to attack the Selectors with a length of wood. She felt it grow inside her, overwhelming, irresistible...

"Go on, go back!" Zonda came forward until they were almost butting foreheads.

Kiet didn't move, didn't say a thing. The look in her eyes was more ferocious than anything she could have said. Zonda seemed to become aware of it with a start.

"You're crazy!" she said.

But she dropped her aggression and drew back. A few moments later, she retreated to her own tent.

"You keep watching me and Ferren, you might see things you wish you hadn't," was her parting shot, as she vanished in through the flap of her tent.

She was still peering out, however. When Ferren came along a little later, she made her reappearance.

"Here's your tent, next to mine," she told him.

He nodded, and took in Kiet's head looking out from the tent on the other side of his. "Next to both of you." He addressed them equally. "Everything's been settled for the meeting tomorrow. Big decisions to be made. See you in the morning."

And with that he disappeared into his own tent.

3

K iet woke the next morning and didn't know where she was. Feeling the fur-snails under her, seeing the frame and covering of the tent, she remembered her new sleeping-place from last night. But it still seemed wrong. Somehow, the world was out of kilter and twisted around.

"What's happened to us, Peeper?" she asked the Morph on his zither.

She wriggled to the flap of her tent and looked out. The sky was above and the ground below, but surely the sun wasn't meant to be in that part of the sky? And the left-to-right slope of the velvety ground, the appearance of the river and the riverbank beyond—nothing was quite the same as yesterday.

Then she realised that she was facing the other side of the river. Her tent must have turned all the way round in the night!

She crawled out into the open. Ferren was already up, sitting watching the sun, while Zonda was still in her tent. Kiet studied the whole row of tents and shook her head in amazement. Every tent had rotated all the way round like her own.

Ferren came over to her, grinning. "A bit disoriented?"

"It's the fur-snails, isn't it?"

"Yes, they've shifted in the night." He pointed to a nearby pole. "Did you see how our tents are moored?"

Kiet had hardly thought about the poles before, but now registered the fact that each tent had a corresponding pole. When Ferren pointed again, she saw the rope that attached the frame of each tent to its pole.

"I didn't see any ropes last night," she said.

"They were there, but flat on the ground. Now they're stretched out tight. The ground's sunk down for this part of the island." He went to the pole that moored Kiet's tent and held his hand about a foot above the velvety surface of fur-snails. "They're lower now, but they came up to here last night."

Kiet thought about it. "But the poles don't move."

"No, they're anchored in the bedrock under the fur-snails. If the Fusselfolk didn't moor their tents, they'd all end up in the river."

"Whew!" Kiet whistled. "What a strange way to live!"

Ferren laughed. "They'd probably say the same about living in nests in a thicket. You want to see something else?"

She followed him to the top of the ridge and looked out over the other side of the island. The entire tribe of Fusselfolk stood lined up behind their Fusselfather in some sort of ceremony. They were shaking themselves, one arm or leg at a time, as if shaking kinks out of their systems.

"What—?" Kiet began, but Ferren hushed her.

"Wait for the important part," he said.

The important part of the ceremony involved the long, pointed stones that every tribesman or tribeswoman carried on a cord round their neck. They lifted the cords over their heads and dangled the stones a foot in front of their faces. For a minute, the stones swung side to side like so many pendulums, and the Fusselfolk echoed the motion with a side-to-side swaying of their own. Then, as the stones settled gradually to a stillness, the Fusselfolk settled too. They concluded the ceremony with a drawn-out exhalation like a sigh of relief.

"They call it, 'taking their bearings'," Ferren explained. "They have to do it first thing every morning. Now they're ready for a new day."

Kiet nodded. "I suppose it makes sense if you live on top of fur-snails."

She felt ready for a new day herself. Last night's confrontation with Zonda belonged in the past, and Zonda's derisive words no longer troubled her. She could still talk with Ferren—in fact, it seemed the most natural thing in the world. It was as though they'd known each other for ages.

They talked on for a while about the movement of fur-snails under their feet. Kiet discovered with surprise that she'd already adjusted to keeping her balance. Her legs made small adjustments automatically, and she didn't even need to think about it. Then they talked about the forthcoming meeting, for which Ferren had high hopes but no definite plans. Kiet was confident that the representatives and People had come round to the young Nesters' way of thinking.

"Everything's going to change!" she declared. "You'll see!"

Talking of the meeting reminded Ferren that he still had matters to discuss with Miriael and Shanna. As he went off to wake them up, Kiet called out after him.

"The ground will be shifting under everyone's feet!" She pointed to the black, velvety ground of fur-snails. "You'll see!"

4

As Ferren had told Kiet, he had no definite plans for the meeting. He was sure the young Nesters and probably the People would support big changes, but he couldn't predict the mood of the representatives. If they could be persuaded to fight against the Humen, he'd do all he could to encourage them, but if they were still cautious, he'd bide his time until they were less fearful.

The meeting began with representatives, People and young Nesters sitting in a circle. Members of the Fusselfolk who weren't otherwise busy sat in a wider circle around them. It was agreed from the very start that this meeting was not just an assembly of representatives—anyone had the right to speak.

"Does that include us?" asked the Fusselfather.

Ferren exchanged glances with Miriael. "Yes, why not Fusselfolk too? If you think you understand the issues."

The Fusselfather stroked his purple-stained beard. "Agreed. Only if we understand the issues."

The next hurdle turned out to be no hurdle at all. No one seemed to remember Skail's claim that representatives should have as many votes as their tribes had members, but everyone remembered the concession that non-representatives should be able vote.

"Fusselfolk won't vote unless we really understand the issues," said the Fusselfather.

Then it was straight on to business. With all eyes upon him, Ferren again took the lead.

"So, this meeting continues on the work of the first assembly of the Residual Alliance," he declared. "What's our next step?"

Representatives, People and young Nesters hadn't thought through the next step, but they were very sure about what it *shouldn't* be.

"No negotiating with the Humen!"

"We'll never listen to them again!"

"Nor that evil angel!"

"Down with them all!"

Ferren rejoiced at the reaction. "You don't want to stay low or small or out of sight?" he asked.

"Never!"

"They're our enemy!"

"Hiding doesn't work!"

"Fight back!"

"Make them pay!"

The Fusselfolk looked bewildered. The Fusselfather raised a hand and spoke in his usual dignified manner.

"Can someone explain, please? Are you saying that tribes like us can *fight* against the Humen?"

"Fight and win!" Zonda pumped a fist. "My tribe built a shelter against Humen force-fields that would've destroyed us. We saw them destroyed instead."

"My tribe trapped a Selector and smashed him in bits." Moireen of the Sea-folk nodded towards Ferren and Miriael. "With their help."

"Three of us took on a Queen-Hyper and beat her by ourselves!" cried Stogget.

"And *we* brought down Doctor Saniette!" Gibby pointed to Kiet.

"She set fire to him. A hundred Humen Doctors all in one!"

The young Nesters cheered and whooped, the People and representatives joined in. Twelve-year-old Tadge whooped loudest of all.

"We'll beat the Humen!" he yelled. "We'll beat them better than Heaven ever did!"

"*That's* our next step!" proclaimed Anniga of the Nod-bodies.

"We ought to make an alliance with Heaven," said Zonda.

The hubbub fell away, and everyone stared at her. They weren't opposed so much as simply stunned by the idea.

"Why are you all gaping at me?" Zonda scowled. "Heaven and us— we have the same enemy, don't we?"

Ferren was on tenterhooks. This was beyond even his highest hopes.

Representatives, People and young Nesters looked at one another with a question in their eyes. "Could we?" "Should we?" "With *Heaven?*"

Stogget was the first to voice a doubt. "We don't need Celestial help, do we? Skail always said…"

He broke off in the face of disapproving murmurs and even a few hisses. The mention of Skail's name was enough to push everyone in the opposite direction.

"It's not only what *we* need, it's what *they* need," said Shanna. She appealed to Miriael. "It could change the balance of the war, couldn't it?"

"Ye-es." Miriael seemed uncertain, though not about her answer to the question. "It could make all the difference."

"As long as it's not another fake alliance," said Pinnet of the Tunnellers. "We don't want to get cheated like that Queen-Hyper cheated us,"

Shanna turned to Miriael again. "Well?"

Miriael shook her head slowly. "There'd be no fear of that. Heaven has strict ethical principles. They *can't* lie or cheat. Whatever they say they'll do, they will."

"And you can talk to Heaven for us, can't you?" Shanna continued to appeal to Miriael. "You have a way of making contact?"

"Yes, in a visionary dream," the angel agreed. "I can try if you want me to."

Ferren scanned the inner circle of survivors and outer circle of Fusselfolk. "Do we want her to?" he asked. "What do we think? Shall we take a vote on it? It deserves a vote, it's a big decision."

In the end, though, the vote was never actually counted. When Ferren asked those opposed to raise a hand, not a single hand went up. When he asked for those in favour to raise a hand, there was a great shout of acclamation. A forest of hands went up, including many Fusselfolk hands, but everyone was too excited to wait while they were counted.

The meeting had gone like a dream. Ferren turned to Miriael with a huge grin. "How about that? The ground just shifted under our feet."

Miriael remained serious. "I'll try for a visionary dream tonight," she said.

5

Kiet was floating on air after the meeting. The fact that Zonda had been the one to make the crucial suggestion didn't spoil her elation in the least. But she felt suddenly uneasy when she saw Zonda draw Ferren aside for a private conversation.

Everyone stood round in excited groups talking about the vote. Kiet herself was half in and half out of a conversation with Miriael and Shanna, Rhinn and Tadge. Miriael had been explaining the problems of making contact through a visionary dream.

"It's not like an ordinary dream, you see. I'm in Heaven, but I don't have a dream-body there. I'm mostly invisible to most of the angels."

"You've done it before, though," Shanna put in.

"Twice. But I have to be lucky."

Kiet listened with one ear, while watching Ferren and Zonda out of the corner of her eye. No doubt he was congratulating her on the role she'd played in the meeting, and she was lapping it up.

By the time Kiet came back to what Miriael was saying, the angel was speaking mostly to Shanna. "The real difficulty will be Heaven's traditional attitude to Residuals. I know because I used to share it. That's why I don't…"

Zonda had started whispering to Ferren, and their heads were very close together. Kiet took in nothing more of the conversation between

Miriael and Shanna. Then Ferren laughed, and Zonda took his hand. In the next moment, they were slipping away without a word to anyone.

Where is she leading him? Kiet wondered in an agony of apprehension.

She still stood on the edge of her own group, but Miriael and Shanna had ceased to exist in her mind. Her thoughts had gone off following Ferren and Zonda, who were heading towards the tents—and after a minute or two more, she set off in the same direction. She didn't decide to do it, she hated herself for doing it, but her legs seemed to carry her anyway.

I'll just stroll past, she told herself. *It's none of my business what they do, really.*

She walked along the row of tents, but Ferren and Zonda had vanished from view. There was no sign of them until she came right up to Zonda's tent. Then she saw Ferren's foot sticking out through the flap.

A painful feeling knotted her chest. If Ferren was in Zonda's tent, then Zonda was in there with him. And the tents were so small, they must be squeezing up very tight to fit in…

Just strolling past, strolling past, strolling past. She repeated the phrase like a refrain in her head.

The tent bulged at the sides where their bodies pressed against the frame and covering. There appeared to be wriggling as if seeking out the best position. Then Zonda laughed and Ferren laughed with her. Kiet caught her breath at the horrible intimacy of their laughter.

That's it, then, she told herself. *Zonda's got what she wanted.*

She froze as the tent flap opened and something flew out, soft like a fabric.

"We don't need *that!*" Zonda cried gaily from within.

For a moment, Kiet thought it was an item of clothing she saw on the ground. Then she realised it was a blanket of fusselfur, like the one in her own tent.

It'll be clothes next, she thought.

She swung on her heel and strode off. She felt she could never get far enough away, no matter how far she walked. Strange sounds of activity were coming from the tent behind her…

6

When Zonda had said, "Come with me, and I'll show you something," Ferren had no idea what she meant. He was so buoyed up after the meeting, he hardly cared anyway.

"What, inside your tent?" he cried, as she crawled in through the flap and beckoned him to follow.

"Best place," she replied.

He crawled in behind her and squeezed alongside. The light inside was dim after the brightness of the morning.

"Now lie on your back like this," she instructed.

Ferren lay on his back. He held his arm in tight to his side, but with Zonda spreading herself out, they couldn't avoid touching.

"Now shake yourself about," she told him, and began to shake herself all over.

Ferren stared in amazement. She wobbled and bounced and jiggled, always in the same spot.

"What does that do?" he asked when she stopped.

She was laughing helplessly, and he laughed with her. "You'll see," she said, as soon as she could draw breath again. "Wait a minute, I'll make more room."

She gathered up the rolled-up fusselfur blanket from under her head and heaved it out through the flap of her tent.

"Now, go on," she instructed. "You try it."

Ferren shook himself all over, as Zonda had done. At first, he was conscious mostly of the contact of her arm against his; then he became aware of the fur-snails moving with a new kind of motion underneath him. The jiggling of his body excited them too. Soon the silky-soft creatures were jiggling as much as he was, brushing against him faster and faster. It was like being on a velvet sea of rolling waves.

"They tickle!" he laughed.

Zonda let out a low, exultant laugh. "Now both of us!" she cried, and started jiggling again too.

Ferren had stopped worrying about touching Zonda's arm, which moved against his arm at the side as the fur-snails moved against him underneath. The interior of the tent grew hot and airless, yet still they kept shaking and jiggling, wilder and wilder. The whole world became a single warm caress.

He was hardly thinking at all, but a scene floated into his mind. He was lying on warm sandstone by a pool, while dragonflies darted and hovered in the air and sunlight sparkled on the water. Complete contentment...

He stopped moving and let the agitation of the fur-snails continue underneath him. Then, gradually, all the other movements slowed too: the silky-softness under his body, the arm and hip and leg pressing against him at the side. He heard panting breath close to his ear, but no longer thought about who was doing the panting. Everything merged with the scene that had floated into his mind.

Was it a memory of the past? Another time of complete contentment? He had the idea there was a girl by the pool, and something to do with sweet, juicy pears...

A hand crept over his chest, and an arm held him close. A voice was whispering into his ear.

"Do you know what I'm thinking? I'm remembering our nights under the blanket in the old Home Ground. When you used to snuggle up against me."

Ferren compared the scene in his mind to his memories of the old Home Ground. No, the scene was somewhere else.

"You were always doing it," the voice insisted. "I think you wanted more than just a snuggle. I think you wanted *this.*"

A face hung over Ferren's face, and he felt a girl's warm breath on his cheeks. Suddenly he was thinking of deep brown eyes, white teeth and dark red hair...

"Lie still," said the voice. "Enjoy it."

Then two lips closed over his in a kiss.

For a moment, he lost himself in the sensation. Then his mind kicked in. He *hadn't* kissed the girl he was thinking of. This wasn't a memory, this was the present.

He opened his eyes and realised. This was Zonda

He turned his head aside, breaking the kiss.

Zonda breathed in and out, languorously. "There," she murmured. "What do you think of that?"

Again she moved to kiss him, again he turned his head aside. This time, the rebuff was obvious.

"What is it?" An edge had come into her voice.

"I don't... This isn't... It's all wrong." His feelings were growing clearer, but he couldn't put them into words.

Zonda levered herself up and scowled down at him. "Stop thinking about your angel. She's only in your head. I'm real flesh and blood, like you. I'm here, I'm real."

It was true, Zonda was very, very real. But there was someone else who was real, and now he knew who. That scene in his mind had happened when he was with the Nesters. He'd never guessed at the time, but *then* was the exact moment when...

"I can't," he told Zonda.

An ugly look came over her face. "*Can't?* I thought you were a bit more than that. Still a little boy at heart, are you?"

"It isn't—"

"Get out of my tent, then. Go on. Get out."

Ferren felt bad inside, yet he couldn't explain. He'd done the wrong thing with Zonda, giving her the wrong impression. But it was too late now. He backed out of her tent and let the flap fall shut behind him.

He felt bad inside, yet at the same time he was exultant. He'd just made an overwhelming discovery. There *was* someone he loved, not Miriael or Zonda, but someone with dark red hair, deep brown eyes and very white teeth.

It was—and always had been—Kiet.

7

In a visionary dream, Miriael was physically asleep on the Earth, but spiritually awake in Heaven. Even though her experience was drifty and dreamlike, the Heaven she visited was the real Heaven, exactly as it was in the present. To get into the state for such a dream, she needed to fall asleep while holding a picture of Heaven vividly in her mind. But it wasn't easy, and the scene she'd been picturing wasn't necessarily the same as the scene she ended up in.

Tonight, hours passed while she tried to focus on one scene after another. Several times, she almost drifted off into ordinary sleep. Then it happened.

Suddenly she was standing on the battlements not far from the Kingdom Gates. Two mighty towers framed ancient doors of burnished bronze. She could see the wall curving down to the Field of Meresin, then up over the green hills of Hanaphon. In the distance was the snow-white peak of Mount Shoah.

Not far from the Pavilions of the Rose, she thought. The Pavilions of the Rose were where her old companions of the Twenty-Second Company were stationed…

No sooner had she had that thought than her desire in the dream seemed to carry her there. Now she was on the Plain of Ashod, facing south to the Imma Beth Citadel. All around were the Pavilions of the Rose, their conical tops striped red and gold. Her heart leaped to see on every flag and banner the motto of the Twenty-Second Company: *Laus Ac Gloria.*

She passed between pavilions. Much was as she remembered it, but there had been changes too. She felt an absurd longing to embrace it all, to hug it to herself. So right and beautiful!

A troop of Junior Angels marching towards her brought her back to her task. Although she should have been in plain view, under the special conditions of the dream she was invisible to them. Their robes were an intense shade of yellow, the spears in their hands were like a glittering forest.

But low-ranking angels had never seen her in visionary dreams. Previously, she'd been visible to an Aeon serving on the Hebdomad, to the Chancellor of Schools on the Third Altitude and to Asmodai, who had once been very high in status. She needed to seek out an angel of superior rank.

She turned and found herself in a different part of the Plain, facing a war-pavilion striped purple and gold. It flew two flags, one with the motto of the Twenty-Second Company, the other with the personal motto of the Company's commander: *Prorsus Ad Victoriam*. Might Commander Elubatel be able to see her?

The movement of the dream carried her instantly inside the pavilion. Elubatel stood over a long table spread with maps and scrolls. He wore a silver breastplate and the crimson robes of the Order of Potentates. At present, he was dictating to a Junior Angel who knelt at the table and wrote on a parchment scroll with a feathery quill.

With a boldness she'd never possessed in her Heavenly life, she came forward and interrupted the dictation with a ringing cry. "Commander Elubatel! Sir!"

But Elubatel continued to dictate as though he hadn't heard a thing. She remembered then that one part of her had been more often visible than any other: her hair. She moved to stand before Elubatel, face to face, and shook her head until her long, golden hair flew out all around.

No use. He looked straight through her, and his voice flowed on without a break. What else could she do?

Elubatel finished his dictation, gave final instructions to the Junior Angel, then turned to leave. In desperation, Miriael reached out a hand to intercept him, but her hand passed through his arm. He must have felt nothing—and neither did she. She was a mere ghost in her own dream.

She watched his retreating back as he went out. The Junior Angel put down his quill, blew on the scroll to dry the ink, then rolled it up and tucked it under his arm. In another moment, he had followed Elubatel, and Miriael was left alone in the pavilion.

She refused to despair. If she couldn't be heard or seen, was there some other way she could leave a message? Watching the Junior Angel take dictation had given her an idea.

She approached the table, where there were several unused scrolls, along with the quill and inkpot. Her attempt to pick up the quill was a complete failure; her fingers met right through it as though it wasn't there. But as she stooped forward, the tips of her hair brushed the edge of the table—and she was able to feel *that*. Her hair really did have some sort of existence in this visionary dream.

With mounting excitement, she took a cluster of golden strands and swished them back and forth over the table top. A faint sensation every time! She had started with the idea of writing a message—now she had the means to do it!

Still holding the strands of her hair, she gathered the tips like a brush, dipped her brush into the inkpot and drew it out again. Yes, the strands were black with ink.

She chose one unused parchment scroll and began making marks on it with her hair. She could produce only the roughest brushstrokes and had to return over and again to the inkpot for more ink. It was infinitely slow, laborious work. Still she kept at it, stroke after stroke, until she had produced a whole message.

MIRIAEL

NEWS

TALK

URGENT

The letters were huge and took up the whole scroll, but they were readable. Surely someone would read them, surely Elubatel would understand and act!

Falling out of the visionary dream proved much easier than falling in. Even as she stood admiring her handiwork, she started to feel the weight of her real, sleeping body on Earth. She gave in to the heaviness and let it pull at her. Soon she was experiencing the folds of her robe, the warm air in her tent, the furry texture of fur-snails.

The interior of Elubatel's pavilion wavered and blurred. For a few minutes, she was between two worlds. Then she dropped right out of Heaven and back into her own body.

When she woke the next morning, the first thing she did was examine the strands of her hair. Some of the tips were still black with ink.

8

Ferren had made his discovery, and he was bursting to let it out. Could Kiet feel the same way about him? He had spent half the night remembering favourable indications, balancing them against not-so-favourable indications. But he had hope.

He waited until after the breakfast meal, when Kiet was heading back towards her tent. Then he caught her up.

"Feel like a walk?" he suggested.

She didn't look at him. "What, on this tiny island?"

"We can follow the water's edge all the way round. Yes?"

She didn't say no, and came with him when he set off. He wasn't so much interested in walking as in telling her his feelings. But he held them back until they were out of anyone's earshot.

"Wasn't it amazing, how the meeting went yesterday?" he said.

"Yes."

"I never expected it. Did you?"

"No."

Kiet seemed to be in a peculiar mood. He kept on talking, but it was a one-way conversation.

Approaching the downstream end of the island, he looked out across the water at the broad, brown banks on either side of the river. No one could overhear them here. He slowed his pace, and Kiet slowed too.

"It was Zonda made it possible," she brought out suddenly.

He had been wondering how to broach the real subject on his mind. "Made what possible?"

"Forming an alliance with Heaven, of course. What you were talking about. Zonda suggested it."

"Right. She did too."

"Did you plan it with her?"

"No. I didn't have definite plans. Didn't I tell you that?"

"Oh, *me*. I don't matter," she muttered.

Ferren stopped in his tracks. He didn't understand the reason behind her words, but he saw his opportunity. "You do. You matter very, very much to—"

"I expect you felt very grateful to her," she interrupted.

"What? Yes. No. I suppose so."

"I hope you told her that."

He shook his head. "I don't want to talk about Zonda. I'd rather talk about—"

"You seemed very happy talking to her after the meeting," Kiet pointed out.

Why was it so difficult to talk to Kiet about herself? Why did she have to keep talking about Zonda?

"What did you do afterwards?" she asked.

"Nothing," he answered automatically.

"Not with Zonda?"

"No."

"You must've gone back to your tent on your own, then."

Ferren couldn't come at an outright lie, so he shrugged. The shrug was meant to convey that he couldn't remember and it wasn't important.

"Strange," she said. "Because I saw your foot sticking out of Zonda's tent. And I heard the two of you together inside."

In all this time, she'd barely looked him in the eye—but now she did. The anger and accusation flaring in *her* eyes made him take a backwards step. It was like a violent slap in the face.

"All right, but—"

"But what?"

"It wasn't—"

"It *was!*"

"I mean…"

He was desperate to explain what had happened with Zonda, but she wouldn't let him. A moment ago, he'd felt completely in the right; now he felt as guilty as if he were completely in the wrong.

"Don't deny it!" she shouted. "At least have the honesty of your own behaviour! You disgust me!"

She stepped closer and seemed about to deliver an actual slap. Instead, she spun suddenly on her heel and stalked off.

Ferren blinked and stood there stunned. His mind was empty, his thoughts scattered in all directions. His heart felt even emptier.

9

M iriael.

Had somebody called her name? Miriael opened her eyes in the middle of the night and saw a brightness hovering above her. She couldn't tell if it was inside her tent or piercing through the velvety roof. It had the shape of a glowing hand.

Then the finger of the hand beckoned to her with a commanding gesture. As it moved slowly away, she knew she was being summoned.

Still half asleep, she followed where it led. She came out through the flap of her tent…crossed over the fur-snails…descended the slope to the river's edge…

She had no qualms about following. The purity of light that shone from the hand told her this had to be a celestial summons. When the finger beckoned to her to cross the water, she waded straight in.

It was as if the whole experience was happening to someone else. The water felt neither cold nor warm nor anything. She came up onto the riverbank on the other side, walked across bare, smooth clay and arrived at an undergrowth of rushes. Two oval, angelic auras glimmered beyond the rushes.

So this must be Heaven's answer to her message! Miriael shook off the lingering tendrils of sleep.

Her excitement dropped a little when she came closer. Commander Elubatel wasn't one of the two, nor any high-ranking angel. These two wore the yellow robes of Junior Angels, the same level that she herself had been. Their auras were dimmed to a subdued level of brightness.

They gazed at a point several inches above her head and introduced themselves. "Junior Messenger Angel Kered."

"And Junior Messenger Angel Osael."

"We were sent to hear the reason for your message." Kered's emphasis on the word 'sent' made it clear they hadn't wished to come. "You have news?"

I have to win them over, Miriael told herself. *I have to persuade them to persuade their superiors.*

"News about the Residuals on Earth," she began. "They've turned against the Humen. Now they think of themselves as being on the same side as Heaven."

Seeing the supercilious look that came into the angels' eyes when she mentioned Residuals, she held back from mentioning an actual alliance.

"You'd know all about what they think, I suppose," said Osael.

Miriael ignored the tone. "Yes, I've seen them close up, and I've seen what they can do. They've been reduced to ignorance, but they're not stupid in themselves. All they need is the self-belief and motivation."

"Yes, well…" Kered shook his head dismissively.

"You know what happened to Doctor Saniette?" Miriael hurried on. "They were the ones who set fire to him. A team of them broke into the Bankstown Camp, rescued me and destroyed Doctor Saniette at the same time. That's the sort of thing they can do. Don't you believe me?"

"We neither believe nor disbelieve," answered Kered. "We certainly don't believe merely because *you* say so."

"If the Residuals choose you as their advocate, they made a poor choice," said Osael.

Miriael shrank under the contempt. Of course, they despised her loss of proper spirituality. In their eyes, her part-physicalised body was corrupt and degraded. Still she struggled to win them over.

"All right. But that's only me. I know you disapprove of what I've become. But I'm only the channel for their proposal. Please don't reject an alliance with them just because—"

"Did you say *alliance?*" Their eyebrows shot up in surprise, their mouths turned down in disdain.

"They can help us, they really can," Miriael insisted. "I may be a poor advocate since I lost my spirituality, but you should listen to them."

The two angels exchanged glances, but they weren't considering the proposal. They frowned as they turned back to her.

"You did much worse than lose your spirituality," said Kered.

"Much, much worse," said Osael.

And then Miriael understood. "Asmodai?" she asked in a whisper. "You know about that?"

Kered's voice was cold. "You helped him, didn't you? The power he has now is thanks to you."

How did they know? Miriael felt utterly humiliated.

"You found him Morphs for his flying wing, I believe," said Osael.

"I never guessed what he was doing," Miriael muttered. "He used me, then betrayed me to the Humen. I hate him now."

"Are you sure?"

"What do you mean?"

"Are you sure you hate him? Why did you help him in the first place?"

Miriael looked from one to the other and saw only accusation in their eyes. "I don't know."

Their silent accusation continued to pin her down. "I suppose I fell in love with him," she admitted.

"*Fell* in love," said Osael. "What sort of love is that?"

"Not the everlasting love that angels feel," said Kered.

"No, a different sort of love," Miriael agreed humbly. "Individual love. I think it was because of my body changing."

"Your *hybrid* body," said Osael. "Part-spiritual, part-physical."

"Yes. But those feelings for him are finished now."

"Are you sure?" Kered asked for the second time.

"Can you promise?" Osael demanded.

Miriael wanted to say yes, she was sure, she could promise. But, with their eyes upon her, the promise died in her throat.

"I don't know," she confessed. "It was very intense at the time, but it ought to be gone by now. Humans have this sort of love. I don't understand how it works."

"So you *can't* be sure," Kered insisted.

"It was never rational. Nor moral, nor ethical." Miriael hung her head.

"Yes, you may well hide your face," Kered told her. "The shame of it."

Every word was like a hammer blow beating her into the ground.

"Fortunately for *you*, our armies can deal with the threat of Asmodai," said Osael. "You gave him power, but Heaven will take it back again."

"We have no need of help," added Kered. "Not yours, nor the Residuals you live in the dirt with."

Miriael was aware of their intensifying auras as they prepared to depart. Then she heard the wind-like rush as they shot up into the sky. But she couldn't raise her eyes to watch, she didn't have the will. In that moment, she could only hang her head in shame.

10

The weather was a mirror of Ferren's mood. The sky had clouded over during the night, and the world had turned grey and drizzly. The fur-snails were slick and slippery under his feet as he wandered about in the wet.

He didn't look to talk, but people kept chatting to him. One brief conversation was with Floy of the Fusselfolk, who appeared puzzled. He was carrying a small bowl filled with oil, which he held up to show Ferren.

"Do you know why they want this? Not for cooking, I'm sure."

"Who wants it?"

"Those young people with you. Nesters, aren't they?"

"Yes." Ferren shrugged. "No, I don't know."

Floy continued on his way, and Ferren was left alone with his thoughts again.

Half an hour later, though, he saw a group of young Nesters gathered in front of one particular tent, all whispering excitedly together. He wouldn't have approached if Kiet had been among the group, but he saw at a glance that she wasn't.

"Whose tent is that?" he asked Rhinn.

"Bross's tent." Her long, serious face looked unusually girlish, almost giggly.

"They're doing Second Intimacies," Tadge piped up beside her.

"Shush!" Rhinn made a move to cuff him, but she was struggling not to laugh.

Ferren had heard the phrase or something similar before. He didn't know what it meant—but he vaguely recalled that it involved Kiet.

"Who's doing it?" he asked.

"Kiet with Bross!" cried Tadge.

"It's a Nester thing," said Rhinn. "You wouldn't understand."

"Why is it called Intimacies?"

Tadge would have answered and Rhinn would have stopped him—

but then Gibby, Flens and Ethany joined the conversation.

"They've been going for ages!" laughed Gibby.

"They must be really into each other," commented Flens.

"What a pair they'll make!" cried Ethany—and her face flushed red as she said it.

Ferren still didn't understand Second Intimacies, but all his forebodings had turned into realities. He understood enough to see that he'd never stood a chance with Kiet.

"Are they mated, then?" he asked dully.

"No, not until Third Intimacies," answered Rhinn.

"Don't ask what *that* is!" laughed Gibby. "Only for Nesters to know!"

"I don't want to know," said Ferren, still in the same dull, flat voice.

At that moment, the flap of Bross's tent went up, and Kiet came out. Ferren gaped.

She was glistening all over with oil. Arms, legs, feet, neck, every visible inch of her skin had been oiled. She rose to her feet and shook herself in the light drizzle.

The other young Nesters clapped and whistled. The expression on Kiet's face was indescribable: self-conscious yet proud, abashed yet defiant. A moment later, Bross followed her out. Although his hands glistened, he had no oil on the rest of his body.

"First Intimacies is she oils him, Second Intimacies is he oils her," Ethany explained in an aside to Ferren.

Kiet hadn't been looking at anyone before, but she saw Ferren now. There was no change in her expression as she looked away again. When Bross stood upright, she took hold of his hand. The other Nesters cheered and whistled with redoubled enthusiasm.

Ferren had never felt more alone in his life.

11

After the visit of Kered and Osael, Miriael had been reluctant to tell anyone of her humiliation. Shanna knew about the message left for Elubatel, but didn't know it had been answered. As long as the drizzle continued, Miriael stayed hidden away in her tent.

Then the drizzle stopped in the middle of the day. It was no surprise that Shanna came calling soon after.

"Miriael? Are you there? Any news?"

Miriael came forward, head and shoulders through the flap of her tent. Seeing she wasn't going to emerge further, Shanna lowered herself to the ground outside.

"Any news?"

There was no escape, and Miriael reported the whole exchange with Kered and Osael. She could sense Shanna's sympathy, which made the telling easier as she went on.

"So I was the very worst person to speak to Heaven about an alliance," she concluded.

"You were also the *only* person who could," Shanna reminded her.

"Perhaps they suspect I might still be working to help Asmodai. Even now."

Shanna snorted. "As if! You're the most honourable, moral, high-minded person I ever met."

The words were balm to Miriael's bruised feelings. But she voiced another doubt. "What about what we heard from Ferren and the others? That Asmodai was still looking for me?"

"That's his problem, not yours."

"But maybe *he* thinks—"

"Forget it. In the past. All over now." Shanna had a wonderfully blunt way of demolishing irrelevancies. "You shouldn't let them get under your skin, you know. Stop bothering what other angels think. You shouldn't be so humble. You're always willing to bow to authority."

Miriael smiled sadly. "It's the way I used to live. The way we all used to live. No one can be simply independent when you touch spirits and share thoughts all the time."

"I don't know about that. Maybe it was different then. But they're completely wrong about you now."

Miriael's smile brightened. "You think I should take lessons from Residuals?"

"I think you should take lessons from *me*. Don't let them push you around. They're no better than you. And they're ignorant in comparison because you've lived on the Earth. You know about all sorts of things outside their experience."

"They ought to listen to me?"

"Of course they ought. Believe in yourself."

"I will."

"You mean it?"

"I do. Thank you."

Miriael did mean it, and she did feel grateful. Shanna's support mattered a great deal, and her advice was usually good. Little by little, Miriael had come to rely on her almost as an equal.

They talked on for a while, then Shanna rose to her feet. She surveyed the sky, which was finally starting to clear.

"Looks like the weather's improving," she commented, as she turned and went off.

Miriael retreated back into her tent. Shame and humiliation no longer burned inside her. Heaven's point of view wasn't necessarily the true point of view—and Kered and Osael's definitely wasn't.

I'm changing, she told herself. *I'm thinking like a Residual.*

It came to her then that she hadn't dwelt on old memories of Heaven for weeks. There had been a time when she was always feeling nostalgic for her previous life. Now she hardly even missed the spirit-to-spirit contact and universal love of the angelic community.

She was still mulling over the change when Shanna called to her through the flap of her tent.

"Miriael! Miriael! Come out! You have to see this!"

Miriael responded instantly to the urgent tone. As she emerged from her tent, she saw that Residuals everywhere were gazing at the sky, all heads turned in the same direction. The afternoon was far gone, yet the light was brighter on one side of the sky—the side where everyone was looking.

She rose to her feet and looked too. There in the distance, many, many miles away, a grey pillar of cloud reached up from the Earth to the sky.

A dozen questioners swung towards Miriael as soon as they saw her.

"What is that thing?"

"Is it the Humen?"

"What are they doing?"

"Isn't that where their Camp is?"

Miriael studied the pillar of cloud. She couldn't see the base of it, nor whether it touched the underside of Heaven, but she remembered that Asmodai had the power to control the weather and create clouds.

"I don't know what it's for," she said. "But yes, that's where the Bankstown Camp is. So definitely the Humen, and probably Asmodai."

12

Thinking like a Residual... Miriael had made up her mind. She wouldn't bow down to authority, she wouldn't worry what other angels thought of her. She needed to find out about the pillar of cloud, and right now they must surely all be talking about it. If she went up to Heaven in a visionary dream, she could listen and learn the facts—and for once her invisibility would be an advantage, not an obstacle.

It's what Shanna would do, she thought. *Determination and self-belief.*

In the silence of the night, she composed herself for bodily sleep while focusing her mind on pictures of Heaven. This time was much easier than the last. As if emerging from a faint, she found herself in another Heavenly scene—not one of the ones she'd been picturing.

Soft, opalescent light drifted down through the air like a very fine rain. She waited for the scene to clarify. She seemed to be standing beside a gently flowing river...

She realised then that she was in the Gardens of Prosopus. The river could only be the River Anaphar, white and creamy as milk. She had visited the Gardens only once before, but they were famous throughout Heaven as the source of manna, the celestial food of angels. And there were manna bushes all around, she now saw. The rain of light was condensing on their twigs and branches to form tiny white droplets. When the droplets solidified, they would be the manna itself, sweet as honey and subtle as air.

Looking round for the angels who gathered the manna, she saw several groups not far away, wearing the green robes of the Order of Virtues or the burgundy robes of the Order of Dominions. They gathered the manna in baskets, some singing, others talking as they worked.

By the strange logic of the dream, Miriael only had to wish...and she found herself close to a group of talkers. They were discussing the manna harvest and provisions for the Heavenly armies and which battle companies were being sent to which zone. Yet although their talk touched repeatedly on the war against the Humen, nobody mentioned the pillar of cloud.

It was the same when Miriael attached herself to other groups. Every conversation was as placid as though nothing very important had happened, certainly nothing worth worrying about. Miriael caught a reference to Asmodai and his switch of sides, but there was still no reference to the pillar of cloud. Either they hadn't been told or the news didn't seem significant to them.

Miriael grew more and more frustrated. Surely someone somewhere had to be worried and taking action to deal with the situation? Surely the War Council on the Sixth Altitude must be holding crisis meetings right now?

Once again, desire drove the movement of her dream. Thinking of the War Council on the Sixth Altitude, she left behind the Gardens of Prosopus on the Third and soared upwards. Altitude after Altitude went by in a rush.

On the Fourth Altitude, she saw the Heavenly Byzantium, with its ten encircling walls as if suspended vertically one above the other. Countless mighty turrets, cupolas and spires crowded behind the walls, every surface encrusted with sparkling precious stones. She passed right through the blue roof of the Fourth Altitude and came to the Fifth.

The volume of sound here took her breath away: a glorious thunder of singing and organ music. She looked out on a vast curving wall of a thousand angels, rising by tiers, candles in their hands. As each section of the choir joined in the harmony, their candles flared with a golden light. Miriael's heart swelled at the magnificence of the music...

But already she was ascending above them. She glimpsed sweeping balustrades and balconies as she passed through the roof of the Fifth

Altitude. Then she was on the Sixth Altitude, higher in Heaven than she'd ever been before. The rarified spiritual atmosphere made her feel light-headed and light-chested. The only level above this was the Seventh Altitude, which had been closed off for many hundreds of years.

She was standing on marble steps that went up to a massive double door of bronze. On the lintel above the door were words engraved: THE GREAT SOUTH HALL. She knew by reputation that this was one of the places where the War Council met.

Did she dare?

She mounted step by step and put her ear to the crack between the wings of the door. Solemn, serious voices were talking inside—solemn and serious enough to be talking about the most worrying new development in the war.

She *did* dare! She took a deep breath and let the dream carry her on into the Great South Hall.

13

The interior of the Hall was a miracle to behold. Circular in shape, it was surrounded on all sides by columns that curved inwards and forked into smaller branches, then smaller branches again. Miriael guessed that she was gazing at an upper extension of the famous Tree of Life. A living light flowed inside the columns like a circulation of the veins.

In the spaces between the branches were a million leaves—at least, they appeared as leaves, though silvery white and flickering. When Miriael looked more closely, she saw that they were actually Blessed Souls perched on the branches of the Tree. The whole vault was in perpetual motion with the fluttering of their wings.

Seven great hierarchs sat or stood around a table of gold. Miriael recognised Shemael, Jehoel and Anaitis, who'd often come down to lower Altitudes. She also saw the same high Aeon she'd encountered in a previous visionary dream, flanked by a pair of purple-robed Seraphim. And then there was Uriel...

The Regent of the South had once visited Miriael on the Earth, and his features were as she remembered them, etched like a crag of rock. Spiritual light streamed from his limbs, from his sixfold wings and from the terrible Sword of Judgement at his side. He'd threatened Miriael with that Sword on his previous visit, yet hadn't judged her guilty in the end.

No one saw her or heard her as she stepped forward to listen to their conversation. This was the southern chapter of the War Council, without Michael, Gabriel and Raphael, but the southern chapter was responsible for the southern sector where the pillar of cloud had appeared. And the discussion *was* about a significant new development in the war.

"How do they ever hope to break in?" demanded one of the Seraphim.

Shemael nodded. "They don't seem to remember the last time they got as far as the underside of Heaven."

"Humen arrogance," said the Aeon. "They never learn."

The Council members stood, half turning towards Uriel, who pursed his lips as he listened. Then he broke his silence.

"Nonetheless, we should send reinforcements to the area."

"Already on their way," said Jehoel at once.

"Local reinforcements, of course," added Anaitis. "We'll be ready if they try to creep up through passages in the ether. We've marked every exit, and we'll be waiting above to pick off intruders."

"So where are our forces now?" asked Uriel.

The Aeon answered. "Covering a mile around the point where we expect the top of the tower to arrive."

"Let us show you," said Jehoel, and stepped across to a map on the table.

Uriel and the others followed, but Miriael stayed where she was. She wasn't interested in the detailed deployment of Heaven's forces— she was interested in the Aeon's reference to a 'tower'. Not a pillar of cloud, but a tower. She wished they'd talk more about it.

But Jehoel was now pointing with his finger. "Forty-Fifth Company here. Twenty-Seventh Company here. Fourteenth and Thirty-First Companies along the Val Jehenna here. All prepared for action."

A *blam!-blam!-blam!* on the door interrupted the discussion. In the next second, without waiting for a response, an angel burst in. Her hair flew wildly around her head, and her robes were in disarray. She flung out her arms and called out across the Hall.

"Terrible news! It's—"

All the hierarchs frowned, and the Aeon cut her short. "Who are you? Introduce yourself properly when you enter this Hall!"

"But the Humen—"

"*Introduce yourself!*"

The angel paused, gasping. "Junior Warrior Angel Tamael of the Twenty-Seventh Company. A message from Commander Paschar. The Humen have broken into the First Altitude and established a beachhead in the Val Jehenna!"

Miriael had thought the hierarchs over-confident, but she'd never expected this. So soon! So easily!

The hierarchs were shocked too, but their reaction took a strange turn. "No panic." Shemael addressed the others. "The main thing is not to show panic."

"We'll deal with this," said the Aeon. "How dare they!"

Anaitis focused on Junior Warrior Angel Tamael. "Calm down now. It's all under control."

"How did it happen?" asked Uriel.

"That flying wing drove right up through the floor of the First Altitude and dropped off Doctors and Hypers. They punched two holes down through the ether for the tower to attach to. It shot up so fast—"

"What do you mean, 'shot up'?" snapped one of the Seraphim. "How could it?"

"*What* tower?" muttered Miriael in frustration.

It was meant as a question to herself, but the words came out aloud.

"Who said that?" demanded Uriel.

The hierarchs looked at one another, then looked in the direction from which the words had come.

Miriael had been unseen and unheard for so long, she'd almost forgotten she wasn't *totally* imperceptible. Without thinking, she retreated a step—and the movement gave her away even more.

"I see something golden," said Shemael, staring hard

"Like an angel's hair," agreed the Aeon.

"Someone's there," said Anaitis. "It's a spy."

Miriael protested. "I'm *not* a spy!"

Uriel came round the table towards her. He gestured Tamael aside.

"Stand back," he said. "I'll make this mystery appear."

14

hree paces away, Uriel unfurled his sixfold wings. Out and out they spread, to an incredible size

"If you're not a spy, don't move," he said.

He covered the last three paces and curved his wings around her. She found herself wrapped in an enclosure of brilliant, feathery white.

"Ah, *there* you are." Uriel nodded and addressed the hierarchs behind him. "Can you all see her now?"

They clustered close and peered at her as if over the top of a hedge.

"It *is* an angel!"

"But without the radiance!"

The space within the encircling wings seemed strangely hushed and still. Miriael was aware of Uriel studying her intently.

"I remember you," he said at last. "You're Miriael, the angel who fell to the Earth and survived. You're here in a visionary dream, aren't you?"

"Yes," Miriael agreed.

"Why?"

"I wanted to understand about the pillar of cloud and what you're doing about it. Except now you're all talking about a tower."

"The cloud is an outer cover, and the tower is the metal structure inside it," said Uriel. "As for what we're doing about it—" his brows descended in a bristling line "—not enough, apparently."

The other hierarchs were still working out connections to Miriael.

"If she's the angel who survived on Earth," said Jehoel slowly, "then she must be the same angel who helped the apostate Asmodai who's helping the Humen."

"And the same angel who came to Heaven in a visionary dream two nights ago." Anaitis spoke scornfully. "I received a full report from Commander Elubatel."

Miriael faced them over the top of Uriel's wings. She *would* believe in herself and not be humble. "I only helped Asmodai before I found out what he was. And Commander Elubatel's messengers *ought* to have listened to me."

"She's been foolish in many ways," said Uriel. "But I'm sure she's not a spy."

"I'm not." Miriael's courage was growing moment by moment. "And you all ought to listen to me. You talk about Asmodai helping the Humen, but he's doing much more than helping. He's leading them and controlling them. He's the mastermind behind them breaking into Heaven."

Jehoel shook his head angrily. "You shouldn't have heard that."

"We'll soon have it under control," said one of the Seraphim.

"Yes, and a moment ago you were saying they had no hope of breaking in. I heard that too. You underestimate Asmodai."

"We defeated the Satan in the past, and we shall do the same with this new apostate," said the Seraph.

"The Satan was proud and rebellious, but Asmodai's a warped intellect. He's far more clever and dangerous."

"In what ways?" Uriel demanded.

Miriael thought. "Well, you know that souls of the human dead power his flying wing?"

"Thanks to you," said Jehoel.

"Yes, but did you realise that Morphs are a completely new form of spiritual energy? He's discovered it and harnessed it. His flying wing is probably indestructible."

"It certainly broke through the floor of the First Altitude," Uriel conceded.

"He'll overreach himself," said the Aeon. "If he tries to bring a whole army up to Heaven, the ether will crack under the weight. Like it did in the time of the Great Collapse."

Miriael shook her head. "No! He knows about the Great Collapse.

He knows everything about Heaven. Do you think he hasn't worked out a way to stop the ether cracking? That's what I'm saying! All the things you think will stop him… He wouldn't have launched his attack if he didn't already have the answers."

The feathers of Uriel's wings swished around her, and he uttered a deep, thoughtful sound as if clearing his throat. "And what would *you* do about it?"

"You need all the help you can get," she told him.

"Hah!" Anaitis curled her lip. "She means making an alliance with the Residuals."

Incredulous looks appeared on every face. "*Alliance?*"

"With *Residuals?*"

Anaitis explained.

"It was in Elubatel's report. She was offering *us* an alliance with *them.* I took it no further, naturally."

Uriel's aquiline features and piercing eyes were so close to Miriael that she could scarcely focus. She took a deep breath. "That's right. You need an alliance with anyone that can help you."

"How?" asked Uriel.

"Residuals would be a new force in the war." Miriael blinked as the archangel's face seemed to swim before her. "Asmodai has brought in the Morphs, so you'd bring in the Residuals."

"Go on."

But Uriel's voice sounded suddenly faint and faraway. Miriael struggled to go on. When she looked at the other hierarchs peering at her over his wings, their faces were growing indistinct. She must have been growing indistinct to them too, because they sounded puzzled as well as faraway.

"What did she say?"

"I couldn't hear."

"She seems to be fading."

Miriael tried to raise her voice. "Don't you see? The Humen have their beachhead in Heaven, so we'd be your beachhead on Earth. Me and them…"

It was no use. They were shaking their heads as she faded out of her visionary dream. She felt the weight of her real body below pulling her down from Heaven.

Not now, she thought. *Please not now.*

But although Uriel's wings wrapped tighter around her, he couldn't hold her up. She was sure she was dropping back down through level after level. There was an impression of tremendous speed and worlds flashing past.

Falling...falling...

A whiteness of feathers still surrounded her, but the feathers themselves were a blur.

Falling...falling...falling...falling...

15

Miriael came back to the Earth with a thump. It was always jarring mentally, but this time it seemed physical too. She felt as if all the breath had been knocked out of her body.

She should have been lying on fur-snails inside her tent, but she was somehow out in the open. Instead of velvety softness, uncomfortable projections dug into her back. There were stars overhead and a feathery whiteness encompassing her all around. For a moment, she didn't know where she was.

Then Uriel stepped back and parted his wings. He had come down too! She had returned to the island of the Fusselfolk, but one of the four greatest archangels was still with her!

He furled his wings and waited for her to recover her breath. She realised that the projections digging into her back were the collapsed ribs of her own tent. She had come down on top of it! How was that even possible?

She sat up. Uriel took another backwards step and folded his arms.

"You followed me!" she exclaimed.

He nodded. "I haven't finished hearing what you had to say. You were proposing an alliance between Heaven and the Residuals. Why would we want Residuals as allies?"

"Because they're on the same side as you. At war with the same enemy. They'll be attacking from behind, where Asmodai and the Humen aren't expecting them."

"Yes, but they're still only Residuals."

So Miriael told him all the things that Residuals had already achieved, including the break-in to the Bankstown Camp and the destruction of Doctor Saniette. Uriel's eyes widened in surprise, but Miriael could see that he believed her.

"They surprised the Humen under Doctor Saniette, and they'll surprise the Humen under Asmodai," she concluded. "He knows everything about Heaven and what *you* can do, but he doesn't know about Residuals."

"Hmm. There is that."

At least he was thinking about it. Miriael waited in silence.

"Here's what I can do," he said at last. "This invasion of the Val Jehenna will require a full meeting of the War Council. I'll summon the North, East and West chapters, if it hasn't already been done. Also Michael, Gabriel and Raphael. I'll present your case to them all as one proposed element in our counter-strategy. But I can't promise anything." He pursed his lips and sighed. "You know the attitude. The mere ideas of allying ourselves with Residuals… Are you asking for a formal alliance?"

"Formal?"

"Written out and signed by all parties. That's how alliances are normally made."

"Yes, if it's the normal way. Like that."

Uriel heaved another sigh. "I'll do what I can. We can only hope."

"Thank you."

"Don't thank me yet. Failure's more likely than success."

"Thank you for believing in me, anyway."

"Yes, well… If I fail, I'll try to send a messenger to tell you."

His aura intensified as he prepared to shoot skywards. He pressed his palms together in prayer and raised his eyes up to Heaven.

"Goodbye, good luck," said Miriael, more to herself than him.

In the next moment he was gone, leaving Miriael with only the dazzle of his departure. She blinked, temporarily blinded, and realised with surprise how fast her heart was beating.

We can only hope. She repeated his words in her mind. *And I'll hope as hard as I can hope.*

She levered herself up from her collapsed tent. The ribs had been pushed over but not actually broken, so it should be possible to re-erect them. She was feeling for them through the covering when she sensed she wasn't alone.

She swung and stared into the darkness. A dozen pairs of eyes looked back at her. The brightness of Uriel's aura had awoken many of the Residuals.

"That was Uriel," she told them. "He came down after my visionary dream."

Little by little, they crept forward. It was no surprise that Ferren, Shanna and Kiet were at the forefront.

"Did he say yes to an alliance?" asked Ferren.

Miriael shook her head. "He can't say yes by himself. It'll take all four archangels and a full meeting of the War Council. But wait till tomorrow, then I'll tell everyone. There's a lot of news to tell."

16

Next day, the survivors and Fusselfolk heard the extraordinary news that Heaven had been invaded. Everyone had the same questions: how had Asmodai and the Humen broken in? what was the tower? and when would the archangels decide about an alliance?

Ferren looked at the pillar of cloud and tried to imagine a tower inside it. The cloud seemed to reach up a little higher today than it had yesterday.

After Miriael's news, it was hard to settle to anything. The Fusselfolk had their normal tasks to keep them busy, but Ferren and the others could only wait. They kept looking up at the sky all morning, but there was no sign from Heaven, neither Uriel descending nor a messenger from Uriel.

In the middle of the day, a change took place in the sky around the top of the pillar of cloud. Ethany saw it first, and cried out in horror and disgust. A livid stain had appeared on the blue of the sky like some sort of disease or infection. It was yellowy green in colour and glowed with an eerie phosphorescence.

"Must be part of the invasion," groaned Shanna.

"Ugh!" Dwinna of the Clanfeathers shuddered. "It's hideous!"

When Ferren asked Miriael, she could only shake her head. "The Humen must have infected the ether. I don't know how or why."

All afternoon, the stain hung over them like a foul omen. It also grew wider around the top of the pillar. The moment-by-moment increase was imperceptible, although Tadge swore he could see it happening. Hour by hour, though, there was no doubt that the yellowy green was spreading out over the blue.

Ferren couldn't stop himself glancing over his shoulder to check on it. Again and again, he grimaced and tore his eyes away. In the end, he retreated inside his tent to try and stop thinking about it.

Still he couldn't find peace. If he stopped thinking about the stain, he started thinking about Heaven's delay over deciding on an alliance. And if he stopped thinking about *that*, he started thinking about Kiet…

Then he became aware of voices very close to the side of his tent. They were young voices, quiet but excited, and they came right through the tent's fabric covering. He could hear every intonation, though not what they were actually saying.

He lay listening for a while; then his curiosity got the better of him. He crept out and peered round into the passage between his tent and the next. Gibby and Tadge, flat on their bellies, twisted their necks and looked back at him.

"Shh!" hissed Gibby, and pointed towards the other side of the ridge behind the tents.

Ferren squeezed in alongside them. Twenty yards away was Bross, doing push-ups.

"He's in training," Gibby explained in a whisper. "Second-best wrestler in the Nesters, but he's going to be first."

"He has to beat Stogget," added Tadge.

Ferren was amazed that anyone could focus their thoughts on

something like wrestling. Bross finished his push-ups and went on to squats, then lunges, then push-ups again. He had done about forty more push-ups when Zonda appeared from a different direction. Ferren, Gibby and Tadge kept their heads down and stayed watching.

Zonda was curious and not shy about asking. She came down the slope to Bross and stood over him.

"What are you doing?"

Bross didn't answer or even look at her. Rhythmically, he sucked in air and expelled it in regular grunts. Zonda sat down beside him.

"You're wet with sweat," she told him. "Pooh! You smell of sweat too."

Bross's face wore an expression of intense concentration. The muscles bulged and shifted under his skin as he arched up and down, up and down, up and down.

Zonda pouted. "Don't think I'll go away if you ignore me," she said. "*Nobody* ignores me."

She leaned across and pressed down on the small of his back just as he was about to push up. Instead of levering up straight, his body bent in the middle. He had lost rhythm, and his breath came out in a *whuff!*

"See? I'm stronger than you," she laughed.

He lay flat and looked round at her. "Not fair," he protested.

"What's it all for, anyway? Do you want to impress the girls?"

"I don't care about girls. I have to keep fit."

"You don't care?" She considered. "Seems a funny time to bother about keeping fit."

"I have to bother. I'm a wrestler."

"A wrestler." Zonda looked him up and down. "Hmm. Do you want to teach me?"

"What?"

"Wrestling. I'm strong. I'd be good at it."

"I don't—"

"Yes, come on, first lesson. Are you scared I might beat you?"

Ferren had seen enough and began to back away. Gibby turned to him before he could disappear.

"Is she always like that?" she asked.

"Yes. Always."

183

"Phew!" Gibby pulled her dainty features into a grotesque face. "Kiet had better watch out, then, or she'll never get to Third Intimacies."

Ferren carried that comment with him as he went off. For a few minutes, it lifted his spirits; then he looked up at the sky and the stain, and his spirits drooped once again. The patch of yellowy green was larger than ever.

The Humen must be winning, he thought. *What's stopping Heaven saying yes to an alliance? Why are they taking so long about it?*

17

The angels came down an hour after sunset. Ferren had almost given up hope, though he still watched and waited outside with Miriael and Shanna. Everyone else had retired to their tents for the night.

Miriael, with her sharper angelic sight, saw the lights first. She was instantly ecstatic.

"This is good! Many lights, not just a single messenger! This is very, very good! Quick, rouse everyone up!"

Ferren, squinting hard, made out what looked like a fuzzy constellation in a far-off corner of the sky. But it was moving against the static background of the stars...

He jumped to his feet and began going round the tents. Again and again, he stuck his head in through the flap and called out, "Wake up! Get up! Visit from Heaven!" Miriael and Shanna were doing the same.

Between tents, he also kept an eye on the sky. The fuzz of the constellation had now become a score of separate lights. Some seemed closer and lower than others, while the largest was more of a lit-up shape than a source of light. It seemed to flicker round the edges as Ferren stared at it.

He didn't hesitate when he came to Kiet's tent. He might have had qualms talking to her at other times, but not now. "Wake up! Get up!

Visit from Heaven!" He roused her, then Zonda, the same as everyone else.

The next time he looked, the lit-up shape was a bright, tasselled canopy, and the flicker round its edges came from a host of white, fluttering wings. He had seen wings like that taking part in the great battle over the People's old Home Ground—'Blessed Souls,' Miriael had called them. They descended over the downstream end of the island, hovering and holding up the canopy ten feet above the ground.

Meanwhile, the awakened Residuals crept forward to observe—but not too far forward. They congregated around the last few tents facing towards the downstream end of the island.

After the descent of the canopy came the descent of the heraldic angels. They carried long, shining trumpets, but blew no note upon them. Instead, they began to sing very quietly, a background murmur of hymning.

Next came half a dozen hierarchs, their auras twice as radiant as those of the heraldic angels. They took up position around the sides of the canopy. The light from so many auras merged to create a single pool of dazzling radiance.

Ferren completed his final wake-up call and came forward to join the observers. Mostly, they sat or lay on the ground, shielding their eyes, ready to flee at the first sign of danger. But not the young Nesters, and not Miriael or Shanna. Ferren went up to stand with his sister and the angel.

"It's really happening," he whispered in awe. "They've decided on an alliance!"

Miriael was smiling. "Yes, and Heaven never does things by halves. This is a full, formal ceremony."

Even as she spoke, the greatest wonder of all appeared: four archangels seated on four golden thrones. They were borne down through the air by more white, fluttering wings. Lower and lower they came, then in under the canopy. Thrones and sandalled feet were just inches above the black, velvety fur-snails, yet the beating wings still kept them aloft without touching.

"That's Michael, the Viceroy of Heaven." Miriael spoke in an undertone to both Ferren and Shanna, nodding towards one throned archangel.

"And Gabriel, the spirit of truth. Raphael the healer. And Uriel of the South, who summoned them." She indicated the other three in turn.

Ferren could hardly look into the light. He had encountered Uriel once before, but the four mightiest archangels all together… Even after his eyes adjusted, the power emanating from the four seated figures was a humming vibration in the air that made it difficult to breathe.

"They're waiting for us," said Miriael.

Ferren drew back half a pace. "Not me."

"Yes, you most of all. You represent the Residuals. They're not making an alliance with *me*." Miriael turned to Shanna on her other side. "And you can be a second representative. Come on."

She stepped forward, leaving the two of them to follow. Ferren looked at his sister, and saw that she was bemused but not visibly afraid. He took courage and advanced with her, three paces behind Miriael. The vibration of power intensified to an electrostatic tingle as they approached.

Six paces from the canopy, Miriael halted and waited for Ferren and Shanna to come level. Then she dropped gracefully to her knees and bowed her head to the four archangels. Ferren and Shanna did the same, more awkwardly.

"Arise," said a deep, sonorous voice.

They rose. It was the Archangel Michael who had spoken, and he spoke again when they were back on their feet.

"We agree to an alliance between Heaven and the Residuals," he said.

"Strange world, strange times," added the Archangel Gabriel.

Ferren hardly dared look into their faces, which seemed like pale, upward-streaming flames. He focused on their resplendent robes, the silver breastplate on Michael's chest and the many sparkling rings on Gabriel's fingers.

Then Uriel addressed Miriael. "It is as you said. We need all the help we can get."

"You haven't thrown back the invaders?"

Miriael's question produced grim looks and frowns all around. Crackles of lightning discharged from the limbs and wings of the four great archangels.

"They're bringing a whole army up onto the First Altitude," answered Uriel. "Fully equipped, with types of soldiers and weapons never seen before."

"And the ether supports them?"

"Yes, they spray some foul chemical to make it more solid."

"Which also poisons every flower and plant and tree." Raphael shuddered. "The Val Jehenna…"

"So we welcome any contribution Residuals can make." Michael paused, drew breath and brought out the words. "We shall be grateful."

Ferren sensed that the archangel's eyes were upon him. *It's up to me to say something,* he thought.

"The Residuals are willing," he said in a loud voice.

"Thank you." Again, Michael's words sounded sincere, even if he had to force himself to utter them. "You expect a formal contract of alliance, I believe?"

Ferren didn't understand, but Miriael spoke up. "Yes. Written and signed. Did you bring it with you?"

Michael turned to her. "It hasn't been written yet, since we don't know the terms."

"Metatron is here to write it now," said Raphael. "At your dictation."

Miriael's eyes went wide. "You want me to dictate it?"

Raphael nodded. "Let it be in your own words. We shall consent to all things reasonable."

One of the hierarchs came forward to stand in front of the archangels. His robes were of a rich burgundy colour, his beard was long and silvery. He carried a parchment scrolled under his arm, a quill in one hand and an inkpot in the other.

"Metatron, the Angel of Record and Register." He announced himself with a slight inclination of the head.

A small desktop had followed him forward, a table without legs. Born up by four pairs of wings, it positioned itself in mid-air before him. He set out his inkpot, spread the parchment on the table, then turned to Miriael.

"Begin," he said.

18

"They're so…so… I can't say what they are."

"I thought they'd be more scary."

"They're more a sort of…*tremendous*."

Kiet, watching from a distance with the other young Nesters, knew exactly what they meant. Looking at the great archangels was like looking through an opening into infinity.

"It makes you want to laugh and shout and cry all at the same time," she said.

"Yes, like your heart's filled full and overflowing," agreed Ethany.

"Like music," said Gibby. "The most wonderful music that ever was."

They were too far away to hear what was being said, but they watched the silver-bearded hierarch write as Miriael spoke. Kiet's gaze wandered to Ferren nearby, and she remembered the time when she'd stood side by side with him facing the radiance of a great archangel. In the end, she'd even taken the lead in addressing Uriel…

Flens must have been remembering the same scene, which the young Nesters had observed from a distance. "You ought to be up there too," he told her. "Like that other time. You and Ferren."

"No need," Kiet said firmly. "He has his sister. That's enough."

Then Rhinn clicked her tongue. "*Now* what's going on?" she asked.

The silver-bearded hierarch had finished writing. He stood back, and the winged desk bearing the parchment floated across from him to Ferren. The hierarch offered his quill, but Ferren shook his head.

"Of course he can't write," muttered Kiet. "What do they expect?"

There was a brief conversation between Miriael and the archangels, followed by a brief conversation between Miriael and Ferren. Then Ferren picked up the inkpot, put his thumb over the top, turned it quickly upside down, then right way up again. Next, he leaned forward over the desk and applied his thumb to the parchment. The silver-bearded hierarch murmured approval, and the great archangels nodded in confirmation.

Then Ferren handed over the inkpot to his sister. Shanna repeated the process and marked the parchment with a second thumbprint.

"That's the alliance made, then," commented Bross.

But Miriael hadn't finished. Turning towards the tents, she called out into the darkness. "Anyone else to sign? You can do it with your thumb."

"Yes," cried a familiar voice. "Me!"

Kiet needed no further prompt when she saw Zonda jump to her feet and step forward. "Me too!" she cried.

In the end, ten Residuals queued up before the winged desk, including the Fusselfather, Dwinna of the Clanfeathers and all the young Nesters. Kiet was second in the queue behind Zonda. She had to narrow her eyes against the dazzling brightness as she studied the hierarchs and great archangels.

She had the impression that they were studying her too. Not hostile or scornful or superior, but simply curious about their new allies. Some of them were even smiling. And Uriel… By the expression in his eyes and the faint nod of his head, he *recognised* her!

When it was her turn, she took the inkpot from Zonda, inked her thumb and added a fourth thumbprint alongside the neat set of marks already on the parchment. She didn't actually hear the sound of applause, yet somehow the air seemed to ring with celebration.

Zonda walked ahead of her back to the other waiting Residuals. She was walking so slowly that Kiet soon caught up and saw the rapt, trance-like look on her face.

Yes, me too, thought Kiet…and for the moment, her negative feelings about Zonda were entirely forgotten.

She came back to her previous spot, but there was no one to sit with; all the young Nesters were queued up in front of the signing table. Then a sudden thought jumped into her mind.

"Peeper!" she exclaimed, and snapped her fingers. Of course he'd want to see the archangels too!

She strode to her own tent at the far end of the row, opened the flap and dived in. She reached for the zither in the darkness.

"Peeper! Wake up! You mustn't miss this!"

"Not aslee-eep," came the plaintive reply. "You left me-e-ee!"

"Sorry." She gathered up the zither, backed out of the tent and headed towards her previous spot again.

By now, the young Nesters had all returned, and the queue of the Residuals had gone. Michael, Gabriel, Raphael and Uriel were no longer on their thrones, but stood talking to Miriael. Ferren and Shanna listened respectfully from a pace further back.

"Let me see-ee!" piped Peeper.

Kiet held the zither over her head, turned towards the light. "The great archangels are visiting us," she told him. "We're allies with them now."

Peeper saw—and was wildly excited. "Ooo-oo-ooh! Ooo-oo-ooh! Ooo-oo-oo-oo-ooh!" He was incapable of words.

The winged desk wafted across to hover in front of Michael, who took up the quill and signed his name on the parchment. One by one, Gabriel, Raphael and Uriel also signed. Then the desk floated back to the silver-bearded patriarch, who checked over the parchment and rolled it up.

The discussion between Miriael and the archangels continued a few minutes more, after which the archangels returned to their thrones. Miriael, Ferren and Shanna stepped back from the canopy. Then the whole company of angels put their hands together in prayer and intoned a long, deep, resonant "*Amen*".

As the resonance died away, the radiance intensified until Kiet was forced to close her eyes. She could only hear: a fluttering of wings like a mighty wind, then a rush and a roar. When she opened her eyes a few moments later, the canopy and angels were soaring high in the sky. A few moments more, and there was nothing to see but the blackness of the night.

Peeper was still making tiny sounds, but quieter now. Kiet lowered the zither.

"Did you like that, little one?" she asked, in the special crooning voice she used for him.

Peeper's "oohs" turned into words. "Beau-oo-oo-tiful! So-o-o-o beau-oo-oo-tiful!"

"Weren't the archangels wonderful?"

"Blessed Souls! Blessed Souls! Blessed So-o-o-ouls!"

She didn't understand at first. "You liked some of the other angels better?"

"Blessed So-o-o-ouls! Beau-oo-oo-tiful wings! So-o-o white!"

She realised then that he meant the fluttering wings that had held up the canopy, thrones and desk.

"Blessed So-o-o-ouls!" he fluted on. "Souls of the hu-u-u-men dead! Like me-e-e-e!"

"Like you?"

"Me-e-e-e! Me-e-e in Heaven!"

Finally, it made sense to her. The Blessed Souls must be human souls from before the time when Heaven closed off entry. If a Morph like Peeper could ascend into Heaven, he'd become a pair of white wings like the ones they'd just seen.

She made up a hopeful, cheering song for him.

> "One day you'll be there, little one,
> Up where you ought to be.
> You'll have your wings to fly around
> So white and bright and free."

19

The morning air seemed somehow fresher after the night's visitation, but the stain was still there around the top of the pillar of cloud. So far as Ferren could tell, it was no longer expanding, but appeared even more lurid in colour than before.

They assembled after the breakfast meal, with representatives, People and young Nesters in an inner circle, Fusselfolk in an outer circle around them. Today, the entire tribe of Fusselfolk was present at the meeting.

Miriael spoke first and reported what the four archangels had told her while the signing was going on. She described a rampart that Heaven was constructing on the First Altitude to contain the invaders. "And meanwhile, they're assembling forces from far and wide for a counter-attack."

Ferren, who had heard it before, asked a question about something he hadn't heard. "What about us? How do they want us to help?"

"They didn't say." Miriael pursed her lips. "They don't really know what we can do. They'd like us to gather and pass on information about the Humen on Earth, of course. But they don't expect us to fight the Humen face to face."

"Why not?" demanded Tadge.

"Because we can't. One thing to do is build up the Residual Alliance again. Send messengers to every tribe and have them ready for war."

Ferren spoke up. "But that'll take months. Weeks, anyway. The invaders might have conquered Heaven by then. What can we do to stop them now?"

No sooner had he asked than he saw the answer—and so did all the young Nesters.

"Sabotage!" many voices cried in unison.

Miriael turned to Shanna with a smile. They had both already reached the same conclusion.

"Yes, we can sabotage them and slow them down." Shanna nodded. "If they're still sending up military forces, we can sabotage their equipment and machines on the ground. And we can interrupt their supplies for the forces up there."

"Sabotage their trains and transports?" Miriael suggested.

"Exactly."

"You're the expert," said Miriael. "Would you lead us?"

"A team? Yes, we could do real damage with a whole team. I could teach my sabotage tricks and skills." Shanna surveyed the inner circle of representatives, People and young Nesters, the outer circle of Fusselfolk. "But not everyone here. Too many. A dozen would be about the right size for a team."

"Me!" "Me!" "Me!" Eager voices called out, and hands shot up.

Miriael shook her head. "A dozen, she said. And there's another job to be done too—going out to the tribes, spreading the word and gathering an army of Residuals willing to fight. That'll be just as important in the end."

Ferren sprang to his feet. "All those wanting to volunteer should raise a hand. Then Shanna can pick her team, and everyone not on it goes out to gather more volunteers."

There were some good-humoured grumbles of disappointment, but it made sense. All those in the inner circle waved hands in the air, while more than half of the Fusselfolk also volunteered.

Shanna picked her team, starting inevitably with Ferren and Miriael. Then she chose someone from every group: Zonda from the People, Floy from the Fusselfolk, and Dwinna and Stogget from the representatives. Young Nesters made up the rest of her team: Kiet, Flens, Bross, Gibby, Ethany, Rhinn and Tadge. "They learned how to creep around in the Humen Camp," she explained. "I need them because they have the experience."

With more good-humoured grumbles, the other volunteers accepted her decision, while Shanna accepted that the team had somehow swelled out to fourteen. "All right, still manageable," she agreed.

Then Miriael went off with the volunteers not chosen for the team to spell out their job with the other tribes. The Fusselfather went off to arrange provisions for all volunteers. Tadge looked up at the stain in the sky and shook his fist at it.

"We'll teach you!" he shouted. "You filth! You'll have us to deal with now! Us and Heaven! You're finished!"

20

It was strange walking on solid land after so many days of living with the restless rotation of fur-snails. Ferren found himself swaying from side to side and took a while to regain a sense of balance on ground that stayed motionless under his feet.

The team headed in the direction of the pillar of cloud until they came to an overbridge. "All overbridges lead to the Bankstown Camp," Miriael told them, so they used this one as a guide and walked parallel. For hour after hour, the gaunt, black structure remained deserted, with no traffic along the top of any kind.

The next day, they decided to walk along the top themselves.

"Much faster and easier," said Ferren. "We can hide if we see anyone in the distance."

It was what he'd done on his original journey to the Bankstown Camp. By day, they kept a constant watch and walked close to the edge of the roadway, ready to dive over and disappear at the first hint of danger. By night, they climbed down and found safe places to sleep underneath.

On the second night, Shanna came up next to Ferren for a brother-and-sister talk.

"What's happening between you and Kiet, little brother?" she demanded in a whisper. "Have you fallen out?"

Ferren grimaced inwardly. "I suppose so."

"We need you working together, you know. Like you did as joint leaders when you came to rescue Miriael. Now I never see you talk to her."

"No, she spends all her time talking to Peeper."

"Ah, the Morph on the zither."

"Yes. She doesn't want to talk to me. I've tried."

"Have you? Have you tried really hard?"

He sidestepped the question. "She's with Bross now, anyway. They've done Second Intimacies together."

"Hmm. I don't know what that is, but I don't think it matters much to Bross. He's always with Zonda now. Haven't you noticed?"

Ferren *had* noticed, but didn't know what it meant. "He's still matched up with Kiet. That's how Nester society works."

Shanna shook her head and scowled. "All right. Tomorrow, I'll ask Kiet about Second Intimacies and find out how much it matters to her."

Next day, Shanna fell in beside Kiet and talked as they walked along. Ferren watched out of the corner of his eye and waited for his sister to report. Later, when she fell in beside *him*, the news was both good and bad.

"Second Intimacies is a step towards bonding, but not a commitment," Shanna told him. "Kiet's very offhand, the way she talks about it. I think she sees Bross as just a friend. But…"

"But what?"

"She really resents *you*. I mentioned your name, and she was ready to bite my head off. What did you do?"

"Nothing."

"Nothing?"

"Nothing much."

"Let's hear it. *All* of it."

Ferren had never been able to keep secrets from his big sister. He told her about the night when he'd joined Zonda in her tent, and how he'd tried to deny it to Kiet the next morning. "But she'd seen us together."

"What happened? You and Zonda?"

"Some kissing. Nothing else. She started it. I didn't want it, and she turned huffy."

"Then what?"

"I went back to my own tent."

"Are you sure? Look me in the eye."

Ferren looked his sister straight in the eye and repeated it.

"Did you tell that to Kiet?"

"She never gave me the chance. And now she won't talk to me at all."

"Hmm." Shanna pursed her lips. "I wonder if she'll listen to me. Maybe I can convince her."

"How?"

But Shanna wouldn't say. "I'll try when the moment's right," she told him.

The moment was right later the same day. Ferren was walking behind when he saw Shanna fall in beside Kiet once again. The signs weren't good: the stiffness of Kiet's back and the thrust of her jaw seemed like a rebuff right from the start.

When Shanna reported, she seemed annoyed with him and equally annoyed with Kiet. "I don't know what's wrong with the pair of you! Why can't you act like sensible human beings?"

"She didn't believe you?"

"Maybe she did. I couldn't tell. She doesn't forgive you, anyway."

"She's still angry."

"Who knows? She says she isn't. According to her, she doesn't want anything more to do with boys, not ever. When I told her you really like her, she said you ought to focus on fighting against the Humen, same as she does."

Ferren felt utterly deflated. *I more than like her, I love her,* he thought. But even to his big sister, he couldn't confess that.

"All right, I'll do that," he said dully. "I'll stop thinking about her and focus on fighting the Humen."

Shanna looked at him, then looked away with a snort of frustration. She lengthened her stride to walk on by herself.

By now, they were coming close to the Camp. The pillar of cloud seemed to reach up for miles, and the stain in the sky was right over their heads. Shanna had no more long conversations with Ferren or Kiet, but a great many long conversations with Miriael.

For one more day, they continued along the top of the overbridge, then hid underneath for the night. In the morning, Miriael announced a decision she'd reached in consultation with Shanna.

"We think it's time to stay down on the ground. It's too exposed walking along the top now. And we have something to tell you about this tower in the cloud."

21

The sabotage team clustered around Miriael and Shanna under the overbridge. Massive blocks of concrete supported the pylons, with dark-leafed weeds growing between the blocks.

"We suspected it days ago, and now we're almost certain," Miriael began. "The pillar of cloud doesn't rise up from inside the Bankstown Camp, but from the construction site outside. The same site where you had your base, where we stayed after you rescued me."

"We went back there to watch Heaven's attack on the Camp," Shanna put in.

"And we saw Asmodai come out to inspect one particular place afterwards," Miriael went on. "The rest of the site was for storing the materials, but this fenced-off zone was where the actual constructing went on."

A memory clicked over in Ferren's mind. "Did you say, 'fenced-off zone'?"

"Yes."

"We saw it on the way in, when we were coming to rescue you. Right?" He appealed to the young Nesters, who nodded in confirmation.

"Good, you know the place, then." Miriael smiled grimly. "It was busy before, but it turned into a frenzy of activity after Asmodai inspected. Workers, lights, transport machines—it never stopped, day or night."

"The thing they were building was right in the middle," added Shanna. "We went in to investigate, and Miriael saw it."

"Yes, it must have been the foundation. It went deep underground, but not very high above ground. Somehow they extended it upwards incredibly fast."

"It turned into the tower," Shanna concluded. "We're sure that's where it is."

There was a long moment of reflective silence. Then Zonda spoke up.

"What does that mean for us?"

As the expert saboteur, Shanna responded. "Our goal is to interrupt supplies and troops going up in the tower. So we go to the fenced-off zone and check out possible forms of sabotage there."

"Woohoo!" Gibby pumped a fist. "Do we get to see the tower inside the cloud?"

Shanna and Miriael exchanged glances. "That depends," said Miriael.

They continued their advance, underneath the overbridge. Progress was much slower wading through the weeds, which were often thick and tangled. All day they pushed forward, and heard only two squads of Hypers and one transport vehicle passing along on top. But they could feel the vibration in the ground that came from the throb of Humen machinery. The Camp wasn't far ahead, and nor was the construction site.

It was mid-afternoon when the wire canopies over the Camp came into view. While the wire canopies were directly in front of them, the pillar of cloud was now more to the side. Miriael called a halt, and they surveyed the cloud from the shadow of the pylons.

"We'll need to cut across to it," she said. "I think we should wait for nightfall. It'll be more risky the closer we get."

"Let's take a better look now, though," Flens suggested. "Let's climb up and see where we'll be going in the dark."

Ferren agreed. "Yes, safe enough. We could look out from just below the deck."

They headed for the nearest pylon and climbed up into the metal frame that supported the deck of the overbridge. When they peered out, the pillar of cloud seemed more overwhelming than ever: several hundred yards wide and impossibly high. It was separated from their overbridge by two further overbridges, which blocked their view of its base.

But Rhinn was puzzled. "If that's the construction site, where are all the stacks?"

Ferren shared the feeling. The stacks should have been tall enough to appear above the overbridges.

"They've been dismantled," Miriael explained. "They were stacks of building materials, so now they've all gone into building the tower." She turned to Shanna. "The good thing is, we're on the side away from the main gates to the zone."

"Yes, the quiet side, for creeping in through the same back gate." Shanna nodded. "And the other good thing is, the edge of the cloud looks like it comes down to cover the gate and the fence.

Miriael laughed. "Asmodai would've meant it to hide the tower, but now it'll hide us too. We can do what we did last time."

"*All* of what we did?"

"Why not? Except this time you ride under the train as well."

Ferren, listening, had no idea what they were talking about. The two of them seemed to have taken complete charge of the sabotage mission.

22

The night was dark and quiet apart from the glow that illuminated the pillar of cloud, apart from the rumbling, clanking, mechanical sounds going on inside it. It seemed that all Humen energies had been concentrated upon this single tower and the supreme objective of an invasion of Heaven.

The sabotage team cut across under the two intervening overbridges. They crouched low as they moved, ready to drop flat at any moment, but there was no one near enough to see them.

When they looked out from under the last overbridge, the base of the cloud was directly in front of them. By night, it looked more grey than white, with wispy tendrils of vapour drifting out around the main column. Individual lights glowed through in colours of orange, yellow and green, all blurred and many moving. More lights moved along the overbridge on the other side, as a constant stream of transport vehicles travelled between the Camp and the tower.

"Some bits of cover there," said Shanna, pointing.

Ferren followed her gaze to what remained of the construction site before them. Although the great stacks had gone, there were numerous small piles of leftover construction materials. They could cross the final distance to the cloud by flitting from one bit of cover to another.

Shanna picked the route and led the way. She not only took advantage of the construction materials but of a convenient trench running in their direction. The young Nesters kept close to the less experienced Dwinna, Floy, Zonda and Stogget, telling them when to dart forward, when to stop and hide. Ferren and Miriael brought up the rear.

Finally, they reached the safety of the cloud and stopped to recover their breath. All sight was dimmed and all sound muffled in the grey obscurity. Ferren felt the water vapour damp on his skin.

"It's like ordinary cloud, then," said Ethany.

"It is," Miriael agreed. "Artificially created and shaped by Asmodai, artificially kept in place. But in itself, it's the same as any other cloud."

"Perfect for us breaking into the zone," said Ferren.

Miriael held up a hand. "Yes, but wait for Shanna."

Ferren scanned the shadowy figures standing around and realised that his sister wasn't among them.

"She's gone to find a back gate in the fence," Miriael explained. "She'll open it for us."

They waited in patience, and at last Shanna returned, snapping her fingers.

"Follow me," she told them.

They followed her deeper into the cloud and came soon to a high wire fence. The gate stood open, and they trooped through after her. Ferren guessed she'd opened the lock by communicating with a Plasmatic inside, and the young Nesters had seen her perform the trick before. The others didn't think to question it.

The noise of machinery was louder now, though it seemed to come and go in the cloud. The lights were brighter too, though still blurred. The activity was concentrated in the centre of the zone. Everyone copied Shanna's crouching, stealthy gait as she led them around the outskirts close to the wire fence.

When they dropped down behind a pile of sheet metal rolls, Miriael laughed. "So it's still here!"

Shanna grinned back at her. "Maybe they keep restocking the pile."

"So you'll find a train and...?"

"All the same as last time. Only I'll be quicker climbing in underneath."

Miriael turned to the others. "We're going to reconnoitre possible places to sabotage. You'll be hidden here, just stay till we get back."

"How long?" Ferren asked.

Miriael and Shanna looked at one another.

"Half an hour," said Miriael.

"Not more than an hour," said Shanna.

"What?" "No!" Exclamations of protest came from all sides.

"Shush, voices down," said Miriael. "We'll be riding to the tower in the undercarriage of a train, then out through the main gates. Then we have to wait for a chance to get down and come back round to the back gate again. So..."

"An hour," said Shanna.

"Why can't we come too?" asked Kiet.

"You wouldn't recognise places to sabotage," answered Shanna.

"Nor would Miriael," Kiet answered back.

"I want to see the tower," said Tadge.

"And me!" "So do I!" "Me too!"

Miriael consulted silently with Shanna. Ferren studied their expressions.

"I think you're going because *you* want to see the tower," he said to Miriael.

A faint smile appeared in Miriael's face, echoed a moment later by a smile on Shanna's.

"I suppose they could all fit into the undercarriage," said Shanna.

"As long as they stay out of sight," said Miriael.

"Hurrah!" cried Tadge. "We're coming too!"

So it was decided, and Shanna vanished into the cloud in search of a suitable train. Miriael explained the procedure to everyone else: how Shanna would instruct the Plasmatics in the engine and drive the train out here to them; how they had to dive in between the wheels and climb up into the undercarriage; then how they had to keep quiet and invisible after the Hypers took charge of the engine again.

It was many minutes later when a train loomed out of the cloud and slowed to a stop alongside the pile of sheet metal rolls.

"Now!" hissed Miriael. "You know what to do! Go!"

23

Miriael's head throbbed with the rumble of wheels and grinding of axles as their train rolled towards the centre of the zone. Everything had gone perfectly to plan. The Residuals had climbed up into the undercarriage of the last trolley of the train; Shanna had climbed up into the first trolley, then wriggled her way along to join them. Now the whole sabotage team lay tightly packed between springs and struts and crossbars. No doubt they had all found peepholes at the side, as Miriael had herself.

The zone was in many ways different to the last time she'd ridden under a trolley. The same mechanical noises and the same bright lights— but she had the impression that the operation had become slicker and more efficient. Peering out into the cloud, she saw shadowy formations of well-drilled Hypers marching to orders and transport vehicles of many kinds trundling back and forth.

Before they were building the system, now it's fully functioning, she thought. *Everything's a cog in a well-oiled machine.*

As the train approached the centre of the zone, they passed stationary trains laden like their own with steel boxes, drums and cylinders. The noise outside intensified: bangs and rattles, clangs and creaks. When the brightness of floodlights came right into the undercarriage, she drew back a little from her peephole.

Did everyone understand the importance of staying hidden? Had she stressed it enough to them?

Then the train started to slow, and the sound changed under its wheels. Miriael looked down through the undercarriage and saw that solid ground had given way to the iron grilles she remembered. The vast cavern below the slots was as she remembered it too, though less brightly lit than before.

When she turned back to her peephole at the side, she discovered that the cloud had gone. The train had entered the hollow core of the pillar, and she could see clearly under the floodlights. She glimpsed Hypers, white-coated Doctors, a row of machines coming forward...

They hadn't quite reached the central structure when their train shuddered to a halt, trolleys bumping one into another. The machines that had come forward swung out long arms, while an amplified voice rattled out orders in mathematical formulae.

"24p x 12% + 8.9ab...3.45 + 4x − 16(4y - z)..."

Then came a great thumping, clanking and scraping directly over their heads. The trolley and its undercarriage shook and rocked.

They're unloading the cargo with cranes, thought Miriael. *The whole train all at the same time.*

The sounds moved across to the other side of the train, where there were more crunching clashes of metal on metal. The Residuals swivelled round to lie facing that way, and Miriael did too. When she peered through a peephole, she saw a shining track of rollers, ten yards wide, running along the ground next to the train. Already the track was half-filled with steel boxes and drums unloaded from their train.

Miriael glanced towards Shanna, who lay ahead of her in the undercarriage. Had she spotted possible forms of sabotage yet? Perhaps to the cranes? Perhaps to the track of rollers?

"Hey, what are you doing!" hissed a voice from somewhere behind in the undercarriage.

The voice belonged to Rhinn, and the hiss was directed at Tadge.

Miriael twisted her neck to look back along the track. With horror, she saw that Tadge had climbed down from the trolley and onto the rollers.

"Idiot!" cried several other voices.

"Just taking a look," Tadge called over his shoulder.

He advanced further across the track past boxes and drums. Then he tilted his head and raised his eyes, facing forward. He was looking at the tower, of course...

"Wow!" he gasped. "You have to see it from here!"

"Come back, you little fool!" Rhinn clambered after him, then Kiet after Rhinn and Ferren after Kiet.

Tadge turned and saw them. "All right, all right. Coming."

He went to step back when there was a whirr of machinery, and the rollers rotated under his feet. Suddenly, the whole track was moving forward, carrying boxes, drums and cylinders. Tadge tumbled over and fell flat on his face. Rhinn, Kiet and Ferren tried to stay upright, then went sprawling too. They were all carried along with the cargo.

Miriael lowered herself from the undercarriage and looked out between the wheels of the train. Helpless and aghast, she watched them go past one by one.

Then, just as abruptly as it had started moving, the track came to a stop. From somewhere ahead came a resounding CLANGG!

Like Miriael, the other Residuals had dropped from the undercarriage to the ground. As soon as the track stopped moving, they jumped out onto the rollers and ran forward to help. Miriael went with them, crouching low. With her greater height, she might be in view of the Hypers or Doctors operating the cranes.

Ferren, Kiet, Rhinn and Tadge were still struggling to rise. The rollers were difficult to balance on even when the track was motionless. The others came up, held out hands and hauled them to their feet.

No sooner were they upright than the track jolted into motion once more—and threw everyone down on the rollers. Miriael heard voices all around.

"Get ready!"

"If it stops again!"

"Straight off!"

Everyone wriggled to the side of the track. They didn't look up at the tower, though they were surely almost under it by now. The rollers carried them towards the engine of their train, level with the first trolley which was now empty of cargo. Then another sudden stop.

The CLANGGGG! that followed was even louder than the last.

They were up on all fours and about to spring back between the wheels of their train when it accelerated forward. They froze and stared. Impossible to dart in underneath when the wheels were moving!

Then Miriael recognised a new danger, too: as soon as the last trolley had gone past, they would all be exposed to Hypers and Doctors on the other side.

"Hide!" she called out. "Quick! They'll see us in a minute!"

Everyone understood—just in time. They swung round and sprang for cover behind the boxes, drums and cylinders. They were all hidden by the time the last trolley moved away. In the same moment, the machinery of the track whirred into action, swept their feet from under them and carried them forward once again.

Miriael found herself flat on her back. She looked up and saw gigantic, tubular legs spanned by horizontal girders. They were coming in under the tower. On the girder that passed over her head she saw a great blade of steel and a bulb of glass containing grey matter of some kind.

In the next moment she was looking right up inside the frame of the tower. She took in an instant impression of cables hanging down, coloured lights attached to the frame, a cage of wire—and all rising up to an unbelievable height.

"There's a hole!" someone called out ahead. "We're going into a hole!"

Miriael grabbed hold of a steel box beside her and struggled to stand on the rotating rollers. She almost fell when the rollers came to a sudden dead halt. The stop-go track had stopped again.

There was another almighty CLANGGGG!!—only this time behind her. She twisted and saw that the great steel blade had descended across the track. They were trapped inside the tower.

"Go back!" "No, forward!" "Back!" "Forward!"

Scrambling to their feet, the sabotage team called out and milled in all directions. Wire mesh caged them in at the sides, the steel blade made a barrier behind, and there was some sort of hole to the front.

Then the blade advanced, pushing boxes, drums, cylinders and Residuals forward into the hole.

"Don't get crushed!" cried Miriael, and stepped forward before the blade could reach her. She could see the hole herself now, a square of darkness as wide as the track, where the ground opened up at the end of the rollers. Swiftly, inexorably, they were all being swept into it.

Either get crushed or fall to our deaths, thought Miriael.

Then she saw something coming up in the hole: a square platform exactly the same size as the hole itself. The advancing blade shunted boxes, drums and cylinders onto it—and Miriael and the Residuals along with the cargo.

In the next moment, the platform continued to ascend and carried them up inside the tower.

24

Up and up and up... Almost immediately, they were closed in by a mesh of wire like an endless vertical cage. Horizontal girders went past on the other side of the wire, coloured lights cast glows and shadows across their faces.

Ferren and Kiet had ended up closest to Miriael. Kiet gazed around in wonder.

"So this is how their tower works," she said.

"This is it," Miriael agreed. "Moving platforms to transport troops and equipment up to Heaven."

"And we're going up there too."

"No getting off now," said Ferren. "Let's check round and see if everyone's all right."

Miriael was about to go with them, but Shanna suddenly appeared and beckoned to her. "Let me show you something!"

Miriael followed past steel boxes and drums to a corner of the platform. Looking out through the wire cage here, they looked out at one of the tower's giant tubular legs.

"See how it's made." Shanna pointed.

Miriael saw what she meant. The tubular legs were constructed in twenty-foot segments, and the top of each segment fitted snugly into the bottom of the next.

"They slide over one another," said Shanna.

"Mmm." Miriael pursed her lips thoughtfully. "So that's the answer."

"What answer?"

"To the mystery of how the Humen could put up this tower so fast. They didn't have to keep bolting new segments on at the top, they expanded them telescopically."

"Mmm." Shanna looked thoughtful too.

They were still studying the tubular leg when the coloured lights gave out. Clearly, only the base of the tower was illuminated. Miriael's eyes adjusted to the faint moonlight that filtered in through the encompassing cloud.

Then Ferren and Kiet reappeared.

"All safe, all fourteen of us," Ferren announced.

"Nobody even injured," added Kiet.

"That's a relief." Miriael smiled. "Can you gather everyone together, then? We should talk about what to do next."

"We'll bring everyone to the middle of the platform," said Kiet.

They hurried off, while Miriael and Shanna made their own way to the middle of the platform. Several Residuals were already there, and Shanna set them to work moving drums and cylinders aside to clear more space. The steel boxes were too heavy for anyone to shift.

When Gibby and Ethany turned up, they were buzzing with news of their own.

"Guess what? There's a second cage over on that side!"

"And platforms coming down!"

"All empty!"

Miriael listened and nodded. "It makes sense. "A continuous cycle of platforms going up and coming down. Twin shafts in the same tower. We'll take a proper look in the morning."

The task of moving drums and cylinders went much faster when Stogget and Bross turned up. Soon, everyone found a place to sit on the cold metal platform, all waiting to hear from Miriael. She sensed a mix of emotions among them: excitement, concern, hope and, most of all, uncertainty.

She strove to renew their motivation. "This wasn't what we planned, but we can make it work. We're still saboteurs, but now we do our sabotage up in Heaven. We'll be right behind the invaders' front lines."

Ferren caught on and backed her up. "Even better!" he cried.

"Yes, even better," Miriael agreed. "Because we can damage their equipment just before they want to use it."

"More dangerous, though," said Rhinn.

"Who cares?" cried Tadge. "We'll be the heroes who won the war!"

"Not *you!*" Zonda cut him down. "You'll still be the idiot who can't do what he's told."

Scowls were aimed at Tadge from all sides. "Yes, shut up, Tadge!" "No sense!" "Stupid thing to do!"

Tadge put his head down. "It's even better this way," he mumbled to himself. "She *said* so."

The only one not scowling was Rhinn. "Enough! I haven't finished telling him off yet. No one else needs do it."

Kiet turned to Miriael. "Will you let the archangels know what's happening?"

"Yes, good idea," Miriael agreed at once. "We can coordinate moves if they're attacking the Humen in front and we're sabotaging from behind. I'll try for a visionary dream." She looked round. "Anyone else ready to sleep?"

They looked at one another and yawned. Now that the adrenalin had worn off, they were all drooping with weariness.

"What about arriving in Heaven?" asked Ferren.

"Not for a long time yet," she told him. "At the speed we're travelling, it'll be tomorrow before we get there. Probably late tomorrow."

The gathering broke up, and everyone went off to find a spot to sleep. Miriael chose a space between two steel boxes, and Shanna, as always, came with her. She was grateful for the company.

25

Blackness, utter blackness.

Miriael didn't know where she was. She'd fallen asleep picturing the Great South Hall—which was no guarantee that a visionary dream would take her there. But this unnatural night wasn't like any part of Heaven anywhere.

Then she was gazing out in another direction…and now there *were* lights, tiny and twinkling, on the plain before her. There was a different kind of light higher up too, a long, thin band of pale, pure brightness. Surely the eternal, early morning light of Heaven! But why only a sliver of it? And why so far up in the sky?

Staring harder, she began to perceive silhouettes in the landscape— in particular, a rocky crag that reared up sharply from the plain. A crag in the distinctive shape of the head of a lion…unmistakable! It could only be the Rock of the Tabernacle, and she must have come to the Val Jehenna.

Then understanding dawned. She'd heard it reported in the Great South Hall, that the Val Jehenna was the invaders' beachhead on the First Altitude. So this was the Val Jehenna under Humen occupation! A darkened, sinister version of the Val Jehenna! She felt sick at heart.

But she had a purpose to accomplish. Since she'd come to the wrong part of Heaven, she needed to wish herself up to the right part. She turned her mind to Michael, Gabriel, Raphael and Uriel on the Sixth Altitude…

The dream carried her not upwards but forward to the Rock of the Tabernacle. Now she saw a construction on top of the crag that had never existed before: a raised deck with a railing all round. She almost cried out in horror when she saw who was on it.

Asmodai!

Even at a distance, she recognised his flowing, fine-spun hair and his new black robes. He stood at the front of the deck, radiating spiritual energy, while three Doctors in their wheelchairs sat illuminated in his light.

She strove to wish herself somewhere else, anywhere else, but the wishing didn't work. The dream carried her to the back of the deck, behind Asmodai and the Doctors. They were talking strategy—or Asmodai was talking and the Doctors were agreeing.

"Yes, I expect they're busy plotting away behind their rampart." He swept a hand across the darkness below the thin band of Heavenly light. "Probably building up for a counter-attack. I think I'll let them make the attempt. They'll be more vulnerable when they come out in the open."

Miriael might have listened in to the information if she hadn't been wholly focused on getting away. *Go back,* she willed herself. *Go back, go back, go back.*

Instead, she glided even closer, only a few paces away. Asmodai broke off all at once in the middle of what he was saying, whirled round and scanned the space where she was standing.

A smile slowly formed on his beautiful lips. "Well, well. What have we here?"

I'm not here, I'm invisible in Heaven, thought Miriael. *You can't see me.*

But Asmodai had seen her in Heaven once before, and he saw her again now—or at least the gold of her hair. He stared intently, and his smile widened.

"Ah, my poor little Miriael!" He turned to the Doctors. "It seems she couldn't stay away."

One of the Doctors spoke into a box on the arm of his chair. "*What can you see?*"

"This—" Asmodai pointed straight at her "—is the angel I've been searching for. I implanted a connection between the two of us, but she's been trying to hide. Now she's come to me in a visionary dream. She couldn't hide from her own feelings."

The Doctors made vague noises in their crackling, amplified voices, and Asmodai continued to address them. But Miriael understood it was her he was talking to.

"She's an angel in love, you see. A fascinating case. No normal angel can feel the sort of love she feels for me. But she's corrupted by living on the Earth. She's mortal enough to fall hopelessly, passionately in love."

He swung to the doctors with a laugh. "You wouldn't remember such love, would you? Perhaps, many centuries ago, when you were still capable of human feeling…"

He swung back to Miriael. "Yes, my dear, abnormal angel. Your wishes brought you to me, in spite of yourself. You know how a visionary dream works. You'd leave right now if you could, wouldn't you? Try it."

Miriael *was* trying to leave, desperately, but the dream held her trapped.

"You really think…" she began, then stopped as he cupped a hand to his ear.

"Yes, go on," he said. "I can hear you."

"You really think I could love you after what you did to me?"

Asmodai turned, smiling, to the Doctors again. "Ah, I betrayed her, you see. Completely deceived her and traded her off. She knows what I did, and what I am. She knows that, as a being of pure spirit, I can never have any personal feeling for her. Yet it makes no difference to her kind of love. A delicious paradox! I find it quite enchanting."

He returned his gaze to Miriael, and the deep, lambent pools of his eyes drank her in.

"Do you know why I've been searching for you, my poor Miriael? I'd like to give you the chance to fall in love with me all over again. So far, you've only fallen in love with my beauty, but soon you'll be able to fall in love with my power and majesty. When I become the conqueror of Heaven, and every angel acknowledges my supremacy—think how much you'll be in love with me then!"

"No, no, no!" She struggled to shout him down. But although he could hear her, it was as though her voice had no volume.

"Did you know you're my favourite audience?" he went on. "You have a special capacity to appreciate me, I believe. I want to watch you watching me with that delightful look of adoration in your eyes. I have to admit, I've missed that look. I shall enjoy every minute of it."

Miriael had started to shake. Asmodai came forward a step and reached out to her with thumb and forefinger. He was focused on a strand of her hair, and meant to take hold of it.

Back and forth, up and down, more and more violently she shook. Someone was doing it to her—Asmodai? But his hand was steady as his thumb and forefinger closed on a golden strand of her hair. Closed on it—and passed right through it. She heard him breathe a murmur of disappointment.

She was coming out of the dream, returning to reality. It was her body down on the Earth that was being shaken. As though from a great distance, she heard Asmodai's voice saying, "I'll come for you wherever you are…"

Reality turned out to be Shanna shaking her by the arms. As Asmodai's voice faded, Shanna's replaced it.

"Good, all finished now. You were having some sort of nightmare in your visionary dream. Shouting, 'No, no, no!' over and over."

Miriael's head cleared, and she felt the hard metal of the platform under her back. She struggled to sit up.

"I never managed to speak to any of the great archangels," she confessed.

Shanna helped her lean back against one of the steel boxes. "I guessed that. Don't worry about it."

26

When Ferren promised his sister he'd stop thinking about Kiet and focus on fighting the Humen, he'd seriously meant it. And when he was caught up in the drama of hiding in the train's undercarriage or getting swept along on the rollers, he *could* focus. Yet still the thought of Kiet resurfaced in every quieter moment. And tonight he had a lot of quieter moments.

His thoughts of Kiet were painfully sharpened by the prospect of death. Their sabotage mission would be far more dangerous in Heaven, Rhinn had been right about that. He might die or Kiet might die or they both might die. Yet he'd never managed to tell her how he felt about her. The possibility of dying with all of that left unsaid gnawed away at his insides.

I love Kiet, I love Kiet, I love Kiet. He'd said it a thousand times to himself, but never to her. Perhaps she wouldn't believe him, perhaps she'd still blame him over Zonda, or perhaps she wouldn't care anyway. But the secret was bursting to come out. How could he die without letting her know?

All through the night he slept and woke, then slept and woke again. When he was awake, he listened to the constant sounds of the platform ascending: clicks and creaks and the hiss of cables running through wheels. Every sound seemed to be counting down the moments to their arrival in Heaven. There would be no chance to speak to Kiet once they'd arrived.

By the time dawn came around, he had made up his mind. This feeling was the biggest thing in his life; he *couldn't* keep it locked up inside.

The actual sunrise wasn't visible, only a greater brightness of light through the cloud. A breeze was blowing, and the air felt thin and chill. He waited until he heard a general murmur of rousing, movement and voices. Then he stretched, rose and went in search of Kiet.

He found her in a cosy spot surrounded by drums and cylinders. She was sitting up yawning, with Peeper's zither beside her. Obviously, she'd only just woken up.

She frowned quizzically when he squatted before her.

"What?"

He refused to be put off by her tone. He hoped there was no one else close enough to hear, though he didn't care if they did.

"I want to talk about me and you."

"Oh? I'm included, am I?"

"All right. Just me, then."

She sniffed and said nothing. He couldn't think of a way to lead up to his secret, so he came right out with it.

"I love you."

She stared at him, then looked away. "*Love* me? Love *me?*" She seemed to be collecting her thoughts. "I don't like your idea of love."

He didn't know what to say. She stared at him intently.

"Is this love like the same as you loved Zonda? A hot bit of fun for the night?"

He shook his head. "That was a mistake."

"Is it the same as you loved Miriael? Pure loyal devotion?"

He shook his head again.

"Hnh!" She snorted. "You just want me to be another of your mistakes."

Although she sounded angry, the look on her face seemed more confused. He took a deep breath.

"It was always you. No one else. Only I couldn't see it."

She glanced around and lowered her voice. "All right, enough. People can hear you."

"I don't care." He jumped to his feet. "Let them. I'm not ashamed."

It was an extraordinary sensation, as though he'd plunged off a waterfall and left his stomach behind. A rush that was part exhilaration, part terror, part relief. He didn't know what he felt, but certainly not ashamed.

"I mean it," he said. "I love you."

Then he spun on his heel and rushed off. His heart pounded, and he was almost too giddy to walk straight. He returned to his sleeping spot and sank down on the hard metal floor next to one of the steel boxes.

"I mean it," he said to her image in his mind, as though making some kind of challenge. Somehow the feeling was even stronger for having been uttered.

Half an hour later, he was still in the same spot when Flens stuck his head round the corner.

"Come and have breakfast!" the young Nester grinned. "There's a syrupy stuff in those drums—Shanna discovered it. You just have to turn on the tap and drink."

Ferren remembered the fuel for Plasmatics from his first expedition inside the Humen Camp. He rose and followed Flens to where a large group had gathered round one of the drums. The group didn't include Kiet, he noted.

He took his turn under the tap and gulped down half a dozen mouthfuls. The taste was as he remembered it, sweet and slightly fruity. He wiped his mouth, then returned to his sleeping spot.

There was somebody already there. Kiet! She patted a space on the floor beside her.

His jaw dropped. "What are you…?"

"Come and sit," she said.

He couldn't interpret her expression, but she didn't look confused and she didn't look angry. As he stood there wondering, she clicked her tongue impatiently.

"You took your time," she told him.

At first he thought she meant the time he'd been away having a drink of the syrupy liquid. Then she explained.

"Time to work out your feelings." Again she patted the floor beside her. "Are you going to sit or not?"

Ferren's astonished heart was starting to sing. He sat down beside her, not quite touching. He inhaled the scent of her hair—glorious, dark red hair.

"When did you work it out?" she asked.

"I...um..." He could have told her it was when Zonda kissed him, but instinct warned him to keep quiet about that.

"*I've* known for ages," she said.

"About me loving you?" He didn't understand.

"No." She laughed. "That I loved you, of course."

"Oh. I never knew."

"You wouldn't."

He laughed too, for no particular reason. She moved up closer.

"Let's just sit here," she said. "It's nice like this."

He put his arm round her shoulder, and she snuggled against him. When they leaned heads together, he heard her murmur approval. It was amazing how they fitted so well against one another.

As if she was always meant to be there, he thought.

27

After a while, Kiet remembered she'd left Peeper behind.

"I should go back, or he'll be getting anxious," she said. "Will you come with me?"

Ferren grinned. *As if she needed to ask!*

They walked to where Kiet had left Peeper's zither propped up against a cylinder. She sat down, lifted the zither and rested it on her lap. Ferren sat close and wrapped an arm round her again. For hours, there was nothing else to do, and nothing else he wanted to do. Time passed in a kind of trance.

As the day wore on, the air grew colder, and the breeze blew harder. The light coming through the cloud grew first brighter, then softer and more mellow. Twice they rose to drink more of the syrupy liquid. Ferren turned on the tap for Kiet, and she did the same for him.

When they came back to Peeper after their second drink, Kiet looked at the zither and pursed her lips.

"It won't be easy to carry him when we're creeping round behind the Humen front lines," she said. "I wish there was a better way."

"Tie the zither round your neck," Ferren suggested.

"What with?"

"My sister will have some cord or string." Ferren felt capable of solving any problem. "She has all sorts of useful things like that."

They went looking for Shanna and found her, as expected, sitting with Miriael. What they didn't expect was to find the two of them arguing.

"I think it's a very bad idea," Miriael was saying. "How can you be sure it's Plasmatics?"

"What else could it be?"

"It's still all guesswork. A hundred to one chance."

"But if it works..."

"It won't."

"But if it does..."

Shanna and Miriael became aware of their audience, and broke off. There was a moment of awkward silence before Ferren uttered his request.

"Er, do you have anything so that Kiet can tie the zither round her neck?"

Shanna not only had a cord, but a knife with which to cut off a suitable length. Ferren accepted the cord, and he and Kiet went off to fix up the zither by themselves.

"Wonder what that was about?" he said. "Miriael sounded really annoyed."

"But Shanna wasn't going to give in." Kiet shrugged. "Best leave them to it."

They tied the cord to the frame of the zither, and Kiet hung it round her neck for practice. Peeper uttered a peep of satisfaction at the new arrangement.

The platform's smooth motion continued to carry them steadily upwards. By now, the light was not only less bright, but starting to take on an ominous tinge of yellowy green colour—the colour of the stain that had spread out over the sky.

"Nearly there now," said Kiet.

A little later, Shanna came round to call everyone together, while Miriael sang out from the middle of the platform.

"Everyone here! Here now!"

A few minutes later, everyone sat listening while Miriael addressed them.

"We'll soon arrive at the underside of Heaven, the floor of the First Altitude. I don't know what we'll find there now, but I can tell you how it used to be. It's made of ether, and the Humen have done something with chemicals to harden it. But it should still have cracks and passages for crawling up through.

"The thing is, we want to jump off somehow before this platform comes out at the top on the First Altitude. If we're still on it then, there'll be Hypers and maybe Doctors waiting to unload the cargo we've come up with. We don't want to be seen, and we don't want to fight."

"We're not armed for a fight," put in Shanna.

"Exactly. So we hope for a chance to jump off." Miriael scanned the sabotage team. "Any questions?"

There were no immediate questions, and she didn't give them time to reflect.

"Get ready, then. We'll be arriving in about ten minutes."

28

Ferren still didn't know what Miriael and Shanna had been arguing about. He went with Kiet as she walked aside and lifted the zither to her ear. Peeper was communicating in excited, fluting tones, too softly for Ferren to hear.

"What's he saying?"

Kiet looked up through the shaft of the wire cage, but there was little to see except the bottom of another platform ascending fifty feet above them. She shook her head and turned to Ferren.

"Let's go to the edge of the platform. Peeper wants to see the underside of Heaven. We'll get a better view there."

They made their way between steel boxes, drums and cylinders. The edge of the platform seemed more than ever exposed in the wind now blowing. Around the tower, the cloud swirled and billowed, yet stayed always in the same place.

Kiet held the zither next to the enclosing cage for Peeper to look through the wires. Ferren twisted his neck to look upwards too. The wires going past blurred the view, but he could see a small patch of Heaven within the cloud—stained and livid and yellowy green.

"Looks horrible," he commented.

"Shush!" Kiet nodded towards the invisible Morph on his zither. "Don't spoil it for him. He's just excited to be so close."

"Why?"

"It's his home. He ought to be up there as a Blessed Soul. At least he's going to see it now."

"Right. Of course." Ferren clicked his tongue at himself for asking. "What about you? Excited?"

"More nervous."

"Me too."

"But we'll survive."

"We *have* to," he said. *Because now we have so much to live for,* he added mentally.

Peeper had been uttering quiet, happy "oohs', but his sounds changed all at once to a frantic "eee!-eee!-eee!-eee!" The chittering was too fast for Ferren to understand—but Kiet understood.

"It's his friends," she told Ferren. "Where?" she asked Peeper.

She looked up through the wire of the cage again, and gasped. Ferren looked up and saw it too. Appearing faintly through the cloud was something darker that rested flat against the underside of Heaven. Even half obscured, there was no mistaking that delta shape. Asmodai's flying wing was attached to Heaven like a gigantic bat!

Shanna's voice rang out from another part of the platform. "Everyone this side! Quick now!"

Still Ferren and Kiet stayed staring as if hypnotised. They were now so close that they could see where the great tubes of the tower terminated against the underside of Heaven. At the same time, the cloud thinned out, and the flying wing showed through clearer and clearer. Ferren could even distinguish the pale spot of Asmodai's glass bubble near the point of the delta.

Shanna shouted again. "Preparing to leave!"

"All here?" cried Miriael.

The cage of wire came to an end just before they reached the underside of Heaven. For one split second, Ferren and Kiet glimpsed the point of the delta and Asmodai's glass bubble—which was empty. Then they swung and ran in the direction of another shout from Shanna.

They flew across the platform as walls closed in all around. The light changed, and sounds of creaking metal and moving cables boomed like thunder, multiplied through a thousand echoes. The platform was now going up inside a kind of tunnel.

Young Nesters, People and representatives stood lined up along one side. Miriael turned at the sound of pounding footsteps.

"We saw the flying wing!" Kiet cried out to her.

But Miriael wasn't interested. "Where've you been? We're jumping off."

"*Jump!*" shouted Shanna in the same moment.

Residuals threw themselves off from the edge. The great tubes and the cage of wire had finished, but the shaft continued up through the tunnel, and so did the frame on which the platform ran. The jumpers landed on girders of the frame and clung on.

"Now you!" Miriael ordered. Ferren and Kiet advanced to the edge with Shanna and Miriael.

"*Jump!*" Shanna shouted again.

Ferren launched himself towards the nearest girder and clamped arms around it. Kiet, Miriael and Shanna clung on safely alongside. Behind their backs, the platform continued to ascend through the floor of the First Altitude.

PART FOUR

WAR IN HEAVEN

1

Ferren stared at the wall in front of him, which was pitted with fissures and cavities. He could lean forward and touch it from the girder to which he clung. Miriael had called the substance of Heaven "ether', though the word meant nothing to him. It looked translucent and crystalline, like ice, with an eerie inward light. But it was now dirty ice, stained to a yellowy green colour. When he sniffed the air, it smelled of strange chemicals.

The sabotage team had ended up on two levels. Those who had jumped second were higher on the frame than those who had jumped first. Ferren heard excited cries from below.

"Hey! There's a big hole here!"

"I'm going in!"

"Me too!"

"See where it goes!"

Looking down, Ferren saw Flens swing himself across into a crevice in the ether, followed by Gibby, then Ethany. He also saw another platform coming up after the one they'd just abandoned. It carried no troops, only canisters and machines of various kinds.

"No openings here," said Shanna, who was studying the wall on their higher level.

"Hello!" a voice called down a few moments later. It was Flens sticking his head out from a hole that was higher up again.

"Passages everywhere!" cried Gibby's muffled voice behind him.

"Just what we want," said Miriael. "We'll burrow through the ether.

Stay together and keep heading upwards."

The upper group climbed to the hole where Flens had stuck out his head; the lower group disappeared into the original crevice. The platform with the canisters and machines went past behind them, and another cargo-carrying platform came into view below.

Ferren made the crossing from frame to wall and found himself in a passage on his hands and knees. Kiet and Shanna were ahead of him, Miriael behind. Although the ether had the smoothness of ice, it didn't feel cold. The yellowy green discoloration ran through its pure translucence like a disease.

"What is it?" he asked Miriael, turning and pointing to one particularly foul-looking stain.

"Some sort of coagulant, I suppose." The angel grimaced. "To fix the ether and hold it together. Keep going."

The passages were sometimes wide and sometimes narrow. The team could barely squeeze through in some places; in others, they walked upright through small chambers. There were countless intersections and routes to choose from. The young Nesters leading the way turned left and right and left, but always upwards wherever possible.

It seemed an age later when the advance stopped, and a whisper came down from the front of the line.

"They've arrived at the surface." Ferren repeated the information to Miriael. "There's a board over the top. What now?"

"Tell them to creep out and hide and wait. Check for Humen first."

Ferren passed on Miriael's response and heard it travel back to the front. A little later, he heard the scrape of a board moved aside. Then the line moved forward again. It was a very slow and cautious progress over the last twenty yards.

Ferren followed Shanna up the final slope. The light now entering the passage from outside was an artificial, yellowish light. He saw Kiet climb out and disappear ahead.

Then Shanna stopped and stepped to the side. "You go next," she told Ferren.

He was eager to catch up with Kiet and didn't question it. He assumed Shanna wanted to drop back in order to keep company with Miriael.

He moved up to the end of the passage, raised his head and peered out. They weren't in the open yet, but inside some vast roofed space like a warehouse or depot. He took in pallets piled high with cartons and sacks, military equipment wrapped under nets—and Kiet, crouching in the shelter of the nearest pile of cartons. He hoisted himself up and ran across to her.

2

"Where are the others?"

Kiet hooked a thumb. "Back there."

Ferren looked and saw that the rest of the team had gathered in a well-hidden spot between piles of sacks and some lumpish machine under a khaki tarpaulin. But he was in no hurry to join them. He squatted down next to Kiet.

"What is this place?" he asked.

"Don't know, but I think it's where they unload the platforms." She pointed to pulleys and hooks that dangled from rails overhead. "And listen to the noise."

There was a tremendous grinding and clanking of heavy machinery in another part of the depot. Shouts and commands rang back and forth from the same direction. Much closer, Ferren heard the whirr of some particular engine and the straining sounds of the Plasmatics that propelled it. *Urghh-hish! Urghh-hish Urghh-hish!* But Plasmatics couldn't give them away, and there were no Hypers nearby.

"Where are Miriael and Shanna?" Kiet asked. "Why are they taking so long?"

Ferren wondered too. He looked back to the exit from the passages—and in the next moment, Miriael appeared. She sprang from the hole, pushed the board back in place, then hurried across to join them. But only Miriael.

"Where's my sister?"

The angel looked annoyed. "Gone off on her own," she replied.

"What? Why?"

"She has an idea for something to do against the Humen."

It didn't make sense to Ferren. "But we're all doing something against the Humen. We need her to show us how to sabotage their equipment."

"I know. I couldn't persuade her out of it."

"When will she be back?"

"When her idea doesn't work, I suppose."

"So what do we do till then?"

"The best we can." Miriael shrugged. "Think of our own forms of sabotage. She said you'd come up with ideas."

"*Me?*"

"She said you should take her place, and I'd help you. I know about Heaven, but I know nothing about sabotage. She was sure you'd be good at it."

"Phuh!" Ferren snorted in anger and despair.

Kiet put a hand on his arm. "You can do it. If your sister learned, you will too."

"Huh!" Ferren snorted again—less despairing though no less angry. "She had years to learn."

"Yes, but you've got Miriael helping you. And me. Come on. You'll try."

"You have to," said Miriael.

Ferren pulled a face. "All right. Let's join the others."

They darted across to where the others waited beside the tarpaulin-shrouded machine. They were all eager to move on, and for the moment nobody noticed that Shanna was missing.

Ferren and Kiet took the lead and made their way past piled-up pallets, stacked equipment, boxes and drums. They checked ahead at every corner, but saw no Hypers. Soon they came to the wall of the depot and followed it round to a sliding door.

Luckily, it wasn't locked. Ferren and Kiet slid it a little way open, then waited as the others passed through. Gasps of shock told them there was something wrong on the other side. And why wasn't more light coming in through the gap?

Kiet followed Miriael out the door, and Ferren followed Kiet. The scene before their eyes was dark and desolate.

"What is this?"

"This can't be Heaven!"

"I thought it was a bright place!"

The questions were directed towards Miriael, who alone seemed unsurprised.

"Heaven *is* a bright place," she told them. "Only not this part of it. This is the Val Jehenna, where the Humen have taken over."

"It's a bit bright over there." Flens pointed to a thin, high band of light in the distance, showing through under the roof of the sky.

"Yes, that's divine light from the rest of Heaven," Miriael agreed. "But Heaven must have closed down the First Heavenly Sun. It would normally shine over our heads here, and the Val Jehenna would be green and beautiful."

"Not now." Gibby shuddered. "Horrible place!"

"This was the scene of my last visionary dream," Miriael went on, gazing towards the thin band of light. "I think there's a barrier below the light—that'll be the great rampart the War Council was building, to block off the Val Jehenna from the rest of Heaven."

"Where's the Humen army?" asked Dwinna.

"Close to the rampart, I expect. Their front lines, anyway. On the other side of the Rock of the Tabernacle." Miriael pointed to a strangely shaped crag that stuck up in the middle of the plain.

"What do we sabotage?" Zonda wanted to know. She looked around. "Where's Shanna?"

Miriael sighed. "We'll have to do without her."

There were groans and disbelieving protests. But even as Miriael opened her mouth to explain, a train of laden trolleys emerged from the depot by a larger exit. Several Hypers marched beside it, casting beams of torchlight.

"We need to get away from here first," said Ferren. "She can explain as we go."

3

Moving quickly and quietly, the team left the depot behind. The ground all around smelled of chemicals and was crusted with what looked like hardened tar. Here and there were patches of withered grass and the blackened blossoms of dead, fallen flowers.

With Ferren and Kiet leading, the team detoured away from the route of the train and its accompanying Hypers. The lights of other convoys were travelling along the same route, which was evidently a main highway between the top of the tower, the Rock of the Tabernacle and the Humen front lines.

Meanwhile, Miriael was explaining Shanna's absence to the others, repeating what she'd already told Ferren and Kiet. Ferren wondered if she was also telling them that Shanna had designated *him* to take her place.

He heard from Miriael herself a few minutes later, when she strode forward to join the two at the front.

"They're not happy about Shanna," she reported. "But they trust you. Especially the young Nesters. They said it would be like the rescue team, when you all broke into the Bankstown Camp to save me from Doctor Saniette."

"That was me and Kiet as leaders together," said Ferren.

"Yes, I think that's what they meant. Now you can be co-leaders for sabotage."

Ferren grinned, and saw a secret smile on Kiet's face, too.

A few hundred yards from the depot, they came upon massive hoses running across the ground. A hundred yards further again, they found that every hose ended in a tripod structure with a rotor on top. The rotors whirled round and round, spraying liquid with a fine, swishing sound like rain.

Ferren wrinkled his nose and inhaled the fumes. "It's the chemicals."

Miriael nodded. "So this is how they do it. They spray the ground to keep it solid."

"If we had a knife, we could cut the hoses and do some sabotage," Kiet suggested

"But we don't have a knife," said Ferren.

"It would take an axe or a saw to cut through *those* hoses," added Miriael.

Regretfully, they dropped the idea and detoured further away from the sprays.

Some while later, they saw an abandoned vehicle, all burned-out ribs and chassis. Later again, they passed more bits of wreckage and many curious chunks of a honeycomb-like material. Ferren had seen Hypers smashed apart before, and recognised the kind of material they were made of under their rubber suits.

"There must've been terrible fighting here," he commented.

"Why no angels' bodies?" Kiet asked Miriael. "It can't be only the Humen that got slaughtered."

"No. Angels too."

"Where?"

Miriael stepped aside to something dull and drab lying flat on the ground. It looked like a rag until she picked it up and spread it out; then it turned out to be a wide piece of colourless fabric.

"The robe of an angel," she said.

Ferren stared at Miriael's yellow robes, and Kiet asked the question he was about to ask: "Why doesn't it have a colour, then?"

"Our robes lose their colour when their owner's extinguished. 'Extinguished' is what happens to a being of pure spirit, you see. No body to leave behind."

"Oh," said Ferren and Kiet in the same breath. Even at a glance, there were hundreds of rag-like bits of fabric lying around.

They continued on parallel to the main highway. Now they could see tiny, twinkling lights against the darkness that Miriael had described as a rampart blocking off the Val Jehenna from the rest of Heaven. Miriael herself seemed more interested in the crag that she'd called the Rock of the Tabernacle.

But that's not our destination, thought Ferren with a frown.

Again, Kiet asked the question before he could ask it himself. "Where are we going?"

Miriael shrugged. "I don't know. Looking for sabotage possibilities." She gestures towards the twinkling lights. "Those are the Humen front lines, I assume."

"But we're supposed to be doing our sabotage *behind* their front lines. Aren't we?"

"Probably. That's for you to decide. I can only guide you with my knowledge of Heaven."

Ferren and Kiet looked at one another, then scanned the landscape.

Two hundred yards ahead, the Rock of the Tabernacle lay to their left, a cluster of low Humen structures to their right.

"What's that?" asked Ferren, pointing. "Like some sort of military encampment."

"Could be something to sabotage in there," said Kiet.

"Could be," Miriael responded to their questioning looks with a non-committal tone.

"Let's make a start, then," said Kiet.

"We'll investigate," said Ferren.

4

There were a score of marquees in the encampment, and half a dozen silvery, hemispherical domes. Hypers were moving about in the passages between the marquees, but they made so much noise they were easy to avoid. The mysterious hemispheres became the first target of the sabotage team's attention.

Approaching one, they discovered the reason for its silvery appearance: the entire surface was coated in shiny metallic foil. A low, droning whine emanated from equipment operating within.

"Perhaps it's a secret weapon," whispered Kiet.

Then Gibby applied her fingernails and made a second discovery.

"You can scratch it off," she announced. "There's glass underneath."

Soon everyone was scratching away, making peepholes in the foil. Ferren brought his eye right up against the glass to see through.

Inside was a rounded chamber filled with wispy, brown fibres of what looked like wool. Two giant metal combs cycled in ceaseless circles, raking through the fibres and looping them around some small object suspended in the middle. The object glimmered like jewellery and looked like an inscription— a set of numbers, letters and symbols. Ferren squinted at it, but he couldn't read ordinary writing let alone a mathematical formula.

"What is that thing?" muttered Kiet, who was peering through her peephole next to his.

"Don't know, but they're building it up," he muttered back.

With every cycle, the combs wound more fibres around the inscription, and the central woolly mass grew bigger and bigger. At the same time, the suspended object at its heart glimmered less and less brightly.

Ferren waited until the inscription was completely submerged before he stepped back. Most of the others had already abandoned their peepholes.

"Not much of a secret weapon," sniffed Zonda. "What could that do?"

"We could still sabotage it," said Stogget.

"What, break in through the glass?" Kiet shook her head doubtfully.

In fact, the glass was too thick to shatter. Stogget pounded on it with his fists in vain.

"We could cut _these._" Ethany, who'd been exploring around, pointed to a pair of cables that ran in under the side of the hemisphere.

One cable was red, one yellow, and both were sheathed in heavy plastic. Ferren took a close look and shook his head.

"We'd need a proper tool for cutting them," he said.

"Same problem again," sighed Rhinn.

"So we *find* a tool," said Kiet. "Let's start looking."

"Hold on." Ferren scanned the team. "Where's Miriael?"

Floy of the Fusselfolk cleared his throat. "Er, she said she'd be back in five minutes. She wanted to investigate something somewhere else."

"Investigate what?" Ferren demanded.

"That rock sticking up. The Rock of the Tabernacle."

Zonda snorted. "She'll be more than five minutes getting *there.*"

Ferren didn't understand. What was so special about the Rock of the Tabernacle? Why now? Did Miriael have something more important than sabotage to do? And if it was so important, why shouldn't the whole team come? She'd been in a strange mood, he'd noticed…

"Come on," Kiet broke in on his thoughts. "We're searching for a cutting tool. We can find that without her."

Then Flens broke in on *her.* "Shush! Everyone quiet!"

He had turned away from the hemisphere and was staring through the gap between two marquees. Now they all heard it: a sound of groaning, a rattle of wheels and the tread of heavy boots.

In the next moment, a Hyper came into view, pushing a hospital trolley. Unusually, he was clad from head to foot in white rubber, which Ferren recognised as the costume of a medical assistant. A second Hyper, clad in the usual black, lay on top of the trolley groaning in agony. They were briefly visible in the gap before they passed by.

"Let's follow," hissed Kiet. "I have a good feeling about this."

5

The team watched from the shadows as the medical assistant Hyper wheeled his trolley past two marquees. There were plastic windows in the canvas walls, but all were darkened—until the third marquee. Light spilled from the interior as the Hyper wheeled his trolley in at the entrance of the third marquee.

"Let's look in from the side," whispered Kiet.

With Kiet and Ferren leading, the team circled round by narrower passages and approached the third marquee from behind. Very cautiously, they raised their heads to peer in through the plastic windows.

Inside were two white-coated Doctors, exactly the same as all the other Doctors Ferren had ever seen. Their faces were like grey, crumpled paper, the backs of their heads were swathed in bandages. They sat in their wheelchairs on opposite sides of the trolley that had just been wheeled in.

On top of the trolley, the black-suited Hyper's groans had turned to curses and protests. One Doctor leaned forward and unscrewed the plug in his forehead, while the second Doctor plunged some sort of measuring instrument into the hole as soon as the plug came away. Then both Doctors examined the gauge on the instrument.

"Only three quarters of a psycholitre left in him," said the first Doctor, his whisper of a voice amplified to an artificial volume.

"Still worth reusing," said the second Doctor.

The first Doctor pulled across a stand from which dangled a tube of clear plastic and fitted the end of the tube over the hole. Ferren watched as an uncanny, multi-coloured jelly started to flow along the tube to a storage flask nearby.

They're extracting psycholitres, he thought with a shiver. *Taking them out of one Hyper to reuse in another.*

The curses and protests from the condemned Hyper stopped as soon as the extraction began. When it was finished, a medical assistant pushed the trolley to another part of the marquee, where more medical assistants waited. They took hold of the now-empty body and rolled it from the trolley onto a metal-topped table.

Next, they turned to a bench of tools and picked out a selection of shears, saws and cleavers. Ferren noticed a huge bin beside the table already half full of Hyper body parts. No doubt they would dismember the body and reuse the honeycomb material too...

A nudge from Kiet made him jump. "Cutting tools," she whispered.

She was pointing to the bench, on which many shears, saws and cleavers still remained. Of course—exactly what they were looking for!

"We'll need a distraction." Kiet addressed her next whisper to everyone. "I know how to do it."

She dropped down below the level of the plastic windows, and everyone dropped down to listen.

Five minutes later, the plan was in place. Ferren wasn't happy because Kiet insisted on taking the riskiest role for herself, but as she said, it was her plan. Kiet, Ferren and Stogget circled round the tent to the side that was next to the bench of tools. The others all stayed where they were, with Zonda in charge.

Ferren's task was to watch through a plastic window and give the signals. Near his feet, Kiet stretched out flat on the ground, and Stogget knelt beside her. Inside the marquee, the medical assistants were busy cutting and sawing on the metal-topped table, while the Doctors sat slumped and motionless in their wheelchairs.

Ready to begin! Ferren peeked through his window and saw Zonda looking back at him from her window on the opposite side. He gave a thumbs-up, Zonda disappeared—and in the next moment, a tremendous beating noise started up. The canvas wall billowed as Zonda and the others whacked and smacked it with the flats of their hands.

"Now!" Ferren whispered down to Kiet, and gave Stogget a nudge with his knee. Immediately, Stogget pulled up the bottom edge of the canvas, and Kiet slid forward underneath. Ferren went back to peeking through his window.

He couldn't see Kiet because the bench of tools was so close to this side of the marquee—which was part of the plan. He knew she'd come out under the bench top and was now rising up on all fours. Meanwhile, Doctors and Hypers all stared in the opposite direction. The noise of beating on the canvas wall continued like a kind of thunder.

"What is it?"

"Who's doing that?"

As several Hypers started across to investigate, Ferren saw Kiet's hand reach up from under the bench top. She felt around this way and that, searching by touch for a suitable cutting tool.

Quick! Take any one! he urged her in his mind.

But she didn't. Her fingers fumbled over a pair of shears and rejected them. Further and further she explored along the bench top. When she arrived at a steel hacksaw, he was ready to scream.

Yes! That one! Now!

Then a new hospital trolley came in through the entrance—and the Hyper who was wheeling it *wasn't* looking towards the billowing and beating on the other side of the marquee. Instead, his attention fell instantly upon the bench, the figure underneath it and the hand that still hadn't closed over the hacksaw.

"Hey! Who's that? Intruder!"

His snarling shout swung every pair of eyes towards himself, then towards the direction he was pointing. Ferren dropped down out of sight, signalled to Stogget with a jab of his knee and hissed, "Out now!"

Stogget reacted fast. He reached in under the canvas, gripped Kiet by the ankles and pulled her out from the marquee with one great tug. She was flat on her belly again as she emerged. Ferren and Stogget together grabbed her under the armpits and hoisted her upright.

"Run!" gasped Ferren.

There were shouts from within, then a crash like an overturning trolley. Ferren dashed down passages between marquees with Kiet and Stogget at his heels. He could only hope that Zonda and the others were running too.

6

Miriael walked fast, eyes fixed upon the Rock of the Tabernacle. Sometimes she stumbled over bits of broken metal, chunks of honeycomb material and even the robes of extinguished angels, yet she hardly noticed. She was approaching the raised deck at the front of the crag facing the rampart.

She had a vague sense that there were important reasons for wanting to investigate. After all, this was the command centre for the Humen invasion, so if any communications could be sabotaged here... But she didn't consider her reasons too deeply.

She didn't approach directly, but veered to the side. So far, she had seen no glow of light emanating from the front of the crag, but she still hadn't viewed the whole deck. She continued on a little further, then a little further, then a little further again.

Finally, the evidence was before her eyes. Four white-coated Doctors sat in their wheelchairs on the deck, but *he* wasn't there. She shook her head as if coming out of a trance.

Why had she wanted to see Asmodai? Because that was her real reason, she couldn't deny it. What would she have done if he had been there? Was it just to set eyes on his face again?

Suddenly, she didn't understand herself at all. She felt foolish and confused, alone and exposed on the darkened plain. When she looked around, she realised she'd come much, much further than she'd ever intended. She turned on her heel to return to the Residuals.

She'd gone hardly a step when she noticed a dead flower under her feet. It was like every other flower in the Val Jehenna, fallen and shrivelled. But this one she noticed. She stooped and plucked it up.

She couldn't even tell what colour the petals had been. She remembered the Val Jehenna as one of the most beautiful places on the First Altitude, with flowers like scattered stars, yellow, pink and golden. Sometimes she had come here with warrior angels of her company when they were off duty…

The sadness that had been building ever since she'd entered this desolate, devastated version of the Val Jehenna rose over her like a wave. She sank to the ground and submerged in a welter of memories.

Memories of the serene and glorious landscape that had once existed…memories of Asmodai in his radiant beauty when she'd first fallen in love with him…memories of Asmodai on the deck of the Rock uttering terrible words…pronouncing her ultimate humiliation… memories of the wonderful feeling of being in love when she'd first discovered it…memories of everything lost and gone…

She was still gazing through tear-bleared eyes at the flower between her fingers when a sudden noise dragged her from her stupor.

Wraaaahhh! Wraaaahhh! Wraaaahhh!

It was an alarm siren, and it came from the direction of the encampment with the silvery hemispheres and marquees. Ferren and the others must be in trouble! Now she could hear a hubbub of activity and a clamour of shouting. Were those shadows sprinting away from the encampment over the plain? She dropped the flower and rose to her feet.

Wraaaahhh! Wraaaahhh! Wraaaahhh!

7

Ferren's only goal was to escape from the encampment as fast as possible. Rushing along passages between the marquees, he, Kiet and Stogget ran into Zonda and her group rushing the same way.

"Found you!" gasped Zonda. "Where do we—"

Wraaaahhh! Wraaaahhh! Wraaaahhh!

Her words were drowned out by the ear-splitting blare of a siren. Everyone jumped at the sound and fled down the nearest passage—which luckily led them straight out of the encampment.

They raced on across the open plain. Ahead of them were the tiny, twinkling lights of the Humen front lines, the black barrier of the rampart and the sliver of Heavenly light coming in over the top of the barrier. Ferren didn't care about the direction, so long as they could run off far enough before Hypers started looking for them outside the encampment.

The siren wasn't the only sound; now there were cries and shouts coming from the marquees behind them. For three hundred yards they ran like the wind. Sometimes they tripped and fell over battlefield debris, but scrambled back up and ran on.

Darkness sheltered them for three hundred yards. Then thin pencil beams of light leaped out and fanned across the plain. One searchlight probed on their side of the encampment, but it was still some way to their right. Ferren swung his arm in a signal to keep running.

They ran on as far as they could. Then Ferren glanced over his shoulder, saw that the searchlight was almost upon them and yelled a warning.

"Get down, lie flat, don't move!"

Everyone flung themselves flat and froze. A moment later, the searchlight beam swept across. Intense light exposed every inch of the ground in stark black-and-white.

Ferren held his breath. They would be seen, for sure—but not necessarily seen as human beings. At this distance, they might be mistaken for bits of wreckage or lumps of honeycomb material or fallen Celestial robes. He could only hope…

Slowly, slowly, the beam passed over and swung further away to the left. There were gasps and sighs of relief from a dozen throats.

Ferren sprang to his feet. "Run on! Far as we can before it comes back!"

Once more they ran—another hundred yards. The searchlight completed its sweep to the left, reversed direction and began to approach once more. Ferren no longer needed to shout a warning; they were all keeping watch over their shoulders now. They dived flat to the ground and held themselves motionless as the beam passed across from left to right and continued on its way.

It became a kind of pattern. Three times more they ran a hundred yards in the darkness, then dropped to the ground and lay still. Kiet was next to Ferren whenever they threw themselves down.

"How long do we keep doing this?" she asked him after the fourth time.

"Don't know. Until they stop searching."

"We'll run into the Humen army soon."

Ferren looked ahead and saw how much brighter the twinkling lights had become. It was true, they'd already covered more than half the distance to the front lines.

"We ought to hide," said Kiet. "What about that vehicle there?"

"Where?" Ferren couldn't tell where she was looking, and she couldn't point while holding herself motionless.

"On our left. Fifty paces."

Ferren shifted his head, swivelled his eyes and saw it. The vehicle had been abandoned, one of the biggest wrecked machines they'd seen. It looked like some sort of armoured transport vehicle, a long steel box with caterpillar tracks. Although seemingly intact, it lay upside down with its chassis exposed.

"Right, we hide." He grinned at Kiet—and in the next moment, the searchlight moved away.

He jumped to his feet as darkness engulfed them all again. "Follow us! This way!" he cried.

"We'll hide!" Kiet called out over her shoulder as she ran with him to the transport vehicle. "Inside this thing!"

They made for a door that hung ajar on one side of the vehicle. Ferren and Kiet dived in, and the others dived in after them. The last one in pulled the door shut.

The searchlight returned a moment later. The box-like interior had no windows, but it had ventilation louvres, and the light came in through slats along one side. Everywhere was bare metal—if there had ever been furnishings, they'd been stripped out when the vehicle was abandoned. What had been its roof was now the floor, and its floor the roof.

Light and shadows shifted from left to right as the searchlight swept across; when it had gone, the darkness was total. There was only the smell of stale air, the feel of cold metal and the echoing sound of their own movements.

Kiet spoke up in the darkness. "I can't see anyone coming after us.

Maybe they're still searching the marquees."

Ferren realised she was peering through one of the louvres, and did the same himself. If there were Hypers out searching the plain, sooner or later they would be caught in the beams. But there were no Hypers.

He was still watching when the siren fell silent a few minutes later. A few minutes later again, the searchlights went off.

"They've given up!" cried Kiet.

Tadge whooped in triumph, and everyone began talking at once.

"Quiet!" Rhinn's hiss cut across the chatter. "What's that?"

In the hush that followed, Ferren heard it too: a sound of hurrying footsteps. Light footsteps, though, not the boots of a Hyper. Could it be…?

The footsteps came close and circled round to the door of the vehicle. With a squeak and scrape, the handle turned—

"It's me," said Miriael, as the door swung open.

For a moment, her winged silhouette was visible in the doorway as she stooped to enter. Then she closed the door behind her.

"I've been watching you since you ran from the encampment," she explained. "I was coming to meet your route, then I saw you hide here. What happened?"

Everyone took it in turns to tell the story of the Doctors and the bench of tools, the distraction that had worked and the arrival of a trolley-wheeling Hyper that had brought their plan undone.

"So we still don't have a cutting tool for our sabotage," Kiet concluded. "We *still* can't begin."

"Hmm." Miriael shook her head. "It's not going well, is it?"

She hadn't said anything about the success or failure of her own investigation, Ferren noted. He was wondering how to ask when, all at once, another kind of light banished the darkness.

"It's the First Heavenly Sun!" Miriael exclaimed, and clapped her hands. "They've lit up the First Heavenly Sun again!"

Pure and fresh, soft and spreading, the new light came in through louvres on both sides of the vehicle. The Residuals gazed at one another's faces in wonder. Ferren blinked and laughed.

"I wonder what it's for," murmured Miriael.

8

Ferren swung to the louvre where he'd looked out before. Now the Rock of the Tabernacle stood out sharp and clear, and the wreckage and debris scattered on the plain was clearly visible. But he had eyes only for the beautiful blue of the sky. He twisted his neck to see the source of the light, and there, almost directly overhead, was the First Heavenly Sun. It looked like a flower that had just unfolded to disclose a centre of glowing, golden brightness.

"Phew, look at that!" whistled Kiet, peering out through the louvres next to him.

A sound like a peal of thunder broke in on their admiration.

"What's this?" cried someone from the other side of the vehicle.

The thunder turned into a deep, solemn chant.

"Whose faces are those?"

Everyone was now looking out towards the rampart and the front lines of the Humen army. Ferren switched sides and found himself a louvre to look out in the same direction. He took in a wall two hundred feet high with battlements at the top—that was the rampart. He took in a black mass of Hypers below, glittering with weapons, milling around under the light—that was the Humen army.

But the most extraordinary sight was the line of four gigantic faces that had appeared before the rampart. Faces framed by flowing white hair and flowing white beards, faces without bodies, faces as huge as the rampart was high. Four sets of lips moved and uttered the booming chant.

Miriael raised her voice to explain. "Those are the faces of the four Great Patriarchs. I think Heaven's about to launch a counter-attack."

Her words came true a moment later. All at once, a multitude of shining angels came forward over the battlements. They echoed the chant of the Patriarchs in their pure, melodic voices. Then, like a waterfall of brightness, they began the two-hundred-foot descent to the ground.

An ugly, angry roar rose from the Humen lines. Ferren heard shouts of command, followed by sounds of machinery and engines springing to life. The milling confusion was rapidly reforming into an organised defence.

"Oh, look!" cried Miriael. "Heaven's using Stones of Wrath too!"

Ferren stared at the new phenomenon she called Stones of Wrath. Groups of angels carried them over the battlements: spherical crystals twenty feet in diameter, cut into sharp-edged facets. The angels lowered them in cradles of silver wire down the front of the rampart.

Miriael laughed in delight. "They must be from our Western forces! They haven't been used since we defeated Doctor Mengis and Doctor Genelle!"

By now, the first wave of warrior angels had reached the ground. Ferren could no longer see them over the top of the Humen army, but he heard sounds of fighting as the two sides clashed. The clamour swelled until even the chant of the Great Patriarchs was drowned out.

Then the amplified voice of a Doctor rang out across the battlefield: "*Coldfire! Launch the coldfire!*"

A dozen sizzling lines of fire shot up from the ground, soared to the roof of the First Altitude and erupted in flames. Further and further the flames spread out, devouring air and sky.

"What've they done now?" gasped someone in alarm.

Miriael was no longer laughing. "Autogenic coldfire. It feeds off itself. I've seen it before, but never on such a scale."

"Will it burn us?" asked someone else.

"It would if it came down to the ground," answered Miriael. "But then it would burn the Hypers, too. I expect they'll leave it as a layer in mid-air to limit our powers of flight. They'll want to make our warrior angels fight at ground level."

Ferren watched as ripples of coldfire washed back and forth overhead. There was no heat, only billows of flame like seething foam. By the time the fire reached the rampart, the angelic horde had already completed its descent.

Now the clamour of battle redoubled in volume. Ferren could hear screams and detonations and screeches of metal, he could distinguish Humen war cries from Heavenly battle hymns. He saw Hypers hurrying this way and that behind the lines, he blinked at flashes and glows that lit up the air above the heads of the Humen army. But the fighting at the front was out of his view.

"What's *happening?*" he cried in frustration.

Miriael answered from her place further along the louvres. "We'll have to wait and see," she said.

9

Time passed, and still they couldn't tell what was happening. Once, Ferren glimpsed the turret of a mechanical monster pouring smoke; later, he saw the top of a Stone of Wrath rolling into the Humen lines. Strangest of all were the musical notes like guitar strings breaking, which didn't seem to belong on a battlefield at all.

Then the amplified, artificial voice of a Doctor blared forth. "*Fall back, all troops! Orderly retreat! Fall back!*"

There was a moment of silence inside the transport vehicle—then everyone whooped and cheered.

"Yahoo!" Tadge whooped loudest of all. "We've won! We've *won!*"

Miriael laughed. "No, but we're winning."

Staring out through his louvre, Ferren saw the Humen army begin to withdraw. Although it was an orderly retreat, not a rout, it was a very hurried one. All along the line, Hypers flooded back from the fighting, away from the rampart. Now several mechanical monsters were visible, and a few Queen-Hypers among the Hypers.

"*Orderly retreat! Maintain ranks! Officers, keep your troops in formation!*"

In no time at all, the first troops to withdraw had come almost as far as the upside-down transport machine. Officers barked orders, Hypers snarled curses in the direction of the advancing Heavenly host. But there was no panic yet. The Humen troops still held their weapons raised and ready to fire—flamethrowers and other unfamiliar devices.

Then Miriael spoke up. "They'll go past as long as we stay hidden."

"Just don't let them see you looking out," warned Ferren.

Everyone would have liked to keep watching, but they understood the risk and drew away from the louvres on the battlefield side. They heard the thunder of boots pounding the ground, a whole army of boots approaching. Then the light coming in through the louvres dimmed, and Hyper soldiers began to go past around either end of the transport vehicle. Miriael put a finger to her lips for silence

"*Far enough, officers!*" Once more, the amplified Doctor's voice blared forth. "*Halt your troops! Regroup and reform! Form a defensive line against the enemy!*"

Ferren groaned inwardly. All around, the boots came to a halt, then shuffled over the ground in different directions. Officers barked new orders, and Hyper soldiers responded with snarling, jeering sounds that might have meant anything.

Then a rasping voice called out very close: "Hey, lads, what about this? Grab it before anyone else does!"

In the next moment came a tremendous thumping and bumping against the sides and on top of the transport vehicle. The interior echoed with reverberations. The sabotage team exchanged troubled looks as they realised what was happening: a group of Hypers had decided to use the vehicle as a defensive shield for themselves.

Just so long as they keep to the outside, thought Ferren. He listened to the sounds of some climbing up onto the chassis overhead, while others stayed sheltering behind the vehicle on the ground. The ones on the ground grumbled loudly among themselves, and their voices came in through the louvres on that side.

"Easy to say 'form a defensive line'."

"Doctors ought to be sending us reinforcements."

"Doctors say whatever the big leader wants 'em to say. Anything to please *him.*"

"Why doesn't he come and help us himself?"

Ferren understood that they were speaking about Asmodai. Then, suddenly, the tone changed.

"Get ready! Hold yer fire! Let 'em get close, then blast 'em!"

On the other side of the vehicle, a battle-hymn filled the air.

"*Onward, onward, onward!*
Angels to the fore!

Ours will be the victory
In our righteous war!"

The angels weren't far away now. Ferren clenched his fists and willed them forward. Then he noticed what Kiet was doing. She had dropped down below the level of the louvres on the battlefield side, but she held up the zither so that Peeper could look out. Of course, the Morph was invisible and the zither was only a frame with strings—so there was no risk involved.

When he saw Kiet lower the zither to her ear and nod her head, he guessed that she was listening and Peeper was reporting. He went across and dropped down beside her. Peeper's cheeps and chirrups were so quiet, they were almost inaudible.

"What's he saying?"

Kiet whispered back a moment later. "There's a line of Hypers and a Queen-Hyper right in front of us. The angels are coming forward with their spears, all bright with light. Very close—"

Her whisper was drowned out as the battle-hymn rose to a crescendo, followed by a burst of sharp, splitting sounds, followed by a roaring whoosh. Then came an almighty racket as the Humen army fired back. There were yells and screams, dull explosions and strange, single musical notes. Inside the metal box of the vehicle, the din was deafening.

Kiet raised the zither to the louvres again. On the other side of the vehicle, Hypers were shouting in panic.

"They're falling back around us!"

"We'll get cut off!"

"We oughter fall back while we can!"

Yes, drop back! Ferren willed them to go. *Drop back, drop back, drop back, drop—*

"Hey!" A different kind of shout rang out. "Who's this in here?"

Ferren swung in the direction of the shout, on the other side of the vehicle. The eyeslits of a black rubber-clad head were peering in through one of the louvres there. They'd been spotted!

In the next moment, the eyeslits withdrew and the barrel of a weapon thrust in through the same louvre. Kiet was the first to react. She dropped the zither, sprang across and seized the protruding end of the barrel.

The weapon was a flamethrower, and she wrenched it sideways, trying to redirect it away from anyone inside. The Hyper on the other end let out a furious roar and fired regardless. A jet of yellow flame shot from the nozzle and narrowly missed Rhinn and Tadge. As they leaped away, Kiet struggled to push the barrel downwards.

But the Hyper pushed back. Flame continued to spurt from the nozzle, filling the inside of the metal box with smoke.

Ferren leaped forward to help. Kiet's face had twisted in agony, and she let him take her place, gripping the end of the barrel. He understood her agony the moment his hands touched the metal of the nozzle— which was burning hot.

He kept pushing downwards, then sideways, then downwards again. He could only last a few moments more, and Kiet, wringing her hands, could hardly take over again. Out of the corner of his eye, he saw other weapons already starting to thrust in through the louvres…

"*Hosanna!*

Hosanna!

Hosanna in excelsis!"

The singing was suddenly right next to the transport vehicle. The front line of angels had arrived! The flamethrower that Ferren gripped went slack in his hands, and its flame cut out. He let go of the barrel and blew on his palms.

Dimly, he heard Hypers yelling, "Fall back! Fall back!" Some screamed in pain, some bumped and thumped as they scrambled down from the chassis overhead. He blinked away the smoke stinging his eyes and saw Kiet grinning with joy and relief.

"*Hosanna!*

Hosanna!

Hosanna in excelsis!"

The singing flowed all around the transport vehicle. He had never heard a sound so beautiful.

10

"Everyone all right?" Ferren called out.

The answers came back mingled with laughter, sobs of thankfulness and coughing in the smoke. Everyone had survived unharmed.

Stirred by a single thought, they crossed to look out at the angels who'd swept past and the Hypers who'd been driven back. Ferren joined Kiet at the same louvre where they'd fought to deflect the flamethrower.

Already, the main force of angels had moved on, but a couple still lingered near the transport vehicle. A Hyper lay on the ground, seemingly unable to rise—perhaps he'd injured himself jumping down from the chassis. The two angels wore casques on their heads, carried spears in their hands, and their wings were like a white dazzle of snow. The Hyper writhed in his black rubber suit, screaming obscenities at them.

The radiance of one angel intensified, brighter and brighter. Then she raised her spear and jabbed down towards the Hyper. But the point didn't make contact; instead, a bolt of spiritual energy poured through the spear-shaft, shot out from the spear-tip and struck deep into the black-clad chest. There was an explosive *whumpf!* and a violent eruption of shimmering, multi-coloured vapour.

"So that's what their spears are for," muttered Kiet.

A few moments later, the vapour had dispersed, the angel's radiance had returned to a normal level and all that remained of the Hyper's body were scattered chunks of charred honeycomb.

The angels turned and sped after their comrades, who were now fighting a hundred yards away. The Heavenly army continued to sing hosannas; the wild yells and cries from the Humen army sounded close to panic.

Then Zonda called out from the other end of their metal box: "Hey, it's safe now! Let's have a look outside!"

She flung the door wide, and they all streamed out into the open.

Ferren surveyed the war-ravaged scene and took in patches of burnt grass, gouges in the ground and the remnants of shattered bodies.

"Whoo!" cried Tadge, darting forward. "This is mine!"

He snatched up a weapon that lay beside one broken Hyper. Rhinn frowned and made a move to take it off him.

"It's a Humen weapon," she said.

"So?" Tadge clutched it all the more tightly. "We oughter be armed."

Rhinn shook her head. "Remember what happened to Skail?"

Everyone remembered Skail's flamethrower—and how Miriael had warned against Humen weapons at the time. Now, though, she seemed thoughtful.

"That's a spike-gun you've holding," she said, studying it. "You wouldn't know how to fire it."

"Easy, I'd pull the trigger," Tadge retorted, and pointed to a trigger on the underside of the weapon.

"Hmm, yes. All right, you would know how to fire it." Miriael nodded, chewed at her lip, then appeared to reach a conclusion. "I think he's right," she told everyone. "I drop my objection to Humen weapons. You should arm yourselves if you can."

"We can," said Ferren, and swung an arm to encompass all the weapons that Hypers had dropped in their retreat.

"Then *fight* with them!" cried Tadge.

Everyone exchanged glances. Tadge hoisted his weapon and aimed at nothing in particular.

"Fight! Fight! Fight!" he whooped.

Miriael scanned every face. "Fight on the side of the angels? Fight the Humen with their own weapons?"

"Yes!" Zonda supported Tadge. "We weren't very good at sabotage. Let's be fighters instead!"

Ferren laughed. "We can't sabotage things behind enemy lines anyway."

Kiet completed the thought. "Because we're not behind enemy lines anymore!"

There was no need to take a vote. Everyone cheered and pumped fists in the air. "Fight! Fight! Fight!"

Miriael smiled and clapped her hands. "Right, then. Find weapons for yourselves."

They all fanned out to search. Ferren had a quicker idea, and hurried to the louvre where the Hyper had fired into the transport vehicle. As he expected, the flamethrower lay on the ground below, where it had dropped after he and the Hyper let go of it.

With his new weapon under his arm, he rejoined Miriael and Tadge.

"You're not looking for something yourself?" he asked the angel.

Miriael grimaced with a little laugh. "Not me. I couldn't bear the touch."

Kiet rejoined them a few minutes later, carrying an odd-looking weapon with a perforated barrel. Miriael examined it and nodded.

"That's a tracer gun. Rapid-fire, for close quarters fighting. The Hypers use them—"

She broke off as the amplified voice of a Doctor blared forth yet again.

"*Halt the retreat! Hold your ground! Another defensive line! Confront and resist!*"

Ferren could locate the source of the voice now. It came from the crag that Miriael had called the Rock of the Tabernacle. At the front of the crag was a raised deck, in which sat four white-coated figures in wheelchairs.

"They're desperate to make a stand now," said Miriael, who was gazing in the same direction. "Our army's almost reached their command centre. They can't afford to lose that."

A moment later, a succession of trumpet notes split the air.

"And now we're deploying for an ultimate push." Miriael interpreted the trumpeters' signal. "This will be the decisive confrontation." She rose on tiptoe to look out further than Ferren could see across the battlefield. "I think that's our commander for this sector over there, and his trumpeters with him."

She dropped back on her heels. More and more of the Residuals had come up with their newly acquired weapons over the past few minutes.

"Does everyone have a weapon now?" she asked.

Ferren checked and counted. "Yes, and everyone's back."

"Then let's go and talk to the sector commander." She pointed the direction. "We'll find out where we can be most help for the ultimate push."

11

Many companies of angels were still coming forward behind the front line of Heaven's advance. They were all charged to the brim with spiritual energy, their features clear as water, an eagerness for battle in their blue eyes. Remote and elevated, they hardly seemed to notice the incongruous band of Residuals.

"Ah, I can see the Archon Marioch," said Miriael, peering ahead as she led the way. "He must be the commander here."

Ferren couldn't see for himself until they came closer. Then he gasped at the sight of a magnificent chariot of burnished gold, inlaid with red and turquoise jewels. To the rear of it stood six angels bearing trumpets and six angels bearing flags and banners. And in front... He blinked and looked again. Instead of horses, two gigantic birds rested in harness in front of the chariot, two gigantic birds with wings of bronze, hooked beaks and glittering plumage.

Miriael turned to explain. "Those birds are the Eagles of the Apocalypse."

She approached the chariot in a straight line, whereas Ferren and the others detoured and kept well away from the Eagles. The mighty birds observed their progress with wary eyes and dug their talons deeper into the ground.

It wasn't only the Eagles that watched them with suspicion. The six trumpeter angels and six flag-bearing angels were equally unwelcoming. Ferren saw raised eyebrows, narrowed eyes and downturned mouths. The Archon Marioch was the most scornful of all.

From the height of his chariot, he looked down on Miriael and swept his gaze across the Residuals. His eyes were piercing, his robes a deep green, and he carried a golden rod in his hand. Ferren had the impression that his robes pulsated in the radiance that streamed from his limbs.

"Yes?" He addressed Miriael in a faraway tone of voice.

She gestured towards the Residuals clustering behind her. "These are your new allies. Their representatives signed a formal treaty with

Heaven's highest archangels."

"I heard about it." His tone remained unyielding. "And?"

"They're here to fight for you."

"Fight for us? *Them?*"

"And me too."

Marioch curled his lip. "Fighting with those Humen weapons, I suppose?"

Miriael ignored the contempt. "So we need you to deploy us to the front line."

"What, alongside my warrior angels?" His eyes widened in genuine surprise.

"Yes."

"No." Marioch waved a hand to dismiss them. "Do your own fighting, if you think you can. And now, excuse me, I have a battle to win."

"Wait!" Zonda pushed forward, simmering with outrage. "We can *help* you!"

Marioch raked her with a scornful look, but he had no intention of answering. He turned to his trumpeter angels—when a high-pitched sound came from the zither that Kiet carried on a cord round her neck.

"*Eee!-eeeeee!*"

It was Peeper, and he was wildly agitated. Kiet bent over the stringed instrument in alarm.

"What is it, little one?"

But the high-pitched sound continued without words. Marioch and his subordinates frowned in disapproval.

"I think he's in pain," Kiet explained. A moment later, she winced herself. "Oh! I can feel it too." She turned to Ferren. "It's his friends and colleagues. Can't you feel it?"

Ferren guessed and looked up, but there was nothing there yet. Only the feeling: a jangling, scraping friction along the nerves, a sense of being pinned and trapped and tortured for all eternity...

Then the vast wing appeared. It was travelling very low, and more slowly than Ferren had ever seen before. The point and the glass bubble passed by fifty feet away, while the side of the delta cut across the First Heavenly Sun and cast everything in shadow.

Ferren ducked and shrank, as even the angels ducked and shrank.

When he raised his eyes again, the underside of the wing looked different to other times, with a dozen bulging, brown shapes slung below. But he had no chance to work out what they were—a tremendous flapping and beating made him whirl round.

It was the two Eagles of the Apocalypse, panicked by the shadow of Asmodai's vast wing. With an explosive flurry of their own wings, they took off in opposite directions.

Everything happened in a split second. The chariot jerked forward, Marioch tumbled out at the back, the straps of the harness tautened and snapped. As the Eagles sped off on separate trajectories, the chariot settled down still upright on its wheels, but twenty yards further on. Subordinate angels hurried forward to help their leader to his feet.

"Asmodai has joined the battle!" Miriael shouted at them.

The trailing edge of the delta passed over, uncovering the sun once again. Ferren turned back to watch it glide across the battlefield. It hadn't gone far when one of the brown, bulging shapes detached from its underside and drifted groundward. Then another. And another. They were like large puffs of brown smoke, and they reminded him of something...

They must be a kind of secret weapon, he thought, *and they've been dropped to attack Heaven's army from the rear. Although they don't look much like secret weapons...*

Then it came back to him. These were the things they'd seen being created inside the silver hemispheres. The same shade of brown, the same woolliness!

"You see what they are?" He turned to Kiet. "You remember, in the silver hemispheres?"

But Kiet was preoccupied with Peeper. She held his zither close to her face and addressed him in a quiet, crooning voice. Trying to soothe and calm him, no doubt. He turned to Marioch, who seemed still dazed, and the other angels, who had fallen into fluttering confusion.

"Now we'll show you what we can do!" he shouted at them. "We'll deploy ourselves! We can deal with those woolly things!" He turned to the Residuals, who were gazing in all directions. "Right? We know their secret! Come on!" He swung an arm and pointed to where the nearest woolly mass had landed.

"Bring Peeper with you!" he called out to Kiet over his shoulder, as he set off running.

12

At first, Kiet had spoken to Peeper in order to soothe him, but later she'd listened. Once he'd overcome his immediate reaction to the flying wing, the Morph had an idea to propose. Kiet had raised many doubts, but in the end she'd nodded.

"I'll tell Miriael and the others when the moment's right. When I think they might agree."

Kiet lowered the zither to hang on its cord over her chest, then looked around. The scene had changed in the time she'd been talking to Peeper. Miriael still stood close by, but the Residuals clustered in a group several paces away, talking furiously among themselves. Marioch and his trumpeters and flag-bearers formed another group, further away again.

Then Kiet remembered Ferren calling out to her about something, though she hadn't heard what. So far as she could see, he wasn't with the other Residuals, nor anywhere else either. She stepped across to Miriael.

"Where's Ferren?"

"Ferren?" Miriael responded automatically, her attention still faraway. Then she adjusted to the question. "Ferren. I think he ran off somewhere over there." She pointed in the opposite direction to the frontline combat.

"Why there?"

"Asmodai's secret weapons, I suppose. Didn't you see? A dozen of them dropped to attack Heaven's army from the rear."

Kiet hadn't seen, and shook her head. "Shouldn't we join Ferren?"

"We *should* have. Only he ran off and disappeared too fast. I don't think anyone knows what he's doing."

"Oh. So we wait for him to come back here?"

"That's what *I'll* be doing." Miriael nodded towards the group of Residuals. "I expect they'll—"

The blare of a Doctor's amplified voice cut across her. "*Forward, armies of the Earth! Our overlord has come! We have the advantage, and the enemy is vulnerable! Our cipherdogs have landed to undermine them from behind! Seize the moment! Advance at the front! Destroy them utterly!*"

A great clamour rose up from the Humen army in response. The arrival of the flying wing had inspired them with new confidence. Hypers' war cries drowned out the hosannas and battle hymns of the angels. Was the Heavenly frontline already starting to waver?

Marioch's flag-bearers raised their standards higher in the air, and his trumpeters blew a three-note flourish of command. Then they marched off with their commander towards the front line. To Kiet's eyes, though, there was a sense of desperation in the way they held up their chins and thrust out their chests.

A moment later, the group of Residuals set off after them. Kiet watched them go, but wasn't tempted to follow. She was thinking about Peeper's idea.

"No, I'll wait here with you," she said in answer to Miriael's question. "Where's Asmodai?"

Miriael pointed to the side of the battlefield where she'd been gazing out before. "I saw him come down over there. I can't see him now. But listen."

There were many different sounds across the battlefield, but Kiet focused her attention where Miriael pointed. What she heard was a distant murmur—a murmur made up of a thousand angelic voices wailing and crying. And behind the murmur, a strange, faint swish or a hiss.

"What is it?" Kiet asked.

"I don't know, but it seems to be moving around."

Their view was blocked by scattered bands of angels that had come to a standstill in a state of indecision. Many appeared to be looking and listening in the same direction as Miriael and Kiet.

"We need to get up higher," said Kiet, and her gaze lit upon Marioch's abandoned chariot. "That'll do!"

"I'm not sure…" Miriael seemed reluctant about mounting an archon's chariot.

"Yes, come on. Nobody cares."

Kiet made her way to the back of the chariot and sprang up the three steps that went up to the driver's floor. Miriael overcame her scruples and ascended a minute later.

The battlefield was no longer a tidy alignment of opposing forces but a confused swirl of many separate conflicts. The Humen had broken through Heaven's front line in several places, and swarms of Hypers now surged into the space behind. Kiet took it all in at a glance, then turned to look for Asmodai.

The first thing she saw was a wide, mowed track, dotted with the tatters of angels' robes. It was as though some great scythe had swept across the ground and laid everything flat. She followed the track around and came to the great delta that was doing the mowing.

"He's cutting them down with his wing!" she gasped.

"Evil, evil, evil." Miriael uttered a sound like a strangled sob.

Kiet rose on tiptoe for a better look. Now she could see an eerie blue light that played over the leading edge of the wing. The angels in their ranks stood motionless as it glided towards them, seemingly hypnotised. It threw up a spray of fine detritus as it cut them down.

"Why don't they do something?" Kiet could have cried with frustration. "Why don't they lie flat on the ground? Maybe it would pass over them!"

Miriael only groaned. "Warrior angels don't lie flat on the ground. It's not in our training."

Kiet dropped back on the soles of her feet. "Heaven's losing everywhere, isn't it? Front...rear...side...everywhere."

Miriael nodded mutely, tears in her eyes.

"The great archangels will be frantic enough for any answer, don't you think?"

Another mute nod.

"Peeper has an idea." Kiet held up the zither, and the Morph uttered a single, affirmative peep. "But it can only work if you contact Heaven first."

"Contact Heaven? *Now?*"

"You'll have to have one of your visionary dreams."

"You mean, fall asleep in the middle of a battle?"

"Yes."

Miriael grimaced. "Last time, I never even reached the right part of Heaven."

"Will you try?"

"Tell me about this idea."

"All right, me and Peeper will explain it to you. Right, Peeper?"

The Morph uttered another loud peep.

13

Ferren kept on running even after he realised no one was following. Perhaps they hadn't heard or understood. But ahead was a cleared space between the companies of angels, and he glimpsed a fuzzy, brown shape at the centre of it.

I'll just deal with this one, he thought. *If it works, I can tell the angels how to deal with the rest.*

Approaching the cleared space, he discovered it wasn't as empty as he'd first thought. Angels who were still standing had retreated thirty yards away from the woolly mass, but there were also angels who had sunk to their knees or lay listlessly on their sides closer in. They seemed barely able to hold up their heads, and their robes had lost most of their colour.

"Let me through, please!" he cried.

He came forward through the ring of standing angels and threaded a way between those slumped to the ground.

"Don't," said a female voice.

He looked and saw a warrior angel whose robes might once have been maroon. She lay propped on one elbow, her face very pale and her eyelids drooping.

"Don't go any nearer or you'll die," she warned. "What are you?"

Ferren paused. He was amazed that an angel could speak to him without the usual scornful superiority, and even seemed to care for his welfare.

"I'm a Residual, and we signed a treaty to make us your allies. I'm coming to help with *that.*" He pointed to the brown, woolly mass.

"The cipherdog?" She shook her head sadly, feebly. "It's too powerful. It sucks out our spiritual energy."

"I'm not sure I have any of that. I have a soul—can it suck out a soul?"

"I don't know. But you can't destroy it, anyway." Her eyes focused on the flamethrower in his hands. "That won't do any good. The stuff it's made of won't catch fire. We've tried. We've tried everything."

"I have another way."

Again, a slow, sad shake of her head. "It's not alive. It's a nothingness. It doesn't have a heart or a head."

"It has a centre, though. And I know what it is." He realised that her head had dropped down and she was no longer listening. "I'll show you afterwards."

He continued his advance towards the cipherdog. It was a shapeless, billowing, brown mass, about twenty feet wide, the same size as the interior of one of the silvery hemispheres. It made a roar like a distant wind as it moved slowly over the ground. Sometimes its bulges resembled clawed legs or a snout or a fanged mouth, but only for an instant; then they merged back into the mass.

A yard away, he tried the flamethrower, shooting a jet of flame straight into the thing. After the angel's warning, he wasn't surprised when the flame was snuffed out as if under a blanket. He was more surprised when the woolly mass bulged out towards him and engulfed the barrel of the weapon. He felt the flamethrower being pulled from his grip, then borne off deeper into the brown murk.

He hadn't expected to fight the thing from outside anyway. He stared at the cipherdog, took a deep breath and plunged forward into it.

The fibres were infinitely soft and infinitely dry, as though the air had been filled with padding. Suddenly, all sound and sight were muffled, and the external world ceased to exist. He pushed forward, and the fibres yielded to his movements. With his hands held out in front of him, he swept from side to side at about the right height.

He was searching for what he'd seen when they'd watched the making of a cipherdog: a small object like a piece of jewellery that the fibres had been spun around. He didn't know how the numbers, letters and symbols of the inscription worked, but he was sure they were the key to the cipherdog's existence.

Sweeping side to side with his hands, he couldn't use them to protect his face. He felt the fibres exploring his nostrils and searching for his mouth with a strange persistence of their own. It was a struggle to keep his eyes open when fibres fingered around his eye-sockets and brushed over his eyeballs. Still he stared into the brown murk, which grew browner and murkier the further he advanced. Everywhere looked exactly the same, nowhere could he see the glimmering inscription he sought.

The woolly mass pressed tighter and tighter around him. He felt he was drowning in it, drowning in dry floss. The fibres had blocked up his nostrils, and when he tried to breathe through his mouth, the air was utterly dead and exhausted. There was no oxygen in his lungs, and his chest hurt.

Still he made wide sweeps with his arms as he staggered about. Everything was starting to turn muddled and dreamy, his feet seemed to be floating over the ground...

Then he touched something hard and small suspended in the middle of the mass. He closed his hand over it, dragged it towards him and pulled off the fibres that came with it. Now he could see a glimmer of numbers, letters and symbols. It was like a tiny glowing ember in his palm, and it felt hot, too.

He would have thrown it to the ground and stamped on it, but he was afraid of losing it in the murk. Instead, he squeezed it in his fist.

Out, out, out! he willed. *Out, out, out!*

Finally, the cipher disintegrated. The inscription of numbers, letters and symbols broke into three parts in his hand, and the heat went out of it.

He could hardly stand upright—but already the fibres were drifting away from his face, floating down. Without its controlling centre, the whole woolly mass had collapsed and deflated. Ferren hung on until the air cleared around him, then sucked in a great refreshing draught.

Soon he stood in the middle of a wide, brown carpet of fallen, woolly fibres. Angels all around gaped in disbelief. Five feet away, he saw the lumpish shape of his flamethrower under the fibres on the ground. He collected his weapon and headed for the angel who'd tried to warn him.

14

"You see? This is what keeps the things alive. You have to find this and destroy it."

Ferren showed the female angel the broken inscription in his hand, then let the pieces fall to the ground. He had the impression she was already recovering spiritual energy; certainly, the maroon colour was coming back into her robes.

"The cipher for a cipherdog," she murmured.

"You'll find it right in the middle, about this far off the ground." He demonstrated the height at which the inscription had hung suspended. "You have to tell all the other angels how to destroy the things."

"If we can keep up our spiritual energy long enough." She seemed uncertain. "Won't you…?"

"No, I have to get back to my friends now. Can you stand?"

The angel made a great effort and rose shakily to her feet.

"I feel the energy coming back," she told Ferren. She turned to the other angels lying on the ground and addressed them in what was meant as a cry but came out as a croak. "Energy coming back! You can stand too!"

"Nah!" A harsh laugh came from the opposite side of the cleared space. "Not after we get to you, you won't!"

A band of half a dozen Hypers stepped forward. The leader's black rubber suit was painted like an anatomy diagram with a white skeleton, grey muscle and red organs.

"Let's finish 'em off, lads!" he roared.

He advanced on the nearest angel, who was visibly sagging where he knelt. When the leader fired a long projectile into the victim's body, what little spiritual energy the angel had left shrank to a dot of radiance on his forehead. Then the radiance went out, accompanied by a single musical note like the breaking of a string. Wings and body vanished instantly into thin air, leaving only his robes, which dropped in a pile to the ground.

Ferren goggled to see for the first time how an angel died. He heard more beautiful, sad notes as Hypers turned their weapons on other weakened angels. The standing angels who formed a ring further back merely watched as if uninvolved.

"Do something!" Ferren appealed. "What's wrong with you? Stop them!"

The angels in the ring seemed to have lost the will to act. Ferren charged across the carpet of soft, brown fibres to confront the lead Hyper himself. He aimed his flamethrower in the same moment that the leader aimed his projectile weapon. But Ferren pulled his trigger first.

A long jet of fire shot out and enveloped the Hyper's head and shoulders. He staggered and dropped his weapon. As his black rubber suit went up in a flare of yellow flame, he turned into a kind of walking candle. Yet he *did* walk, advancing step by step upon Ferren. The black rubber dripped down like tar, and the honeycomb material of his body showed through under the suit. The flamethrower couldn't make him stop.

"Glahh-ugh-glahh!" He uttered a strange, inarticulate, bubbling sound—and Ferren saw that melted rubber had dripped down over his mouthslit. In the next moment, Ferren also saw that melted rubber from his eye-sockets had dripped down over his eyeslits. The Hyper was blinded!

Ferren stopped firing and started to back away. But the Hyper broke into a sudden, stumbling run, lost his balance and toppled towards Ferren with his arms stretched wide. One flailing arm caught Ferren on the chest and knocked him over, too.

As Ferren went down on his back, the Hyper fell crosswise on top of him. Again came that horrible, gurgling sound from the Hyper's mouthslit.

"Glahh-ugh-glahh!"

But Ferren saw his chance. The nozzle of the flamethrower was now so close to the mouthslit... He redirected the nozzle, thrust it through the melted rubber and pulled the trigger.

The jet of fire shot right down the Hyper's gullet. Flames escaped from the corners of his mouthslit and lit up behind his eyeslits. Cracks began to appear in the honeycomb material of his neck and chest, and spurts of black smoke issued from the cracks.

Ferren drew back the flamethrower, pushed the Hyper off him and rolled away just in time. There was a dull *whumpf!* as the body split apart, followed by an eruption of shimmering, rainbow vapour. Ferren's stomach turned at the sight of that vapour, which had been extracted from Residuals like himself. It billowed upwards and dissipated in the air, accompanied by a cloud of black smoke.

He scrambled up on his hands and knees. "Attack them all!" he yelled to the ring of standing angels. "You have the numbers! Attack!"

And this time, the angels acted. As they advanced upon the murdering band, the remaining Hypers decided that the numbers *were* against them, and began a hasty retreat.

Ferren rose to his feet and called across to the female angel who now knew the secret of the cipherdogs. "You have to destroy the rest of those dog-things! Show the other angels how to do it! The cipher in the middle of them!"

The angel nodded uncertainly. Ferren could only hope she'd follow through—he had no more time to spare. He was desperate to get back to Kiet and the others, especially Kiet. He set off running back in the direction he'd come.

The battlefield had become a chaos, with companies of angels rushing this way and that. Perhaps some were rushing to fight against Humen troops that had broken through the front lines, but he suspected that many were simply rushing away. Compared to the eagerness for battle that had shone in their eyes before, now dismay and despair showed openly on every face.

He saw other bands of Hypers too, like the ones who'd been killing the weakened angels. Heaven's forces had been infiltrated by intruders in many places, and there were skirmishes going on everywhere. He kept well away from trouble as he made his way back.

He knew approximately where he was heading, but he needed a glimpse of Marioch's chariot to give him the exact location. And at last he caught sight of it, a glint of bright gold on the other side of a company of marching angels. He pushed through between them, dodging spears and breastplates, and came out into a relative clearing.

Nobody stood near the chariot at all: not Marioch or his trumpeters or flag-bearers, not Miriael or any of the young Nesters, People and representatives. In vain, he scanned around for Kiet's distinctive dark red hair.

And then he spotted a patch of dark red on the ground beside one of the chariot wheels. It was, it had to be, the colour of her hair! And that had to be Kiet herself lying half under the chariot! But why face down? And why so motionless? Surely she couldn't be...

A terrible premonition seized him, and he ran forward in a panic.

15

Zonda and the other Residuals had fought their way forward against the enemy front line. They had the advantage of surprise; the Humen weren't expecting to be attacked with their own spike-guns, tracer-guns and flamethrowers. The spike-guns wielded by Zonda, Gibby, Floy and Tadge were especially effective.

It was Rhinn who shouted a warning. "Hey, where are all the angels? We're on our own!"

"Who cares?" cried Zonda, taking aim at another Hyper. "We're winning!"

Bross, fighting beside her, took a look around. "No, she's right. We're in trouble if we get cut off."

Zonda lowered her spike-gun and looked round too. The angels, including Marioch's trumpeters and flag-bearers, were fifty paces further back.

She snorted with frustration. In the absence of Ferren and Miriael, she'd become the accepted leader—which she considered her natural right anyway. But she listened to Bross.

"All right! Fall back, everyone!" she shouted, and signalled with her arm. "Move it, squirt," she told Tadge, who was still trying to advance.

They retreated as a tight-knit band, with Gibby and Ethany covering the retreat from the rear. The Hyper jeered, but stayed at a wary distance.

By now, the angels' front line had grown very ragged and irregular. Zonda headed straight for Marioch, who stood surrounded by his trumpeters and flag-bearers.

"Why didn't you keep up with us?" she demanded. "We were driving them back. You weren't even trying."

Marioch assumed a haughty expression. "I have the whole front line to think about. If they're not all moving forward, any local advance can become a vulnerability." The haughtiness fell away. "And they're not moving forward. They've already been breached in too many places."

Zonda scoffed. "Just follow us! We'll show you how to do it!"

Then her attention was caught by something approaching: a spherical shape twenty feet in diameter. Angels stepped swiftly out of the way as it bowled towards the Humen front line. It was one of the giant, facetted crystals that Miriael had called Stones of Wrath.

"*Yes!*" Zonda whirled back to Marioch. "*It's* moving forward! We can go with it!"

"The prayers of the Great Patriarchs control the Stones," he answered uncomfortably. "I don't know what it'll do."

"*That!*" cried Zonda, as the Stone accelerated into the Humen front line, rolling over Hypers and crushing them. "This is our chance! Come on!" She turned from Marioch and appealed to all the angels nearby. "Follow us! Follow the Stone!"

She set off running, and the Residuals ran after her. They ran to the spot where the Stone had bowled into the enemy front line. Dull detonations and eruptions of shimmering, multi-coloured vapour marked its progress over the crushed bodies of Hypers. Zonda didn't look back, but she hoped some of the angels were following.

Flames, flares, darts and projectiles from the Hypers' weapons had no impact upon the Stone. These particular Hypers bore shields of mirror-glass to deflect discharging light from the angels' spears, but nothing could deflect the simple weight of the giant crystal. It left in its wake only flat patches of rubber and pulverized honeycomb.

Following the path of the Stone, the Residuals fired short bursts from their weapons at the Hypers who'd managed to fall back on either side. But, hurrying to catch up, they had no time to take proper aim. The Hypers showed their teeth while staying back out of harm's way.

"Whoo-hooo for the Stone!" cried Tadge. "It's unstoppable!"

He spoke too soon. A black, rubber-suited figure came leaping forward, flourishing a gauntlet on her right hand. Taller than an ordinary Hyper, lithe and agile as a cat, features created by red lipstick and white paint—it was a Queen-Hyper.

She paused six feet away from the rolling crystal and swung the hand that wore the gauntlet in a mighty downward stroke. There was no contact— yet four long cuts appeared as if by magic in the crystalline surface.

"How did she do that?" gasped Bross.

The Stone lost momentum and juddered to a halt. The Queen-Hyper strode closer, almost purring with satisfaction. In the next moment, there was a cracking, shattering sound, and the surface between the cuts caved in. The Queen-Hyper positioned herself before the gaping hole, made an upwards spring and dived inside.

16

*N*o-o-o-o-o-o!
A silent scream filled Ferren's mind as he flew forward. He was hardly aware of covering the thirty yards to Kiet's motionless body, hardly aware of flinging himself to the ground beside her. Only her head and shoulders stuck out from under the chariot. Her face was pressed into the ground, and her hair fell over her eyes. He brushed her hair aside—and her eyes were still open.

"Kiet?"

She rolled over a little to look up into *his* eyes. "I was pretending to be dead," she told him. "It's the safest way to be. There were Hypers passing by a minute ago."

He laughed hysterically. His relief was so intense it doubled him up like a pain in his chest. The world swam around him in a blur.

I thought you were really dead," he brought out at last. "I thought it was all over."

"All over?"

"Everything. For me. Without you."

"I was only pretending. You look as white as a ghost."

"I feel…I feel like my heart just stopped. And now it's going crazy."

A frown creased her forehead, and she touched her fingers to his chest. "It's hammering so fast. Slow down. Slow down."

He grinned a foolish, radiant grin and sank to the ground beside her. "I'll be all right now. Better than all right." He felt as though nothing could ever be bad again.

"I'm keeping guard for Miriael," she explained. "She's having a visionary dream. She's asleep under there."

Her gesture directed him to look behind her, underneath the chariot. Stretched out on her back between the wheels lay the angel Miriael. The idea of sleeping in the middle of a battlefield only made him grin some more. Everything was so good…

"It was Peeper's plan," she went on. "Miriael has to talk to the great archangels, and they have to make a promise." She paused. "You're not listening, are you?"

"Not really, no," he agreed. He was inhaling the scent of her hair, which was every bit as good as he remembered it.

"You should hide in under the chariot yourself. You're too visible out here."

"Sorry," he said—meaning sorry for being too visible, sorry for not listening and sorry for inhaling the scent of her hair.

He moved in under the chariot, keeping away from Miriael so as not to disturb her sleep. Kiet remained on guard with her head and shoulders sticking out. His flamethrower lay close beside her, where he'd dropped it in his moment of fear. He watched her…

A minute later, she looked back at him. Then she whispered to Peeper, unhooked the zither from around her neck and propped it up against a wheel of the chariot. She collected his flamethrower along with her tracer-gun and wriggled in under the chariot to join him.

"I'm leaving Peeper on guard," she whispered. "He'll sing out if he sees any Humen come too near."

Ferren waited and wondered.

"You really thought your heart had stopped before?" she asked.

"It was the worst moment of my life. If you'd been dead…"

She was lying very close, mere inches away. She reached up and touched her fingers for the second time to his chest.

"Normal heartbeat now," she told him. "Maybe speeding up just a bit."

She left her hand in place, and they were silent for a while.

"How long before Miriael wakes up?" he murmured.

"I don't know."

"I think—"

"No."

"No what?"

"Don't think."

All at once, her arms wrapped around him. Her eyes were half shut, and his eyelids somehow closed of their own accord. He felt the touch of her lips as her mouth opened to him. In the next moment, he gave himself up to the sensation of their very first kiss.

So soft and sweet and delicious… The world outside ceased to exist. He didn't hear the ongoing roar of battle, the marching feet, the Hypers yelling, the musical notes of angels dying. Nor did he hear the amplified Doctor's voice blaring forth: *"Abandon hope, you forces of Heaven! Your rule is ended! Your realm belongs to Asmodai and the Humen!"*

There was only the experience of their very first kiss.

17

Zonda and the other Residuals were all in place around the Stone of Wrath, waiting for the Queen-Hyper to re-emerge. From within came vicious noises of spitting, hissing and snarling. A milky opacity now blanked out many of the crystal's facetted surfaces.

Marioch and a score of angels were also waiting, fifty yards away. They had followed as far as the gap carved by the Stone in the Humen front line. The Hypers of the front line waited too, observing angels and Residuals and Stone. For the time being, they were content to observe without acting.

Suddenly, a flurry of wings burst from the hole in the Stone with a frantic fluttering. They were a dazzling white, yet also somehow ragged and broken. They flew off erratically as though half stunned.

"Fall back while you have the chance!" Marioch called out to the

Residuals. "Come back and join us. We need your fighting skills!"

Zonda grinned: it was a major concession. She turned and waved. "Queen-Hyper first, then we join."

In the next moment, the Queen-Hyper herself burst forth. She leaped up out of the hole in the crystal, poised on top of the Stone and screeched in triumph. Zonda pulled the trigger of her spike-gun.

The projectile shot straight for the spot where the Queen-Hyper stood, but it was too slow to hit her. The cat-like creature saw it coming, swayed out of the way, then launched through the air straight at Zonda.

Before she knew what was happening, Zonda found herself flat on her back with the Queen-Hyper's boot on her chest. Glittering eyeslits looked down at her, a cruel smile appeared on the red, painted mouthslit. The Queen-Hyper gloated for a moment before killing her victim.

Then strong arms wrapped round her neck and shoulders and pulled her off-balance. Bross had jumped onto her from behind. He was trying to wrestle with her, but he had no chance against her unnatural vitality. In one fluid movement, she whirled, broke his hold and flung him to the ground ten feet away.

In her next movement, she sprang after him, raised her right arm with the gauntlet and prepared to slice him as she had sliced the Stone of Wrath.

Zonda rolled over, desperate to jump to her feet. But instead she caught sight of something on the ground close by, something shiny like a fine, silvery wire. She did the first thing that came into her head—threw herself onto it and clamped it between her teeth.

There was a sudden violent jerk that almost pulled her teeth out of her head and her head off her neck. The Queen-Hyper had tried to swing her gauntlet, but the wire had halted the swing before it began. A taut line of silver, almost invisible, stretched through the air between Zonda's mouth and one fingertip of the gauntlet.

The Queen-Hyper looked round with a hiss. Whether or not she understood what had happened, she saw Zonda on the ground and drew back her arm with a short, sharp jerk. Zonda felt the wire slide between her teeth and clenched down tighter. She nearly cried out as her head was wrenched to the side. But the wire stopped moving—and it was the gauntlet that slipped suddenly right off the Queen-Hyper's hand.

The Queen-Hyper stared from the gauntlet to her hand and back again. So did the Residuals. The secret of the slicing strokes was now plain: thin wires like whips extended from every fingertip of the gauntlet.

The Residuals acted one second before the Queen-Hyper. By the time she stepped forward to retrieve her gantlet, they had formed a ring around it. Confronted by a barrier of raised weapons, she paused.

A rictus of savage frustration passed across her painted features. Then she spun on her heel and stalked off. The Residuals brandished their fists and flourished their weapons. A victorious *Hallelujah!* rang out from the angels around Marioch. The Hypers hung back, temporarily demoralised.

Floy helped Zonda to her feet, and Zonda went over to do the same for Bross. He was winded but uninjured. Then Marioch and his angels rushed up and gathered round. They shook their heads in wonder when Zonda displayed the gauntlet with its trailing, silver wires.

"You defeated her," murmured Marioch. "You really defeated her."

Zonda laughed. "Are *you* joining *us* now?"

"Yes! Yes, we are!" Marioch turned to address his followers. "These Residuals show us the way! We dishonour ourselves when we let them do our fighting for us! We must aspire to equal them in spirit and courage! Win or lose, we fight on to the final end! If Heaven goes down, we go down with honour!"

Zonda shook her head. "I'm not planning to lose," she said firmly.

She surveyed the battlefield, and her eyes lit on the Rock of the Tabernacle with its raised deck and white-coated Doctors. "That's their command centre, isn't it? Let's try and take that!"

With a great cheer, Residuals and angels turned their faces in the direction of the crag called the Rock of the Tabernacle.

18

Miriael awoke and opened her eyes.

I did it, she thought to herself. If only the rest of Peeper's idea could work out as smoothly...

She looked up at the underside of Marioch's golden chariot and remembered she'd fallen asleep in the middle of the great battle on the First Altitude. She rolled over and felt the metal of some Humen weapon digging into her hip. Kiet was lying nearby, and someone else next to her. It was Ferren, she realised, who must have returned from wherever he'd gone...

"Success!" she announced. "I have the agreement of the great arch-angels!"

Kiet and Ferren turned to face her. By the look in their eyes, they'd only just woken up too. Kiet struggled to focus, absorbed what she'd just heard and grinned with delight.

"Wait a minute," she said, and slid out backwards from under the chariot.

Ferren still appeared dazed, Miriael noted, and seemed mystified about what was going on. Perhaps Kiet hadn't got around to explaining the plan.

A moment later, Kiet came back with Peeper on his zither. "He already heard you say," she told Miriael, and the Morph uttered a high fluting sound like the song of a bird.

Miriael turned to the snowflake-like pattern of lines on the zither that her angelic sight alone could see. "Yes, you have their promise, Peeper. I spoke to Uriel and Gabriel, and they promised on behalf of Michael and Rafael as well. So it's up to you now."

Kiet bent over Peeper on his zither and crooned to him softly. "You're so very, very brave, little one. I never knew how brave. Aren't you scared at all?"

"No-o-o-o!" piped the Morph. "Ye-e-e-es! But I'll do it anywa-a-ay!"

Kiet looped the cord of the zither over her neck again, and they all came out from under the chariot. Miriael could tell at a glance that the fighting overall had gone badly for Heaven. Even here, far behind what had been the battlefront, there were skirmishes going on between Hypers and angels, while one armoured mechanical monster ploughed forward a mere fifty yards away. But the monster passed on, and none of the Hypers were looking in their direction.

Kiet sucked in her lips, looked out in all directions and frowned. "How do we find Asmodai?" she asked Miriael. "We need to get close."

Miriael smiled. "Yes, very close. And it's a big battlefield. You and

Peeper didn't foresee that problem?"

"No." Kiet's frown deepened. "Maybe we could climb up on the chariot again?"

"There's a better way. I thought about needing to get close and I believe I have the answer."

"What?"

"I can call for Asmodai to come."

"*What?*"

"There's a connection between us. He implanted it in me when…one time when he was visiting me. I used to be able to summon him then, so with luck I'll be able to summon him now."

Kiet nodded thoughtfully. "And he'll come because he's been searching for you for weeks."

"I suspect he wants to talk to me." Miriael felt strangely elated at the prospect. "Which will keep him quiet while you carry out Peeper's plan. But you and Ferren will need to watch over me until he comes. I need to close my eyes to concentrate."

She glanced round for a suitable spot and decided to sit with her back against the chariot wheel. She arranged herself comfortably on the ground, while Kiet with her tracer-gun and Ferren with his flamethrower stood guard on either side. Then she closed her eyes, formed a mental picture of Asmodai and began to recite the call-phrase under her breath.

"*Veni Asmodai, veni ad me.*"

There were sounds of battle all around, but she shut them out of her mind. Harder and harder she concentrated on every detail of those beautiful features with which she'd once fallen in love. She redoubled the intensity of her appeal until she was almost begging.

"*Veni Asmodai, veni ad me.*
Veni Asmodai, veni ad me."

19

Minute after minute went by, and Ferren was growing more uneasy. While Miriael sat murmuring under her breath with her eyes closed, Hypers in the distance were starting to pay attention. They hadn't attacked yet, but he saw them turn and call out to one another.

Then came a swishing, hissing sound. As it approached, he heard mingled cries and screams, and the plangent notes of angels expiring. The wing was hugging the contours of the ground, so close that it only appeared at the last moment. Its leading edge was a hundred yards wide and scythed through angels and Hypers alike. Asmodai seemed to care as little about the one as the other

Ferren was about to fling himself flat when the nose of the delta lifted slightly. It passed just over their heads, and the temperature of the air dropped suddenly under its shadow. The point came to a stop behind them, hovering inches above the chariot. Asmodai's bulging glass bubble was a mere ten feet in front of them.

Ferren ducked his head and stayed upright on his feet, as did Kiet. It wasn't the first time he'd seen Asmodai inside his bubble, but never so near as this. Close up, the black-robed angel's beauty was breathtaking. Ferren studied his noble brow, his perfect, half-smiling lips, the solemn depths of his eyes and his hair floating in the light that streamed out round his head. Although Ferren hated him, he was awestruck, too. But both Residuals might have been lumps of wood for all the attention Asmodai gave them. He had come for Miriael.

"I am here," he said. "You may open your eyes."

Ferren seemed to hear the voice deep inside his eardrums, calm and sweet and melodious. Asmodai gazed down upon Miriael and intensified his radiance, spreading a pool of soft, golden light over her.

"Look up now, Miriael," he said.

Still leaning back against the chariot wheel, Miriael appeared reluctant to open her eyes. But eventually she did. She looked up at Asmodai with a strange expression that Ferren couldn't interpret at all.

"You came," she said quietly.

They really do have a connection between them, Ferren thought with a grimace.

Then he noticed that Kiet was no longer standing on Miriael's other side. Where had she gone? Was it something to do with this plan that she and Miriael kept talking about?

He wanted to follow, but he couldn't cut across in front of Miriael while she gazed at Asmodai and Asmodai gazed at her. Instead, he slipped off to the side and circled all the way round behind the back of the chariot.

His roundabout route took him out from under the wing, and he was still in the open as he came past the end of the chariot. He found himself looking at the leading edge of the vast delta as it angled diagonally back from point to tail. And there stood Kiet out in the open, halfway back.

He watched as she unlooped the zither from her neck and spoke a few words to Peeper. Then she suddenly ran right up to the leading edge, drew back her arm and flung the zither up on top of the wing. Ferren saw it sail through the air, but couldn't see where it landed.

What a strange thing to do! He would have liked to shout out and question her, but he didn't want anyone else to hear, and Kiet didn't look as though she had any attention to spare. She was now backing off for a better view of the top of the wing.

Ferren did the same. At twenty paces' distance, the wing's upper surface showed itself as a glittering white, very different to the dark grey of the underside. Tiny projections stuck up all over it like miniature fins. At thirty paces' distance, he spotted the zither not far from the centre of the delta. So far as he could see, it was just lying there, caught on the fins.

He waited—and Kiet seemed to be waiting too. He couldn't tell exactly where she was looking, but he knew the Morphs were as invisible to her as to him. Nonetheless, she seemed very, very intent.

For a long time, nothing happened. His thoughts drifted across to Miriael and Asmodai. What was going on between them now?

He crouched low and looked back under the endless expanse of dark, smooth metal that was the underside of the wing. Fifty yards away, Miriael still sat against the wheel of the chariot, looking up towards the bulging shape of the glass bubble. Ferren couldn't tell who was speaking, but they were both still in conversation.

Then Miriael rose from her sitting position, shuffled closer to the bubble—and dropped to her knees. It was as if she were worshipping him!

Ferren was horrified. He forgot about Kiet and the zither, and ran to investigate Miriael and Asmodai. He didn't need a roundabout route this time; if he came in under the wing, he could approach the glass bubble from behind, and Asmodai would never see him.

Even before coming close, he heard the tone of Asmodai's voice, very sweet and very cold. "No, don't bow your head. I prefer to see you looking at me. My poor little Miriael, so helplessly in love."

Miriael raised her head and looked at him. In fact, she seemed to be devouring his face with her eyes, as though she could never get enough of him.

"I'm pleased you've stopped fighting the feeling," the voice continued. "Of course, you had to call for me in the end. There was nothing to do but surrender to it, was there? And soon you'll be able to love me better than ever before."

Asmodai laughed and swirled his black robes. Miriael continued to gaze up at him without a word—and the look in her eyes suggested utter adoration. Ferren shook his head at her, trying to make her stop, trying to snap her out of the enchantment. But she showed not a flicker of awareness that he was there.

"Ah, do you remember how you loved me as a lowly Angel of Strategy when I came down to visit you? How much more you'll have to love me as Heaven's glorious new ruler! I look forward to finding out what your love will drive you to do. How far will you go, I wonder. Will you enjoy finding out too?"

Miriael answered in so low a voice that Ferren had to strain to hear. "Yes," she said.

Again that laugh, setting Ferren's teeth on edge. "Even the most abject acts of devotion?"

"Yes."

Ferren couldn't see Asmodai's face from behind, only his black robes, white wings and radiant hair, but he could imagine the cold, superior expression on his beautiful features. He felt sick to the stomach.

He was so focused on the shameful scene that he didn't hear Kiet coming up behind him. Only when she began waving her arms did he become aware of her presence. He spun round.

"What is it?"

But Kiet only waved her arms all the more furiously. She was signalling to Miriael.

Ferren turned and saw that Miriael was rising to her feet.

20

When Miriael saw Kiet's signal, it was a relief to put her self-discovery into action. Though she had wondered beforehand how she might react to Asmodai face to face, she was very sure of her feelings now. Hearing him talk on and on... He imagined he was telling her about herself, but in every word it was himself he was telling her about.

"Well, I'm glad that's over." She sighed and clicked her tongue. "It was becoming hard to listen to."

His beautiful eyes had widened at the sight of her standing upright. "I didn't say you could stop kneeling."

"No," she agreed. "You're a victim of your own vanity, Asmodai. I've been keeping you talking to distract your attention, that's all."

Still he didn't understand. He glared and spoke in a tone of absolute command. "Kneel to me. *Kneel.*"

"I don't think so. You don't have that power anymore. You lost it when you traded me off to the Humen."

His brows descended in an angry frown. Now he understood, though he couldn't adjust.

"I've been pretending love to you as you pretended love to me," she went on. "For someone so good at deception, you're amazingly easy to deceive, Asmodai. You see what you want to believe. That's your vanity, I suppose."

He leaned forward in the bubble, put his hands flat against the glass and directed the full force of his will on her. She observed with a strange kind of detachment.

I would have done anything for you once, she thought. *When I was new to these part-mortal feelings, then you were my first love. But now...*

It had been so wonderful and exciting to be taken over by that urge to give herself completely and drown in love! But, in truth, Asmodai could never have never matched the size of her feelings for him, not even if he'd been all that he pretended to be. She hadn't understood at the time, but she'd grown more accustomed to her new self since. There were better and more honest forms of love…

Still he was striving to bend her to his will, pressing his face against the glass.

"It's no use, you know," she told him. "You can't make someone love you when there's nothing there."

"*Kneel!*"

Miriael shrugged. "I think you have more need of me than I ever had of you. Your vanity demands a mirror, and you're missing your favourite mirror. That's why you kept searching for me for so long, that's why you were so quick to come when I called in the middle of a battle. It never really made sense, but now it does. I see you at the size you are, Asmodai. Ridiculous, petty vanity, ridiculous craving for adoration. Even if you were able to conquer Heaven, I could never admire you again."

"No? No?" An ugly, vicious expression had replaced the look of superiority on his face. "Then see my power!"

He drew back deeper inside his bubble, and in the next moment the flying wing drew back too. Slowly reversing, it slid away yard by yard. The point passed over Miriael's head, uncovering the sky of the First Altitude. Then the delta changed from moving backwards to moving downwards. It stopped when the leading edge was level with Miriael's neck.

Looking at the edge from a few feet away, Miriael saw a million tiny serrations like metal teeth. She remembered how the wing had scythed through whole battalions of angels while she and Kiet watched from up on the chariot.

"Now! *On your knees!*"

Clearly, the only way to avoid being cut in two was to kneel. Yet somehow she felt inexplicably lighthearted. Nothing he did could change the fact that she'd defeated him. She straightened to stand at her fullest height.

Her lightheartedness persisted even when the teeth came suddenly to life. Like a million tiny scissors, they began moving back and forth, crisscrossing over one another.

"This is power!" Asmodai's melodious voice had sharpened to a sound like a Hyper's rasp. "I can destroy you in the blink of an eye!"

"Then destroy me," answered Miriael.

Inch by inch, the wing came forward. The tiny teeth made a snick-snick-snick sound as they crossed and uncrossed. Miriael stared at them and felt oddly unconcerned.

Two feet away, the teeth stopped scissoring and the wing came to a standstill. Asmodai uttered an angry command, and the forward movement resumed. Then, one foot away, it halted again.

Miriael heard Kiet's voice shouting from somewhere under the wing. "They're doing it, Miriael! Resisting and rebelling!"

"*Procedite! Servite mihi! Procedite! Servite mihi!*" Asmodai thundered his orders in Latin. The only effect was a grinding of metal deep within the wing.

Resisting and rebelling, thought Miriael. *Just in time.*

21

Ferren turned to Kiet. "It's the Morphs, isn't it?"

"Right." She grinned. "Fighting against Asmodai's control. Peeper persuaded them."

Ferren and Kiet had dropped down on all fours when the wing descended lower to the ground. The underside had stopped just two feet above them. Now they could hear strange grating and grinding sounds through the metal.

"That's what you were signalling to Miriael!" Ferren had to shout above the noise.

"Yes, after Peeper signalled to me! Four loud peeps meant—"

Asmodai's furious voice rose above all other sounds. "*Procedite!* Go forward! Forward! *Procedite!*"

The gratings and grindings intensified. A titanic struggle was going on as the Morphs fought to escape Asmodai's will and Asmodai fought to reimpose it.

"*Procedite! Dominus sum!* I am your master! Obey or suffer!"

The Morphs *were* suffering, and Ferren winced in sympathy with their pain. They were shrilling and shrieking now—yet still they didn't go forward. Instead, the nose of the vast delta began to lift up off the ground. Asmodai uttered a terrible, blasphemous curse.

The very air seemed to vibrate with the willpower involved. Slowly, slowly, the nose of the delta continued to rear higher, while the tail remained almost touching the ground. Asmodai's glass bubble came clearly into view, and the black-robed angel inside it. His limbs were straining and rigid, his head thrown back, his fingers outstretched.

"*Descendite! Descendite!* Go down!" he shrieked.

Ferren glanced across and saw that Miriael was still upright beside the chariot. Then Kiet tugged at his arm.

"Come on! Get away!"

She jumped to her feet and ran, and Ferren followed. They ended up not far from the spot where he'd previously viewed the zither on top of the wing. When they stopped to turn and look now, the wing was in a very different condition.

It had risen to stand almost vertical on its tail like a monstrous triangular sail. The once-smooth surface of its metal underside had been everywhere deformed by wave-like corrugations. Asmodai's bubble was a hundred feet above the ground, while the point of the delta seemed as if brushing the sky of the First Altitude. Some remnants of coldfire that were still washing across parted and dissolved around it.

Then Asmodai put forth all his power in a supreme act of will. Ribbons of electricity fanned out from his limbs across the underside of the delta, while the point moved back and forth as if caught in some mighty tug of war. There were sounds of tortured metal, sounds of Morphs wailing in agony. The great wing shook and shuddered, and several plates and panels twisted right off and rained down out of the sky.

Little by little, the nose began to tilt forward. Asmodai let out a screech of triumph.

"He's winning!" groaned Kiet.

Once the movement had begun, it became unstoppable. Lower and lower the nose descended, swinging the delta back down. Ferren stared up as it came rushing towards them, half hypnotised by its gathering speed.

Once more Kiet tugged on Ferren's arm. "Further!" she cried

They sprinted further away. They hadn't gone far when the wing came down behind them. They felt the wind of its fall and heard the thump as it met the ground. Both staggered and fell, then immediately jumped back up.

The wing lay on the ground not quite in its original position, but a bit further forward. Ferren looked for Miriael, but couldn't see her. The wing now covered the place where she'd been standing beside the chariot. Had she been caught and crushed?

"Oh!" gasped Kiet.

Her eyes weren't looking out over the wing, but up to the sky. Ferren looked up too, and saw that Michael, Gabriel, Raphael and Uriel had appeared. Radiant and majestic, they descended between the remnants of coldfire.

A strange hush spread across the battlefield below. They hovered high above the wing, and their voices rang out beautiful, deep and sonorous.

"All praise to you!" said Michael.

"You have done wonders," said Gabriel.

"Success is within your grasp," said Raphael.

"One last effort will do it," said Uriel.

A howl of rage came from Asmodai beneath the wing. But it wasn't him they were addressing.

They're encouraging the Morphs, thought Ferren. *The Morphs aren't beaten yet.*

"Remember our promise," said Michael.

"We look forward to keeping it," said Gabriel.

"Complete the task," said Rafael.

Uriel raised an arm. "And take the betrayer out of Heaven!"

Inch by inch, the wing began to lift up from the ground. The corrugations had become deep troughs and ridges, and there were visible gaps in the wing where the frame showed through.

"*Manete! Nolite movere!* Stay down!" shrieked Asmodai.

Still the wing continued to rise. It wasn't rising from the nose alone this time, but nose and tail together. The screech of metal and the screech of Asmodai's commands were deafening. Ferren sensed more than heard the words that Kiet was growling between gritted teeth.

"They *can*, they *can*, they *can*, they *can do it!*"

She believed it, and he believed it with her. He was even more elated when he caught sight of Miriael crouching beside the chariot. Although the top of the chariot had been crushed down to the level of its wheels, enough had survived to keep the underside of the wing from crushing her.

He joined in Kiet's chant. "They *can*, they *can*, they *can*, they *can do it!*"

Still horizontal, the delta rose higher and higher into the air. The four great archangels had moved aside to let it pass. Like everyone on the battlefield below, they were watching Asmodai in his bubble. He seemed to be writhing as he continued to shriek commands.

"*Oboedite!* Obey! *Descendite!*"

Finally, the wing came to a stop, high up against the roof of the First Altitude. Then its nose tilted down. It was the movement Asmodai had been commanding, and he gloried in his victory.

"Yes! I am the master! *Dominus sum!*"

The tilt steepened to an angle of 45 degrees—and the wing shot forward. Asmodai's cry of victory turned to a scream of despair. Faster and faster, gathering momentum, the great delta went down in a one-way dive. Ferren caught a momentary glimpse of Asmodai doubled up with his arms over his face.

Nose-first, the wing plunged into the floor of the First Altitude. The point pierced through, the whole vast delta crashed through after it. For a moment, everything shook and blurred, followed by a shock-wave of sound.

Ferren found himself suddenly sitting on the ground, with Kiet beside him.

"That's it!" she cried, and clapped her hands. "They've taken him right out of Heaven!"

22

Zonda and the other Residuals were tossed in the air and flung to the ground. They'd watched Asmodai's flying wing rise once and descend, rise a second time, then hurtle down out of control. But they weren't ready for an earthquake as the ground leaped under their feet. There was a stunned silence as the reverberations died away.

One by one, they scrambled to their feet and looked around. They had fought their way nearly to the base of the Rock of the Tabernacle, but had been finally brought to a standstill. Marioch and his angels were close behind them; ahead stood a row of huge black boxes. The fighting that had paused while everyone watched Asmodai crash out of Heaven was now ready to resume.

Except it wasn't… Zonda and the Residuals swung to face the Rock and raised their weapons for another charge. After what they'd just seen, they felt sure of victory. The Hypers, though, were no longer so eager to defend the Rock. When they rose to their feet, their body language expressed resentment rather than aggression. Instead of raising their weapons, they began talking among themselves.

"Organise and defend! Protect your Doctors!"

The voice boomed out from the row of black boxes: amplified, yet somehow tinny and almost hysterical. One of the Doctors on the deck above was bent over the arm of his wheelchair, addressing the troops. The deck itself had developed a tilt under the shaking of the quake, and all the Doctors' wheelchairs had rolled higgledy-piggledy down one end.

In any case, the troops weren't interested. They grimaced and kept talking. Then some of them began walking.

"Cowards!" yelled Stogget. "Where you going? Stop and fight!"

He moved to cut off their route, but they detoured to avoid him.

"Nah, we don't wanna fight you," said one.

"We're sick of this," said another. "We're leaving."

"Yeah, same as our big leader just did."

"Him and his big ideas! Invading Heaven!"

"We're off out of it. Back down to Earth."

Zonda and Bross stepped up alongside Stogget, as more and more Hypers joined the stream of those leaving.

"We could cut them off," Stogget suggested, flexing his brawny wrestler's arms.

"Why bother?" said Bross.

Zonda agreed. "They're all heading to the top of the tower," she said, and pointed over the heads of the retreating Hypers. "Back where we came up."

"Protect your Doctors! Protect your Doctors!"

There was more than one amplified voice now, and they were pleading as much as commanding. But the sound cut off suddenly when a Hyper walking past the black boxes pulled out a wire and broke the connection.

A moment later, Marioch strode forward to join the Residuals. His mouth wasn't smiling, but joy and amazement shone forth from every part of his face.

"It's the same all over the battlefield," he told them. "The Humen have lost hope. Abandoning their weapons, giving up, running away. We've won."

Zonda clapped Bross on the shoulder. "We did it!"

Bross laughed. "Not us! I bet Ferren and Kiet and Miriael did it!"

Now Marioch smiled with his mouth. "All of you! You Residuals saved Heaven for us."

Then the other young Nesters and representatives added themselves to the conversation.

"What now?" asked Ethany. "The fighting's over."

"Yeah, nothing left for us to do," Flens agreed.

"I want to see the hole!" cried Tadge at the top of his voice.

Everyone looked at him. "What hole?"

"Where the wing crashed out!"

They all turned to gaze in the direction where Asmodai's wing had plunged into the floor of the First Altitude.

"Yeah, I suppose it must've made a hole," said Zonda.

"A great big hole!" Tadge insisted.

"Let's go and see," said Bross.

23

"Ah, here come some more of our heroes!" Uriel announced. He had been talking with Miriael, while Ferren and Kiet had been peering down through the hole opened up in the ether by the plummeting delta. Ferren heard the announcement, backed away from the edge and looked over his shoulder. Hands were waving furiously for attention behind the many angels who had gathered around the hole.

"I think it's Zonda and the others," he told Kiet.

Uriel raised his voice. "Let them come forward! Make way and do them honour, you soldiers of Heaven!"

The angels stepped back respectfully and cleared a path to the edge of the hole. Reverential gestures conveyed their deep gratitude as Zonda and Bross led the fighting team forward. By the time Zonda reached Ferren and Kiet, she was laughing and swaggering.

"We came to see where he crashed out," said Bross. "Did you do it?"

Ferren pointed to Kiet. "She did. With Miriael."

Kiet shook her head and grinned. "No. It was Peeper, really."

"Whew!" Tadge had pushed forward far enough to see the size of the hole. "Look at that!"

The hole was a hundred yards wide. Angels circled the jagged edge all around, and below the edge were sheer sides of crystalline ether going down.

"I want to see down below!" Tadge protested, as Rhinn's grip held him back.

"Not safe," she warned, and maintained her grip.

"No, it's safer on all fours," Ferren told them all. "Then you won't lose your balance if you get giddy."

Everyone dropped down on their hands and knees, and shuffled forward to the hole. When they stuck their head out over the edge, they gasped and gulped.

"It's all right," said Kiet. "If you get giddy, just look level for a while. Take slow breaths, and it'll pass."

The Earth was far, far below, in colours of green and brown. There was a cool breeze blowing, driving small, white clouds that cast slowly moving shadows over the map-like landscape. Away to their right was a shoreline edged by the greeny-blue of the sea. It was like hanging suspended from an infinite height above the world.

Several Residuals retreated until they were barely peeking over the edge. Others began pointing and calling out. They recognised the dark green of forests and the lighter green of grasslands, traced the winding course of rivers and the straighter routes of overbridges. Ferren looked down with the rest.

"See that dark spot there?" he said. "That's the crater where Asmodai hit the ground. It looks tiny from here, but it's huge, really. And he's at the bottom of it."

"Is he dead then?" asked Floy.

It was Miriael who answered. Like all the angels around the hole, she remained standing without giddiness. "Not according to Uriel," she said. "A spiritual being like Asmodai can't be killed by the impact of a fall. But his fate has been decided."

"What's that?" asked Dwinna, pointing to another sort of dark spot, close by the first.

"That's the Bankstown Camp," Miriael told her. "See the pillar of cloud going down to it?"

They studied the pillar of cloud. It looked like a mere thread far below, but expanded to a wide, grey funnel as it came up towards the floor of Heaven.

"It's changed," said Ethany

"There are things in it," said Rhinn.

Ferren explained. "It's been changing and drifting ever since we first started to watch. Blowing away in the wind. That's the frame of the tower beginning to show through."

"It's no longer under Asmodai's control, so it's behaving like natural cloud," Miriael completed the explanation.

Minute by minute, the great metal tubes that held up the tower came more clearly into view. Soon the wire cages of the twin shafts inside were also exposed.

"I can see platforms inside!" cried Ethany. "Coming up and going down!"

Gibby whistled. "And Hypers on the ones going down! Look at them trying to escape!"

Ferren could see, too. The platforms going down were laden with Hypers, bodies piled on top of one another as they struggled for a place. At this distance, they looked like masses of black, teeming ants.

"And now they're climbing down the frame!" Gibby whistled again.

In their desperation, Hypers unable to fit on the platforms were starting to clamber down the girders of the frame. Ferren shook his head in disbelief. Didn't they realize they'd be climbing for days?

At that moment, loud sounds of cracking and creaking came from the top of the tower. The great tubes appeared to be moving, and the metal was under some sort of strain. Hypers on the platforms and on the frame shrieked in alarm.

"What is it?" "What's happening?" The Residuals looked at one another.

"Maybe they've overloaded the tower," Ferren suggested. "Maybe it can't take the weight."

"No." Miriael had a huge, incredulous smile on her face. "That's your sister. That's Shanna who did it."

24

With more cracking and creaking sounds, the top of the tower broke away from the underside of Heaven. The great tubes were shrinking telescopically, sliding in on themselves. Girders and wire cages collapsed inside them as they retreated. The platforms had come to a halt; now only a few cables connected platforms and tower to the tunnel through the ether.

"Did you say *Shanna*?" Ferren swung to Miriael. "What did she do?"

"I never believed her. I was so sure her idea wouldn't work." Miriael herself seemed to be struggling to adjust. "She went off to try her own bit of sabotage, do you remember? And I blamed her for not staying to help us! I was so wrong."

A succession of sharp sounds rang out like a volley of shots. The cables had been stretched too far, and now, one by one, they snapped. The tower wobbled and swayed, the tubes continued to retract. Hypers who'd been clinging to the frame lost their hold and plummeted to their doom, screaming.

"It was when she saw the tubes were telescopic," Miriael went on. "She guessed there had to be Plasmatics inside to make them expand. That's how the Humen made the tower go up so quickly. Her idea was to give them the opposite instruction." She pointed and laughed. "So now they're contracting!"

Miriael had been explaining to Ferren, but others had been listening too—including Uriel. A frown now appeared on his stern, aquiline features.

"I still don't understand," he said.

Miriael turned to him. She didn't have his spiritual form of radiance, but she radiated delight.

"All right. You know about the Plasmatics that power all Humen machinery. And perhaps you know those Plasmatics are made from the living tissue of Residuals?"

"We didn't know, but we suspected," Uriel murmured.

"Well, Shanna as a Residual discovered a way to communicate with them and override Humen commands. She can do it by touch and tapping if she can open up the machinery..."

Ferren already understood this part of the explanation, and stopped listening. He focused again on the top of the tower, which had shrunk down several hundred feet below them. It swayed to the left, then to the right, as the tubes retracted at slightly different rates. The Hypers on the platforms screamed and screeched.

"It's going!" yelled Zonda at the top of her voice.

Somewhere lower down, the whole tower was starting to buckle. It slewed round counter-clockwise, tilted and seemed to sag. Then, in slow motion, it toppled to the side. The screams of the Hypers diminished as they were carried further and further away.

Everyone held their breath and watched in awe. For what seemed an eternity, there was no sound but the whisper of the wind. They saw the tower grow smaller and smaller...

"Yes!" Ferren heard Kiet mutter fiercely beside him. "They get their revenge!"

He knew she was thinking of all the Residuals who'd been carried off by Selectors and used to create Plasmatics. Residuals like her parents, Residuals like his own father and mother when he'd been no more than a baby... As Plasmatics, they couldn't be conscious of what they were doing, yet this was their revenge, and they were the instruments of it.

Further and further, the tower dropped away. It was tilting in the direction of the second dark spot—and when it finally fell, it came down right across the Bankstown Camp. There was a long outbreath of satisfaction from everyone watching. The stupendous structure shattered and spread out as it hit the ground, and the debris extended in a long plume over and beyond what had once been the biggest Humen Camp in the southern hemisphere.

Up in Heaven, they were too far away to catch even an echo of the actual crash. After a moment of waiting, Tadge supplied the missing sound.

"Boom!" he said.

A cheer rose up from all round the hole in the floor of the First Altitude. Residuals hugged and clapped one another on the back, trumpeter angels blew a spontaneous fanfare on their trumpets.

Then Ferren heard Uriel speaking to Miriael. "Do you want to go down and see?" the archangel asked.

Ferren disengaged from a hug with Kiet. "Does that include us?"

"Yes, all of you." Incredibly, there was a warm smile on Uriel's granite-like face. "All Residuals should be present since you brought it about. And before we visit the wreckage, I think you should see the end of Asmodai."

Everyone was eager—but also puzzled.

"How do we get down there?" asked Kiet.

"Like this," said Uriel, and clapped his hands.

A host of white wings fluttered towards them out of the sky.

25

"Those are Blessed Souls, aren't they?" Ferren remembered the wings that had carried down the canopy and the thrones of the four great archangels for the ceremony of signing the alliance.

"Indeed they are," said Uriel. "And your means of transport back to Earth. Who would like to be first?"

"Me!" cried Zonda, and stepped forward.

Uriel gestured to the Blessed Souls, and six pairs of wings fluttered down to the first volunteer. Everyone else made room as they caught hold of her by the arms and the cloth wrapped round her waist.

"But you have to come too!" she cried to Bross.

In the next moment, the wings beat the air, and Zonda took off.

"Ooo-er!" she quavered, soaring suddenly above the heads of the crowd.

The wings readjusted her angle so that she hovered horizontally in the air. Bross stepped forward to take next turn, and another half dozen Blessed Souls descended around him.

"Is it scary?" Gibby called out to Zonda.

"Nah…" Zonda began, then gave a little shriek as the wings carried her out over the open hole. "Yii-eee!"

The wings kept her hovering there until Bross had been lifted up and carried out to join her. Then the two of them dropped down through the hole and were lost to view.

Kiet grinned at Ferren with a wild light in her eyes. "Us next!" she cried.

This time, a full dozen Blessed Souls fluttered down. Ferren and Kiet stood side by side and felt tiny touches gripping them under the arms and around the waist.

"They tickle!" laughed Kiet.

The lift-off was so smooth, it was like becoming weightless. Ferren found himself looking down on the heads of Residuals and angels, then swivelling horizontal, then gliding forward as if swimming through the air.

"Whooo!" He gasped at the emptiness under him, the white clouds and panorama of the Earth many, many miles below.

Then all at once they were falling, falling, falling. The rush of their descent took Ferren's breath away and blinded his eyes with tears. He had a moment of real panic, thinking he was dropping like a stone, imagining the terrible smash when he slammed into the ground.

But although he was travelling so fast, he wasn't actually accelerating. The wings were still beating, still controlling his descent. He blinked away the tears and narrowed his eyes against the wind.

The light had changed. No longer the eternal clear light of the Divine Realm, it was the ordinary daylight of an ordinary morning. How much time had gone by while they'd been up in Heaven? From the end of one day to the start of the next? He couldn't think about it right now.

Instead, he looked down and surveyed the same map-like landscape as before, but with the small, white clouds much nearer. Nearer again were the figures of Zonda and Bross, seemingly suspended with outspread arms. The beating wings of Blessed Souls made a white flicker round their bodies.

He twisted his head to look at Kiet, and in the same moment she twisted to look at him. They were still side by side, no more than a few arms' lengths apart. With her dark red hair streaming in the wind, she had never looked so unbelievably beautiful.

She flapped a hand at him and shouted. The wind snatched away her words, but he understood. She wanted to fly closer and touch hands.

"How?" he shouted back—but of course she couldn't hear him, either. He laughed and flapped back at her. He didn't know how to communicate with Blessed Souls.

Yet somehow the Blessed Souls knew what they wanted. They veered in their downward flight, gradually narrowing the distance.

"Just a bit more!" cried Ferren.

He strained to reach out on his side, and Kiet strained on hers. They were both waggling their fingertips—and finally they made contact. It was only the briefest, lightest brush before the Blessed Souls drew them once more apart.

Kiet whooped, and Ferren was now close enough to read her lips. "Another! Do it again!"

The Blessed Souls entered into the spirit of the game. As Ferren and Kiet stretched out wildly with their hands, the wings carried them closer, then further, then closer, then further. Sometimes the two of them managed to touch, sometimes they didn't. They yelled in delight at every success and laughed uncontrollably at every near miss.

Ferren hardly noticed the dampness of the clouds they passed through or the approaching landscape below. He was dizzy with euphoria and wished that the game could go on forever.

But all too soon it ended. The wings beat more strongly, now slowing the speed of their descent. Kiet blew him a kiss, and he blew a kiss back, but there were no more touches or near misses.

When he looked down again, he was amazed that the ground had come so close already. Below was a ploughed field of yellowy-brown clay, with strange conical mounds at regular intervals beside the furrows...

He was still staring at it when it came up and hit him. Forgetting to lower his feet, he landed in a belly-flop, and the air was driven from his lungs. When he rolled onto his back a minute later, Kiet stood over him, laughing.

"Get up, we're here!" she announced, and reached out a hand to help him up.

26

The field, with its furrows and conical mounds, rang a bell in Ferren's memory—maybe from his very first journey to the Humen Camp? But there was one feature he'd certainly never seen before: a bank of earth that rose ten feet above the level ground and curved round for hundreds of yards across the field.

Zonda and Bross wandered across to join them, while more and more Residuals were landing all the time. Miriael, having lost her angelic power of flight, had been carried down with the rest. As everyone gathered and chattered and shared their flying experiences, Gibby suddenly called out in a loud voice.

"Look who!"

It was Shanna coming towards them across the field. Her mouth was wide, her legs were pumping, and she was running like a madwoman..

"She must've seen the wings bringing us down," said Ferren.

"Perhaps she was coming to see where Asmodai crashed," said Dwinna.

"But *then* she saw the wings bringing us down," Ferren insisted.

He waited as long as his patience could bear, then ran to Shanna himself. Miriael was right behind him, but he jumped forward first and seized his sister in a fierce hug.

"You did it!" he cried. "You brought down the tower!"

She patted his back, but had no breath to speak.

By the time he released her, not only Miriael but all the Residuals had come up. They bombarded Shanna with questions, to which she could only respond with gasps of laughter and relief. Then her eyes sought Miriael's.

Miriael had fallen to the back of the press, but she stood head and shoulders above everyone else. Her face glowed with the happiest of smiles.

"I'm so glad I was wrong, and you were right," she said.

"I'm glad ..." Shanna brought out, but could manage no more.

Though the words were mundane, the bond between the two of them was plain to see. The others respected it, and stepped back.

"You have to tell her everything that's happened," Ferren said to Miriael. "Tell her how we knocked Asmodai out of Heaven."

"How Peeper and the Morphs did." Kiet corrected him.

When they turned from celebrating with Shanna, they discovered that the scene had changed behind them. The Blessed Souls had formed themselves into a double line of white wings that led up to the bank of earth like an avenue. At the far end of the avenue stood Uriel, who must have descended from Heaven soon after them.

"That's our way to go, then," said Ferren.

"Looks like he's waiting for us," said Kiet.

They set off along the marked route, Ferren and Kiet at the front and Miriael and Shanna at the rear. Ferren noted that Uriel's radiance no longer spilled out freely all around, as it had in Heaven. Down here in the terrestrial atmosphere, it had acquired a boundary like a skin of light, enclosing the archangel in his own bright oval. Ferren remembered Miriael talking of the aura she should have had when visiting Earth... the aura she'd lost...

Uriel was waiting for them all to join him, but for Miriael in particular. He began by addressing her almost as an equal.

"So we come to the end of one era and the start of another. This continent of Australia will be the first to be freed from the presence of Humen, then others will follow. Heaven will be looking to make many more treaties like the one you arranged here."

Miriael filled in the missing piece. "With other Residuals, you mean."

"Yes, other Residuals on other continents. You could help us, you know."

Miriael said nothing, and after a moment he went on. "If you come back to Heaven, your return will be honoured. You can claim a place for yourself far above your old rank of Junior Warrior Angel. I would propose to include you as a special adviser on the War Council."

"So that I could arrange the treaties?"

"Exactly. As a mediator. An invaluable role."

"But first I'd have to re-spiritualise myself."

"To return to Heaven, yes. But we could help you with that. Much more than we did last time."

Miriael shook her head. "No, I've grown rather fond of terrestrial food. Thank you, but Earth is where I belong now."

"What more can I offer?"

"Nothing. I have a role to play on this continent, and I'd like to play it. When the Humen are driven out, and the tribes here set up their own society, I can help them. I'd like to be *their* special adviser."

"Ah, well." Uriel sighed. "I'm not altogether surprised. It's our loss."

"And our gain," murmured Shanna, who had quietly moved to stand closer to Miriael.

For a while, nobody spoke. Then they became aware of a rushing sound from above. Many more angels were descending, with Michael, Gabriel and Raphael at the head of the host. Michael bore a sceptre, Gabriel a golden orb, and Rafael a bell. They landed on top of the bank of earth, then turned to look down on the other side.

Uriel swung in the same direction. "It is time to deal with the betrayer," he announced. "We shall bring him forth from his hole."

"Where?" asked Zonda.

"In front of you. This bank is the rim of soil forced up around the crater. He hit the ground with tremendous force."

Uriel dropped his hand to the scabbard at his side and drew forth the mighty Sword of Judgement. Then, holding it high before him, he led the way up the slope to the top of the bank.

27

The crater was a gaping hole many hundreds of yards wide. The bank of raised earth made a complete circle around it, and fifty or more angels had taken up position along the top. The depths of the hole were in shadow, beyond the reach of the morning sun; there was something huge at the bottom, but Ferren couldn't make out the details.

Uriel moved round to stand next to Michael, Gabriel and Raphael. With them stood a fifth hierarch, whom Ferren recognised by his burgundy robes and long, silvery beard. It was the same angel who'd written out the contract of alliance between Heaven and the Residuals. At that time, he had carried a parchment scroll and a quill; now he carried a massive, brass-bound book.

"Bring forth the betrayer," Michael intoned in a deep, solemn voice. "Let the ritual begin."

A dozen angels launched off from the top of the bank and flew down into the crater. The light of their auras illuminated what had been previously masked in shadow: Asmodai's flying wing lying at the bottom of the hole. Though smashed and broken into many pieces, it still retained its overall delta shape. The upper surface of the wing glittered faintly in places where it wasn't dimmed with dirt.

The angels hovered above the point of the delta, and one sang out. "Come out in the open, Asmodai the Betrayer!"

There was no movement or response. Asmodai remained in his glass bubble underneath the wing, and presumably intended to stay there.

The angels went lower and sang out again. Then two plunged right down among the wreckage. Ferren blinked at the dazzling flashes that burst from their auras. There was a sound like cracking, splintering glass—and finally Asmodai emerged.

He looked very different to the last time they'd seen him. His black robes were tattered, the circlet had fallen from his brow, and he no longer emanated power and spiritual energy. Although his radiance maintained the oval shape of an aura, it was a low, feeble glow compared to that of the other angels.

"Look up at us, Asmodai!" Michael commanded.

Slowly, unwillingly, Asmodai raised his head. He appeared to be shivering, as though he wasn't adequately protected in the terrestrial atmosphere.

"Asmodai, you have warred against Heaven for the second time," said Gabriel. "Once as a follower of the Satan, now as a leader of our Humen enemies. The first time, you were cast into Hell, but later forgiven. Now you have despised Heaven's mercy and persisted in your evil. You have placed yourself beyond redemption."

Asmodai answered with a drawn-out hiss. "You don't need to punish me. I'm no threat to you now, am I? You can't be afraid of me like this." He hunched his shoulders and spread his arms in a demonstration of harmlessness.

"Unfortunately, not true," said Gabriel. "You recovered your power before, and you would do so again. Your punishment must be final."

"You can trust me!"

"No," Michael told him. "Never again."

The twice-fallen angel hadn't been exactly pleading before, but now his expression twisted into a snarl. "I won't go back to Hell."

"That is not the punishment." Michael's voice was implacable. "We are going to apply Extreme Sanction to you."

"What?" Different emotions contended on Asmodai's face: shock, fear, disbelief, anger, despair.

"Prepare yourself." Michael held up his sceptre in both hands, Gabriel raised his golden orb, Uriel flourished the Sword of Judgement and Rafael struck a resounding note on his bell.

Ferren, who was standing between Kiet and Miriael, whispered a question to the angel. "What does Extreme Sanction mean?"

"Elimination and non-existence," she replied. "Final and forever. Metatron will perform the ritual."

The hierarch with the silvery beard and burgundy robes stepped forward. Ferren was about to ask another question when Asmodai let out a terrible howl.

"No-o-o-o! You can't do that!"

"We can and we will," said Rafael.

"I'm a being of pure spirit! It's against every principle!"

Gabriel shook his head. "Pure spirit, but not purity of spirit, Asmodai. We have learned that spirituality is not the same as ethical goodness. Even physical beings can have more ethical goodness than you."

"Residuals, you mean!" Asmodai made a vicious, spitting sound. "If you can choose beasts like that over—"

Michael cut him off. "No, you won't learn or change, Asmodai. As you've already proved. That is why we must apply Extreme Sanction." He nodded to Metatron. "Proceed."

Metatron opened up his brass-bound book and began leafing through the pages. Miriael leaned over to Ferren and explained in a whisper.

"That's the Universal Register, recording the lives and deeds of every angel."

Metatron arrived at the page he wanted. He held the book aloft so that Asmodai could see.

"This is *your* record," he announced. "A page devoted to the angel Asmodai. Your achievements, your sins, your entire history in Heaven, then Hell, then Heaven again."

Michael, Gabriel, Rafael and Uriel began a solemn chant.

"Excommunicamus et anathematizamus hunc furem, vel hunc malefactorem."

The other angels all round the top of the bank chanted a response. *"Maledictus sit in totis viribus."*

Metatron lowered the book and slammed his fist down on the open page. Asmodai thrashed and writhed back and forth in torment, shrieking. The angels who'd descended to the bottom of the crater moved to form a containing ring around him.

"Sicut aqua ignis extinguitur, sic extinguatur lucerna ejus in secula seculorum."
"Maledictus sit intus et exterius."

At every chanted response, Metatron slammed his fist down on Asmodai's page in the Universal Register. With every blow, Asmodai's face and body grew purple and black as if with bruises. The chant continued until he was darkened all over.

"Insurgat adversus illum coelum cum omnibus virtutibus quae in eo moventur ad damnandum eum."

"Fiat. Fiat. Fiat."

The chant concluded. Metatron raised and gripped the page he'd been striking, then tore the whole sheet out of the book.

Asmodai's shrieks turned to a thin, squeezed sound. His body changed too, in the strangest way. He seemed somehow flattened, no longer fully three-dimensional but more like a picture, without depth.

Metatron stooped and placed his brass-bound book on the ground. Then he took up the page he'd torn out and folded it double.

Asmodai suddenly lost all width, compressed to a vertical band of dark colours. His features were no longer distinguishable, nor even his limbs. His shrieks reduced to a single, continuous high-pitched note.

Then Metatron gripped the folded page in both hands, and, with one swift movement, tore it in half.

Asmodai vanished. It was as though the vertical band had been sucked back between two walls. The high-pitched note receded into an infinitely remote distance, then went out with a tiny pop.

"Amen," intoned Michael, Gabriel, Rafael and Uriel.

"Amen," echoed all the other angels.

28

Ferren felt thankful, though he didn't feel like celebrating. "Good riddance to him," he muttered, and turned to go back down from the top of the bank. But Kiet plucked at his elbow.

"Wait! You're forgetting something. The Morphs are still there."

He swung back and looked where she was pointing. Of course! The Morphs were still at the bottom of the crater. Though no longer under the control of Asmodai's will, they were still attached to the wreckage of the wing.

"Is Peeper there too?" he asked.

"Yes, he'll be with them." Kiet cupped her hands round her mouth and called across to Michael, Gabriel, Rafael and Uriel. "You have a promise to keep!"

The four archangels nodded, and Uriel spoke on behalf of all. "And we shall keep it."

He clapped his hands, and the Blessed Souls that had been hovering in the background came forward around him. He directed them down to the depths of the crater, and they swooped to obey.

"Is this the promise that Miriael came back with?" Ferren asked. "When she was having a visionary dream, while we were...er..."

"Yes, that promise." Kiet grinned. "From Gabriel and Uriel, on behalf of Michael and Rafael, on behalf of the whole War Council. Guess what she got them to promise."

Ferren had already guessed. "To let the Morphs up into Heaven?"

"Exactly. To let them into their Heavenly home, where they can become Blessed Souls instead of lonely outcasts. It's the one and only thing they've always wanted. The one and only thing that could've made them rebel against Asmodai's will. Did you ever wonder how Peeper persuaded them so fast?"

"I did, yes."

"That's how. That was the key."

Miriael, on Ferren's other side, had caught some parts of their conversation, and now joined in.

"They promised to open the Portals of Heaven to all Morphs everywhere across the Earth. Back to the way it used to be with human souls, before the War Council locked them out. It really is the start of a new era. And since it was an argument over the exclusion of souls that made the Supreme Trinity—"

She broke off as a cheeping and chirruping rose up from below. "Something's happening!" cried Kiet.

Everyone leaned forward to peer into the depths of the crater. The white wings of the Blessed Souls, which had been circling around just above the wing, lifted gradually higher and higher. Ferren and Kiet turned to Miriael.

"Is it the Morphs?"

"Can you see them? What are they doing?"

Ordinary Residual eyesight couldn't see the Morphs, but Miriael could. "They're detaching themselves and floating upwards," she said.

The cheeping and chirruping swelled louder, like the song of a thousand birds. The angels who'd descended to deal with Asmodai returned to their original positions on top of the bank. The Blessed Souls hovered in a ring around the sides of the crater.

Miriael pointed to the white wings of the Blessed Souls. "I think they're encouraging them, guiding them upwards. I expect they'll be showing them how to transform into Blessed Souls too."

Ferren couldn't see, but he heard the cheeping and chirruping rise steadily higher as the ring of wings moved upwards. In the past, the voices of Morphs had always sounded sad and plaintive, but these sounds were full of joy. And somehow more and more musical... The Blessed Souls were singing a hymn as they accompanied the Morphs, and the melody of their music somehow crept into the cheeping and chirruping as well.

Soon the sounds came up level with the top of the bank, then floated above it. The white wings flew higher too.

Kiet appealed to Miriael. "Can you see our Peeper?"

Miriael smiled and shook her head. "Among so many Morphs? No, I can't recognise any one of them individually."

By now, everyone was having to lean back to stay watching, as the ring of Blessed Souls spread wider above them. Ferren imagined the Morphs gaining in confidence...starting to fly rather than float...

Then, suddenly, he didn't need to imagine anymore. In the middle of the ring, something white winked into existence. Then another, then another. Flashes of white twinkled against the blue of the sky.

"New wings!" he cried.

"New Blessed Souls!" cried Kiet.

Miriael laughed. "It's the transformation!"

Every flash of white was a newborn pair of fluttering wings. In no time at all, there were hundreds upon hundreds of them, flying round and round in a teeming flock. Ferren cheered, Kiet cheered, all the Residuals cheered. The angels and archangels raised their eyes with beatific expressions and put their hands together in prayer.

It was exhilarating just to see the new Blessed Souls sporting in the air. Like all newborns, they were lively and playful. Their cheeping and chirruping had turned into a glorious harmony of singing voices.

Then Uriel clapped his hands a second time. "Show them the way to Heaven!" he commanded.

The older Blessed Souls rearranged themselves into a double line of hovering wings. Like white beacons, they marked the upwards path to Heaven. At the end of the path, a rift appeared in the sky, a glowing gap in the blue. It was framed by pillars and an arch, and seemed to disclose infinite realms of colour and light.

"The Fourth Portal," murmured Miriael.

The newborns flew up between the beacons, dwindling into the distance. But one pair of wings hung back, then dipped down lower over their heads. Ferren heard a pure singing voice, though he couldn't understand the language of the hymn.

"That's him!" cried Kiet at once. "That's our Peeper!"

Ferren didn't doubt it, especially when the newborn waggled its wings. "He came back to say goodbye!"

They both waved, and so did Miriael and all the Residuals nearby.

Then the wings gave one last waggle, and Peeper spiralled up after his fellow Blessed Souls. The leading newborns were already halfway towards the light of the Fourth Portal.

"He'll be happy now," said Ferren.

"Yes." Kiet made a gulping sound. "He'll be in his true home at last."

Ferren had a lump in his throat, while Kiet had tears streaming down her face. Yet she still managed to compose a final song and sing it out for Peeper.

> "Be always happy, little one,
> No longer lost and lone.
> So many years you've been locked out
> And now you're going home."

APPENDIX 1
CHRONOLOGY OF THE MILLENARY WAR

1961	USSR sends first human into space
1969	US lands first human on the moon
2028	The Venables-Hirsch experiment
2031	Inauguration of Project Olympus
2033	The Trespass upon Heaven
	The Devastation at Mount Horeb
2034	Start of the Age of the Undead
2038	The Depopulation of New York
2075	Many Fallen Angels allowed back into Heaven
2079	Quarrel in Heaven over excluding human souls
	Supreme Trinity withdraws to Seventh Altitude
	War Council of great archangels takes control
2088	The First United Earth Congress
2089–94	The False Truce
2094	The Great Collapse
2223	First appearance of Plasmatics
2228	First appearance of Hypers
2262–91	Construction of the Endless Wall
2436–40	The Weather Wars
2440–2543	The Hundred Years' Blizzard in North America
2755	Humen colonies in the Burning Continents expelled
2904	Foundation of the South American Empire
2912	First appearance of force-fields and boost-beams
2927–45	The Wars of Doctor Mengis and Doctor Genelle
2943–45	The Campaign of the Five Zones
3003–3022	Rise of the ten original Bankstown Doctors
3023	Bankstown Doctors destroyed at Battle of Picton
3024	The destruction of Doctor Saniette

Appendix 2
Angelology: Traditional Lore on Angels in this Book

Traditionally, Heaven is composed of seven distinct Heavens; in this book, Heaven has seven distinct Altitudes. Angels are divided into nine Orders, from Seraphim on the highest level, through Cherubim, Ofanim, Dominions, Virtues, Powers and Principalities, down to the lowest levels of Archangels and Angels. Confusingly, 'angels' also applies to beings of all Orders and 'archangels' to the highest captains of Heaven, so I've renamed the lowest Orders as Junior Angels and Archangels.

Aeon: a celestial power of higher rank, who may be an emanation of God or one of the first beings created by God.

Anaitis: an important female angel also known as Anahita.

Asmodai: a fallen angel who once governed seventy-two legions of infernal spirits in Hell. According to early Church fathers such as St Jerome, followers of Satan would eventually repent and be allowed back into Heaven—which is what happened to Asmodai in *The Ferren Trilogy*.

Elubatel: one of the eight angels of omnipotence.

Gabriel: angel of truth and revelation. Gabriel told Mary that she would bear the Christ-child and dictated the Koran to Muhammed.

Jehoel: the principal angel of fire and Master of the Heavenly choirs.

manna: the food of angels, manna is traditionally produced or stored in the upper Paradise., which lies in the Third Heaven (Third Altitude of Heaven). When fed to the Israelites in the desert, it had a taste 'like wafers made with honey' (Exodus)

Marioch (Marioc): the angel who watched over the writings of Enoch and made sure the Books of Enoch were preserved.

Metatron: no angel has as many names, roles, or cross-identifications as Metatron! I've opted for the version that casts him as the heavenly scribe, a keeper of archives and the brother of Sandalphon.

Michael: Viceroy of Heaven and weigher of souls at the Last Judgement. Michael led the armies of the Lord that drove out the rebel angels. His secret mystery name is Sabbathiel.

[the] Satan: leader of the rebel angels who were cast down into Hell. The word 'Satan' actually means 'adversary', so a more literal translation would be 'the Satan', which is what I've used in *The Ferren Trilogy*.

Raphael: The angel of healing, science and knowledge. He is the Regent of the Sun and the chief of all guardian angels.

Shemael: traditionally, the angel who stands at the windows of Heaven listening for songs of praise rising from the Earth. (He's had to take on a new role by Ferren's time!)

Uriel: the fourth greatest archangel after Michael, Gabriel and Raphael. He controls the South and is included among the Angels of Destruction. As an agent of divine punishment, he wields the mighty Sword of God, re-christened 'the Sword of Judgement' in *The Ferren Trilogy*.

NB Other named angels in the story are also traditional figures—from Christian sources (especially the Apocrypha), Jewish sources (especially the Kabbalah) and Islamic sources (especially Sufi texts). Since those sources give little geographical information on Heaven, I've had to make up almost all the place-names in Heaven.

NBB. Good evidence supports the version I've given as traditional for the above figures, but there are always other versions too. That's just the nature of angelology!

ABOUT THE AUTHOR

Richard was born in Yorkshire, England, then migrated to Australia at the age of twenty-one. He was always trying to write, but could never finish the stories he began. Instead he drifted around as a singer, songwriter and poet, then became a university tutor and finally a university lecturer. But after twenty-five years of writer's block, he finally finished the cult novel, *The Vicar of Morbing Vyle*.

When he contracted his next book to a major publisher, he immediately resigned his lectureship to follow his original dream. Since then, he's produced seventeen books of fantasy, SF and horror/supernatural, ranging from Children's to Young Adult to Adult. Best known internationally for *Worldshaker* and its sequels, he's won many awards in France and Australia.

He lives with partner Aileen near Wollongong, south of Sydney, between golden beaches and green escarpment. Walking Yogi the Labrador while listening to music is his favourite relaxation—when he's not writing like a mad workaholic, catching up all on those wasted twenty-five years...

His Ferren Trilogy website is at www.ferren.com.au and his author website is at www.richardharland.au. You can email him at author@ferren.com.au.

For all aspiring writers, he's put up a comprehensive 145-page guide to writing fantasy fiction at www.writingtips.com.au.

BOOKS BY RICHARD HARLAND

For YA Readers

The Ferren Trilogy:
Ferren and the Angel (Book 1)
Ferren and the Doomsday Mission (Book 2)
Ferren and the Invaders of Heaven (Book 3)

Worldshaker
Liberator
Song of the Slums

For Younger Readers

the Wolf Kingdom quartet:
Escape!
Under Siege
Race to the Ruins
The Heavy Crown
Sassycat
Walter Wants to Be a Werewolf

For Adult Readers

The Vicar of Morbing Vyle
The Black Crusade
the Eddon and Vail series:
The Dark Edge
Taken By Force
Hidden From View

What Reviewers Have Said about *Ferren and the Doomsday Mission*, Book 2 in The Ferren Trilogy.

"[Book 2] carries you through various emotional levels and is filled with a number of exciting events—giving us what we loved about book one but making it feel fresh. Richard Harland has outdone himself again. May the last book in the Ferren trilogy hit its target as hard as these two have."

—*Independent Book Review* (Alexandria Ducksworth)

"Harland paints a vivid and immersive backdrop, delving into a futuristic landscape fraught with political intrigue and moral ambiguity. The thought-provoking exploration of power dynamics and the consequences of humanity's hubris adds depth to the story."

—*Kirkus Reviews*

"The writing is ideal, spot-on for the genre, especially the special languages and sound effects interspersed throughout. The short chapters provide a sense of urgency that will keep readers engaged in the action. Did I mention creativity? I did, but it bears repeating. Seriously out of this world creative! Harland knows how to entertain!"

—*Reader Views* (Sheri Hoyte)